COME
WINTER

a novel

COME
WINTER

C L A R E G U T I E R R E Z

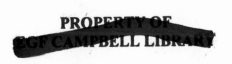

RIVER GROVE
BOOKS

Published by River Grove Books
Austin, TX
www.rivergrovebooks.com

Distributed by River Grove Books

For ordering information or special discounts for bulk purchases, please contact River Grove Books at PO Box 91869, Austin, TX 78709, 512.891.6100.

Design and composition by Greenleaf Book Group
Cover design by Greenleaf Book Group
Cover images: ©istock/y-studio; ©Shutterstock/conrado; ©Shutterstock/Richard Semik

Cataloging-in-Publication data is available.

ISBN: 978-1-63299-015-0
eBook ISBN: 978-1-63299-016-7

First Edition

FOR MY HUSBAND, Beto. His love, support,
and encouragement open the stories in my mind.

THE STAFF AT GREENLEAF BOOK GROUP have been a blessing.
They have perfected the process of publication to a science. From the
initial contact to the last page, they guide, support, and gently inspire.
Thank you, Jonathan, Tyler, Chelsea, Lindsey, and the entire staff.

NOTE FROM AUTHOR

MY WISH IS THAT YOU will enjoy the story of a woman tossed about, who rises to become what fate intended. Her trials are not unlike those of most of the women of her time, though perhaps not all occur with the same woman. Loss of children, hunger, freezing weather, and loss of husbands—all in the midst of horrible diseases. Marriages were arranged for the advancement of families and/or kingdoms. Yet, women found love and nurtured.

Our world, yours and mine, is filled with stories of such women. Not fiction like this, but true stories, with inspiring triumphs and heart-wrenching trials. Women who move quietly through their lives, unnoticed, yet leave a legacy upon which mankind rests.

PROLOGUE

IN THE EIGHTEENTH CENTURY, AS times before and after, people accused of being witches or heretics were burned at the stake. Such a sentence was an unspeakable way to die. The executions frequently took place in public, the better to discourage anyone else from similar activities.

"Not this time, not this victim," the man whispered as he watched the mayhem below. He had never attempted a shot from such a distance. The figure being tied to the stake was praying. As soon as she was secured, the fires were set. Cursing the tears that filled his eyes, he steeled himself for the job at hand. Slowly setting the gun, he found his target through the wisps of smoke and pulled the trigger. The shot went unnoticed; yelling and taunting from the mob below drowned out all other sounds. Mouthing good-bye to the form now slumped at the stake, the man turned and left.

When the victim, now barely visible through the smoke, suddenly sagged against the ties, the mass of onlookers was stilled. "An innocent, for sure," a voice called out. "Saved from such a death by the hand of God." The gathered crowd now backed away, frightened. The men responsible for this burning stumbled against each other in their haste to leave. From somewhere in the sea of bodies, a rock flew, hitting one of the retreating accusers. Other stones followed. "You tried to murder an innocent!" someone cried.

When lightning suddenly lit up a darkened sky, the entire assembly broke and ran. A crack of thunder rolled over them.

ONE

A WORLD AWAY, THE LORD of a castle stood at the kitchen door, studying the captured woman. She was quiet, but not subdued. Her light olive skin was like satin. Under the loose sackcloth she wore, he could tell she was slim, and shorter than the local women. Her arms were firm, her fingers slender and long. Her deep auburn hair, piled in haste on top of her head like a crown, shone with light from the candles and fireplace. Escaped tendrils, damp with perspiration, snaked around the nape of her neck. She did not look up or acknowledge his presence—just kept working.

It was not uncommon for men from Scotland to fight for other countries when money was scarce. Not so many years ago, the lord himself had done so. One of the men he had met during a stint in Italy was a young man named Tabor, Carlos Tabor. Several weeks ago, Carlos had contacted the lord with a special request. He requested his sister be kidnapped before she could reach the English court. Carlos feared for this woman's safety, should she reach that court.

To ride across the border into England was an easy task. Clans did so, especially when there was a need for more women of childbearing age. Telling the lord's men they needed women had immediately garnered support. Carlos had promised he would send for his sister within weeks of her capture. The lord had no idea where the other women wound up. This lady, however, he brought with him.

Every day since the day he had brought her to his castle, the lord had come to watch her as she went about her work in his kitchen. She cooked, cleaned the pots, and swept the stone floors. He wondered how she could be so serene, so calm. She was totally isolated from other humans, except for the servants and men who came to eat in her kitchen. Even then, no one spoke to her. Despite that, she acted as if all were well in her world. She was strangely detached. He wanted to know more about her. *What nonsense I think*, he mused. *They will come for her any day, I'm certain. The sooner the better.* Just the same, he remained in the silence, watching. For some reason, she made him feel as though he were intruding into her small world. *It's the silence*, he thought.

Standing just inside the door, he brought his hands to his hips. "How is it you can be happy here?" he finally asked. His voice sounded harsh in the stillness of the kitchen. It was the first time he'd addressed her.

She stopped moving about and stood, thinking. "Because this is where I am," she answered simply, as if he were nothing but a figment of her imagination. Her voice was soft; her slight accent gave it a melodious lilt. She returned to the vegetables on her chopping board, her hands working the knife with practiced precision.

"You have nothing," he pointed out, pressing on.

The woman did not respond.

Captivated, the lord stood watching, waiting for some answer, until finally he left her. She did not notice his departure.

The next day, he came again. This day, he walked with command and purpose into the room. As always, she was hard at work. "I do not understand . . .," he began, speaking to her turned back. "Look at me when I speak to you!" he ordered when the woman gave no indication she had heard him.

"I cannot." She replied quietly, her back still turned.

"What?" he asked, frowning. "Why not?"

"It is forbidden to look at you. I cannot," the woman said.

"You will look at me!" he persisted. "I give you permission to look at me."

"Do your men know that you have granted such permission?" the woman asked.

He paused. "No."

"Then I cannot," she repeated, her voice still soft. "The punishment is death."

He stepped closer, a look of surprise on his face. "I command you to look

4

at me when I speak to you." He spoke sternly, and his face darkened when she still did not obey.

"The punishment is death," she repeated gently.

Shaking his head, he decided to pursue a different path. "Why are you not frightened or angry? You have nothing you came with."

The woman stopped sweeping. She had no idea how to answer. He was her captor. This was not her country, and life for any woman here was precarious at best. Her own situation was worse than most. Carefully, she said, "I am not unhappy here."

He watched her with such intensity that she stayed quiet for a long moment before returning to her work.

Although he eventually left her, he could not keep her from his mind. *Why should I care if she is happy or not?* He had neither the time nor the patience for women. His mother . . . the memory of her had long gone, but now it reached out to him again. Allowing his mind to feel her gentle touch and remember her soft love, he again felt drawn to the woman working in his kitchen. Every day it was the same. She worked all day cooking for everyone around her, at night leaving for her lone room. What was wrong with him, that he would even notice her? "Damned woman," he muttered. She had taken over his thoughts. He should have sent her on, but he never did. Now he felt he would never send her away, not when she filled his every waking hour. "Damnation!" he cursed. He understood well how this would complicate things.

Several days later, the lord took his place at the kitchen door late in the afternoon. "Today, you look at me when I speak," he commanded. "I do not *ask.*"

Slowly, she turned to him. The face he saw was as near perfect as he could have imagined. Her nose, bone structure, and mouth spoke to her Italian heritage. Her skin was smooth and clear, its golden coloring accentuated by the soft rose that swept over her cheeks. Surrounded by thick black lashes, her eyes found his. He was startled to see they were a deep gold, not the brown he had expected, and that she looked at him with kindness, not with fear. Struggling to regain his command of the situation, he remarked, "You have nothing . . . not family, friends, possessions, or freedom."

The woman lowered her eyes briefly. She didn't know what he wanted her to say. What more could this place take from her? Even death didn't matter now. Too much had happened to her. She raised her eyes to meet his. He was frowning. His eyes were so brown, they seemed black. His graying curls straggled from beneath the flat, gray bonnet covering his head. To the woman, they resembled the edges of an abandoned bird nest. The image made her smile briefly, though she immediately caught herself. If it were a mortal crime to even look at him, how much worse to laugh at him? The smile left her face as quickly as it had appeared. "What would you have me say?"

He searched her eyes, then turned abruptly and left the room without answering. Alone, the woman prayed no one had seen her smile. Perhaps he had missed it too. No matter—what's done is done. She went back to cleaning the kitchen floors. Filling every waking hour with any labor she could find was her only salvation. It made each day pass, and if she got through the days one at a time, she would survive.

Outside, the lord wandered the grounds of the castle. He was powerfully built and stood at six feet. Years of military training and physical activity had left his shoulders broad, his arms and legs muscled, and his belly flat. His hands and face were deeply tanned. His face usually bore an expression of intensity, although laughter sprung from his mouth at the slightest provocation. He wore his thick, wavy hair—dark but with gray beginning to creep up his temples— tied back with a thin strip of leather. His dress bore the mark of a man of his station and financial security. Just now, he had the look of one carrying the weight of a serious problem.

He made his way through the gardens and to the stables. There, he met his only brother, Bruce, who knew the lord's every mood well. Together they saddled up in preparation for a ride. This day they rode with a madness. The horses were foaming at the mouth when the men returned. The lord was not one to misuse his animals, but today something inside him burned.

He had not spoken for the duration of the ride, nor had his brother. Now, however, his brother looked at him keenly. "You are bothered by something. How can I help?"

"You cannot, Bruce. This problem lies within my breast. 'Tis a new feeling for me," he admitted gruffly, with a deep frown.

At this admission, Bruce smiled. He too had seen the woman now housed in his brother's castle. She was beautiful, but not in the way of their own women. Her eyes were so familiar. He felt as if he had known her, though he was certain he had not. She walked as if she owned the land and all on it, carrying herself with a confidence not often seen in common women. To tell the truth, Bruce thought, she walked with such grace that she nearly floated. He doubted she had ever been subject to anyone, man or otherwise. She was not common. "How fares the woman?"

The lord looked at him sharply. "Why do you ask?"

"Oh, worry not, brother," Bruce said with a quick grin. "I have my own woman, and am happy enough. But perhaps you are taken with the woman? It would serve you right. I find this most interesting." Bruce looked like his brother, except he was smaller and wiry. He shared his brother's eye coloring, hair, and demeanor, although he bore no evidence of his brother's burden. He was carefree, laughing easily. His eyes twinkled with mischief, though those eyes could speak of imminent death as the need arose.

"That is well enough, Bruce. It would seem little else interests you of late," the lord answered testily. His brother only laughed.

The lord returned to his castle, determined to speak with the woman again. The kitchen was empty, but her touch was everywhere. All was clean and in order. He stood but a second, thinking. With a decision made, he walked out.

Several weeks passed before he allowed himself to see her again. He needed to see her. He wanted to look into her eyes and see that fleeting smile. This time, he stood at the door a long while before she became aware of his presence. "I wish to speak with you," he said when she noticed him at last, breaking the silence.

"Speak," the woman answered. She stood motionless, looking straight ahead, waiting.

"I will tell you this one more time—you will look at me when I speak to you." He waited until she had turned to him. He felt the familiar wash of warmth at the sight of her face. "Of what do you think, in here, all day alone? Whom do you talk with? You must tell me why you are not afraid or angry . . . something."

The woman's eyes moved from the lord to the tiny window in the kitchen, then back slowly to him. She remembered stories about the clans of Scotland. They were rumored to be crude and ruthless, especially with women from England. The woman spoke quietly, choosing her words carefully. "I said I was not unhappy; I did not say I was unafraid. Angry? Of what use is anger here?"

He could see no signs of fear or malice. She was not mocking, not hopeless, not anything he had come to expect from women kidnapped. She was at peace. He knew he was drawn to her—without hope of reprieve, it would seem. Each meeting made it more so, and yet he could not take her. Not yet.

At this moment, he knew only that he must protect her. He had stopped trying to understand his own feelings. These new feelings made little sense to him, but it mattered not. With a fierceness he would never have believed any woman could inspire in him, he knew he would possess her. *I have yet to know how I will handle this when they come for her, but she will stay,* he promised himself.

"You're worried," the woman murmured, her head tipped slightly to the side as she regarded the man standing before her.

Her words brought him back to the present.

"Something bothers you," she continued. She had not moved toward him, but he felt as if she were standing next to him.

"It does," he acknowledged. Sinking into a chair, he leaned it back against the wall and briefly closed his eyes. "It does," he repeated. At that moment he gave in to the madness that had filled him these past months. She always made him calmer and more assured. "I have much to think of, but now is the time for action, not thinking. If it goes as I believe, I will return in maybe three weeks. If not, well . . ."

"Go in peace. You will return." The woman watched him keenly.

He stood at length without answering, thinking on her words to him, and on how self-assured yet unassuming she was. At last he nodded to her and left.

"Move her to the quarters today," the lord said to the chief of his guard. "I trust you will protect her carefully while I am away. There will be no mercy to the one who might harm her, nor to the one who would allow such."

The chief bowed slightly, puzzled, watching Lord Rhys walk away. He had served Lord Rhys for many years and knew his temper well. It was widely known that no woman had held Lord Rhys before, even though his house was filled with possibilities and even though the lord availed himself of these companions frequently. What was it about this woman that captured this man?

Whatever the case, keeping her safe should prove to be an easy task. No one would dare harm her now that it was clear she was the lord's favorite. The chief immediately searched for the castle's steward.

TWO

WHEN THE WOMAN RETURNED TO her room that evening, she found two men standing outside her door. She recognized one as the castle's steward, but the other was unfamiliar. "You have been moved," the steward announced. "Follow me."

The woman hesitated. She had no desire to leave the area. All she possessed was in her room. Reading her brief pause, the steward continued, "Everything has been moved, by order of my lord." He pointed a thumb at the man beside him. "This is the chief of his guard." Silently, she allowed the two men to lead her up three levels.

When they arrived at the highest level of the citadel, the steward opened a door and motioned for her to enter. She stood in the doorway, unable to step inside the lushly appointed quarters. She felt as if she were stepping across an invisible line into a place from which there would be no return.

Cautiously, she stepped inside. Her eyes were immediately drawn to immense windows. Moving across the rooms, the steward opened the casements, exposing the darkening grounds below. The woman found herself awed. She'd been unaware of the majesty and expanse of the castle until now. She could hear the soft cooing of doves settling in for the night, and people laughing.

After lighting a fire, the steward returned to the door, flanked by the chief. "Whenever you need anything, pull on this cord, and I will be here to assist you," he instructed as he ran his hand over a silk line. He found himself wanting to help her, to let her know she would be fine now, although he guessed she had never doubted this. All these weeks he had watched her as she worked unceasingly. She was so serene. Never before had this old castle been at such peace. His lord's choice was wise. It looked as though he would keep this one. He nodded to her, then left, closing the door behind him. Caty heard the lock clink.

Once she was alone, the woman slowly turned around in the middle of the warm, opulent room. Enormous candles burned in holders on the walls. A large overstuffed bed covered with thick, velvety blankets occupied one wall. On the next wall, she noted several doors without handles. *Allowing for entry without escape, no doubt,* she thought. A heavy iron candleholder and candle sat on a table in one corner. The windows flanked a great fireplace on the third wall, and an outsized chair nearby had blankets thrown over the back. The final wall was broken by a hallway. Walking its short length, she found a door leading to a privy. Previously, she had used the straw piled outside the kitchen door, where all the workers relieved themselves. Gratefulness filled her, and she continued down the hall to another door.

Beyond it she found a smaller sleeping area long since abandoned. At the far wall a window allowed moonlight into the area. A single bed with a simple stand and one lone chair completed the plain furnishings. *This would have been for the servants of whoever slept in these quarters before,* she thought. *Why am I not in here instead of the room beyond?* She knew her place had changed in ways she did not understand. Yet, she was not at court in England. She was an occupant of a place in which she had no desire to stay. She was still not free.

The woman walked slowly back into the chamber, crossing to stand at the windows. For the first time in months, she could see outdoors, not just the wall beyond the tiny window in the kitchen. Below, lit by a full moon now high in a cloudless sky, she could see manicured grounds. Walkways rambled in and out of a large garden that seemed to be waiting patiently for the warmth of spring. Fruit trees formed a backdrop to the east of the grounds. It was so like many other gardens she had walked through. Even the sounds of voices and laughter drifting to her felt comforting and familiar.

Slowly, she turned back to her new room. Her few possessions lay on the large bed. Grasping tightly, she held her coin pouch close, remembering the mother that had given it to her. Her gratitude became tinged with fright as she turned and, with tear-filled eyes, once again surveyed her new cell. The furnishings were regal, with colors of reds, blues, and greens mixed through-out. Heavy fabrics were gracefully draped over walls, keeping the cold of the stones at bay. The floors were covered with thick rugs in a rich rust color. A bulky armoire stood beside the hall. All these things she viewed again. The area was comfortable and welcoming, but she was still a prisoner.

This night, she rested beneath soft blankets, in a soft bed. Drifting off to a troubled sleep, she worried. What was expected of her now? What had hap-pened to the last person who lay down to sleep in this bed?

THREE

WHEN MORNING RAN ITS GENTLE fingers across her face, she opened her eyes. Slowly, at first disoriented, she turned her head to survey the room. It was as she remembered. Hopefully, the change in quarters would not mean she was no longer allowed access to the kitchen. Listening, she could hear voices beyond her door. As yet, no one had tried to enter. At least someone might light the fireplace to take the chill from this place.

She dressed, then pulled the silk string to call for the steward. He knocked shortly thereafter and entered carrying a tray that held bread, fresh fruit, cream, honey, and a small pot and mug. The pot held hot tea. Setting the tray on the round table near the chair, he opened the windows, allowing fresh air to fill the room. He called a chamber boy to clean her privy and then busied himself starting a fire. When all was finished, he bowed and left with the boy. Not a word had been spoken. She wasn't surprised that he had not elaborated upon the reason for her changed living arrangements. *What need would he have to share information with one such as me?* she asked herself.

No matter. For the first time since her captivity, she had hot tea. She knew tea was not something these people were accustomed to drinking and was surprised to see it served now. She had tucked tea away in her belongings, saved. It was the only touch from her world before, now gone so awry. Dragging the big chair closer to the window, she sank down and closed her eyes. *If I pretend, I could imagine I'm back with my family having my morning meal—freely.* She surveyed the room again, slowly. What would happen now? How could she live here? She knew little of this man, but she was certain he had no intentions of letting her go. With clarity and purpose, the woman made her decision. *I must leave*

13

this place, while he is away. I will go to England. If I stay here, I will be forced into this household, and never leave. Suddenly the richly appointed room felt stifling.

Aware that she must take care not to arouse suspicion, the woman began to make plans over the following days. The possibility of escape spurred on the determination that flowed through her veins. Every thought was clear. Each time the steward brought food, she stowed away most of what would not perish immediately. She took note of as much of the castle's schedule as she could from her vantage point. She planned to leave during the day; else she would be lost. *I probably will be anyway*, she admitted to herself as she watched the last rays of sunlight move gracefully across the grounds.

Reviewing in her mind every detail of her escape, she concluded she would leave disguised as a young man. She was slight and strong; if clothed skillfully, she could pass for a young man, surely. The next day, she asked the pageboy for a pair of breeches, claiming she suffered with the cold. Finally he agreed and left her his best pair, convinced by the coins she slipped into his hand. She had also discovered, while meticulously searching her room, that one of the doors without handles pushed open easily to quarters she believed must be the lord's. Each evening since this discovery, she slipped into his rooms, searching for anything that might be of use. She found a back stairway she was certain led out of his chambers. She also found a heavy cloak and a shirt, rough but warm.

Nearly a week had already passed. She could wait no longer for fear he would return. *I am Lady Caterina Tabor. I can do what I need to do*, she told herself. Tomorrow would be the day. Watching the fire, feeling it heat the room, Caty tried to begin her transformation into a boy. Try as she might, she was unable to conceal her long hair beneath the cloak. Any movement brought it falling out onto her shoulders. This would be a problem.

Caty searched the lord's room until she finally found scissors. She remembered how much her father had loved her long hair. *It will grow.* She grasped a handful and cut. Slowly at first, waiting until each lock fell to the floor before grabbing another. As she cut, she forced herself to imagine her life as a free woman, perhaps in England. Now having committed to the procedure, she was hacking at the hair, eager to have it over. Finished at last! Hurriedly gathering all the clippings, she thrust them into the fire. The sizzle and smell of burning hair stopped her wandering mind. Changing quickly, she donned the breeches, the woolen leggings, the shirt, and her own worn shoes. Then she focused on packing, taking only what she could easily carry.

Caty slipped into the lord's chambers through one of the handleless doors and locked it behind her; now the steward would be prevented from entering. She surveyed the room. On his writing table, she found a short dagger. It was small enough to be easily concealed in her cloak. She slid it under her belt. After smudging her face with soot and dirt from the fireplace, hiding her coin pouch, and throwing the cloak over her head, she was ready. Early, as dawn opened its wings to spread the first light, she wrote a note to the lord, listed all she had taken, left what she could as payment, and slipped out the door from his quarters. Just as she imagined, the stairway led directly outside.

Movement proved easier than she had imagined. Covered with the cloak, Caty stole along the castle wall. Once she reached the corner, she moved quickly through the gardens. Few people were out and about that early. No one took notice of the lad clad in the lord's own colors. Following the sounds and smells, she found the stables. It was too early for the grooms to be about, since the lord of the manor would not be around to take his horses out. Heedful of any noise she might make, she opened the gate and picked out a horse. She found herself grateful for the hours her brothers had spent teaching her as she now quickly saddled, mounted, and headed away from the castle proper in what she hoped was a southerly direction. Fighting the impulse to look behind, she felt the rush of freedom. When sunlight finally filled the skies, Caty knew she was headed south, toward England.

FOUR

FOR DAYS, SHE RARELY SAW travelers. She avoided the few roads in the country, following well-worn trails instead. Whenever she heard hoofbeats in the distance, she would ride into the woods and wait. The countryside was turning green; it would soon be lush with emerging grasses and trees whose branches would swell with new buds. Flowers were beginning to open, beckoning to butterflies and bees. Spring blessed the land with sights that awakened memories of balmy days. Birds sang and the warm midday sun promised the eventual arrival of summer. Caty, however, paid little attention to these things. Through day after day of furtive riding, she was driven by fear of recapture and reprisal. Nights were spent huddled beneath her cloak, praying no one would come near her camp and shivering as the air quickly cooled.

Lying in wait for the light of day, Caty would watch as pictures of her life before these times flitted through her memory. Never could she have imagined how parting from her family would unfold. The intermittent conflict in Europe kept men like her father engaged in battle or planning the next one, constantly traveling, leading British troops in the Indies, sailing under the English flag to secure tea markets in China during uprisings, and making quick forays into France to spy. Against custom, Lord Tabor would take his wife and children with him on nearly all of these ventures, setting up makeshift households at each of his posts. Though English by birth, Caty had not spent more than a few weeks in total in her home country. Somehow, through it all, her mother had managed to create a separate haven for her children. Caty was the youngest and the only daughter of Lord Tabor and Lady Isabella, and as such, she had enjoyed the attention and games of her brothers. Her parents allowed her to spend hours with the boys, riding, play-fighting, and exploring. Her father believed that, in an uncertain world, these things might make the difference between life and death.

Eventually, she was the only child left with her parents as Lord Tabor led them across far-flung lands in service of the Crown. Time passed, marked by victories, holidays, and sorrows, eventually taking Caty from childhood to womanhood. Still, her father kept her at home—wherever that happened to be—with Lady Isabella. Caty never minded, nor did she yearn to be wed. She yearned instead for knowledge. She learned about herbs, healing, sickness, and death. Her father saw to it she was as well educated as her brothers. She could read, write, and speak French, Italian, and Latin, along with her mother tongue, English.

At her father's side, she learned to read maps and plan battles. Lord Tabor was well known for his acumen in battle, his cunning use of troops to capitalize on the terrain, and his daring refusal to surrender, no matter how dismal the prospects. Although she kept silent during his meetings, she took in everything. He gladly shared his knowledge with her. This daughter of his looked just like Lady Isabella, the woman he still loved with a heated passion. Loath to send Caty away, he and his wife poured everything they knew into her mind. She took it all in and more, the knowledge falling into her expansive mind like buckets of water dumped into an abyss.

England had been at war with France in the War of the Spanish Succession since 1702. While Marlborough fought the French, alongside the Bavarian and Austrian troops, to save Austria from invasion in 1704, Lord Tabor assisted the British affront against Spain, capturing Gibraltar. In 1706, he received another order from Queen Anne: he was to join Marlborough and fight by his side, as plans were under way to take on the French in an attempt to take the Netherlands. In 1709, Lord Tabor and Marlborough defeated the French again at the Battle of Malplaquet. Through it all, Lady Isabella stayed with her husband. Three years later, Lord Tabor was asked to slip across the French border again. Before accepting, an agreement was reached between Queen Anne and Lord

Tabor: he would be allowed to take his wife and daughter to Rome for a short stay, to visit Lady Isabella's homeland and the land of Caty's childhood.

Before they departed, Lord Tabor called in another favor. At his request, the queen agreed that Caty would come to and serve at court in England. Queen Anne was busy with the business of war and welcomed another well-educated lady to her court. Caty would be safer there than in France, Lord Tabor knew. Time was running out; he needed to get his only daughter away from the events taking shape. Because pockets of fanatics still burned heretics at the stake, Lord Tabor had instructed Caty to keep her Roman Catholic beliefs secret, at least for now. In these times, just who was deemed a heretic depended upon the religious leaning of the zealot. Who could know what would happen in the English realm?

One day during their stay in Rome, Lord Tabor informed Caty that she would be leaving for England before he and her mother returned to France. Her father brushed her hair from her face, kissed her, and reminded her that she was a Tabor and should conduct herself accordingly. Her mother cried softly as Caty left them. So much had changed in a quick turn. Ill at ease with leaving but nevertheless excited by possible adventures at court, Caty rode toward the docks, surrounded by a group of somber, unspeaking protectors. As they drew closer, a dark, oppressive feeling filled her. She could feel the danger. Caty's mother had taught her to heed the feelings she had in her mind, but this time Caty had no idea what to heed.

Now, as she lay on the fields of Scotland, Caty could still see in her mind the silhouetted contour of Italy disappear as she watched from the deck of the ship that night. She stared at the dark form until she could no longer make out the dim shape of her mother's homeland. Caty could remember her mother's gentle caresses, her laughter, and her melodic speech. Caty never spoke of it, but she had heard her father talk of his work in France. Caty's mother was known as a great healer. Caty had also heard the rumblings about witchcraft surrounding her mother. She had sensed the danger her parents would face in France, and knew that this was why she had finally been sent to England. Tears ran down her face as she watched the murky line of land disappear. In her heart, she knew she had truly bid her parents good-bye. Everyone left home, she tried to tell herself, but the ache remained.

Although the men on board that ship had been most kind, Caty heard the whispers about her presence. It was a bad omen to have a woman aboard, even one of noble birth. She kept to herself as much as possible. When the pirate ship attacked them, the crew swore they had been doomed because of Caty. She was hidden below deck, where the captain had dragged her in haste. She lay shaking beneath planks that had been set in place to hide contraband. Even now, she could still hear the steps of a man walking slowly toward the place she lay hidden. He was searching, his foot tapping the boards. Just when it seemed she would be found, he was called away, after losing a verbal battle with another man.

Not daring to move, she had strained to hear what was being said. The fighting seemed fierce, and laced with a great deal of confusion. Caty was too frightened to think. What would she do if this ship sank? Shivering, she held herself and prayed. Perhaps because the ship carried little in the way of valuables, the pirates eventually left them alone, to limp homeward. When the captain came for her, she could see the fight had gone badly. Most of the men were wounded or dead. They were not scattered, as in battle, but lined up. Something was terribly wrong. Caty wondered again why they had been left alive, why the search for her had been abandoned.

Putting the problem out of her mind, she instead focused on the job at hand. The remaining crew now wanted her help. Her skill at salvaging the lives of the wounded kept the captain, albeit begrudgingly, from giving her up. Time crept by. Food and water grew scarce, as weather forced the ship to change course again and again. She ate little and stayed with the wounded, never mingling with the other crew, feeling the animosity from the captain. Nothing could appease him, short of her jumping ship. Caty knew he had something to hide.

The suspicion the captain cast upon her was so pervasive that Caty shuddered to think on it even now. Such rumors could spell death, she knew. As soon as the ship pulled into a small port near Dumfries, Scotland, she left. The captain insisted that the pirates had seized all monies given to him for safekeeping by her father. Secretly, she doubted the pirates ever knew about the chest. Her sense of foreboding grew.

Lady Isabella had assisted Caty in hiding most of her money in the hems of gowns and cloaks. Because of this, Caty was able to pay for a place at the inn. She knew she needed to get away from the rumors and tales now swirling around her thanks to the ship's captain. The English court may not be a safe haven for her, at least not just yet. Queen Anne was Protestant. Her court followed suit. Any excuse to rid the country of a Catholic was taken. Caty knew she would stand little chance of escape, should the stories reach the court with her. Tales of her healing powers were already being whispered among the ship's crew. The captain spoke of his close ties to members of Anne's court. Desperate, Caty removed every hidden coin and jewel and sewed up the hems of her garments. She would need this money to travel deeper into Scotland and make a new life for herself there. Scotland, she was told, would offer wonderful opportunities for a young girl without family. Using nearly all she had left, she purchased a horse and some food and paid for a place with a man leading a group to Glasgow.

They never made Glasgow.

FIVE

TOO LATE TO DO ANYTHING about that now, Caty thought. *Best to think on what I must do to survive*. Shaking the memories off, she saddled up and rode, thinking now of England. Caty believed she had no choice but to try for England again, given her abduction and captivity. Thinking back on the talk she had heard before her capture, Caty realized Glasgow had a large port. If she could make Glasgow, she might book passage on a ship bound for some distant port in England. She would not have to go to court. She would seek work elsewhere.

Now that Caty was a fugitive, her life and everything in it had turned upside down. Each time she felt despair take hold of her, she remembered her mother. She knew Lady Isabella would never have quit. Caty swore not to either. Instead, she focused on what she needed to do to reach England quickly, making lists in her mind. She would have need of a map, and some idea of this land she now traveled. *One would think I would get better at this. I should soon be an expert runaway.* She refused to think on the greatest question: What happens when someone who has run away from a lord is caught?

Preoccupied with these thoughts, Caty failed to hear the sound of approaching horses and men's laughter until the last moment. The sounds came from just beyond a curve in the road. Rousing herself from her mental fog, she sharply turned her horse to ride as deep into the roadside brush as she dared. She dismounted quickly and slipped her hand onto the horse's neck, holding tightly to the reins. She laid a reassuring hand on his nose, whispering to him. After several long moments, a group of men passed on the path, laughing and talking loudly. By their dress and armament, she knew they were English. The careless manner of the riders led Caty to suspect they were not worried about being waylaid. She held her breath as they passed nearby. Waiting until they were well out of view, she finally leaned into her horse, closing her eyes. "Much too close," she said to the steed aloud. "I need to keep a sharper eye, and stop dreaming."

"That you do," agreed a booming male voice from behind.

As a chorus of laughter erupted at the comment, Caty's head jerked up and she spun around, looking for the voice's owner. Her heart fell. He was a thief, surely. Who else would travel within the cover of the thickets? He and his men were hidden well beyond the view of the road, apparently hiding within the same trees and underbrush Caty had chosen. Had she been more alert, she may have moved aside quicker and missed these men also. *Not I, given the luck I am blessed with*, she thought. *I am now snared, like a hare.* Her mind raced. She would await their move.

"For what reason do we find such a young lad alone and in hiding?" the voice continued.

"I think he has run away," another responded amid more laughter. "And would like to go on running, without aggravation from the likes of us."

With that, the men broke through the brush and surrounded Caty. This band was clearly accustomed to living on the road. They were dressed for fighting, not leisure. Though the clothes were dusty, they were of a high quality. The appearance and speech of the apparent leader, however, did not match that of his companions. He spoke learned English but looked ragtag. He was average in height, medium in build, with dark brown hair and blue eyes that twinkled. The man had an easy laugh, but Caty felt he could change that at will. He had a sword at his side, as did each of the men with him. Each man also carried a pistol in his belt and a rifle. It was plain they knew each other well and were close companions, as men of battle become.

The man the others clearly regarded as leader made no move to seize her. Taking a breath, Caty spoke in a troubled voice. "I am lost, sir. I try for Glasgow. 'Tis not safe to be seen alone on these roads. I am not trained in the better arts of defense, sir. I was trained to teach only." Lowering her head, she hoped the man would allow her to simply leave.

"Pray tell me, what do you teach, lad?" he asked, not unkindly. However, when Caty met his eyes, she could tell he did not believe that she taught at all. He stood patiently, waiting for her reply.

Following her instincts, she raised her chin and answered, "I teach Latin, French, and mathematics, sir. I read and write well, in each of those languages. I hope to find employment in Glasgow. Do you know of Glasgow, sir? Would it be much further?"

His eyes narrowed. "Aye, I know Glasgow well. 'Tis too late to travel more this night. Come stay with us, and you may take your leave in the morn. Have you food?"

"Enough," Caty answered. She was afraid that if she looked at him squarely, he would discern she was not a lad. But, fearing more his reaction if she did not face him boldly, she stepped forward and held his gaze.

He frowned slightly, his head cocked to one side as he studied her. Decisively, he turned to the men with him. "Do you see what I see?"

A few nodded in agreement. At this, he strode to her and yanked the cloak from her shoulders. Her short, cropped hair stuck out in every direction and her face was filthy, as were her clothes, but the band's leader knew what he saw. "'Tis not a lad!"

Caty jerked the cloak back from him. "What are the English doing in Scotland, sir?" she fired back at him. "First those men who just passed on the road, now you—for surely you are not Scottish. A Scotsman would never behave in this manner. To think, you English dare to call the Scots uncivilized!" Caty had learned much during her months in the lord's kitchen about the nature of the animosity between the Scottish and English. With this statement, she had taken a great gamble.

The man was taken aback, both by her aggressive action and her words. If she were as educated as she claimed, she could not be of common birth—and her speech confirmed it. As Caty intended, he was insulted that she would grant the Scots greater grace than the English. Bowing deeply, he addressed her sarcastically. "Please forgive me, madam; I meant no disrespect for one of such birth as you. My men and I are humble servants of the Queen, and would that you spend time with us. Perhaps you would do better with proper escort to Glasgow."

Caty stiffened. She certainly did not need them hanging around her, drawing more attention. Worse, she would never be able to fend off all of them. "Pray let me continue on my way unhindered, sir. I must make haste."

"Nay, I cannot do that, lass," he replied. "Now you have my curiosity afire. You will be our guest this evening, and may take your leave in the morn, if I decide it is safe to allow you to leave us. Like you, we would not be captured. Only you know we are about. So you can see why I cannot now let you leave. Come, you will be with us at least this night. Better to be comfortable." He bowed slightly and offered her his hand.

Caty closed her eyes briefly. Bowing ever so slightly, she placed the reins of her horse in his outstretched hand. For the briefest moment, she thought he would toss them back at her; instead, he threw back his head and laughed. Turning, he led her through the watching men and beyond, to tether her mount.

Caty stood stiffly, not certain how she would be received. She slowly turned to look at each man but could see no signs of danger. Nodding to them respectfully, she walked back through them and toward a fallen log. She sat and waited, unsure what to do. As if she were not around, the men all pitched in as they set up camp.

"What name do you go by, lass?" one of the men asked as he knelt to make a fire.

"Lad," she answered, without hesitation. At her reply, the band broke into laughter.

"What name do you go by, *lad*?" he responded.

"No, I go by 'lad.' I have not taken the time to think of a proper name. You, sir? What name do you go by?" With arched brows, she looked him in the eye and waited for an answer. This was met with more good-natured laughter.

The leader answered, "We all go by 'sir.' Let us eat."

With that, everyone sat around and shared cheese, bread, and wine. Caty was given equal share. When the food had been placed in front of her, she stood and walked to her horse. The group suddenly went silent. She could feel them watching, but attempting to escape in this wilderness would not get her to Glasgow. Rummaging in her small pack, she removed some fruit and salted meat she had been saving. Returning, she offered it to the men. Without a word, it was accepted.

As night fell, Caty could feel weariness make its way into her. Although none had given her a reason to suspect they would harm her, she was reluctant to sleep. While the men prepared their bedding, the leader came to her, threw a blanket over her, and walked away. Soon each man had found a place to sleep and the camp grew quiet. Caty could no longer keep her eyes open, and surrendered to the darkness of sleep. At least this night she would be warm.

SIX

THE SOUND OF A GUNSHOT tore through her troubled dreams. Caty bolted up, wide eyed, instantly awake. She was alone. The site was cleaned and everyone gone. The blanket still lay over her. Her horse was tethered nearby. With ears stiff and head raised, he looked beyond the camp. She rose hastily, gathered her cloak and the blanket, saddled her horse, and mounted. Listening intently for any other noise, Caty warily turned the horse back toward the road, alert to every sound and movement around her. She had been lucky last night, but she knew luck was fickle.

Upon reaching the path, she stopped to think and listen. *Better to keep out of sight*, Caty reasoned. She moved into the brush, riding slowly and parallel to the path. She had not ridden far when she heard men riding hard. Quickly pulling her horse up, Caty backed her mount as deep as she could and dismounted. She again placed her hand on the horse's nose and waited.

The first group of Englishmen she had seen the day before rode into view. In their midst was one of the men she had stayed with during the night. He was wounded, beaten, and bloody. Were he not bound to the saddle, he would have fallen off his horse. Caty watched, horrified, as the band rounded the curve, turned from the path, and rode into the thicket toward her. She began to shake. This would not go well if she were found.

The band stopped close to her, and one of their rank threw a rope over a tree limb. He pulled a noose at one end of the rope over the captive's head. Once the rope was secured, he led the captive's horse out from under him, leaving the man suspended, writhing and choking. Not waiting to see him die, the men rode away without even taking his mount. *I think they wish not to explain an extra horse*, Caty thought. Once she was certain the riders were gone, she mounted and came quickly to the man's feet. Maneuvering her horse under him, she was able to guide the man's feet to the saddle as she slipped behind it.

He slid into the saddle, gasping. Her horse began to shy away, and it seemed for a moment that the poor man might be pulled from the horse, his neck still secured by the noose. Caty murmured to her horse, trying to settle him, while she tugged at the rope around the man's neck. Unable to loosen it, she pulled her knife out and cut the binding on his wrists. With his help, she finally sliced through the noose. The man collapsed against her, gulping air. Barely able to support him, Caty rode deeper into the thick growth of trees and brush until she could no longer see where he had hung. Her arms were numb from the effort to keep him astride the horse. She had to stop.

Sliding off her horse, she pulled the man down with her. His weight smashed Caty into the ground, knocking the air from her lungs. For a minute she lay stunned. The man rolled, moaning, to one side, and Caty pulled away. She stood unsteadily. She was surprised to see that his horse had followed them.

Turning back to the man, now sprawled on his back on the forest floor, she examined his wounds. He had a bullet hole in his right upper chest that had bled very little, his neck was bruised, and he had been beaten badly. He moaned whenever she pressed his left side. Caty suspected several of his ribs were broken from the beating he took. Covering him with her cloak and blanket, she searched for some place to lay him. Brushing sticks and rocks away, she piled leaves and soft branches to make a mound. "You must move," she said to him gently. "Try to stand. I can help."

With great effort, he stood, pulling heavily on her. Together, they staggered their way to the pallet. Caty helped him down, placed her small clothing roll beneath his head, and covered him with her cloak. She then wet his lips with a sip of cool water. "I must get a fire started. Please try to stay with me; do not sleep yet, sir. I need to clean your wounds. Sir?"

He was not able to answer. He only moaned. After dragging the saddles off both horses and securing them, Caty made a small clearing and stacked what dry branches and leaves she could find. She needed to get a fire going, whether it smoked or not. Looking through the bags the man's mount had carried, she found flint and started a small flame. Carefully, she nursed it to a suitable fire. She went back through his belongings, hoping to find another shirt.

When this proved unsuccessful, she pulled his bloodied shirt out of his breeches and tore the bottom. Pulling her extra shirt out of her bag, she tore it up, also. When she was done, she had several thick pads and strips. She wet a strip from her own shirt with water and began to clean the blood away. The shot had gone cleanly through him. Binding the shoulder wound as tightly as she could, she sat back on her heels, listened to his breathing, and watched him. His bleeding had slowed even further, his breathing was no longer labored, and he seemed to relax. Relieved the wound was no worse, she let him rest.

Caty kept a careful eye on the man as she gathered wood into a pile nearby. As the night grew cooler, he began to shiver. Heating several larger rocks, she wrapped them in the blanket he had under his saddle and placed them as near to him as possible. She covered him with the blanket his leader had left with her and then layered her own saddle blanket on top. She worked to warm him, rotating the rocks often. All the while, she fed the fire and kept listening. *If they come back and find us, they will surely finish the work they started. If I do not keep him warm, he may die anyway*, she reasoned. *Better to try.*

Through the night, she labored to maintain the fire and keep him warm. He slept deeply. When dawn opened the day, Caty ventured away from the campsite looking for the stream she could hear running. When she found it, the water was cold and sweet. After washing her face and hands, she sat back. *What do I do now? He needs to eat, and his wound needs care. What could have happened to the rest of his friends?* She was certain she had heard only one shot. And she was sure that his friends would not have left him to be taken.

She rose stiffly and returned to camp. She found the man asleep, and still free from fever. A good sign. She returned to the stream, filled the water bag, then walked along the bank, her eyes scanning the ground. Soon, she found what she searched for. The rock was not too large for her to lift and had a deep indention on one side. Hauling her find back to the camp, she placed it on the fire, then filled the indention with water. When it began to boil, she added dried meat and let it continue to boil, working the meat with a broken branch.

The man began to wake. Caty went over and sat beside him, waiting. As he became aware of her presence, he frowned and closed his eyes. He lay quiet for a long time. Opening his eyes again briefly, he gave her a weak smile. "'Tis really you, lad. Thought perhaps I had dreamed you." His voice was broken.

"No dream, sir. You are wounded, but with a few days you should be good to travel. I need to find something more for us to eat, or you will not make it far, I fear. This is not my land. What can I find?"

"How long have we been here?" he asked, his eyes closed once more.

"I found you yesterday. Only since then," Caty answered, watching him.

"You will have no need to look for food, lad. We will be found by this evening." He opened his eyes to look at Caty, visibly struggling to stay with her.

Caty stood up, alarmed. "Then, we must move you!"

"No, my friends will find us. We need not move." His eyes closed again as he faded.

Caty had no choice but to trust his judgment. Just in case he had misspoken, she gathered all their belongings into a pile and tucked it beneath some brush, then saddled the horses. As she worked, she stopped frequently, listening for any sounds from riders. When she was satisfied she had done all she could to give them a quick start, she checked on her broth and brought some to the man. She woke him gently. "Sir, you must try to eat this. It will not taste to your liking I fear, but you must have something."

He opened his eyes and frowned slightly. "What have you?"

"Do not ask. Just drink," Caty instructed.

Using a large leaf, she funneled the liquid into his mouth. He swallowed it. She waited to be certain it was down, then repeated the process. It took a while, but he drank every drop she gave him. "'Tis not bad, m'lady," he commented. He smiled weakly at her. Caty smiled back at him. Trying to disguise herself as a man had fooled neither this man nor his friends. Caty worried it might not fool anyone, though she believed it more dangerous to ride unattended as a woman. Too late now. The die had been cast.

Caty spent the rest of the morning gathering wood for another night. She could not see how they might be found, but time would tell. Meanwhile, she must be prepared in case they were not. Returning to the stream, she watched for fish. Caty pulled off her leggings and shoes, rolled her breeches up as high as she could, and stepped into the cold water near an outcropping of rocks along the bank. Stooping, she stood motionless, poised with her hands in the water.

Patience and perseverance finally rewarded her. By late afternoon, after repeated attempts, she had caught three large fish. She climbed the bank, shivering. Her feet and hands were numb from the cold water. Briefly she thought of the large, soft bed in her captor's castle. Caty shook her head, refusing to think of it further. Upon her return to the camp, she was pleased to see the man still sleeping. She felt his cool forehead and smiled. "You will be fine, I think," she said softly.

Caty cleaned the fish, split them, and hung one above the fire, in the smoke. The other two she laid out on rocks near the fire, turning them frequently. When they were done, she set them aside. "I thank you, dear brothers, for all the things you taught me. Pray I need them seldom," she murmured.

After checking on the horses again, she slowly returned to the fire. Her back ached and she felt filthy, exhausted, and hungry. What would her mother think if she could see her now? In the company of a man she knew not, running from a man who had captured her, yet hoping more men would soon arrive. *The right men of course, if there are such creatures*, she mused, smiling to herself. And to make matters worse, she herself was dressed as a man.

Caty sat down near the fire, leaned against a tree, and closed her eyes. The warmth gently wrapped around her. Just as she drifted off, the sound of crashing brush shook her. Jumping up, she pulled her knife out and slipped into the undergrowth. As the commotion got closer, she recognized one of the voices. She stood silently in the dusk, waiting and watching. She saw the leader of the captive's band appear in the clearing. Seeming to take in the scene quickly, he dismounted. Caty stepped out near the fire.

"You do not make friends easily, I see," she noted sarcastically. "He is sore wounded, but will recover."

The man smiled briefly. "And how is it you find my man, lad? I thought you had to be in Glasgow. I am certain you did not find him in Glasgow." The rest of his men got off their horses and stood around their comrade.

"I was hiding from the cowardly company that took him, but when they hanged him, I was forced to step in."

The leader's face took on a serious look. "M'lady," he said, no longer willing to play games with her name, "'cowardly' is a strong word. What do you so judge them by?"

"The men I know best, had they need to hang him, would have done so wherever he was captured. They would not have beat him first. Truth be told, sir, he would have died from the gunshot had the men I know best captured him."

"I see. The men you saw are the 'peacekeepers' from England. They do little to keep peace, however. Rather, they push Scotland away." He knelt down to check the wounded man. "He is not hot. He looks none the worse."

"Looks do not always tell the tale, sir. He is very weak. He speaks with difficulty, but I believe it will improve with time. He was hanging long enough to be nearly dead. If the men who left him there knew how to make a proper executioner's knot, he would not have survived. He is better now, but not yet recovered."

The leader studied Caty. "Just who are you?"

A call from one of the men near the fire interrupted them. "Did you catch these fish, m'lady?" The man who spoke was standing near the fire, frowning at her.

Leaving the leader's question unanswered, Caty joined the men around the fire. "Yes, I was blessed with older brothers who spent happy hours with me. I learned a great deal during those times. Truly, I would never have believed the things I learned would be of use. How little I knew then."

One of the men smiled at her. "I would have spent many happy hours with you, if I were your brother. I say the hours would be even happier were I *not* your brother."

Caty was glad the darkening hour hid her blush. She nodded to him for the compliment. "Come, I will share what I have with you all, though it be little.

You must save the smoked fish for the one who sleeps. If he cannot eat tonight, it will keep for tomorrow."

Each man added what he carried to the meal, and all ate well. Caty rose several times to check on her charge. He still slept easily.

As the men began to settle down after caring for the stock and adding to the woodpile, the leader asked Caty to sit with them. Knowing she could not take on even one of them in her present state, and in truth too tired to care, she sat down. After a moment of silence, the leader began, "I ask again who you might be. I would know how you happen to be alone like this, a lady dressed as a lad, running from—"

"Are you not from England?" Caty interrupted.

He frowned. "Perhaps." He looked at her, thoughtfully. "We are, but we are not likely to return to England anytime soon."

"You are outlaws?"

He looked toward his men. "No, we work for the Crown. These are troubled times. We would keep peace in Britain. Queen Anne grows older and has great difficulty with Europe, especially France. She should not have concerns with Scotland."

Caty was silent as she watched the flames. She knew only too well the difficulties faced by England. Her father had spent his life defending the country and advancing its interests. England was, as her mother said, a complicated mistress.

"And you?" He looked at her intently.

She could feel each man watching her. Taking a small breath, she began, "I am also English, although I have only spent a few short weeks on her shores. I was raised elsewhere."

"Elsewhere? What does that mean? Where is elsewhere?" he asked.

Wistfully, Caty replied, "My father made trade agreements with China, fought for the Crown in the Indies, and went wherever he was sent. As his family, we traveled with him."

"That is not customary," one of the men said, leaning forward doubtfully. "Why would a man take his family to such places?"

"It was believed," Caty explained, "that to have his family with him would lend a sense of permanency to his posts. It made his work easier. Besides, my mother was not English; she was from Rome. She was not accepted in most English circles."

The leader nodded. "Your father did the same work as we. From the looks of you, your mother must have been a beauty. I would be hard pressed to leave her behind also." He smiled to himself. For a moment all was quiet. "However," he continued, looking at her, "that does not explain how you are here, like that." He gestured to her pitiful appearance.

Not willing to discuss her capture with this Englishman, she nonchalantly explained, "I was sent to England but never arrived. Our ship was overtaken by pirates. What was left of our company made it to shore, and our piteous little group found itself in Scotland. I had it in mind to continue to England, and believed, perhaps incorrectly, it would be far simpler to travel as a man. Here I am—not where I intended."

"That is your story?" he asked skeptically. "I think, m'lady, you leave the important parts out. You are running from someone, I am certain. While I am loath to leave you unprotected, we cannot take you with us. I believe we will keep you safe this night and send you on your way in the morn. Should anyone ask, we never saw one like you. Nor have you seen anyone like us."

Relieved, Caty smiled. "'Tis a fair bargain, sir."

Rising to check on the wounded man again, she discovered he had been awake for a while. "Are you hungry, sir?" she asked.

He smiled weakly. "Yes, I am." The men gathered around him. It was easy to tell that these men were bound together by more than duty. With everyone sitting near, Caty fed him the smoked fish. He ate. "M'lady, I know we must leave you, but you will stay in my heart, as long as it beats. You have been like an angel to me." He reached up and touched Caty's cheek softly. His hand fell down, limp.

"I think it will take more than water and a bite or two of fish to get you going, sir," said Caty. "I shall remember you, too. All of you," she added, looking around the circle of men. She stood, moved to the fire, and cut a few small pieces of cheese for the recovering man. When she returned, he was asleep again. Gently waking him, she coaxed him into eating the rest of the fish and cheese. Once she had dressed the wound again, she cleaned him up as much as possible. At last, she leaned against a tree to rest. One of the men dropped a heavy cloak over her and she closed her eyes.

The next morning, Caty's patient was much better. He was still weak, but he said he felt like he could ride some. As everyone made ready to leave, he returned her cloak to her. The leader stepped swiftly forward, took the garment from her, and held it up.

"Where did you get this? I now remember from where I know this. I thought before, when first we met you, but now am certain, seeing it clearly."

"I left payment for the cloak, although the owner was not present when I bought it," Caty hastily told the men. "I had to get away quickly." The moment she spoke the words, her heart sank. She had not intended to say all she did. It just slipped out. She froze, praying they would not change their minds, praying they would let her leave.

"You run from Dermoth?" He looked at her in disbelief, then turned to his men. They were beginning to chuckle. He laughed outright. "Go, m'lady. Go in peace. Godspeed! You will need it, and more. Sometime I hope to meet you again. Would that I had time to hear your story today, lady. For 'tis surely a good one! I say truly, we will meet again, and I would hear your tale. Until that time, may God keep you!"

Everyone was laughing by this time.

Caty smiled, quickly turned to her horse, mounted, and rode away. She knew not where Dermoth was, but took no chance they might decide to show her. She intended to get to the port in Glasgow as soon as possible. There she would board a ship bound for England.

SEVEN

GRAY CLOUDS HUNG SUSPENDED OVER the land for days. It rained off and on every afternoon, and nights were miserably cold. Winds howled in the morning, howled in the afternoon, and stayed on during the night. Caty desperately wished she had taken something with which to start a fire. She was not certain what direction she traveled. With the sun hidden behind heavy clouds, she rode blind, without guidance. This was not going as planned. It was far more difficult than she had imagined.

Occasionally, she crossed well-traveled roads. It seemed she might be moving toward more populated areas. On the morning of the sixth day, Caty heard horses approaching. Again, she hid and waited for them to pass. Counting ten men, she noted their banner, their armament, and the discipline with which they carried themselves. *These must be more of the Crown's men. Surely I would be safe to go where they stay*, she decided.

She waited until she could no longer see them before setting out, and then stayed far behind. As evening neared, she came upon a very small borough. A neat sign outside the inn proudly proclaimed itself the Inn of Perth. Uniformed soldiers were wandering everywhere. She could not stay in a place so small. Even one new man would be noted. Caty kept riding until she could no longer see her way through the darkness. As was her habit now, she hid in the wooded areas off the roads. Letting her horse loose to graze, Caty sank down against a boulder. *I knew not the time it would take to get to Glasgow. For certain I am hunted now by the lord's men*, she acknowledged. Huddled beneath the cloak, she tried to think. Perhaps the man who once held her captive was already in Glasgow. Perhaps he would give up on her. Shaking her head, Caty knew that

that would never happen. She must go on. Sleep came in fragments, broken up by time spent worrying. By dawn, she was no closer to peace. Instead, she now rode with exhaustion her constant companion.

As she plodded on, the road gave way to a well-traveled trail. That could mean a greater chance she might be apprehended. Anxiously, Caty noted that she was heading south; the water was on her right. This she knew because when she had entered Scotland, the water had been on her left, and she assumed she had been headed north. *What I would not give for a good map*, she thought. Winding along the coastline, she passed Dundee, a place she judged too small to have a port likely to have ships bound for England. She kept moving.

Hours later, while deep in reflection, Caty rode up a craggy shoulder of land that jutted out over the ocean. The winds blew as usual, pushing curls of water, capped in white bonnets, toward the shores. *I think this land is hard. Hard on her people, the forests, and the very rock she clings to.* Her thoughts were interrupted by a plaintive cry. At first she was not certain what she heard. Listening carefully, she waited. Again it sounded. The cry was pitiful. Urging her horse forward, Caty dismounted and carefully peered over the side of the outcropping she stood on.

Below she could see a woman lying at the water's edge. She looked to be unable to stand. When the tide rose, she would certainly drown—and the water was already washing over her feet. Once more, Caty had a feeling of peril, though there appeared to be none for her. Caty turned back and tied her horse. Looking around for signs of inhabitants, she warily slipped down the embankment. In dismay, Caty stood frozen at what she found. The woman was neither ill nor injured; she was captive. Her hair was securely tied to a stake. Her hands were tightly bound and her feet were staked. She looked at Caty, the fear of death distorting her features. Her appearance was of one who had lost a great struggle. The woman cried out in Gaelic. Caty could not understand a word she said, but her fear and pleading were plain enough.

Caty made her way down and freed the woman with her knife. The woman grasped at her desperately, looking around fearfully and continuing to talk. Caty could not imagine what a woman could have done to warrant this punishment. For certain, the men who did it would be back. She seized every cord and stake and scrambled away, dragging the woman along. They splashed through the water's edge; Caty knew that the incoming tide would cover any sign that the woman had not escaped alone. Coming to a rocky point, they clambered up, stepping from rock to rock. When they reached the upper edge of the bank, they both climbed up, taking care to stay on rocks. They eventually reached Caty's horse. Caty mounted and pulled the woman up behind.

So thick was the surrounding foliage that in just moments they were no longer visible. Fearing she could find herself in the same predicament if she were found to have released this woman, Caty stayed away from the road. After riding a while, she selected a spot and buried the stakes and cord as deeply as she could.

Several hours of riding later, they stopped to rest. The woman started to slide off the horse when the sudden chatter and flight of birds alerted Caty to company. Men were arguing loudly. One was angry—very angry. They spoke in a language much like that of the one the woman spoke. The look of fear on the woman's face told Caty that the woman knew who owned the voice. Barely breathing, Caty held her horse firmly. The woman was frozen with fear.

The men seemed to be moving nearer. They came from the same direction Caty and her new companion had, and she guessed they must be after the woman. One spoke in short sentences, while the angry one answered. The woman touched Caty lightly. She pointed to her foot, shaking her head, then pointed to the horse's foot and nodded. Caty realized they were looking for human tracks but only finding horse tracks. Slowly, the men moved away. When they had gone and the birds had resumed their activities, Caty and the woman moved deeper into the woods in the direction opposite that of their hunters. They would spend the night here. Better to be cold again than chance an unwanted meeting.

Once the horse had been tethered, Caty shared what little she had with the woman. The poor thing ate hungrily. Sitting together next to a fallen tree, they covered themselves with Caty's cloak and settled down. They neither slept nor spoke. Grateful for the warmth the woman's body added to hers, Caty wondered what she was to do with the new addition.

Morning's first light found them wearily trudging onward through the forest. She and the woman found berries to eat and shared the last bit of Caty's meat and biscuit. As they walked and rode, the woman pointed out plants, motioning to body parts, indicating possible uses. Caty began to gather some of the plants. Perhaps this woman was also a healer. Shuddering, Caty was reminded of how fragile her existence would be if she were ever accused of witchcraft. Caty and the woman rode in what Caty hoped was a southerly direction. By now, she was so turned around it seemed hopeless. "The cursed clouds. How does one travel in this place?" she said aloud, knowing full well her companion could not understand.

As they rode on, looking for the villages Caty had passed previously, she realized the inlet was now to her left. *I must be headed north again*, she thought. Disheartened, Caty prayed for sun. *If this is spring, I can little imagine what the rest of the year will bring.* Caty shivered. Little by little, she and the woman were beginning to understand each other. After one long session around a fire the woman had started, Caty finally understood that she must continue riding with the water at her left. The woman was adamant, and Caty had little reason to argue the advice.

The poor soul she had released on the beach stirred Caty's heart, and she was not eager to part with her. Even after advancing without sign of detection, the woman frequently looked backward. She was frightened, and Caty felt for her. Where could she go? She, like Caty, had no one to come to her aid. Caty would have liked to talk about the woman's plight with her, but she could barely understand her babbling about the plants.

On this morning, after riding several hours, the woman urged Caty to stop the horse. As she slid off, she kissed Caty's hand. She chattered in her singsong language, motioning again for Caty to continue and keeping an eye on the water. It was apparent that this was a good-bye. With vigorous nods and hand motions, Caty agreed to continue back the way she had come days ago. She gripped the woman's hand gently and smiled. Pressing her last few coins into the woman's hand, Caty watched as she walked away, praying she would be safe. *This land is not a place for women*, Caty decided.

EIGHT

THE NEXT MORNING, CATY HAD only ridden a short distance on a winding road, which snaked through dense groves of trees and underbrush, when she heard men approaching in front of her. She recalled the voices and the language they spoke; these men were likely those who had staked the woman. The thick vegetation shouldering the road on both sides made it impossible to escape. Caty could do little but meet the inevitable confrontation. Her head held high, she continued forward. It took only moments for them to encounter her. She pulled her horse up and waited. Seven men surrounded her. One, who looked to be the leader, spoke to her, harshly. Caty could not understand him. *I fear this will not go well*, she thought.

"My lord, I do not speak your language. Please forgive me, a stranger to this land."

Frowning, the leader spoke again, this time in English. "Who are you and from where do you come?"

"I am lost. I try for Glasgow. When we landed, the water was on my left. I believed it should be on the right, if I were riding south. I fear I am badly turned. Perhaps you would be able to direct me, sir."

The man was unkempt, with wild hair and the mannerisms of a bully. The entire group consisted of men who looked like they cared little for what Caty thought of as civilization. They looked fierce, though none made any threatening movements toward her. Caty had no idea what she should do next. *Would that my brothers were here*, she thought.

With a mocking bow, he replied, "You would grace us with your company, lad?"

Caty had no intention of going with him, given a choice. She decided to take a dangerous step. "I am not a lad. I travel as a lad for safety. I am a lady. My father's family were warriors and fought in other lands. I wish only to get home. He told many stories of the Scotsmen and their bravery. I know about King Robert the Bruce, William Wallace, and even Rob Roy MacGregor." Smiling, she quietly continued, although her heart hammered in her chest. "I would only ask direction from you. I would not keep you from your business, sir."

"Prove you are a lady," he said impassively, his arms folded across his chest. His voice and face had lost their hostility.

Caty sat up straight. "Have I asked you to prove you are a gentleman?"

"Perhaps I would like to prove I am a *man*, and I could prove you are a woman at the same time." He did not speak in jest. His voice was calm. He waited for her reply.

With narrowed eyes leveled at him, she said, "Then you would prove you are *not* a gentleman, sir? Any man can prove that. I believe Scots have honor. What I ask of you is not something any common man can speak to."

He sat back, studying her. "You are the one dressed as a man. Is this not so?"

"Yes it is so. As this is your land, you must know it is not wise to ride about unprotected, with so many . . ."—Caty paused, frowning for effect—"so many other kinds of men about."

At this, he nodded his head. "You speak the truth. Continue with the water on your left. The sun will rise on your left." Without another word, he and his men rode around her and away.

Caty nodded to them as they rode by, then she too rode on. Until she was certain they were not following her, she could hardly breathe. Sweat glistened on her forehead and trickled down her temples. Her jaw ached from gritting her teeth. Still, she rode on, without looking back. As evening came, she rode past Perth again. "I pray I am heading south finally," she murmured.

Riding onward, past the lights, she rode deep into the woods covering the hillside and stopped. While her horse grazed, she sat against the base of a tree, shielded by thick brush. Tears began to stream down her cheeks. The strain of this venture was becoming more than she had ever bargained for. She was hungry, thirsty, dirty, and tired. She could feel herself coming unwound. She covered her shoulders with the cloak and wrapped her arms around herself. Unable to stop her tears, she rocked gently and cried. Overpowering fear kept the moans soft, but the tears fell like a heavy storm. Eventually, she cried herself to sleep.

Caty awoke with a start; her horse had nuzzled her, nearly pushing her over. She looked around, trying to banish the fog from her mind. Stiff and hungry, she stood. It took great effort to saddle up and ride. Her determination had slipped. This day, life in the castle seemed not so bad. It was too late. A choice was made those long days ago. She would meet her destiny.

NINE

EVENTUALLY, SHE CAME TO YET another borough. This one was the largest she had come across. A sign over a public house identified the town as Stirling. This meant little to Caty. She had tried to put as much distance between her captor and herself as possible, but her dash to England was not going like she thought it would. So much had happened. Surely, once she got closer to England, he could not take her readily. Perhaps she could escape to the new colony across the ocean she had heard talk of. Right now, she was hungry, dirty, and destitute. She needed food, safe rest, and work.

The muddy streets of Stirling were filled with people moving about their business. Smoke funneled toward the skies. The alleys reeked with the odor of refuse, both human and household. Men walked along the streets, covering their faces with the lacy cloths popular among the gentry. Women walked alongside the alleys, dodging horses and men. Little notice of a young man on a horse was taken.

Caty shuddered. She had not lived within the confines of a town for as long as she could remember. Her parents had lived on the outskirts of the towns her father fought to control for England. This filth was repugnant, but the town was bustling, and that boded well for one looking to go unnoticed.

Caty stopped at a small bookshop and cautiously entered. It seemed a suitable place to seek employment, and she needed money and food. The proprietor was an aging man, of little patience. As his last customers filed out, she asked quietly if he might need help.

He eyed her without speaking for a long time. "Just what can you do?" he barked, stepping away from her with a frown. "You look ill, lad, and smell foul. Can you read or write?"

"Sir, I can write and read both. I can read maps and do many things. I studied overseas with my family. I am on my own now. Please help me, sir. I will do whatever you ask of me." Caty met his stern gaze without wavering.

Something in the young man's eyes held the older man's. "Fine," he answered gruffly, "we have boxes of books. Shelve them. But first, wash up through there, out the back door."

Caty cleaned her face and hands in the basin she found out back, then began on the books. Moving about quickly, she worked hard, wondering how she could find out just where she was and how much farther she had yet to travel. Near dark, the old man approached her. "Lad, do you have a place to stay this night?" His tone was softer now.

"No, sir," Caty replied quietly.

"There is a room in the back; you can stay there. Take care if you light a fire. Be certain you blow out the candles. Use the water out by the door to clean up. Here, you can have what I did not eat." The old man handed a small package to Caty. "I will see you in the morn." He watched the young man relax. He felt there must surely be a tale about this lad. Something reminded the old man of his own struggles as a young man, trying to make a life after losing his family. "By what name are you called?"

"James, sir. Might I read?" Caty's eyes looked hopefully into the old man's face.

He turned away, hesitating, and then said, "Yes. Take care to close up." Without looking back again, he shuffled out and closed the door behind him.

Caty ate the bread and cheese left by the old man, saving a portion in her small pouch for times ahead. After closing and locking every door, she washed up. The old man had placed a patch of soap and an old towel on the cot in her new room. Never would she take such things for granted again.

Caty began searching through the shop drawers reserved for charts. She ultimately found what she looked for and anxiously pored over the map—but was discouraged to find that Stirling was still a long way from the English border.

The map did explain her earlier confusion about the water, however; she was now on the other side of Scotland. *I've been turned around far too long—in many ways*, she thought. It was apparent she could only stay for a short while if she were to make it to England before her captor caught up with her. She would need to get much closer to a port of some size. Money was the great issue.

Caty made certain the little shop would be ready for business in the morning. Carrying the water basin upstairs, she bathed as best she could. Next, she tried to wash her clothes. The water was filthy by the time she finished. *If I do this every night, they should get clean eventually. So too should I*, she thought to herself with a smile as she lay to sleep.

Earlier in the day the shopkeeper had recommended a stable for her horse. Now Caty worried about how to pay for the horse's upkeep. With great difficulty, she tried to calm her mind and rest. Her time here would be only long enough to earn the money needed to board a ship bound for England, she told herself. She would not chance being shipped as a lady of men's pleasure.

Always, her captor loomed in her mind. Thinking on him, Caty was surprised she could remember every detail of his face. She could still see his dark eyes piercing her own. Though she had not seen him smile, she could imagine it would be a pleasant sight. She could remember his hands and his walk. *What can I be thinking? How could I have taken such note of him? No matter, he is only one of the men I have met.* Caty stared at the ceiling. *For one who so long was without male companionship, it seems I have now been overrun*, she thought as she rolled over.

Now her thoughts drifted to the other men she had met. Some were seemingly devoid of conscience. The group that had befriended her was not, though. Smiling, she realized how comfortable she became with them, and how quickly. They were her father's people. Caty did not yet feel that England was her homeland. Would it ever become so? What was to become of the poor wretched woman she found? Her thoughts refused to settle. The hour was late when she finally slept.

By the second night, she had copied the map she found. For the next several days, Caty cleaned, filed, and did everything she could do to make the shopkeeper more at ease. He now brought her lunch and something for her evening meals. She saved at least half of what she was given. This time she would take no chances.

"How is it, lad, that you wash so much?" the shopkeeper asked one morning.

"My time in other lands gave credence to the idea that to be clean is to stay in good health," Caty explained. She had no idea how he could know the extent to which she cleaned up each evening, but she made a note to be certain not to leave anything behind that could give her other activities away.

The shopkeeper was pleased to find that the young man he had hired was able to find and recommend books and writings to his customers. The lad's presence had brightened the old shop. The shopkeeper was hopeful he could persuade the lad to stay on. When, after two weeks, Caty asked if she might collect what pay she had coming, he was saddened. "Please, sir," Caty said. "I find I must leave. I am certain I owe for the upkeep of my horse, and would like to replace these worn clothes. Might I be able to take my pay?"

The old man sat down. "What would it take for you to stay on here, lad? You know of what you speak and write. You have been a great help to me. I ask that you stay."

Caty's eyes were sad as she answered. "I am sorry to leave you, too. You have been most kind, but I must leave. I cannot stay here."

He frowned. "From what do you run?"

Caty took a deep breath. "I cannot share with you my plight," she said slowly. "It would be better if you knew not what I am about. I must only trouble you for any pay you think I have been worth."

Making a decision, the old man stood up. "You are coming home with me, for a meal at least. I will bring your horse along. Come." When Caty hesitated, the old man took her arm and turned her toward her room. When Caty returned with her few possessions, the old man walked out with her. Together, they walked to the corner, and there he pointed the way to his home, sent Caty ahead, and walked to the stable. Self-consciously, Caty softly knocked on the cottage door. A small, spry old lady with laughing eyes came to the door.

"Your husband asked that I come here to wait for him," Caty announced.

"Certainly, do enter, lad." The lady opened the door to let Caty in, then went about setting the meal together. As she worked, she watched the young man closely. Shaking her head, she finally sat down at the table and motioned for Caty to sit. "Now, lass, you must tell me what trouble you are in. Mayhaps we can help. 'Tis not good to be alone. Not good at all for a lass to be alone."

Caty froze. What had she done to give herself away? Feigning anger, she answered with dignity. "Just why do you call me a lass? Have I a dress or curls? What?"

"No, but you have a woman's eye, my child. Fear not, your secret is safe with me. My man will know it not, unless you choose to share with him."

At that moment, the shopkeeper entered. With only a brief greeting, he sat down, offered a blessing, and began to eat. For a while, little was said. Caty grew increasingly uncomfortable. Finally, she stood, and stated, "Sir, I must leave, before it becomes too dark to see."

At this, the man turned to his wife. "This bairn is in trouble; it would seem he runs from someone or something. Do we have better clothes to offer?"

"Och aye," she said, standing. "I will fetch them."

"Be you certain you would not stay with us? 'Tis a big town, this. You would be lost here. Unless your trouble is with the Kirk," he added, frowning.

Caty shook her head, quickly. "No. Not with the Kirk, sir. Still, it would be better for you and your wife if you knew little about me. Please do not press me for answers, sir."

"Perhaps," the old lady said, "you run from a carlin."

The old man looked at Caty in surprise. "What is this?"

Caty replied slowly. "Sir, I am not what I seem. The less you know, the safer you may be. I could be a lady, but I would never say so. Please, I must leave."

The old man frowned at Caty, trying to understand. *She could be a lady, what does that mean?*

The shopkeeper's wife quickly pulled Caty into a small bedroom, where she had several pairs of breeches laid out, along with shirts and shoes. "Our son died these many years ago. I think he would have liked to see use of these things. Child, you must not wear the cloak; it is too rich for the lad you pretend to be."

Gladly, Caty changed, and bundled the old dirty clothes up. The woman took the bundle from her. "I will see to these, lass," she said softly. "Take care, the roads are not safe."

Caty impulsively kissed the old lady on the cheek. "Thank you for your kindness." Without waiting for a response, she walked back toward the front of the old couple's house.

Handing her a pouch heavy with coins, the shopkeeper opened the door and watched Caty leave. "God go with you!" he called. He did not understand what trouble Caty might be in, but his instinct told him she was a good person, and she needed help.

Riding away, Caty prayed. Having tucked the lord's cloak into a roll to take with her, she was instead covered with a plain, worn cape the woman had given up. Not looking around, she hoped she traveled with a careless air, not a fearful one.

TEN

THE RIDE WAS SLOW AND chilly. The wind blew another storm in. Heavy clouds hid the moon and stars. There were few travelers out. Caty rode as long as she dared before slipping into the surrounding forest. There would be no rest. Bundled with both cloaks, she still shivered through the long night.

As she followed her copy of the map toward Glasgow, Caty stayed close to the shoreline whenever possible. In Glasgow, she planned to book passage on a merchant ship bound for England, or maybe even America, with the other families she had heard were leaving Scotland bound for that new land.

The clouds finally broke as she neared the city. Caty found shelter deeper into the thickets for another night and buried the lord's cloak before she left. It was much heavier than the one she had been given, and she was loath to give it up. Yet, the old woman's words rang true. She was discarding pieces of her captor; better to not draw unnecessary attention.

Riding into Glasgow with the early morning, Caty took stock of what she saw. It was much larger than she imagined. The bay was filled with the masts of many ships. The streets were crammed with houses and people. Even at this early hour, the community was alive. Like the last village, the stench was overwhelming, especially near the alleys. The size of this place made all the unpleasantness heavier. But to Caty's eyes, the city looked beautiful—it was bustling, the port was busy, and once she earned enough money for her passage, she would finally leave this wretched land. To see such life moving past encouraged her. Surely no one would notice one young man looking for work.

She again sought out printing shops or bookstores on the fringes of the area. She passed all manner of shops, each one busy. That spoke well for the possibility of employment. Eventually, finding a bookstore that looked just like what she needed, she stepped inside and made the same request she had made in Stirling. This time, the owner was a younger man. He was thin, fidgety, and constantly brushing away imaginary flies with a delicately held handkerchief. "Just what can you do?"

Caty answered confidently, "I can read, file, clean, print, and anything else you find necessary."

"Fine. You're hired. This place is a mess. Just get it straight. My uncle died and left this to me. I have not a desire to work in this stuffy place, but like what it yields. We can decide tomorrow what more I might need." He glanced around the bookstore. With an air of great importance he added, "I leave for the tavern. Several are meeting to talk, and I would learn from men such as these. I'll be back before you can leave, to lock up. Do not steal from me. I have friends who would like to make an example of thieves. Do you understand?"

"Yes, sir," Caty hastily replied, and immediately began to straighten up around the area. The nervous man left, and she relaxed. She worked the rest of the day, cleaning and bringing order to the small shop. By nightfall, when the owner returned, he stepped into a different shop. He was well pleased, and so stated.

"Where do you sleep?" he asked, frowning.

"I am not certain," Caty admitted. She had thought on the same problem all afternoon.

"Well, the previous owner, er, my uncle, stayed upstairs. You can stay there if you like. I open at seven in the morning. No later. Clean yourself up." With a disgusted little shudder, he turned on his heel and abruptly left.

Caty, left alone in the shop, found herself happy. She had a place to work, could stay out of sight, save money, and not pay for a room. She blew out all but one candle. Carrying it, she walked up the stairs. The two rooms were small and dusty but well hidden from any view. Opening a window to allow the air to circulate, Caty cleaned her new quarters into the night. By morning, it looked as if she had lived there for years—clean, warm, and inviting. Caty had a full bath for the first time in far too long.

When the owner came in, he was pleased to see that Caty had taken the window displays down and put up new ones. Several customers were already waiting outside the store. Few took notice of her. When they had made their purchases and left, Caty asked if she might leave the shop during lunch. "No, you work all day," the owner said curtly. "You are getting free room, you know. I will let you wander about for half an hour each morning, and as long as you like after closing. If you need to go someplace, go now. And by the way, here are the keys. I expect the shop to be opened by the time I arrive each day, and to not close until dark." Dropping the keys into her hand, he waved her away.

Caty nodded and left quickly. As she hurried to the livery stable, the streets were lively, with shops offering powdered wigs, linen undergarments, lace, and other items the gentry would likely buy. Caty went about quite unnoticed. When she got to the stable, she inquired about her horse. It was being fed, and had attracted some attention. Large and well trained, it seemed the stable hand had received several offers for the animal. "He is not for sale at the moment," Caty told the young man. "If I should change my mind, I will bring him to you first. Perhaps we may yet strike a deal." The lad seemed honest, and gladly agreed.

When Caty's work was done the next day, she secured the front door and left by a back door, which she also locked behind her. She walked the distance to the stable. Taking the horse, she paid for its keep. That left her with but the little in her pouch. No matter, she told herself. She would add to it quickly.

Riding out of town, she dismounted, pulled the saddle off, hid it, and then let the animal loose. She hugged his neck as he made soft noises back. At last she forced herself to stand away. When the horse followed, she yelled and ran at him. Still he stood. She threw tiny stones, yelling and waving at him. Eventually, the animal turned and ran off.

After watching until she could no longer see or hear him, Caty slowly walked back to the shop. She slept little that night, but she knew that what she had done was necessary; she was getting rid of anything that could link her to her captor. At the same time, she felt as though she pushed all that mattered away. *I cannot believe this is what my father envisioned*, she thought sadly. *I am so alone.*

Several days went by, the same as those before. The young owner came by every morning and evening. The evening visits were shorter, and Caty could tell he had been drinking. The morning visits were later, and Caty knew he frequently suffered the effects of his nightly bouts wherever he went.

By the end of the second week, Caty felt she should follow the town's Sunday customs. As she sat in Kirk, half listening to the sermon, she suddenly bolted upright. The reverend had been cautioning his congregation to "forget not the Kirk and her needs" and expounding on the temptations of life when he mentioned "this Edinburgh, with its boundless opportunities." Caty was stunned. Could she have heard right? This was not Glasgow? This was Edinburgh? That meant she would have to travel west to get to ships going to the Americas. From Edinburgh, the ships would most likely sail for such ports as those in France or Germany. Those that sailed down the coast to England would likely dock at ports too close to London. More cold, lonely nights to endure. This time without a horse. It would be a walk—a long walk. Her heart sank.

Self-consciously, she glanced around to see if anyone had noticed her distraction. None had. After the church service, she rushed back to the shop and spread her hand-drawn map on the table, next to one from a book of maps. In her race to copy the map, she had mislabeled it, reversing the locations of Glasgow and Edinburgh. The fact that more than one patron from Stirling had informed her that Glasgow was closer than Edinburgh—a fact seemingly contradicted by her map—now made sense. Studying the map, Caty also realized Glasgow was too far from a port of any size, anyway. She had wondered at the time she took to get to this place. Still, Edinburgh was also a port. It might be easier to travel to England from this place, in fact. This could be better. Situated on the east coast, travel with merchant ships might not be as easily had, at least not going to America. However, the settlement was large and certainly busy. She could stay here in disguise for longer. Then she could decide what destination might be best for her. Maybe she could simply cross the border into England and safety. Surely her captor would not venture into England for her.

That afternoon, Caty reworked her plans. Surely the lord would go to Glasgow first, since it was the closest. That would give her more time. She could save money by simply buying as good a ticket as her finances would allow. Then she would try to get to America. *Perhaps this is for the best*, she thought. *Please, God, help me get out of this mess. 'Tis not of my own doing, You know.*

Caty hastened to rise each morning before the owner came to the store for fear he might discover her guise. Every time he came in, she was dressed and downstairs.

ELEVEN

THIS DAY, THE SHOP OWNER watched her work for a long moment; his eyes narrowed. His thin hand waved the ever-present kerchief around his face and head. He had not paid her any undue attention until now. Though her heart was in her throat, she kept busy. Could he tell she was not a man? Was she moving inappropriately? What would she do if he found her out? In her mind, she went over every detail of her attire. What could she have left undone?

"I think you should come with me tonight," he said. "I go to join a group of men discussing life. We can eat afterward." He watched for Caty's response. She agreed, now persuaded she would have to leave. If he drank as usual, she could easily slip away. That afternoon, she packed her things and hid them outside the back door.

As they walked to the lecture, the shop owner talked nervously, taking care not to move too fast. Caty walked alongside him, searching passing faces for any sign that one could see through her disguise.

At length, they came to a place called Crosskeys Tavern. Patrons packed the popular meeting place. The shop owner and Caty joined a group of men already seated around a table, Caty fearing that all the men must be able to hear her heart pound. As the conversation moved, however, she forgot her fear and was drawn into the discussion. Talk of philosophy, review of works by such minds as Alexander Pope, discussion of the plan to remove Latin as the official language of learning, and debate of the need to help Edinburgh grow on an orderly course all fueled intense debate. To her patron's surprise, Caty held her own. By evening's end, she had nearly forgotten her masquerade. But as the men rose to leave, she felt a growing sense of apprehension.

"Would you not consider spending the rest of this evening with me?" the shopkeeper whispered to her as they wound through the darkened streets of Edinburgh, back toward the shop. "I would know you better. I can make you forget you are alone at this time. I can make you forget you must go about dressed as something you are not." Her disguise had failed. He said more, but Caty was taken aback and heard nothing else. Her mind rushed to grasp what he insinuated.

Thinking quickly, Caty tried to gently turn the man away. She needed to keep working at his shop if possible. Knowing she could ill afford to anger or shame him, desperate to keep up her charade to all others, and certainly not willing to be part of whatever he had in mind, she chose her words carefully. "Perhaps I am not the help you need. I feel you misunderstand my dedication to your business, sir. I am not turned the way you might believe. If I have mis-led you, I beg your pardon; such was never my intent."

"No—I, I mean yes, rather," the man stuttered. "It is . . . I am . . . I am sorry. Please forget I spoke to you. Your arrangements are fine with me, as is your work. I beg your forgiveness. I was just—I made a mistake. I would know why you go about dressed as a man," he finished lamely. He looked so miserable that Caty felt sorry for him.

"No matter, your words need not concern you if you will simply allow me to continue working here." she murmured, turning away. They walked the remainder of the distance to the shop in an uncomfortable silence.

Once inside, he spoke again, this time in a quiet, defeated tone. "Sometimes, I think it would be better if I had never been born. I cannot help what I am or the life I want. You are not that kind of woman, I can see now. I misjudged you. There must be some reason you go about as a man. Are you running from the authorities?" He quickly added, "Do not answer. It matters little. I hoped I had found someone who shares my love of books and learning." His eyes narrowed. "I think you do; however, you are not free to share that love with anyone. I can see that."

With that, he left the shop, slamming the door behind him. Caty realized he thought she was indeed running from an obligation to another man. Though discouraged by the ineffectiveness of her disguise, she felt sorry for the man. She knew not how he would react to her when he came back, and she tried to think of where else she could work, or live. After a long period of rumination, Caty decided to try staying at this shop longer. With a heavy heart, she decided to travel to Glasgow should the man make her stay uncomfortable.

She had retrieved her hidden bundle and was going upstairs to her rooms when the man returned. He called to her as he entered the shop. With trepidation, Caty turned on the stairs to face him. Though he had been gone only an hour, he had had too much ale and was still in a mood to talk. "I have carried this secret long enough, I think. The owner of this shop had a beautiful daughter, he did. I believe he cared little for her, but needed her labor. She and I were attracted to each other. It is difficult to keep such a thing a secret for long. When her father found out, he banned me and threatened to send the daughter away. During the argument that followed, the father was killed. Because the father had been very old, the doctor we called cared little for the inconvenience of calling the authorities. He simply said the man was dead and needed to be buried and asked to be paid. The daughter, saddened and guilty over the argument, went out that afternoon—pushed some men into fighting over her. When the fight worsened, she tried to stop it and was accidentally killed. I buried them both the same day." He sank into one of the chairs nearby, looking utterly miserable.

Caty's heart ached for him. "Sometimes life takes turns only our Lord can understand," she said quietly. "You were kind to care for the daughter. I think you did the best you could do, given the circumstances."

He nodded, grateful for understanding. Without further words, he departed once again.

After this encounter, there seemed to be a new closeness between the two of them, born of friendship and Caty's refusal to judge him. He took her with him often, to listen to his friends and others debate the day's issues. He always brought her food, and he frequently came into the shop with friends, to sit around the great table at the shop's center and visit. On occasion he brought her clothes. In keeping with her disguise, they were always simple, though well built, and suitable for a young man of little means.

On one afternoon, he arrived followed by his usual entourage. When all were seated, the debate would begin. Today, a new member strolled in. He was tall and well built, at ease with himself and his surroundings. He moved like one accustomed to leading. He walked with a purpose. His dark eyes took in every detail of the little shop. Surveying the store offhandedly, his eyes immediately found Caty. He frowned and walked slowly around her. Caty felt his stare and, looking up, met his eyes. Without wavering, she inquired, "Do you seek assistance, sir?"

"No," he answered brusquely. "I would ask your name, lad."

"You would," Caty answered, "but I decline to give it. I work for that gentleman seated there." She pointed across the shop to the owner. "I can help you find books, maps, and other manner of written material. If you have need of additional information, you must speak with the owner."

The stranger studied Caty. "I would ask your name, but I believe I already know it. You have your family's eyes, of that I am certain, and their look. I say you are of the family of Tabor. Are you not?"

Caty's mind raced. "And why would it be so important you know who I am?" she retorted. "If you are as certain as you say, you need not ask. How else can I assist you, sir?"

Smiling coolly, he shook his head, turned, and joined the table. As the afternoon progressed, the men continued debating and Caty busied herself with her work. The stranger looked up at her often. When the men rose to leave, she made certain she was not around. After glancing into the main room to ensure that they were gone, she shared her experience with her employer and wondered aloud whether she should leave.

"Oh no, not because of him. I just met him. He is traveling through town and won't be back. You are safe." He paused, seeming to think for a moment. "Lady, are you in trouble? Is there something I should have knowledge of?"

"No, I am not in trouble. At least not in the way you would think," Caty responded. "I am trying to get back to England, but cannot simply walk onto a ship begging for passage. I will not travel as a woman for hire. I would pay my own way. For this, I work. I have done nothing against any law of man or God."

"Then we shall speak of this no more." The owner smiled at his grand scheme to end the problem, though it consisted merely of ignoring it.

Despite her employer's reassurances, Caty could not forget the strange man. He never came into the shop again, but he had recognized her. Why did it matter to him? Perhaps it did not, but how could he know of her family—in Scotland?

In the following weeks, the shop owner began to pay Caty better, and he seldom came by after the midday meal, leaving her to work in peace. On several afternoons she had found a package left on her bed: additional new clothes, to replace her breeches and shirt.

Always, the shop owner was careful to have people present when he was with her. He wanted no talk of dishonor to be directed toward Caty should her disguise be discovered. They simply went on as before. Caty was grateful for her new confidant, even though she knew he cared more for the adventure of having her around than for her herself. He was more than happy to play the part of protector, as long as he did not actually have to protect.

TWELVE

IN AN ELABORATE TENT, LORD Rhys leaned back in his chair. *This is a sad day*, he mused. As usual, his mind wandered back to the woman. He remembered how she had reacted when her party was attacked and taken captive. Even though she was confused and frightened, she began to move about the wounded, rendering aid. She gave every man the same attention, certainly unaware that she was the main target of the attack. That day she had worked all evening and deep into the night. The rest of the women had huddled in a group weeping, but not her. She worked as though there were no danger to her. She gave orders as if she were a commander. He smiled. He was certain men lived because of what she had done for them. He never planned to keep her. That was not the deal. But from the first day he had been captivated by her. Always, she moved about with a serenity he had never before witnessed. That his own men quickly accepted her still mystified him. His people did not easily take to strangers.

I should have brought her with me for this fight, he thought ruefully. No matter, it was over now. His victory had cost him little when compared to what he stood to lose. His lands would be safe for the time being. The world as he knew it was changing, and one day he would not be isolated. Thanks to men such as the learned Scotsman Argyll, crop production was up. Based on Argyll's advice, Rhys had already changed how men worked the land. Other changes would come, soon. His thoughts turned to the woman, who must now be enjoying her new quarters. What must she think of her new surroundings? He gave no thought to what his clan might think of a union between the two of them, or what the woman herself might think. She would be by his side as he moved forward. His dreaming was interrupted by the entrance of his brother, Bruce.

"We lost a few, but nothing compared to what we killed. What do you want done with the captured men, weapons, women, and everything else?" Bruce sat down.

Lord Rhys knew that many of the men now captive were simple laborers. "You are to rule the lands we have added to our holdings today," he told his brother. "Take one section of our men with you. Return the captured men to their families, to work as they did before; this time, they are to pay only half what they paid before, to their new lord—you. The warriors are to be sent to me. When they are ready, you will get them back. The rest is to be divided. One-fourth to you, one-fourth to me, and the rest divided amongst our men. See that everyone receives equal share. I want the one you believe is the leader brought to me, if he is still alive."

Bruce nodded and left the tent. Lord Rhys's men were already intensely loyal; actions like this just cemented the relationship. As Bruce walked back and forth among the prisoners, goods, and animals, something caught his eye. "Take this to our lord," he told one of his men. "He will have use for it."

Minutes later, the lord ran his hand over the chair his brother had sent him. It was quite heavy, though simply made. Instinctively, he knew the woman would like this gift. His brother had done well, as usual. He smiled to himself. "Thank Lord Bruce for me," he said to the man standing before him.

The prisoner believed to be the leader of the defeated clan was brought in, along with another thought to be his brother. The leader's eyes flashed with defiance. Rhys rose. His height forced the clansman to look up. "You are offered service with me. I know that is not what you would want, but I need good fighting men. You are such a man. The lands you fought to overtake belong to the people you see here." Lord Rhys waved toward those of his men visible through the tent opening. "Your men are hungry; your lands yield little. I can help you."

"Why would you?" the clansman challenged.

"Scotland must end its self-destruction. We have to work our way forward, as a nation. To do this, we need leaders, of which you are one. Who fights at your side?" Lord Rhys eyed the clansman critically.

"My brother, but he is of no consequence to you. I make the decision in this, and I say no! I do not stand with you! My people do not stand with you," the clansman finished haughtily.

"You would rather your people starve? The women and children also?"

"Yes, everyone—but we will not. We will survive, as we have always done. You would take our lands, but you will not take my clan." Finished, he stood defiant.

"I already have. I remind you that the lands you fought over do not belong to you. Because of this day, however, you *have* also lost your lands. To the victor go the lands." The lord paused, waiting.

The man stood silent and defiant, still.

"Stand with me, swear allegiance to me, and you may return to your lands, as the leader of them, under my rule. I offer you life and help with your lands. Take both."

"No, I will never stand with one such as you," the man answered.

"I am a Scotsman, the same as you," the lord replied coldly. He nodded to his men. "Kill him."

The leader was dragged away. Outside, the men who had fought with that leader watched silently. Not one came to his defense.

The second captive in Lord Rhys's tent had also watched with eyes of stone as the leader was dragged out. The lord turned to him next. "Are you his brother, as he said?"

"No. There is not a brother," the man replied. "He took this clan when I was very young."

"Yet you would stay with him?" the lord asked curtly.

"They were . . . are my people. I stayed for my people." The man met the lord's eyes without wavering.

"Tell me of your leader," Lord Rhys asked, studying the man with critical eyes.

"He is not my leader," responded the man.

The lord watched the man closely. "Explain," he ordered.

"When he took the clan, he took my father's wife also. He beat and raped her, until one day she died. Her charge to me was to remember my father and care for his people. We are not like other clans."

"How so?" The more this man talked, the more Lord Rhys liked what he saw before him.

"My father left Scotland to fight. My birthplace was Spain. He brought my mother back with him. My mother was treated as an equal by my father." As he spoke, the man's pride in his clan was evident.

"Everyone out," Lord Rhys said. "Bruce, you stay. And he"—he pointed to the captive—"will stay also."

When the tent had cleared, he ordered the man unbound.

"You are made the same offer," Lord Rhys informed the man standing before him.

The man stood tall, unafraid. "I would stand with you. My clan will stand with you."

"On what do you decide?" asked the lord.

"My clan is getting smaller. We are hungry. I could try to fight you, but then what have I gained? If I stand with you, maybe my clan can survive. For that, I stand. I swear allegiance to you. If I have needs, I bring them to you. I bring grievances the same. If you need my services, you have but to ask."

"It is done," Lord Rhys answered. "By what are you called?"

"I am Thain, of Clan Macintosh," the Highlander replied.

"Thain, you are welcome on my lands and in my home." Rhys shook Thain's hand. The Highlander left the tent.

Bruce watched until they were alone. "I trust not some of these men, but Thain, yes," he commented. "He will bring the others to your side, brother."

"That is the one we want on our side. In two days we leave for Dermoth Castle. Let him take his men back. Give him the same orders I gave you. We will bring half of our men and half of his." As Bruce stepped past, Rhys stopped him. "You are my only brother and will take what is ours, when I am gone. I would have all our peoples and those of Thain know you are my successor." Rhys added, "In truth, I need you with me for what I fear is coming to Scotland."

Bruce grasped Rhys's shoulder. "I have no problem with your direction, brother. My family and my home are with you."

Satisfied, Lord Rhys stretched his legs out before the fire. He was going home.

The moment Rhys entered the great room of his castle, he sensed something amiss. "Bruce, what say you about this silence?"

"I feel it also, brother. Though not as danger." Bruce turned around and surveyed the room.

"No, not as danger." His brother strode to the middle and called for the steward. The poor man crept forward. He knelt low, begging forgiveness. "For what do you beg? Speak man!"

"The woman—"

"What about the woman?" Lord Rhys interrupted. When the steward hesitated, the lord grabbed him by the hair and pulled him up. In a low voice, he said again, "I ask, what about the woman?"

"She ran away, sir. At least I think she did." The poor man trembled, remembering well the temper of his lord.

Now the silence was heavy. Suddenly, Bruce broke into laughter. He slapped his leg, nearly rolling with mirth.

"How so, you find this amusing?" challenged Rhys, whirling to face Bruce.

Though his brother's agitation remained, the edge was gone from Rhys's voice, the very reaction Bruce hoped for. "Let us hear how this lady outsmarted you, brother."

Stammering, the steward told of how he had gone back to her quarters; when she did not call for food, he tried to speak with her and found her room empty. The door to the lord's quarters had been locked. The steward was certain she was not there, as one of the lord's horses was also missing. Several men were already looking for her. So far, no one had returned.

"Since you find such humor in this, you will come with me," Lord Rhys barked at Bruce. "We leave within the hour, to bring her back."

Bruce nodded wordlessly, still grinning, and began to leave for the stable. "Just pray it is not my horse she took!" he called back. "This will be great amusement. Poor brother, you have never had your heart pulled from you before. 'Tis nigh time, I say."

Lord Rhys stormed into his rooms. Nothing was amiss. He almost overlooked the note sitting on his desk. He opened it and read:

> My lord, please find it in your heart to forgive me. I cannot stay and be captive in a household that worships differently than I. You are a good man and, it would seem, an able leader. You should have such a woman at your side. I am not that woman. I leave my mother's signet ring as payment for the things I must take, including the mount. My mother was a favorite lady of the Italian court, and as such, this ring has great value. Please do not try to follow; it would do you little good. God go with you and your people.

He crushed the paper in anger and threw it to the floor, then picked up the ring. He could tell it did indeed have value, just by the weight and stones. He pulled a chain from around his neck and slipped the ring onto it. Replacing the chain around his neck, he held the ring tightly. He entered her quarters; his jaws clenched.

The room still smelled of the juniper and flowers she had been given. He crossed the room and stared out the window. Glancing at the fireplace, he noticed a tuft of hair. He bent to pick it up and found he held long strands of shining auburn hair. *She dared to cut her hair?* His anger burned greater, but so did his desire for this lady. She that would defy him, run away from him, and steal his horse. She would be caught and punished. Still . . . *Don't follow you, lass? You should hope I find you before someone else does harm to you.* Determination filled him.

Changed and on fresh mounts, Lord Rhys, Bruce, and several men left the castle. "Just where do you think she went, brother?"

"Where would you go, Bruce?"

"Probably to England. You would have less chance of reaching me there," Bruce reasoned. "Of course, she knows you not, brother. England, in truth, offers but little protection."

"Hmm. She will need protection against *me*. She is not as wise as she thinks."

"On what do you base that?" asked Bruce.

"Were she wise, she would not have run away," his brother replied simply.

At this, Bruce laughed again. "I see."

Lord Rhys scowled. "What do you see, Bruce?"

"I see she has smacked you as with a griddle," Bruce answered merrily. "Your pride is fair wounded, I say."

"Take heed of what *I* say. She will not do this again." The lord's face was set.

With Bruce still chuckling, they rode on. Knowing well the trails, Lord Rhys and his company continued through the night. Early morning, Rhys was met by one of his grooms, who led a steed. "What have you there?"

"'Tis the missing horse, m'lord. Making its way home, I feel. No sign of the lady. A fine horse, this one. A wonder 'tis still loose, it is."

The lord frowned. If his calculations were correct, she had been gone about three, maybe four weeks. The horse had not been ridden in a while, as it was unkempt and cared little for the lines now holding it firm. Fear that she had already boarded a boat fueled his anger.

"Brother," said Bruce, "you know not where she may be bound? We lose time if we travel the wrong way."

"If I may, m'lord," the young man interjected, "I think she must be headed to Edinburgh. The other groom and I split up in Stirling. He left for Glasgow and I for Edinburgh. Found the horse outside Edinburgh. She was not seen in Stirling, but the horse was. I stopped by the stables in Stirling, on my way back. The horse was in the company of a thin lad who worked for a while at a bookshop but is no longer there. I think this lad is not a lad . . ."

"Yes, I agree. But were she in Stirling, why go to Edinburgh?" the lord countered glumly. "Is not Glasgow closer? Had she reached Glasgow, she could be boarded for England by now."

"'Tis true, Glasgow is a shorter ride from Stirling, but I found the horse on the road to Edinburgh. If she were in Glasgow, you would have heard by now. You would have heard from the stable hand first had he found her. I think the lady is headed to Edinburgh."

"You did well." The lord tossed a handful of coins to the man. "Take the horse back to the—no, wait!" He quickly changed horses, mounting that which had belonged to the woman. He handed over the other horse and rode off. Bruce and the other men quickly caught up. "Tonight we rest the horses," Lord Rhys called to them as they rode. "Tomorrow, we make Stirling."

THIRTEEN

RIDING INTO STIRLING, THE MEN split up, with plans to meet at a local tavern after dark. They were to begin working the outskirts of the town, checking with every shop. Rhys knew the woman would not chance going into town proper if she could find work near the safer edges. "She goes as a lad," he growled to himself.

When the men convened at the tavern that night, none had the woman in tow. After ordering food and ale, Bruce announced, "The old man at the bookstore close to the stable indeed had a lad working for him, but he swears he never paid a woman. Never saw a woman. Only a man, and that one left. Where the man left for, he claims not to know. I believe him. Of course, you will want to talk with him yourself."

Lord Rhys said nothing. He stared gloomily into the ale before him.

"If you would come, the man told me where he lives, and would gladly speak with you."

Behind the lord's men, at another dark table, a stranger sat unnoticed. He idly fingered his cup, swirling the ale inside. His eyes were downcast, and he never looked up, even as he took long drafts from the mug. When the woman came to refill it, he shook his head. He would need to think clearly. With eyes that spoke of practiced intrigue, he studied the now empty mug. At last, he raised his head, glanced at the men seated in front of him, and smiled to himself. He would have to inform his lord that they were not the only ones searching for Lady Tabor. In his assessment, these men would be well practiced at battle. The ease with which they carried their weapons spoke volumes. No matter, for the lady had already left. *Which is precisely what I should do, now,* the man thought.

Once the food arrived for Lord Rhys's table, everyone ate in silence. Bruce and the other men held little thought about the reasons their lord had for chasing this woman. All had seen her the first time she was captured. She was beautiful, but she was just a woman. It was enough that the lord was intent on getting her back. That made this a vacation for them—better than fighting, at least for a while.

When each had eaten his fill, the men arranged for lodging while Bruce and his brother left to speak with the bookstore keeper. Leaving the tavern, they were stopped by an Englishman with his men. Rhys had known this man for years, and trusted him.

"Lord Rhys, what brings you to fair Stirling?" said the Englishman as they shook hands. "Come, share a good drink of wine with us. We've much to tell." The man looked steadily at Lord Rhys. His men all chuckled and went inside the public house, leaving the man outside with the lord and his brother.

"Of what do you speak? I am to meet with someone shortly." Lord Rhys had the distinct impression that his friend knew something, perhaps about the woman.

"I would not keep you long, sir. Might I ask if the black horse in the stable is for sale?" the Englishman inquired, grinning.

"No," answered Lord Rhys, frowning. "How do you know of that horse?" Bruce's hand slipped to his sword. Both men were now listening intently.

The Englishman laughed again. "You have a real lady, this time, Rhys. Although no one will hear so from me, nor from any of my men. Take care not to lose her; she is not familiar with this land."

"I ask again, how come you to know of the horse, and the lady?" Now Lord Rhys was tense. He liked this man and knew him to be honest and trustworthy, but he also knew his reputation with women, one rivaled only by his own brother, Bruce. He could feel the jealousy begin to cloud his thinking.

As if reading his mind, the Englishman shook his head. "Do not think so, Rhys. She goes as a man, or rather a small lad. If not for her, one of my men would have died at the hands of the English peacekeepers, as they call themselves."

"'Tis a sad title for men who care little for peace. They have well deserved reputations for cruel and unjust treatment of the Scots," Rhys added. "Tell me why you think the lady belongs to me."

"Only her cloak of your colors led me to know from where she was running. You will have a spirited life with that lady, sir. I'm surprised to see you here, without her, since you have the horse," the Englishman noted.

Now more relaxed, Rhys explained. "She must have let the horse loose. One of my men found it, trying to find its way home."

The Englishman frowned. "She said she was bound for Glasgow. Perhaps it is not so strange, since she knows not this land." Thrusting his hand out, he added, "I wish you and her well. She is a prize, for certain. Looks just like her brothers." The men shook hands once again, then parted.

Lord Rhys and Bruce resumed their journey to the shopkeeper's house. "One must wonder what story is behind that tale," Bruce noted cheerily as they walked. "Who are her brothers?"

Rhys simply shook his head. Bruce already suspected he knew her brothers— at least one of them.

After knocking at the shopkeeper's door, Rhys and Bruce were met by the old man. He bid them enter, and inside, his wife offered ale. Accepting the offer, all three men sat down. The old lady served the men, then slipped into another part of the house.

"I have come a great distance to inquire about the lad you had in your service, not long ago. He was slender of build and well educated," Rhys said quietly.

"Ah, the one with the special eyes." The old man looked intently at the lord, as he spoke. "He was a good worker and very honest. I was sorry to see him go. He would be a good man to keep, I think."

The lord nodded. "That he would. I would find him and bring him home."

"Might I ask, m'lord, is the young man in trouble?"

"Nay, the bairn is not in trouble, but for running away," Rhys answered.

The old man paused. "May I speak frankly, m'lord?"

"What do you wish to say to me?" Rhys responded.

"Some people are likened to gifts. A man could do no better than to care for something of such value as that." The old man squinted at Rhys.

"I shall keep that in mind," Rhys answered dryly, standing to take his leave.

On the way back to the house of lodging, Bruce spoke up. "You were right, brother. She would be in Edinburgh by now, surely. The groom's find proves that. The horse would not have been on the Edinburgh road were she in Glasgow. We should move quickly if we are to stop her from boarding a ship."

"What is this? Do I detect a note of concern from my brother the jester?" Rhys observed sarcastically.

"Only for you, my lord, only for you. Say what you may, you are smitten. No wonder, for she is a braw lass, for certain. Life will be stern indeed for the rest of us if she slips through your fingers," Bruce admitted. His brother merely growled.

Leaving early the next morning, the men rode long hours and stopped only late at night in a clearing near the road to rest the horses. They left early again the next morning. They arrived at Edinburgh early afternoon the second day. The men would split up, agreeing to meet at an inn located near the stables at dark. "If she is found, not a hand is to be laid on her," Lord Rhys declared to his men. "I do not want her to know she is found out. Am I clear? Bruce, if you let on, I will whip you, too, I swear!"

Bruce shook his head, smiling. "Your word is our command, brother."

Bruce loved Edinburgh, with its never-ending bustle and wide social diversity. He liked the dances, music, and of course, the ladies. This could be a grand time, if only Rhys failed to find his lady for a couple of days. As in Stirling, the men split up to pursue their quarry. This time, Bruce took the area that included Crosskeys Tavern, off Canongate, a section of Edinburgh he knew well. He believed that here the lady could fade into the commotion quite easily. Bruce roamed the streets around his area, watching the people and wandering into several establishments. He saw no sign of Caty, but did not expect to. She would be careful not to walk about during the day. It was nearly evening when Bruce finally entered Crosskeys Tavern. Near the back of the room, he watched as several men joined a group already crowded around a great round table. The talk was lively, with friendly arguments frequently erupting. Bruce heard several men ask for the "skinny lad" that apparently accompanied another of the men. Bruce moved closer, to a small table near the group. The man questioned was already drinking heavily. He reminded those present that he had a bookstore to keep open, and that the lad was working.

When a maid passed with more wine, Bruce paid her extra to ask the shop-keeper to join him. The man could not pass up the possibility of a free drink, and gladly joined Bruce, his ever-present kerchief in hand. The man was thin, nervous, and giddy. He looked to have never worked with his hand, and Bruce doubted he could work with his mind.

After more wine, Bruce got his information. It was evident the shopkeeper thought kindly of the woman, though he spoke of her as if she were a man. Following the shopkeeper's directions, Bruce left the tavern and crossed the street. The shop was easy to find. Its front door was open, flanked by great windows displaying books, maps, and other papers. Bruce stood to one side of the window and surveyed what was visible. Caty was there, moving in and out of his view while she cleaned. He was taken aback momentarily by the short mop of hair that flew in all directions from her head. There could be no doubt though; it was her. Bruce found himself, as usual, wishing he could control his brother's temper. *The woman is very easy to look at, even as a lad, and she is well educated; it looks to be a good match for Rhys*, he noted to himself, smiling. *'Tis certain she will have a fight to settle when Rhys gets his hands on her.*

Her shirt barely hid the fact that she was a woman. The pants did a bet-ter job, but it was all for naught when she walked. Never before had he seen a woman who walked as if afloat. Such grace. No, this was definitely not a man. The owner had to have known she was a woman. Smiling to himself, he toyed with the idea of going into the shop, just to see how she would react. But he soon remembered his brother's admonitions and thought better of it.

He decided to instead wander about and see what he could find out about the owner of the bookshop.

What he found out intrigued him. It was rumored the shop owner had come into the business under poor circumstances. There was talk of the killing of the previous owner, though nothing had ever been proved. Even now, the young man was at risk of losing the shop. He liked to gamble, and lost frequently. Although the bookstore was busy, his debt was growing fast. *Better to let my brother know soon, as the lady could be in a risky situation with this shopkeeper,* Bruce decided.

Slowly making his way back to meet Rhys, Bruce glanced at a man walking toward him. He knew this man from somewhere, but where could he have seen him before? He could not remember, but he was certain he had seen him someplace. The man nodded briefly as they passed. Resisting the urge to turn around, Bruce casually crossed the street and turned to walk the same direction as the man. The man passed the bookstore, paused, and then entered. With pursed lips, Bruce contemplated what he should do. He could not follow the man; the lady would surely recognize him. Did the lady know the man? Shaking his head, he decided not. Then, suddenly, he remembered just where he had last seen this man. He knew the man had been in Stirling, at the same inn where he and Rhys had been. That meant he may have only just arrived here, also. Bruce felt positive this Englishman knew the lady. *I need to find Rhys.*

Caty watched the man enter. She remembered him only too well. While her employer had insisted that this man would not return, Caty saw him open the door again at dusk, look around, and with purpose head toward her. Silently praying the owner would return this evening for once, she stood firmly behind the old counter bracing for whatever would come. The man paused, then walked about the store for a short while, as if confirming his suspicion that she was alone. He walked toward her. Refusing to be intimidated, she stood her ground. When he spoke, however, his manner and voice were even and respectful. "I do not suppose you would share with a stranger the intention of your employment at this place. I am not your adversary, lad. I would only ask whether you want for anything, and whether you are safe here?"

Caty frowned. "Who are you, sir? Why do you ask about me? Should I know you?"

"No, to everything—I only wish to be assured of your safety," he replied.

"I do not understand, sir. Why would that matter to you?" Caty asked.

"Are you safe here?" he persisted, watching her closely.

"I am safe," Caty responded quietly. The man nodded, then left without another word.

Standing, looking after him, Caty tried to place him. Other than the time he had come to the store before, she could not. Once he spoke, she had no fear of him, but she was quite certain he knew she was not a lad. He looked to be about the age of several of her brothers. He was a mystery to her. *Remember, you are to worry only over those things you can change. This is not of that category*, she reminded herself. Pensively, she closed the shop and mounted the steps to her room. She could not get his face out of her head. To whom did he answer? Perhaps it was time she moved on.

Caty lay in bed that night watching darkness drape over her window. There had been a time when the shadows frightened her. Her brother Roberto would always come to her, holding her until the fears left her. She had no idea where any of her brothers were now, and feared her parents were dead. As they often did, Caty's thoughts turned to her mother. Her mother had treated several French soldiers during the last conflict, which had seen the French expelled from the Netherlands. A captured French officer, who had vowed he would see Caty's mother condemned for her "spells," had escaped that same night.

FOURTEEN

RHYS FIRST VISITED WITH THE men at the livery stable. The younger stable hand there took in the lord's cloak and mount with an intense, disbelieving look; Rhys was certain he recognized his horse. "You like my steed?"

"Y-yes, m'lord," the man stammered. "'Tis a fine animal." Though the stable hand hastened to assist, Rhys could easily tell he was uncomfortable, even frightened.

"Would you know where I can find the lad that left this animal to fend for itself?"

"No sir," the nervous man swore. "He came not, after he took the horse out."

"Hmm. I am certain you will let me know if you see him, correct?"

"Of course, sir." The young man nodded, eager to please. "Where would I find you, sir?"

"That matters not. I will come to see you again, soon. It will be worth your while if you remember any other details." Rhys noted the shadow that came over the man's eyes, and had no illusions about the likelihood of this young man giving him information. It would never happen.

"Humph, even disguised as a man, people like her," he muttered under his breath.

Rhys walked the length of the street, looking in shops as he passed, then turned back to find Bruce and his men. He was certain Caty was still here in Edinburgh. He could feel her. *Damnation! What is it about that woman? My troubles would be gone if I but sent her on her way.* Even as he thought it, he knew it was a useless summation. He could never send her away now. She was his. Every-thing had changed. *I fulfilled my part of the bargain. She is safe with me.* With disgust, he shook his head. She was safe—if he could catch her. With determined step, he headed for his brother.

Caty had fallen into a routine. She worked long hours and stayed close to the shop. Her occasional forays into the community were pleasant enough. By this time, people took little notice of her. Her employer trusted her completely now and left her alone. His business had gone up substantially since she arrived, and he did not intend to change the situation. He never let on to the people frequenting his shop, or to the men they met occasionally at Crosskeys Tavern, that she was anyone other than the lad he had hired to help. She was free to read and entertain herself as she saw fit, in keeping with her guise. She kept her hair trimmed and played her part, even when alone.

The owner was coming in later and later, if at all. He had taken to gambling and liked to think he had great social influence. Caty made no comment; she merely worked and tried to stay out of his way. He paid her well, but she knew his debts were growing. Trying to help, she had begun to keep the shop opened later. To her, it seemed only a matter of time before he would be forced to let her go. Several men had already been in to inquire for his whereabouts. If he could only stay out of trouble until she bought her ticket. Slowly, the stack of coins she saved was growing larger. Once Caty had walked down along the docks. She knew she would have to settle for somewhere along the eastern English coast. The more money, the farther she could sail. After watching peo-ple purchase tickets from a small round hut, Caty had asked about passenger charges. Right now, she could sail as far as Sunderland. She hoped to make it farther—perhaps as far south as Scarborough. The farther, the better.

As the setting sun gave up its last rays of light to the dancing dust particles, Caty began to close the shop down. The stranger who had come in the day before had not returned. Caty began to relax again. After locking the front door, she stepped up to close the window coverings, just as she always did. She latched one side, then began pulling the other side to, glancing out at the scene beyond before her view was obstructed. Gasping, she stared at a figure storming down the street. *It cannot be! The lord, here? With his brother!* In horror, Caty watched as the four men walked slowly up the street and crossed toward the shop.

She hardly looked at the three with him; her eyes were fixed on the lord. He looked dark and brooding. All the men were armed. After quickly pulling the window covering tight and blowing out the candles, Caty stood and watched through the cracks of the shutters. She held her breath as they paused at the door. They knocked, waited and knocked again, then tried the door. She heard Bruce tell his brother that they would return in the morrow, early. She watched as the lord's party retreated back across the street, and then stood frozen at the window, struggling to gather her thoughts. "I will not be here when they return," she whispered to herself. "I must leave tonight."

She flew up the stairs, tossed what little she owned into a small bag, pulled her pouch of coins out, and stuffed it into her cloak. Leaving the keys and a scribbled note on the table, she slipped out the back door, covered with her cloak. Caty hurried across the alley behind the bookshop. She would try to buy a place on any ship leaving this evening. She could hide someplace until she arranged to board. "How could he have known I am here?" she muttered, pulling the cloak tighter around herself. In all her time in Edinburgh, she had not ventured far from the bookstore, except for one trek to the docks. She knew the general direction of the docks but would be hard pressed to not get lost in the looming darkness.

As she moved along the streets and alleys, she frequently looked behind her. Edinburgh was now opening its doors to night visitors, with eager anticipation of easy money. Some merchants stayed open late if they also served food and drink. These establishments were best avoided, as were the houses that catered to men. Caty veered away from wandering residents.

She walked steadily but carefully toward the shipyard, trying to sidestep the piles of human waste and other refuse that littered the way. The air was heavy with the foul odors of the streets. Because Edinburgh was a bustling town, filled with citizenry and relentless activity, Caty was able to move along without undue attention. Men and women moved along, intent on their destinations, paying no attention to other pedestrians. Clutching the knife hidden beneath her wrap, she tried to blend into the crowds. Her movements and speed were hindered by the knowledge that robbery was common, especially in the alleyways. She moved quickly beneath lighted windows, scanning the men she passed and looking for any threatening movements. The sounds of homes slowing down for the night reached the streets below, but Caty, gripped by a sense of urgency, heard nothing.

It was almost an hour after she started for the docks that Caty noticed a man trailing her. She was certain he had not been following her earlier. She was nearly safe; if only she could lose him before she got to the shipyard. He walked along the opposite side of the street, but never let her out of his sight. If she slowed, he slowed; if she moved faster, so did he. He made no attempt to cover his intense game of cat and mouse. Caty felt he must be one of her captor's men.

She ducked into a tavern and shoved her way toward the back. Her fear of capture outweighed her fear of the men around her. She chose the most inconspicuous corner of the room and stopped to look back at the tavern's entrance. After several minutes, he still had not entered. Relaxing somewhat, she turned to look for a rear exit. Instead, she spotted her pursuer near the back, smiling at her.

Caty was beginning to get angry. This was not a game to her. Leaving the relative safety of the tavern, she hit the streets again. Finally, in desperation, she ducked onto another darkened street. Once she was out of the lamplight, she began to run. Turning after several minutes to look for the man, she was relieved to see he was nowhere in sight. She spun around and ran full into a different man. She would have fallen but for his arm about her. Gasping, she pushed against him to move away, groping for her knife.

"I think not," the man softly admonished her. Caty's heart dropped. She stood within the steely grip of the lord. She could not see his eyes, but she felt them burning into her. Speechless, she loosened her grip on the knife, her shoulders slumped, and she had to clench her teeth to keep the tears from coming. Her knife clattered to the cobblestone street. He picked it up, examined it, then shook his head before slipping it into his waistband. Rhys was joined by Bruce and two other men, one of whom was Caty's original pursuer.

Caty spoke not a word, and neither did Rhys. He grasped her arm and led her firmly out of the side street and onto another and yet another, weaving his way swiftly, trailed by his brother and the two other men. It was obvious he knew the town well, as he moved without hesitating. *If I were dressed as a woman, he could not drag me along like this,* she thought. *I should never have changed. Not that it matters now.*

After what seemed an eternity, they arrived at the stables. Five horses stood ready to take riders. One was the horse Caty had tried to send home. She recognized the young man holding the horses, too. He looked on helplessly. She knew he wanted to help, but there was not any way he could without putting himself in danger.

The lord lifted Caty roughly upon a horse and handed the reins to her. With teeth clenched, she desperately kicked the animal as hard as she could. It lunged, startled, nearly trampling over Lord Rhys and pushing aside the rest of the horses. With his mane flying, the animal ran. Caty leaned down, gripping his mane and the reins. The horse jumped easily over the fence surrounding the stable, with Caty clinging on frantically.

Her fear of being caught was stronger than her fear of falling with the animal, so she urged the horse on harder. She stuck to the horse as the animal raced through the streets and toward the edge of town. Just as she thought she might get away, she heard thundering hoofs behind her and soon felt someone jerk her from her horse. The rider pulled his mount up shortly. As she left the saddle, another rider grasped at the bridle of her horse, running with it. Both animals slowed, and the frightened horse was controlled.

Bruce looked over at his brother, eyes twinkling, shaking his head. "'Twill be a good life, my lord!" In spite of himself, Rhys admired her courage. That she would still try to escape angered him even more, but her horsemanship and daring thrilled him. Still, he had to break her.

Caty had been slung harshly over the horse, in front of her captor, and he held her firmly in place while his men gathered. The few people about the edge of the borough stopped to stare. Caty was thankful she looked like a boy and that she could see no one. As the group left the town, he still held her upended before him. Then, to Caty's horror, he urged his horse into a full gallop. Unable to protect her face very well, and positioned in a way that gave him full advantage, she was helplessly jostled about. His leg and the leather strap that secured the stirrup struck her face repeatedly. Though she struggled to push herself up, it was useless; he kept her pinned. His horse, though laden with this unusual package, pushed on. When they had ridden well beyond the town, Rhys pulled up. His anger made him clench his jaw, to control the urge to strike her. By this time, Caty, still draped uncomfortably over his mount, was begging him to let her down.

"Nay. I can trust you to run. You have shown that. You are just getting a small taste, my lady. You'll soon learn to respect my temper. You will never run from me again, of that you may be certain. In case you had forgotten, you do belong to me. You will obey me. Until I am certain you understand that, you will put up with whatever I decide is best." His voice was level and angry.

Bruce shook his head disapprovingly but remained silent. On this count, his brother was right. She would need to be accustomed to his temper. Yet he felt bad, watching her sad plight. Rhys's men had never seen their lord behave in such a manner, especially over a woman. Both had been with Rhys and Bruce when Caty was taken. They remembered her well. They remembered the aid she had rendered to them when she was taken. She had shown her spirit then, too. To them, it came as no surprise that she would fight the lord. Unbeknownst to Caty, her behavior this day had made her two more friends. The party moved out again.

After a while, Caty, having given up any semblance of dignity, spoke loudly, but with calm. "My lord, would that you could find it within yourself to right me. Blood pours from my face. I would seem to have little blood left."

Immediately pulling his horse up, Rhys slid off and pulled her from the animal's back. Caty's head pounded and she stumbled when he stood her up. She was surprised to see the alarm on his face. True to her word, she was bleeding profusely from her nose and a split lip. Both eyes were beginning to swell. Pulling at a small kerchief he had at his waist, he dabbed the blood, then handed the kerchief to her.

Bruce rode up and handed Caty a skin of cold water. Shooting him a grateful glance, she tried to stop the bleeding and clean up her face. When she pulled her cap off, she could tell her hair was soaked from the blood that had run into it, leaving it matted. Using the cap, she tried to clean her face. Caty felt the lord watching her intently, but she would not meet his eyes. She was angry now. She refused to let him see her anger.

Once she had finished, Rhys took the cap from her and threw it down behind him. After a short while, he mounted, and leaning down, offered his hand. For an instant, Caty thought of running. She turned and looked around her.

"I would not try, lady." The lord's voice was steely and cold.

Though Caty thought of slapping his hand away, she simply took hold, and he swung her up onto his horse in front of him. Again, the group started off. She tried unsuccessfully to keep from leaning against him. She could feel Rhys smiling cynically down at her head. "Even now, you rebel, lady. You have lost, but give not an inch. I will break you, you will see," he promised.

Caty vowed never to tell him, but for the first time in weeks, she felt secure. The uncertainty of every day had been more than she imagined, as had been the flight. Caty was tired of the charade of character and constant vigilance. At least she could be herself again. She could relax. Eventually, the motion of the horse and the warmth of the man's arms lulled her gently to sleep.

Glancing down at her, Lord Rhys marveled at her beauty, even though she was battered and bloody. Her head lay in the cup of his shoulder, supported by his arm. Her face was turned toward him, and he could see the long lashes, strong cheekbones, and delicate nose. Her lips were full and, with slumber, had formed into a gentle smile. He felt a stab of guilt at his treatment of her. Rather, he wanted to brush her short hair from her brow and kiss the bruises. Rhys could feel desire for the woman gripping his very being. His anger was abated, and he wanted only to hold her, thus, forever.

As they pulled up to cross a brook, Bruce broke the silence. "Brother, we should stop for the night. We can leave early in the morning. The lady needs sleep, as do the horses. Especially yours, with its double load." His voice carried a merry note.

"Humph . . . I think perhaps it is you that are tired, Bruce. No matter, we shall stay the night here."

Caty had awoken when the horse stopped moving. She looked around, not recognizing anything, and was for a moment confused. Then memory gushed back. She sat very still, not certain what she should do next. Rhys lowered her gently to the ground and dismounted. She stretched; her head still ached and her lips were swollen. She could barely see out of her left eye. Gingerly, she patted her face. She stepped away from the men and began to gather wood for a fire. Bending over caused her head to ache worse. She held her head with one hand while she searched for dry wood with the other. One of the men gathered firewood alongside her. With sympathy in his face, he watched her struggle, and finally he spoke to her softly. "Come, m'lady. We can get the fire started. You must be tired. You will find food and blankets there." He nodded respectfully toward the site where the other man and Bruce were starting a fire.

"Thank you, sir." She was surprised at his concern, but grateful for it.

Stopping at the edge of the brook, Caty dunked her head into the cold water. When she raised it up, gasping, she felt light-headed. The water revived her, however, and she repeated the motion until she could no longer feel the clumping of the blood in her hair. She cleaned her face as well. Tenderly, she felt her lips, then tried to move her teeth. They still felt intact. Shivering, she rose and fluffed her short hair. With a deep breath, she turned to face her captors.

The lord was pouring water into skins. Caty walked toward him. Fixing her eyes on him, she spoke quietly. "My lord, while you have great reason not to trust me, you must also have reason to understand my decision to leave. I cannot undo what is done, but I do swear to you, I will run no more. You have more important things to do, I believe, than look for me. If it would please you, I will be ready when you say, on the morrow." To herself, she thought, *I have no desire to see just how you would restrain me this night.*

Caty's statement caught him off guard. His heart was moved to pity, but he would not let her see. Her hair was damp and stuck out about her head like a bush. Her lip was puffed out and both eyes were nearly swollen closed. There was smeared blood around her neck. Indeed, she looked as if she had been in a fight. Again, he was struck by how calm and at ease she still seemed. He knew better than any what it took for her to speak to him this way. Like him, she was also of noble birth, unaccustomed to all she had been through. She was, however, accustomed to doing what she pleased. Rhys looked at her for a moment. When he spoke, his voice was calm, quiet, and firm. "I am not yet certain what I will do about you. However, the rest of this ride will be more pleasant, for everyone, I believe." He started to turn away, then turned back, looking at her through narrowed eyes. "You are never to cut your hair again," he added. Shaking his head with disgust, he left.

As Caty watched him leave, she stuck her tongue out at him. When she turned back to the fire, she was horrified to see Bruce laughing. Her eyes met his. He had to have seen her. He grinned with obvious approval, then went about his business.

Caty began to put together the bread, cheese, and wine the men had set out. She served the men, taking care to serve the lord first. He could not take his eyes off her. When at last she looked to lie down, she saw the small shelter made for her. Inside, she found a bundle of coverings, enough to make a bed. Gratefully, she slipped inside and quickly fell asleep, too tired to think of what would become of her now.

When she awoke in the morning, the men were already stirring. Her head no longer ached. Her lip was still swollen and both eyes were bruised, though the swelling had gone down some. All in all, she was none the worse for the wretched ride. She took another trip to the brook, washing her face and neck carefully. She fluffed her short hair with her fingers, then tried to straighten her clothes.

Back at the fire, she began to put together something to break fast with. Rhys watched her. He walked to where she squatted as she mixed the meats and breads. "You will ride the horse you would have let go." Although his words were reproachful, she could hear a smile in his voice.

"For truth, I would prefer that. The world looks better upright, sir." Glancing up at him, she caught the grin.

Rhys was uncertain how this woman could mend his anger so quickly and easily. He was certain, though, that her presence was his to command. *And command I will, lady,* he thought with satisfaction, *make no mistake. 'Twill be a fine awakening for you, I think.*

Caty spoke softly to the horse as she petted it. "We spent good time together, you and I," she whispered to the animal. It nuzzled her. Mounting easily without help, she turned to see the men watching her. She nodded to them, her cheeks reddening.

As they rode, the lord pushed them to move ever faster. She was unsure what stirred him, but she followed suit. When they stopped to eat during midday, he cautioned his men. "We move on. Storm clouds fill the skies, and I would not like to be left in a storm on another's lands. As long as we can, we move."

The skies grew ever darker as thunder and lightning shook the earth. The rain came next; buckets of stinging pellets poured onto everything in its path. The party continued to push hard, but the horses were beginning to slip on the rocky trail as the rain assailed them. At length, Rhys pulled up. "This is too dangerous. We might lose a horse."

"Or a woman," quipped Bruce. Caty winced. Ignoring the grinning Bruce, Rhys rode deep into the thicket before dismounting.

While one of the men cared for the horses, the rest, using the heavy swords at their sides, began to cut branches. Soon, a lean-to was in place. The thick branches of the trees kept the rain at bay. They ate dried hunks of meat and biscuits. Everyone huddled close together for warmth. Caty tried to sit alone, but the lord pulled her between Bruce and him. She slept very little that night, but was warmer than she was the last. The rain stopped at early morn. Shortly thereafter, the group was on the move once again.

Rhys was pleased that the woman had not asked for special consideration even once. She rode with them at whatever pace he set. She moved easily with the horse and handled the animal effortlessly. He had decided well. He had gotten much more than he bargained for. Somehow he must make her understand that she belonged *with* him, not just *to* him.

At midmorning, the rain started up again. Caty was miserable. The winds, partnered with the rains, made for cold travel. Her teeth chattered and she shook beneath the flimsy cloak she wore. Her shivering was becoming so intense, she feared she might fall from the horse.

Riding up closely, Lord Rhys swung his heavy cloak around Caty's shoulders, to hide the swell her breasts made beneath the wet shirt and thin cloak. Unaware that this kindness had been on behalf of her appearance, Caty was grateful for the warmth. They trekked on. By the time they reached the castle, they had ridden in and out of rain for several days. Every rider was soaked to the skin.

FIFTEEN

CATY SLID OFF THE HORSE and staggered into the great room, following the men. Without speaking, Rhys led her up the stairs to her quarters, closing the door behind her. Too tired and cold to do much more, she stripped off her filthy, wet clothing, pulled a heavy blanket over herself, and lay curled on the bed, shivering.

Without a knock, the door to her room flew open, and the lord strode in; he spoke sternly. "You and I are not finished with this matter. I do not know yet what I will do, but you will be punished. I think the discussion will begin now." He feared that if he did not address the past several weeks now, he would never bring it up again. He had to take the issue on now, while he was wet, cold, and angry again, having been forced to ride through the storm because of her.

Striding resolutely to the bed, he jerked the blanket from her. Gasping, Caty desperately clung to the corner of the wrap as it spun away.

He looked at her, stunned. Her beauty took his breath from him. Her slender, graceful form huddled on the bed. He found he could not move. Crushed and humiliated, Caty pulled at the fallen wrap, trying to cover herself. He pulled the blanket down again and, slowly, his eyes took in every detail. Caty felt her face burn.

Gathering his wits about him, he sat on the bed and pulled her to him, wrapping the blanket tightly around her. His voice was husky with yearning. "'Tis not a good thing to stay with you and see you in this state. I say that these last few weeks will be gone, between us. We start over, you and I. You belong to me. You are mine. You must understand and accept that. You will never run from me again, lass, never!" When he finished, he gently laid her back down and left the room.

In a few moments, he returned. Without looking her way, he filled the fireplace with wood and lit it. Soon a warm glow filled the room. Turning to her, he finally spoke softly, "You are more beautiful than I ever imagined. I think of you often. Sleep well, my lady."

Caty trembled beneath the blankets. Her first blush of shame was replaced with a strange feeling. She began to understand her mother's warning: "You have more power as a woman than any man. One day you will see. Take care not to use it so much it becomes common."

The next morning, women came in bearing cloth of all colors. Caty picked out several pieces, stood for measurements, and added some instruction regarding structure. She waited for their return, hoping she could assist further, but she waited in vain. Her door was still locked. Caty wondered if she would ever be allowed to leave the room at will.

The lord did not come to her room for the next week. Caty decided to tread carefully. She amused herself by watching the activity taking place on the grounds below, listening to the birds—anything to help the time pass. When he finally did come, he followed the steward, who had asked permission to enter with a midday meal. Rhys knew she would be uncomfortable after their last meeting. He chose to pass it over. With authority, he began, "You will not leave me. I trust you understand that now. I must leave again. I would expect to find you here when I return." He longed to hold her. Instead, he stood with his hands on his hips and watched her. What could he do about her actions? Why had he chosen to overlook her escape attempt? *Why?* He knew it was because he loved her and wanted her. *I only know she is mine—and whatever drove me to take her no longer matters. I know only that I love this woman. I, once believed never to feel such things, love.*

"Go in peace, my lord. I will be here when you return. You need not concern yourself with my activities." Caty's voice was quiet, self-assured.

At that, he nodded and left. He knew she would keep her word. He could now concentrate on matters at hand. Nonetheless, he also knew every night would be filled with her image and the burning desire she had ignited.

The next morning, Caty awoke early to the sounds coming from below. Dressing quickly, she tried the door, only to find it unlocked. Not willing to do anything that might result in the door being locked again, she pulled the cord and waited. As the steward had promised when he first took her to the rooms, he answered her call. "I wish to go to the kitchen," she told him. "I must hurry or I will be late." She stepped toward the door.

"You are not to return to the kitchen. Perhaps you would like something else?" The steward stood in the doorway, waiting.

"You do not understand. I would like to go to work," Caty explained.

"That is not possible. You may not return to the lower level unescorted yet." The steward was beginning to look worried.

"Why?" Caty asked, pressing him. She simply could not just sit around all day. The only area she knew was the kitchen. What harm could there be in such a request?

"Everything has changed. Your position has changed," he insisted.

"My position?" Caty's face gave way to anxiety, as she bit her lower lip. To have him speak of the change aloud made Caty's stomach turn.

The poor man didn't answer. Instead he asked, "Do you have any other way I might serve you?" He was beginning to wring his hands.

Caty shook her head. As he turned to leave, she said quickly, "Yes, there is something. How do I get down to the grounds below?"

"I'll bring up something for you to break fast with. You do not go to the grounds alone." With that, he left before she could ask for something else he could not provide.

Caty paced the floor of her room, and slowly felt herself becoming increasingly agitated. Caty would not be deterred from leaving her quarters. She knew that flight was no longer an option—she had given her word—but she refused to stay in the confines of the room. She spent several days studying the grounds from her windows. She made lists of improvements she could make in the management of the castle. She knew from her time in the kitchen that there were too few servants inside the castle proper to serve the lord's needs. And while she had seen some women, none of them spoke or had even acknowledged her. Now that she thought about it, they had only come to the kitchen to eat. Not one had spoken to her. *That will change!* she promised herself.

One morning, when the steward answered her call, Caty stepped outside the door and closed it behind her resolutely. "Today, I am going to the kitchen. I cannot simply sit around all day; I'll go quite insane. I am very grateful for the new room and all it offers, but I must do something. After much thought, I have decided I will return to the kitchen. I expect I will probably leave about the same time as usual this evening." As she spoke, she was already dashing down the stairs. The poor old steward hurried to catch up.

"You cannot do this! Someone else can do whatever you need done, but you shouldn't be in the kitchen, working, alone . . ." His voice trailed off as he struggled to keep up with her.

"If you're worrying about your lordship—"

"Yes, m'lady, I am. I know he will be angry when he finds out you have been in his kitchen." The man huffed with the effort of moving his rotund body down the steps at her breakneck speed. "He has a fiery temper, m'lady," he wheezed.

"Then do not tell him. I will tell him myself," Caty advised without looking back.

"I have never kept anything from him. You surprise me to suggest such a thing," he blurted. Hanging on to the wall, he gasped for breath.

Caty stopped for a moment and turned her eyes on him. "I would never suggest you or anyone else ever keep anything from him," she said gently. "However, I do think he would find it harder to be angry with me, a foreigner and a woman, than with you. You have been very kind to me, and I sought only to keep you from his anger, which if it comes at all should be directed to me. Please forgive me. You must do whatever you think best." *I doubt he will think twice about being angry with me, but this poor man need not know that.*

The man was taken aback. That she would ask his forgiveness made him feel somehow indebted to her. Indeed, Lord Rhys had chosen wisely. Still, he would not be happy with her wanderings. Why could the lord not be happy in the company of someone with a milder leaning? This one was moving too quickly for him; she had already reached the first floor and was headed for the kitchen. At this level, the halls and rooms were bustling with activity, and he gave up any hope he had of returning the woman to her room. As Caty began moving happily about the kitchen, cleaning up and preparing meals, he and several guards kept careful watch over her. The steward's only hope was for the quick return of the lord of the manor. But he was not expected for another two weeks.

For the next week, Caty spent every day in the kitchen. The steward notified the chief guard, who with the steward and several other men spent his days in the kitchen, and word spread about the master's favorite. What few women were in the castle tried to catch a glimpse of her. The story of the lord's recapture of her was on every tongue. She still spoke to no one, except the steward, and even then only when they were alone.

For Caty, the days were much more tolerable. After the week, though, she was increasingly aware that she had placed the steward, her only confidant, in a dangerous position. She could tell he was becoming increasingly anxious, hovering around her. Each night, she tried to rationalize her work in the kitchen. Had it not saved her sanity, and helped the household too? She had to admit, finally, that it could not be worth this man's life or his liberty. As she led the way up the stairs on this evening, she made a decision.

"I have thought a great deal about how what I do might affect you," she said to the steward. "I have decided I cannot in good conscience place you at any risk. I will no longer work downstairs. Perhaps, if you find time tomorrow, I could walk about the gardens. Thank you for the care you've provided for me." With a nod, Caty entered her rooms and closed the door. The steward, left in the hallway, found himself immensely relieved, but also puzzled. She was strange, this one. No matter, it was resolved.

When the sun splashed her room with light, Caty awoke. As usual, she could hear sounds coming from below. In spite of this, she struggled to rise. For the first time since her captivity, she felt lost. She had nothing to do; how could she make the time go by?

Caty closed her eyes and lost herself in a mental picture of her grandmother's house in Rome. Green grass, blue skies, and clean air. She was free to wander anywhere she wished. After a long while, she opened her eyes. Above her she could see the patterns created by the sun shining through the stained-glass windows. As the shapes glided slowly across the ceiling, her eyes moved around the room, taking in the colors. With dogged determination, she pushed back the bed coverings, dressed, and called for the steward. "Would you know where I might get paper and paints?" she asked when he stepped into the room.

"Of course," he answered, then disappeared.

He returned shortly, arms laden with tablets of paper, small pots of paint, and brushes. She smiled at him, taking the items and thanking him before closing the door. Left alone, she carefully pulled the small table close to the window and sat down. She leaned back into the chair and closed her eyes. After several moments of concentration, she picked up a quill and ink and began to sketch. When the steward returned with her morning tray and the young boy to clean her privy, Caty sketched still. As night fell, she realized she could no longer see the paper in front of her. Standing, she stretched and moved about the room. The days would be easier.

The steward reported on Caty's activities to the chief of the guard each day, and as time passed, both men were drawn deeper under her spell. These gruff old men would die for her. They didn't know why they felt this way, but neither did they question this fact. Caty gently moved them. She was never angry, demanding, or demeaning. They felt her respect. Yet she conveyed a sense of strength and resolve. In their minds, since she belonged to the lord, she was a part of this castle and their clan. She belonged to them, also.

At first, other than the steward, only the lad sent nightly to clean the privy spoke with her. He was not certain how to react after her brief escape, but Caty acted as if the incident had never happened. She never mentioned the breeches or her escape. Neither did he. Soon he forgot he was uncomfortable, and went about his duties chattering happily. She and the young boy began to form a bond, grown from a shared frustration with life's events.

She also continued to speak with the steward, asking his opinion about such things as the coming weather, the colors in her drawings, and the placement of her furnishings. In the beginning, he had spoken but little, giving one-word answers when he could. However, with persistence, Caty had him bringing her up to date on all the castle happenings, and even reporting on the varying personalities of its inhabitants. What few ladies she encountered when the steward was not able to wait on her were pleasant once they knew she was not of a mind to scold them or demand anything of them. Little by little, Caty built her support system.

SIXTEEN

RHYS COULD SEE THE SIMPLE walls of his castle, the bothies of his people, and the livestock dotting the countryside. Pride swelled within him. All this and more belonged to him. He protected each one. He alone could keep their lands intact, could move them safely into the future—a future in which they would stand with other clans as equals, in spite of the English. As usual, his thoughts turned to the woman. He was impatient to see her. He smiled at the memory of her sleeping on his shoulder. Rhys knew he was not of a mind to cause her any more stress. With any luck, she would feel the same toward him.

An hour later, Caty was startled to hear a door open. She froze; since she had returned, no one had come into her quarters uninvited. His frame filled the door; then he was at her side. She jumped to her feet, dropping the palette. He stooped to pick it up and studied it before returning it to her. She kept silent. He turned and walked back into the hall, spoke to someone, and returned to her room with another chair. He calmly asked her to sit, and after she did so he followed suit. "You're doing well?"

"Yes, thank you," she answered. She was impressed with the change in him. The richly woven clothing fit well. Until now, she had seen him in clothes made for battle or travel. He moved smoothly, like a cat, with ease and grace. Clearly, he was more comfortable. His salt-and-pepper hair was combed and he looked more at ease with himself. Neither spoke for a while.

Then he turned to her. "You approve of your quarters?" There was an air of resolve about him.

"Yes, I do, thank you." Caty eyed him with a touch of suspicion.

"I understand you have been working in the kitchen. Please listen carefully to what I am about to say to you. You must never move about without an escort, until I approve. The steward has been assigned to you. He will see to it that anything you need is provided, and will also coordinate the guards for your protection. He will find women to wait on you. You will be the target of much talk and castle intrigue. No matter. I have made a decision, and we move forward. Whenever I can, I will take you out, riding, walking, whatever. Never are you to go alone. Do you understand?"

She studied him, frowning. "I hear you, and certainly will do whatever you would like me to do, but no, I do not understand. Why am I at such risk? Certainly, there is no one left alive to tell of my past or capture."

Lord Rhys smiled in spite of himself. He knew she would be the object of speculation—an English woman in the court of a lord of Scotland. "It's your future that would be the item most of concern. While possession is apparently not of your culture, it is of mine. You are here now, and you do belong to me." His voice softened. "You have made a great change in me. I will protect you, and with time . . ."

The woman started, then lowered her head as the meaning of his words came to her. Shocked, she sat in silence. Surely he didn't think she could ever love him. More to the point, certainly he couldn't still want to bed her. *I will not be a mistress for anyone*, she thought, her mind and her heart racing. Afraid he would see her thoughts in her eyes, she remained still and silent.

Finally, she raised her eyes to meet his. He looked deep into her heart, it seemed. "I know you think it impossible to care for me, but I know differently," he said softly.

"Indeed, you realize how impossible this is for me," Caty murmured. "Not just because of our countries but, more important to me, because of my religion. We're so different."

"Are we?" he asked. "Do you even know what my religious beliefs are, or anything about my country?" He had never let her know that he knew she was English. Her coloring did not lean that way, but he knew much about this intriguing lady.

"No. Honestly, no. I do know mine, though. I have seen nothing of mine here. Your people have been most kind, but . . ." Her voice trailed off.

He studied her for a long time. He marveled that she did not waver under his gaze. He remembered the times when he could not get her to look at him until he demanded she turn. She simply waited, watching him. He rose abruptly and walked to the door. "I would like to show you the gardens. Please come."

He stood waiting for her to pass. She was grateful he had chosen not to press her. She didn't want to feel any more awkward than she already felt. He led her to one of the side doors in her room. Pushing it open, they stepped into a large study. They walked through and came to a wide, curved stairway that led to the great room below. He took her through the great room, to another side door. Stepping out into the sunshine, Caty breathed deeply.

In spite of herself, she felt pleased with the walk that ensued. The area was filled with all manner of activity. Men and horses moved about. Women with small children hurried on their way. Lord Rhys took her arm and led her down the paths, along pools and fountains. Flowers were beginning to bloom. Roses and other flowers Caty had yet to learn the names of were all shyly opening their buds to be seen. The two of them moved slowly, and he talked about how the garden evolved. He seemed relaxed. She listened to him, watching his face as he spoke of his mother and her gardens.

At the far end of the grounds, they came upon a larger pool. The water was beautiful. Impulsively, she leaned down on the side. She dipped her hand into the water, surprised to find it so warm. "I suppose it would be unseemly for me to swim sometime," she commented wistfully, more to herself than to him.

"Not at all." He smiled at her. The memory of her naked body still burned within him. "I think I would like that. You must be certain that only I am with you, however." Throughout his travels to different lands, he'd often watched women swimming in pools of cool water. It was a custom he thought most interesting.

He felt a sudden need to make her feel that this was her home. "You will soon have ladies to care for you."

Caty frowned at him. "Please, I do not need to have anyone in attendance.

I can do what little I am allowed to do for myself. I am not comfortable with someone around me all the time." *And in truth I wish to remain apart from these people*, she added silently.

"I am sorry, but you have no choice in this matter," he answered firmly. She could tell by his tone that the subject was closed.

He suspected that, in reality, she was quite used to having someone by her side continually. Her resistance was more likely born of her feeling disconnected to his people. But he understood that the more people he placed around her, at her service, the quicker she would be at ease. He wanted her to be at ease, the sooner the better.

After a moment of silence, she took a deep breath. "I would like to do something more active. I cannot simply sit around all day. You do not want me to cook anymore; perhaps my meals were not to your liking. At any rate, it gave me something to do each day. Now, I just sit and paint or sketch. I am certain *you* would not like that for a moment. A short while I can take, but days on end, I do not believe so."

He studied her. Ignoring her comments, he asked, "Tell me, why have you never been frightened here? How do you stay so at ease? Yet you would run from me. I remember well the day we took you. I watched you move about. You thought only of the injured men. Yes, you tried to leave once, but now that you are back, you appear comfortable. Why are you this way?"

"I'm going to believe you will at least consider my request." She smiled wryly. She walked a short distance and then turned to him. "I have learned to work on only those things I can control, and not allow the rest to change who or what I am, or at least what I believe myself to be. I believe that your men are essentially good men. I have yet to meet many women, but believe they are probably good also."

"How can you say that?" Rhys laughed dryly. "Women are more treacherous than men. Not many can be trusted, I have found." They reached a small bench, and Caty sat down. He stood with one foot on the bench, resting his arm on his knee, watching her. She was always in his mind, and now he wanted to take her. Her face was upturned, and serious. Her eyes held his. He had to squeeze his hand hard to keep from pulling her to him.

"If your men are good, it is because they had good mothers," she gently replied.

He smiled slightly and nodded. *I shall have a lifetime to learn all she thinks.* "Perhaps. Perhaps it is as you say," he said in a low voice. "I say men are good because they are called to a greater cause, touched by a greater being, if they are so lucky."

Caty smiled in triumph. "And could not that greater being be a woman?"

At her answer, he laughed in agreement. "So you think you have won, lady?" he asked, teasingly.

Their conversation was interrupted by a call. As a man hurried toward them, he called out, "There is news, m'lord, from the Northern Highlands!"

The lord nodded in answer, then turned to Caty. "We must go now. I will have a late meal with you. Please tell the steward what you would like. He already knows what I will have." He reached for her hand, helped her up, and walked back with her hand still in his firm grasp. When they reached the entrance of the great room, he opened the huge door. Raising her hand, he gently kissed it and held it to his lips. When he released her, she stepped through the door and heard it close. One of the castle pages met her and walked with her to her chamber.

SEVENTEEN

CATY STOOD AT THE WINDOW. She paced back and forth. Finally, she sat down. *What do I do now? Does it even matter?* She could not run away again. She had given her word. And even if she could, just where would she go? She shook her head. He was so unusual. Still, she was not as uneasy with him. *Perhaps it is I that am unusual,* she thought. She stood gazing out the window, lost in memories of her mother.

A knock at her door roused her. She found the steward outside, with a beautiful wooden rocker. He brought it inside and asked where she would like to have it placed. "This is for me?" she asked.

"Yes. Perhaps you would like to have it near the window for the morning and evening lights. The corner would work well. I'll see you get a table to set next to it. It is a gift from our lord. Also, please tell me what you would like for your evening meal."

Caty smiled at him. "I'm not very hungry this evening. Perhaps a small bit of fruit with my tea. Thank you for bringing the chair. You are very kind."

Every trip to Caty's quarters bound the steward closer to her. He knew he would do anything she asked. With the threat of fighting among the clans increasing, the steward had ordered extra men to watch her quarters. He would not allow any harm to come to her. Although he had borne the wrath of his lord when she ran away, he would do all in his power to keep her safe—and to keep her in this castle.

He also had in mind a woman to assist her. He would speak with his lordship about it this evening. Hopefully, Rhys would take her soon and end the swirl of talk around the castle.

Once the steward had gone, Caty sat down in the rocker. She leaned back and began to rock. Her mind wandered aimlessly. She drifted off to sleep. A knock at her door woke her. She was surprised to find her room dark. Stumbling as she moved to the door, she met the steward and the serving boy, who carried a large tray. It was laden with meats, vegetables, and fruits. Baskets of bread and jellies and jugs of wine rounded out the menu. "My goodness—who all is coming to dine with us?"

The steward smiled. "Only His Grace. He does like his evening meal." He quickly set about starting a fire in the fireplace. Lighting candles around the room, he inspected the area. Once finished, he nodded in approval and left her.

Caty felt she should change into something different, but what? More important, why? She must do nothing to let him think she was shifting her position or changing her mind. Perhaps something more severe. Pulling a plain black gown from the chest, she dressed. Her hair was its own boss and flew about her head in every direction. *I shall be grateful when it grows long enough to control*, she noted to herself.

She chose simple pearls from her little stash that was tucked in her coin pouch. She gently touched the finger where her mother's ring had rested not so long ago, before she had left it as payment. He never spoke of the ring, nor did he wear it. *I think he did not care for it. I may ask him to return the ring, if he remains kind with me.*

Soon Rhys arrived through the door from his study and quarters. He smiled when he saw her. Crossing the room, he took her hand and turned her around. Now she felt awkward. The gown, meant to put him off, had succeeded instead in pleasing him. To move the moment along, she asked about the study.

"I love to read," said Rhys. "A man does well who learns of past mistakes or successes and is able to use such information. Of course, you may enter anytime you wish. The books are in English and Latin. If you think of something you would like to read and cannot find it, just let me know. I read every evening. It pleases me that you too like to read."

She had missed again. Pleasing him was not something she wanted. "If it suits you sir, be seated. From the food presented, I think you must be famished."

As he ate, he watched her. She ate a small dish of fruit, drank hot tea. She asked how his trip had gone and if his men were well.

He frowned. "Why would you care how my men fare?"

"When one goes into battle, as I must assume you did based upon our conversation before you left—and before I left—one sustains injuries. From what I have seen, your men would not hesitate to die for you or perhaps your cause, so it is natural I would ask about them."

Her soft rebuke had surprised him. She was right; he had spoken of his heavy mind before he left the first time. "They are well."

She knew she had caught him off guard and made a mental note to take care with his suspicious leaning. Pushing on, she asked, "Did you capture many?"

He looked at her intently for several moments. "I am not used to any woman asking me questions about what I do or how I do it. I think I do not mind your interest. Yes, I did capture what I set out for." He proceeded to discuss the battle they had fought while she was running away. He told her what he had taken, and how he had distributed the spoils. He also discussed his more recent skirmish. The woman listened. When he had finished, she nodded approval.

"I'm pleased and proud of you." The moment she spoke the words, she realized how it must sound to him. She certainly did not want him to know it would matter to her, what he did. She held her breath—the words had just left her of their own accord. How would he feel? How could she have even thought such a thing, let alone spoken the words to him? She could feel the heat of her face.

The man spoke softly, his head cocked. "You please me to even ask. I can tell you ask from interest, not for conversation's sake. I think you are moving." He smiled.

The woman felt herself blush deeper. She stood and began to pick up the remnants of their dinner. "You must be very tired. Thank you for spending time with me. I will spend some time in your study tomorrow, if I'm not troubling anyone."

Before he knew it, she had gently moved him to the door. He left, more than a little angry. Never before had anyone ever dismissed him, certainly not any woman. She had done it so well, so smoothly, he barely realized it. Again he smiled in spite of himself. She would take a little while, but she would be well worth the time and effort. The thought grew in him. What changes would she envision for his home and the surrounding area? How would the rest of his people receive her? It promised to be most interesting. Dismissed—she had even walked him to the door!

"Not next time," he promised.

EIGHTEEN

CATY LAY STILL. MORNING LIGHT was working its way into her rooms. Though she had spent all night thinking, she was in the same place as when she began. If only he would consent to letting her go. Even as her mind spoke the wish, she knew in her heart it could never be. So this was where she would spend her days? A prisoner in a beautiful prison, but a prisoner nonetheless. Closing her eyes, she tried to clear her mind. She must not think of forever, only the next few days. Always the next few days. That she could handle. She realized that the anxious feeling she had carried for so long was gone. What was happening to her?

It was late afternoon before he came in. As usual, he simply opened the door, without knocking. Caty was at the window, drawing, and did not hear him enter. Every door or window that would open was flung wide. A breeze blew the heavy drapes and the sounds of the birds in his garden blended with her soft singing. He stood motionless. *How could she be unhappy and still sing? She must be more content than even she would admit.* He strode into the room.

When she saw him, she blushed. "I'm sorry, I didn't hear you knock."

"That's because I did not knock. One has no inclination to knock on one's own door." He smiled at her.

Caty didn't answer immediately. Finally, after studying him, she observed, "You look very tired. Perhaps you couldn't sleep?"

He sank into his chair, now a part of the room's furnishings. "You're observant—I didn't sleep. Of course, from what you told the steward, neither did you. We should have spent the long night keeping each other company."

Caty didn't respond, but Rhys didn't mind. He was working his way with her.

"What did you do today?" he asked.

"Well, my activities were a little hindered by my location," she answered sarcastically, "but I did sketch and paint. I think I would also like some writing paper. It's very peaceful here. May I ask just where 'here' is?"

The man was quiet for a while. "I think not. I would rather show you than talk of where you are. I'll leave you briefly, to change. Wear something warm." With that, he strode from her with purpose. She moved quickly once the door had closed. The thought of leaving her quarters for a short while stirred her much more than the thought of him coming back in while she was changing.

When he returned, he carried with him a beautiful silver chain. Crossing the room, he lifted a tapestry and, to her surprise, she saw a door she had never before discovered. "This door will take you to the grounds or the stables. Only leave this way if you feel you are in danger. Be certain to lay the cloth back into place so that it will not appear loose. I have brought you a key to open a lock. The chain is strong and should hold up well." He slipped the chain over her head. She shivered involuntarily as his hand brushed the nape of her neck. "The key fits a box you will find in my chambers. Later I will show you. Now, please come with me."

He was impatient to see how she would react to her trip. Rhys proudly walked with her across the grounds. Caty's hair was growing out now, though she had attempted to tuck it under a woven cap. She wore a loose blouse over a flowing skirt and sturdy shoes. A soft woolen cape covered her.

As they walked, Caty was acutely aware of the glances she provoked. Out of respect, the men did not stare, but the women did. They did not seem unkind, just immensely curious. This was not her country and these were not her people, yet she could not lose herself. He had not instructed her to do otherwise, so she strode confidently along next to him.

Rhys observed her change and smiled to himself. *She walks like a queen; I know she will touch my people.*

When they arrived at the stables, Caty struggled to hide her excitement.

"Would you care to ride?" Lord Rhys asked. "More to the point, would you care to ride *with* me and not *away* from me?"

"Certainly, my lord. I gave you my word, and would be bound by it." A small crowd of men had gathered outside the stables, watching curiously. She recognized a few from her time in the kitchen. They all seemed to know her, though. She was certain the story of her escape had been shared by all.

The lord instructed the stable hand to bring Caty her mount. The animal was sleek, shiny, and spirited, with a full mane and the color of red clay. Snorting, prancing, and shying away from the men standing around, the horse refused to allow the stable hand to saddle him.

Rhys started toward the animal, but Caty stepped forward quickly, moving in front of him. The poor stable hand gasped as she approached the horse, hoping he would not be blamed if she were injured.

"Fear not, sir," Caty said to the young man. "I have spent many hours with such beasts. I think they have gentle hearts, when all is said and done. Let me try." Her voice was low and quiet. She stood close to the horse, talking and petting it gently. Her soft voice began to calm him. As the animal began to nuzzle her, she bent to lift the saddle, but it was taken from her. With ease, Rhys threw the blanket and saddle upon the horse's back. Caty continued to speak with the horse. After adjustments were made to her saddle, the lord offered his hand, she mounted, and they were off. Caty could hear the murmuring of the crowd as they rode away.

"You affect animals the same way you affect people, I see," Lord Rhys called to her. "When we are done for the day, I would know from where you gain this skill." He smiled at her.

Now, as he took her around the land surrounding the castle, he spoke of the history of the area and its people. Caty was so caught up in the structures, activities, and sights, she forgot to be worried about her impression on his people or the coming night. The hills were lush and green. The fields were dotted with cattle and sheep. Farmers worked the land. The town around his castle was made of huts of various sizes, a few small shops, stables, and outdoor stalls. Chimneys jutting from the thatched roofs sent smoke gently curling skyward. The afternoon passed quickly. She frequently patted the horse when they paused. Once they had returned to the stables, she dismounted and rubbed his ears and nose. "What do you call this horse?"

"The horse has no name," Lord Rhys replied without looking at her. "He was just taken into my stable. Call him what you will. He is yours."

"Does that mean I can ride when I please?" Caty asked hopefully.

He turned to face her. "No. It means the horse is yours. If you wish to ride, you may arrange to do so with me. You are not to be about without me."

"I think I shall call him Saltillo. That's what color he is. He is a wonderful animal. Thank you very much. I should like to visit him often. May I?" Her eyes were bright, her face flushed.

The sight of her standing there took his heartbeat away. "I think that would be fine, if my brother or I am with you. But you are not to come here alone." It was easy to tell she liked horses. She rode well. What else would he find out about this lady if he asked? He intended to find out. Soon.

"You don't trust me, do you?" Caty asked, her head tilted and a small frown creasing her brow. Her eyes were sad. "It is I who should harbor a great deal of distrust, I believe. I was not brought here willingly."

Rhys turned, regarding her for a moment. "You are not the one I distrust, little one. You are a woman and in a different land. You may be safe or be in great danger, both because you belong to me. For these reasons, you will do as I say. I must be certain you will; I cannot spend my time worrying about you. I'd rather think pleasant thoughts about you." He smiled at her blush.

She turned quickly and started for the castle. His long stride moved him beside her in an instant. Again, he took her arm, placed her hand on his arm, and led her away. They walked in silence.

The air was clean and crisp as night fell. Stars lit up the sky and quiet voices filled the crevices of the buildings. Laughter slipped its way through the open windows, making the dark feel warm and inviting. He was pleased to note that, although she had a long stride for one so short, she walked smoothly, easily, as if floating. Her head was held high, and while he could not see her features, he was certain she was smiling. His heart filled. She clearly was the one he had waited so long for. In that instant, he knew he would never let her go, nor be without her.

Caty was grateful for the urgent message that took her captor from her side upon reaching their quarters. He was all business as he opened her door. Before he left her, he said teasingly, "Of course, there is still the matter of your punishment to consider." Then, in earnest, he continued, "But you please me, lady. You are a good rider and gentle lady. Sleep well and I will be with you in the morning." Lifting her hand, he softly kissed it. He turned and continued walking with the men who had come for him, talking in a low voice. Caty slipped quickly into her room and closed the door behind her.

It had taken over an hour to persuade the steward to allow her to bathe; now Caty felt she could do so without interruption. The fear that she would somehow contract a dreaded fever because she bathed seemed outrageous to her. Both her parents were fastidious about their cleanliness, having learned its benefits from Lord Tabor's stays in China. The steward had eventually sent in several ladies with a tub and water, and after she had soaked in it and the ladies had left, Caty wandered around the room in the dark, wrapped in a soft robe. The fireplace cast a warm glow.

She stood at the window, taken with the stars and night sounds. How simple and safe it all seemed in the night. It was the harsh light of day that brought her to her knees. How could she spend her life like this? What choice would she have? Was this really so bad? Shaking her head, she sought to dispel such thoughts. Of course her life with the lord would be awful. She and he were such different creatures. Although he had nearly always been gentle with her, she knew only too well that he had another side.

Lying in bed, Caty closed her eyes. She, too, would always remember the night he took her party. Everyone was from different countries and had different schemes, and one hardly knew the other. Yet, when lightning struck, each had done their best to stave off the inevitable. The lord's men outnumbered them, and certainly outfought them. Caty's party was made up of wanderers for the most part, and none were ready to fight or even really knew how. His men had been swift. It seemed everything was over as it began. She could still see the bodies lying around. What few men had hired on with them as escorts were dead. Only a few of the lord's men had been wounded, while most of the men left alive in her group were injured. She couldn't remember when the women were taken or where, but she recalled trying to help anyone she could quickly get to. When she finally stopped, it was morning.

Caty had been exhausted and couldn't even struggle when she was taken. She was hardly aware of the ride to the castle, only awakening in the little room, alone, cold, and frightened. Even then, she knew how to find a measure of peace. Time and her feeling of isolation had moved her deeply. She had believed there would be no escape. Best to do something to make the time pass.

Now, Caty realized she had one chance to survive what must be coming. She would take that chance. Perhaps. Come what may.

NINETEEN

MORNINGS WERE SOFT AND GENTLE this time of year. The sounds of birds and the heavy perfume from the garden made it seem she were someplace else. Not so. She rolled over, unwilling to rise and face another day. Her resolve was tired, she was tired, and for the first time, Caty could feel the chain of hopelessness pull. *No, I won't give in to this feeling*, she told herself. *I will make of each day what I can, but I will not quit. Never.* With a struggling spirit, she finished her prayers and dressed.

After calling for the steward, Caty pulled her cloak about her. The hand that held the gift was hidden. When her call was answered, she greeted the steward with a smile. "Please take me to the stables. I know this is short notice, but I want to be certain to see Saltillo before he is moved, as I am certain he will be, since I understand he is no longer in my lord's herd. I am not certain where he might be stabled. I promise I will be quick. Tomorrow, perhaps we could run down there again if he is still there, at about the same time, if it's convenient for you."

As always, the steward was caught off guard. He could escort her, since Lord Rhys had just recently given him permission to do so, foreseeing the possibility of just such a request. But he hadn't planned to dash off to the stables. Yet, her quiet smile and demeanor left him unable to even think of this as untimely or demanding. "Certainly, m'lady. Please follow me." With hesitancy in his heart, he prayed Rhys would not return and ask for her.

At the stables, Caty found that Saltillo remembered her gentle touch and voice. When she called to him, he turned, his ears alert, walked to her, and nuzzled her hand. When she pulled her other hand from the folds of her cloak, he found several carrots. While he ate, she continued to pet him and talk to him. When he finished the carrots, she gave him slices of apple she had tucked into a pocket of the cloak.

After her treats were gone, she climbed through the fence and slipped into the corral with the horse. "No m'lady, you mustn't!" the steward said with urgency. "No one but His Grace or his groom is allowed to enter the corral. Please—you must not let anyone see you there. That's most unseemly for a lady!" The poor man was wringing his hands in agitation. He could not simply go after her. He could not touch her. One could not simply grab the lord's lady. Admittedly, there was little chance of that, since he would never be able to fit through the corral logs. "Lady, please . . . ," he moaned.

Caty slipped her arms around the horse, spoke into his ear, then quickly slid back through the logs. "I did not know such actions would be prohibited. Please accept my apology. I would not endanger our trips to see him. We can return now; thank you for allowing me this small pleasure."

When they arrived back at her quarters, she again thanked him. After she left him, he stood looking at her door, shaking his head. "Luck was with us this time, lady," he said under his breath. "Your lord is not about yet." He walked away, rubbing his arthritic hands together. What kind of man would have ever let her leave his country, travel without family, and then not fight heaven and earth to get her back? Perhaps she had no family. Instinct told him he was correct.

Caty cautiously opened the door that led to the lord's library. She knew that once he left to conduct his business, he seldom returned to his quarters, and certainly never before late afternoon. She stood in the center of the room, awed by the sheer number of books. The books in English were shelved together, covering one wall. She began to read titles. Finding one she liked, she sat at the table. As she fell deep into the book, the time slipped away. She was startled to hear footsteps.

"I see you have found pleasure in something I love," said Lord Rhys's voice.

"That pleases me. What are you reading?" Crossing to her side and taking the book from her, he examined what she had chosen. He turned to peer at the woman. That she would try to learn more about him and his people also pleased him.

The book she had found, written years earlier, was still relevant. He turned it over in his hands. In his mind's eye, even now, he could see the man working over his desk, recording all he knew, to be certain these people he loved so much would have their story told. This woman brought him the same kind of peace the old man had given him.

He sat at the table with her. Handing the book back to her, he said, "What you will learn from the pages of this book will paint a beautiful picture of my lands. The tapestry that my people make is more diverse than any country in our world. It has been just so for many, many years. This is what I live for, to protect them and preserve their way of life. You were meant to be with me, I am certain. In time, the things you now view as restraints will come to be like a blanket on a cold night. Something you long for. Surely you must see the way my men already treat you and respond to you. Soon everyone will know that you are my lady, and that you are a part of them."

Caty sat frozen, hardly daring to breathe. She had not expected this. Every fiber in her being longed to run. Yet, there was not any place for her to go. She knew she must calm her racing heart and hold the tears that threatened to rob her of her dignity. He could never know how this vision of the future crushed her, even though she had expected this. Had he not come after her when she ran away? His words made her verdict final. If she were to maintain her composure, she must leave his presence. Rising, she tried to speak without trembling. "You have given me much to think on. I would like to read the book, and perhaps when I've finished, we can talk."

He stood when she did. "Where are you going? You can read here."

"I'm not feeling well. I haven't felt very well this afternoon. Please excuse me." She grasped the book and retreated to her rooms, as fast as she dared.

He watched her go. Something he had said upset her a great deal. But what? Surely she already knew she would not ever leave this place, or him. He had plotted her capture and was successful, then had gone after her when she would have escaped. How long would it take her to know that this was where she belonged? He was growing impatient. Just when he thought she was coming to him, she slipped away again. Maybe he should just take her. He strode from the room, angrily slamming the door.

The next morning, Caty awoke to silence. *Even the birds know my despair.* As Caty lay in thought, she caught the distant rumble of thunder. For a moment, she lay motionless. With the second roll, she felt alive again. Dressing quickly, she rang for the steward.

He came. At her request to visit the stables again, he cringed. He knew from experience that he would be unable to control Caty. "I cannot take you there, lady. However, Lord Rhys's brother is near; I will notify Lord Bruce you wish to see him."

When Bruce arrived, he bowed slightly. She returned the salutation with a small curtsy. "You wished to see me?" Bruce asked. He had his brother's handsome face, but without the lines of authority etched about it. His smile lit up his eyes and warmed his features. He watched her intently. Caty knew he approved of her.

"Yes, I wish to go to the stables to see my horse, before it rains. Is that possible?"

"Certainly." He turned and led the way, down different corridors and out toward the stables.

When she called to Saltillo, the animal came toward her immediately. He made soft sounds but was nervous. "Why does he move about so?" she asked Bruce. "Is he afraid of the rain?"

"The horse is not from this place. Remember our ride in the storm? Here, the rain is not such a small thing. We have many rains, and when they come, they come hard and long. The land, with its rivers to fill and mountains to wash, is reluctant to let the storm move on."

Bruce watched as she began to softly stroke and speak to the horse. Slowly, the animal settled down as it moved closer to the woman. The man marveled at how easily she affected the horse, the same horse that had thrown several riders the day they captured him. When the woman made movements to saddle the horse, Bruce stopped her. "You cannot think to ride now. 'Tis not only the storm, but without my brother it would be very improper. Not to mention you endanger my neck, too." He spoke hastily and with a tone that, not unlike his brother's, left no room for any different action.

"Please forgive my ignorance of your customs. I am not accustomed to waiting for permission before I do anything. Perhaps my lord would be better off sending me back to my own people." She laughed softly.

"You are with your own people," he answered simply.

Caty made no reply. She stayed with the horse until they were certain the storm was imminent. Reluctantly, she moved toward the castle.

The animal whinnied after her. Turning, she began walking back to the stables with resolve. "I cannot leave him," she told Bruce. "I will stay with him in his stall, until the storm has passed."

Her sudden change startled Bruce. He quickly realized he could not win this argument without forcefully taking her back. While he knew his brother seldom corrected him, he was certain that touching this woman was not something he should do. Uncertain, he stood still.

Caty turned to him. "Please tell your brother where I am, as I would not wish him to worry about me. I will be with Saltillo, and will stay out of sight." He was left with no choice. Either he physically hauled her back, or risked his brother's wrath for leaving her. Eventually, he posted himself outside the stable.

This woman was headstrong, not like any woman he had ever known. He watched as she stroked the horse and murmured into its ear. The horse calmed. The storm raged, and Bruce got soaked. As the rain pelted his face with stinging force, his good humor washed down onto the ground, which was rapidly growing muddy around him. "Be warned, Rhys—next time I will take her back, even if I must haul her as a sack," he muttered.

Back in the castle, Lord Rhys searched for the woman but found her quarters empty. The steward reported that she had requested to go to the stables, and that his brother had taken her. Grabbing a heavy wrap, Lord Rhys ran into the storm. Upon reaching the stables, he found his brother posted outside, soaked and shivering. Bruce's relief at seeing Rhys was evident. Neither spoke. No one could hear or be heard above the storm anyway. Bruce nodded toward the stalls, then ducked his head and ran for the shelter of the castle.

Rhys entered to find the woman holding the horse. She was speaking softly; the animal was standing still, leaning in toward her. As she spoke, she gently laid her hand on him, all the while holding his mane firm with her free hand. Rhys stood quietly, watching. He had never known a woman to care about horses, let alone care *for* one. The animal responded to her touch. If she moved away, the animal followed her, nuzzling her. She spoke also to the horses in the adjoining stall. They too had moved toward her, and stood as she moved about and touched each one. Her own animal stood near, watching her. They seemed to have forgotten the storm. She did indeed have a gift. He had heard much about it when he agreed to kidnap her. Each day, it became more evident.

As the winds died down, she began to move away toward the gate. Her horse followed as long as he could, then whinnied as she stepped out and closed the gate. When Rhys spoke to her, she turned, startled. "How long have you been with me?"

"Long enough," he answered gently. As always when he saw her, any anger he might have felt left him. Draping her with his wrap, he helped her step over the large puddle that had formed near the corral. He reached for her hand and led her out toward the shelter of the castle. "You may come see your horse often," he said. "You must only come with my brother or with me, never alone or with anyone else. Understood?" Rhys knew Caty's independence might overrule her thinking. His steward had shared her run to the stables yesterday. While he had no qualms regarding his steward escorting her, the steward was older, was slower, and would not be able to assist her if the need arose. Rhys had not planned on Caty dashing about.

Caty nodded but did not speak. She turned once to look back at the stable.

Her horse was watching her leave. "Please," she slipped away from Lord Rhys and ran back to the stable for a last word. He shook his head slightly. She was always running, dashing, walking away from him, without even thinking to ask if she could leave. Of itself, the action seemed not so troubling. That it didn't bother him, however, was troubling to great degree. He made a decision.

"We will talk this evening," he told her when she had returned to his side. "You must freshen up. I will dine with you in your quarters tonight. We will talk then. Should you find you suddenly feel ill, no matter. I will happily send for my physician to assist you. He is very good, actually." He wickedly smiled down at her. He had her this time. Caty held her breath while he spoke about the structures they passed. His mood lightened with each step, though she was silent. He knew she had been unprepared for his plans. He had won the first battle, he thought, smiling to himself. *Soon, my lady, you will truly be mine.*

When he left her at her door, she found that the fire had warmed the room. Candles cast waving glows onto the walls, as if mocking her plight. She wanted to cry but would not allow herself to become the object of his sympathy. Instead, she decided to take great pains to pick out the ugliest gown she could find. Her armoire had been filled with them—surely she could find one that would deter his attraction. Unable to decide, she called for the steward. "Do you have anyone that can assist me with my wardrobe?" she asked when he appeared.

He smiled at her. "Indeed I do, my lady. I will send for her at once." Finally! She asked for something he could easily provide.

A soft knock on her door announced the presence of her lady-in-waiting, Rosaling. The steward introduced them. "My lady," said the woman as she curtsied. "How can I be of service to you?"

Caty immediately felt comfortable. Rosaling, or Rose as she was called, was an elderly woman with kind eyes and a ready smile. Short and stout, she carried an air of one who knew how to take care of business. Her face bore the lines of laughter as well as the furrows of frowns.

"I am expecting His Grace soon, to dine with me. I really have no idea just what to wear. I mean, I don't want to appear overbearing in dress or manner, but I do want to appear in control. I think." Caty looked at Rose hopefully.

Rose smiled. "I can help, m'lady. Here, let us have a look into the possibilities." With that, she moved to the bureau and began to search. After a short while, she removed a striking blue gown with smooth gathers just below the bodice, which was a brocade of the same color. The bodice began high at her neck and flowed to the empire waist, blending with the material of the skirt. Caty would be well covered. The material was silky and hung full, gently hiding her body. The sleeves were long and straight until the cuffs, which hung loose and graceful. The color made Caty's large eyes stand out. Rose deftly brushed her short hair loose. It fell in ringlets, surrounding her face and beginning to trail down her neck. "There!" said Rose with satisfaction. "You are beautiful, but not easy."

"I am called Caty. Please, come again in the morning, and maybe this evening also, if you're not too tired. I could use the company. Unless it might be a trouble for your husband." Caty suddenly yearned for company.

"He died three years ago. I have been called by the steward to care for you. I once cared for our lord's sister before she was sent to be married. Her husband requested no one accompany her—sadly."

"Hmm. It seems the men in your country understand a woman as little as the men from my country." Caty called the steward and requested Rose's belongings be moved into the small room included in her quarters.

As a final act, to avoid the soft, seductive glow of her room, she and Rose moved to Rhys's study. This would be her battleground. When the steward arrived with the evening meal, Rose deftly relieved him of it and followed her mistress into the study. She then moved about lighting the fire and every candle she could find. "He must not feel too sure of himself, m'lady." Already, Caty knew she would be close to Rose. She laughed as Rose added several candles from Caty's chambers to those in the study. When she had finished, the room was ablaze with light. "Bright as the day, m'lady. Keep his mind on what he is eating, we will."

When Rhys arrived, he was surprised to find Caty with Rose in the study. "Why are we not having our meal in your chambers? Did I not make myself clear?" he asked gruffly.

"It did not seem the proper place to have a meal. I felt certain you would not mind sharing the time with me in this room. Please accept my gratitude for the service of my lady-in-waiting, Rose." Rose curtsied deeply.

Caty sensed that Rhys felt awkward. Not accustomed to having anyone around when he was with Caty, he was angry. Quietly, she spoke to him. "My lord, it would be unseemly to always spend your time in my chambers, would it not? If I am to stay here, it is my hope your people are comfortable and proud of me, not talking behind closed doors. I have thought about this a great deal, and with your approval, would like to have our meals in the great room, below." The words flew out as soon as the idea hit her mind. It would be much easier to fend off Rhys in the great room.

He looked at her sharply. "You agree to stay then?"

"I agree that I have no choice, and would do nothing to give your court or clan reason to think any less of you," she countered smoothly. "As a woman, I know I am of little consequence to anyone. You, however, are the one they must rely on and follow. It will not be said you are keeping someone hid away."

"Hmm. You make a good argument, m'lady. So be it. Rose, you will see to it that our meals are taken in the great room. Heaven knows it has never seen much 'great.' Perhaps it is time that changes. Now, leave us. I wish to have a word with your lady." She immediately began to back toward the door when he spoke again. "Rose." He paused. "It is good to see you again."

Rose bowed and left the room, closing the doors behind her. Caty found herself alone with him again. Her heart pounded. She feared he could hear it. *Please help me keep him at bay a while longer. Perhaps he will tire of the game, and let me go,* her mind whispered. He looked into her eyes. Her gaze never wavered. She waited for him to speak again. *Speak!* she thought. *I shall go mad waiting. This cannot be happening.*

Rhys reached across the table and took her hand in his. His touch was warm and strong. Caty was glad she no longer trembled when he took her hand. Still he didn't speak. She looked down briefly, then back up to look into his eyes. Meeting his gaze, she spoke. "Please tell me what is on your mind, sir. You are much too serious this evening. Have I done something to anger you?"

Swiftly he responded, "Certainly you know what plays in my mind always. I think of you every minute and hour. I believe you could grow to love me. I am certain of it. I need you to help me. My people need you. My lands are small compared with what you may be familiar with, but they have been with my family for generations. I must be constantly aware of everything around me, to keep my people safe. I need someone who can tend to my home, my grounds, and all that I have, when I leave, as I do often. You are the one I need."

"How can that be?" she asked. "You know nothing about me. I may be a servant for all you know. How could I care for someone who kidnapped me, killed everyone in my party, and held me prisoner for these long months? How could your people care about me? They know me not. Most importantly, the issue of our religions is one I could never take lightly." Caty stopped and watched Lord Rhys. *There. It is out. Let him do with it as he will.*

"My people will love you; my men already do. Anyone who has contact with you cares for you. Yes, I took you prisoner, but I have treated you well, have I not? It is the custom in this land to kidnap a wife, if need be. It needed to be. As I noted before, you do not even know what religion I practice. You cannot pass judgment." Silently he added, *Besides, I know all about you. That is why I took you.*

Caty sat still. He was right. In everything he said, he was right. *He says he took a wife. It is over. He planned on this all the while.* She knew he waited for her response. Slowly, her eyes met his. "My name is Caterina. I was named for my mother's mother. My mother's people were from Rome. I am called Caty."

He frowned. "How is it you have not wed?"

"I was not . . ." Caty struggled to find the words.

"You were from the other side of the sheets?" It was not uncommon for children born out of wedlock to be raised by the wandering husband's wife.

"No, I was not!" Caty answered immediately. Noting the shadow that passed his eyes, she added, "Not that it should matter, since I came to you not by my own choice, and certainly not under any pretenses."

Frowning, he leaned forward. "You were betrothed?"

Caty sat back. She was shocked. "Heavens, no. It's just . . ." She hesitated. He listened patiently. His eyes were soft and kindly. "I believe my parents both perished. Perhaps because of their religious beliefs. Strange, the things man does in the name of God." Caty's eyes misted and she grew quiet.

"Yes, I agree." He knew all about her parents. It was the promise to her brother that brought about the raid on her party in the first place. Every man of any worth in England knew of Lord Tabor's deeds, bravery, and loyalty to the Crown. Only the Crown seemed oblivious. To Her Majesty's advisers, Lord Tabor was expendable. As was his family.

Rhys knew better. He leaned back into the chair to watch her. He was glad she had never known any other man. He suspected as much; there was something about the confident way she handled herself, without waiting for or needing approval. She had never given him reason to think on her past. She was not even aware of the effect she had on men. The blue gown she wore this night was like the setting for a rare stone, allowing the jewel to take the center. He decided she must wear her hair uncovered and loose whenever they were alone. *Alone, ah yes.* He stood. Caty stood also, moving quickly to her chambers, calling to Rose as she entered. To her surprise, he followed. Grateful for her lady-in-waiting, she walked to the fire. He followed, squatting to lay several more logs onto the hearth. Turning to Rose, he commanded, "Leave us."

TWENTY

HE STRODE TO THE DOOR and locked it behind Rose. Caty could feel her heart racing. He returned to the fire and warmed himself. "I am called Rhys Dermoth."

Caty looked up at him sharply. "You are called Dermoth? Dermoth is your name?" The English man and his band had laughed at some secret riddle when the Englishman had pulled her cloak from her. *He knew then who I ran from. He must know Rhys Dermoth.*

"Yes, I am called Dermoth. You know of Dermoth?" He frowned quizzically and studied her.

"No, I heard the name before, but did not understand it was a family name. I . . . I thought it referred to a place." She answered quickly. She was in no position to discuss her adventures with him.

"It is a place as well. Your home is called Dermoth Castle. I have one brother, whom you have met, Bruce. My sister married and left this land. We have no one else alive. Our family has held these lands for many generations. Even with fighting around our borders, we have been able to escape destruction. There have been unspeakable acts in all of Scotland, in the name of religion. My family, also, felt the blows. However, we have survived. I intend to see that we prosper, at last."

He looked directly at her. His voice was soft but firm. "It matters not to me where you came from nor who your family was. I can see you are kind, gentle, and honest. That speaks well for your mother. You will be with me to see to it that my people can move beyond what they have suffered. We will speak of this again, soon." He moved to stand over her. "For this moment, you must remember—all you have seen since you've come to me is mine, including you, lady." He smiled as he gently brushed her face with his hand. Yawning, he strode to the bed and began undressing.

"What . . . what are you doing?" Caty asked, horrified. Surely he wouldn't force her. Yet, she was his, as he had so aptly pointed out.

"I, lady, am making ready to sleep. You may sleep in the chair if you do not desire to lie with me, but you will not enter the hall. I will wait for you." With that, he was naked, and lay down.

She refused to watch him and turned to the fire, standing there, frozen. Behind her, she could hear him chuckling. She refused to lie with someone not of her choice. In her heart of hearts, she knew this to be impossible. Only the poorest were able to choose whom they wed. Most women were a commodity. A way to bind families and fortunes. How could she be of use to him without family or fortune?

After a long while, she turned slowly. To her relief, he slept. She quietly tiptoed to the bed. Unable to resist, she stood watching him. His hair lay all around his head. His face, relaxed in sleep, was kind and carried no sign of distress. In spite of herself, Caty smiled. *He's not bad to gaze upon, but I just cannot— can I?* She could see his broad shoulders, muscled arms, strong chest, and . . . Shaking her head, she refused to look upon him further. Laying a blanket gently over him, she slipped away.

Early morning light woke Rhys. He realized Caty had not been on the bed all night, nor was she in the chair. With anger rising, he strode without covering to open the hall door. All was dark and quiet on this floor. Frowning, he returned to the chamber. Rhys opened the door to the study. Finding it empty, he slowly opened the door to his own bedchamber. To his surprise, there she lay. Curled under the soft blankets, still dressed, sleeping soundly. Standing over her, he had to restrain himself. How easy it would be to bed her now. He held back. He listened to her rhythmic breathing. Her long lashes still held a few tears. Her hair, grown out slightly, stuck out with abandon around her head. Slowly, he pulled the coverlet up closer around her, leaving her to rest.

Entering Caty's chamber again, Rhys dressed, then called Rose. "Let my lady sleep late. When she awakens, have the steward notify me. Please bring in several other young women you think would care for her alongside you, Rose. This will be a special day." He smiled to himself. *Tonight, you are mine, lass.*

Rose watched Lord Rhys. He was happier than she had seen him in a long, long time. She knew her lady had not slept with him, although it was clear that Caty had softened toward him the last several weeks. *About time*, Rose thought. *She could do no better than his lordship.* She happily began to clean the chamber and ready it for a bath. This was indeed a special occasion, although she feared her lady might not see it that way at first. *No matter. This place has a great need of m'lady. I must do all in my power to keep her safe and make this a home for her.*

Caty awoke as the sounds of activity reached the bed. Sitting up, she was momentarily disoriented. Looking around, she gasped. Fearing he would find her in his chambers, she slid off the large bed and ran quickly to the closed door. She gently pushed it aside and surveyed the empty study. Inside, she found Rose humming happily. "Is he gone, Rose?"

"Aye, m'lady. He slept like a wee one, all the night. You would like a bath? 'Twill be a cold day coming soon. Too cold for bathing and such. The water is warmed, and the fire is full." Rose had already set out towels to warm, several buckets of water were heating, and the tub awaited water.

Having slept in her gown, Caty had to admit that a bath would feel good. "Yes, Rose, quickly; I don't wish to be found in such a state."

Rose frowned. "Of course, m'lady. I'll lay a fresh gown out. Here, let me help you, and do not be a'lying too long." Rose opened the door and pulled the string to summon the steward. "The lady is up!" she said when he entered after a light tap at the door. The steward nodded, backing away. When he was gone, Rose washed Caty's hair and rinsed her off, pouring water scented with oils over her.

When Caty stood, she was grateful for the warmed blanket Rose wrapped around her. Seated near the fire, she closed her eyes as Rose dried her hair. "Rose, check his room without delay. He must not know I slept in his bed. I'm quite positive that he would like that." Caty shook her head as she remembered her near miss the previous night. "It's just what he would want."

"That's not the whole of what I would like, lady," said a male voice from behind them. There he stood, his frame filling the doorway. "I would much prefer to be in the bed with you. And I shall be. Since you are so comfortable there, I'm certain you will rest easy lying with me." The firm look in his eyes gave Caty a sinking feeling. Rhys smiled in appreciation of her shapely legs peeking out from beneath the coverlet. "I believe it is time to find a weaver for you. You will need new gowns. Take your time this day, my lady. This is the first day of June, and today we wed."

Caty jumped to her feet. "What? Oh, I can't—please! Please . . ." Her voice trailed off.

Rhys walked to her. He held her face and gaze firm. "I have been more than patient, have I not? I could have bedded you the first night."

"I, I know," Caty answered haltingly. "But . . . but what if I am unable to give you a child?" Her mind raced, trying to find some reason he might not want her. "Perhaps you would do better with someone younger than I."

Rhys frowned. "A child? I could bed any woman I please to give me children. My heir is not from me, but is my father's children, by birth order. Next in line after me will be Bruce. After him, if need be, there are many boys." He smiled. "Bruce is very busy with his woman."

Caty blushed again but pushed forward. "I can't wed you. My religion—"

He interrupted brusquely, "I fail to see how that is of concern to me. You will work it out with your God, I'm positive. It's to be today. Until then . . ." He took her hand and lifted it to his lips. He then released her hand and started to leave, but instead took her face in his hands and kissed her full on her mouth. The kiss was long, soft, and warm. "That will have to hold you until later, my love," he said with a smile. Caty could do little to hide the blush. His smile broadened.

As the door closed, Caty sank into her chair. "This cannot be. I will not wed this man. I am a Catholic. I cannot do this!"

"There, there, little one." Rose held her. "You must trust our lordship. He will take care of you. You will see. Everything will be as you wish."

"How? How can that be?" Caty asked softly. Unmoved, Rose began to groom and dress her. Caty moved as if in a trance. She shed no tears; it would be useless to cry over something she could not stop. As Rose went about choosing the best gown, putting soft touches to her hair and brushing off her shoes, Caty sat impassive. In the early afternoon, a knock at the door from the steward gave Caty a horrible, sickly feeling.

"'Tis time, m'lady," Rose instructed gently after consulting in hushed tones with the steward. As her lady-in-waiting led her out the door, Caty paused and surveyed the chamber. Then, slowly, she and Rose, led by the steward, made their way down the stairs to the great room, and Caty resolved that neither Lord Rhys nor anyone else would know of the turmoil in her heart and soul. She wore a soft, cream-colored gown, with a moderate squared neckline. A stiff, full collar rounded the neckline, dropping to a deep V that overlapped the bodice in front. From each shoulder and under the back of her collar, a filmy gossamer material hung to the floor, flowing behind her as she walked. The dress had great gathers round her tiny waist, and the skirt grazed the floor. The sleeves were full, gathering to wide bands at her wrists. A crown of flowers sent to her by Rhys sat upon her head, and from it flowed more of the gossamer material. It fell below her waist, edged with small mother-of-pearl beads.

At the bottom of the stair, rather than entering the great room from the door nearest, the steward led them through the kitchen and outside to the main entrance. She lifted her head, took a deep breath, and paused at the sight of the room filled with people. Gracefully, lifting her gown, she entered the room. As she came in, a hush fell upon the people and filled every corner of the great room. Caty could see the dancing patterns the sunlight made on the floor. The rays of sunlight seemed oddly out of place with her heart. Bruce met her at the door, bowed, and took her hand gently. "Lady, allow me." His eyes were filled with frank admiration. He winked at her and smiled. "Fear not, lady—I mean, sister. These many people are here for you." Firmly, he placed her hand on his arm and turned with her to begin the walk down the aisle. As the couple passed through the room, the people stood up. Murmurs drifted to her as she walked by the people of Dermoth lands.

Rhys stood at the front. He was freshly shaven, with his mustache and beard neatly trimmed. His hair was pulled back and tied carefully. His breeches and heavy shirt were the color of Caty's gown, as was the heavy cloak he wore about his shoulder, held by a sleek golden braid. A sword hung loosely at his side. On the middle finger of each hand, he wore enormous signet rings, thick gold with large stones. One was deep emerald and one was fire ruby. His eyes were ablaze, and it was plain he wanted this maiden. Bravely, Caty met his gaze without hesitation. Again, he marveled at her calm. When Bruce and Caty reached Rhys, Bruce handed her to his brother, bowing to both. Rhys took her hand in his, set her hand on his arm, and turned to the front. He could feel Caty trembling. A man stepped from behind a back panel in the great room and strode to the makeshift altar that had been set up. Caty slowly took in the man and his garb. She gasped. This man was surely a priest. She turned to Rhys but he looked straight ahead. The ceremony began. As she took her vows, she looked to Rhys. His eyes were kind and filled with emotion. His touch was tender. Caty's heart felt easier. Her greatest concern was solved. She would not have to hide her religion. The priest and ceremony were both Catholic. Carefully, she signed her name on the document presented her. She had no choice in this union, but he was of her religion. God would see to the rest.

Once the ceremony had drawn to a close, food was brought out. Gathering around the laden table, people began to fill the hall with laughter and talk. Musicians wandered along the edge of the room, playing softly. Rhys took Caty's hand. He looked down at her, smiling. "You are beautiful, lady."

"Thank you, Lord Rhys," Caty murmured as Rhys led her to his table.

"Listen to what you hear here and tell me your thoughts. Many of these men are my closest advisers." His voice dropped to a whisper. "Do not be unsettled. These men already genuinely care for you."

"Why did you not tell me you were of the same faith?" she whispered back. Now her golden eyes searched his face.

"I wanted to see how deeply you care about your beliefs. Besides, I knew for me it mattered not, but for you—it was of great importance. One day, you will grow to love me. Our differences are few, and soon will become unnoticeable."

Caty smiled as she looked at his hand holding hers. "Perhaps, Your Grace," she said. Perhaps he was right. One great burden had been lifted, for certain. Time would tell. He led her to the head of the table now set for them. She sat at his side. Gigantic trays of food were being brought out, as were pitchers of wine.

Rhys raised her hand to his lips and kissed it gently. "You are trembling, lady. Do you fear me?" he asked kindly, his voice soft, for her ears only.

Caty, blushing, couldn't meet his eyes. "Nay, my lord. I know not why I do this when your hand touches me."

Rhys smiled. "I do. Soon you will also. Now our guests need our attention."

The castle had not held such celebration in several generations. Caty was awed by the people who filled every free space. She searched the faces, wondering if by chance she might remember anyone from her time in the kitchen. She turned to see Rhys watching her again. She smiled back at her new husband.

"We shall dance," Rhys said after a while, standing to offer her his hand. He bowed deeply. Caty stood, and the great hall went silent. He led her to the front of the table. With his right arm around her waist, he swept the hall with his left. "I present to you your lady, Lady Caty, my wife." A loud cheer rose from the hall. Gracefully, Caty curtsied to them, took Rhys's arm, and stepped onto the floor. "Lady Caty, how I have waited for this moment. A lifetime." The musicians now moved nearer the head table, and began to play louder. With that, the couple danced together. Initially, most of the people in attendance just watched. This type of dancing was a novelty for them, something they knew their lord had brought back from England. Times were surely changing. Slowly at first, a few couples joined them. Soon, the floor was packed with pairs trying to learn this new activity.

When they were seated again, the men and women began approaching to offer congratulations. Caty spoke to each, and gave her hand to each. Several ladies cast sidelong glances toward her new brother-in-law. Once she caught him winking at an admiring woman. Noticing Caty's attention, Bruce laughed and said, "Life is short, my lady. Best to fill each day." All the women apparently knew him well, but he also watched the men carefully. It seemed to Caty that he looked not for allies, but for trouble. She turned back to survey the crowd. She saw that most watched her.

Caty resolved to spend more time with the staff of this castle. She would meet with the steward first thing each morning. Experience told her that the steward always knew what was going on. Returning to her observation of the room, she saw that most of the men in attendance were relaxed, but a small group stood aside, simply watching. She saw that Bruce watched this group warily. A feeling came over Caty. She little understood how or when she would be nudged by what her mother called their "gift," but it was coming to her now.

TWENTY-ONE

"RHYS," CATY SAID QUIETLY AS she turned to her new husband, "do you see that group of men watching us?" She darted her eyes to her right, where the men stood. "Do they mean danger for you?"

Rhys stole a look in the direction she had indicated. "No. They are from the Northern Highlands. Their clans are much farther north. We see not eye to eye regarding our country's future. I doubt they will cause any trouble. They merely wish to see who I wed."

Several minutes later, one of the men came forward. Perhaps he had caught Caty looking. After speaking briefly with Rhys, he turned to her. In a singsong voice, he welcomed her to Scotland, with wishes for a happy and fruitful marriage. Caty inhaled sharply. Looking into her eyes was the very man she had talked out of taking her on the road so many months before near Perth, he who seemed to be in search of the Gaelic-speaking woman she had freed, he who had asked her to prove her womanhood. She knew he remembered her.

"You are for certain a lady," he said, smiling. After a quick bow, he left. As he neared the end of the hall, the rest of the group joined him and made their exit. Relieved they were gone, Caty made a mental note to talk with her husband about them. She saw Rhys frown slightly in the wake of their departure, but he was interrupted by other guests before he could share his thoughts. Glancing at Bruce, she noticed him studying her, a questioning look on his face, too. She smiled sweetly at him. She would talk with her husband first.

After several hours of talking with guests, Rhys leaned to her. "Perhaps we could slip away?"

Caty smiled. "Nay, lord, I doubt you could ever slip away from these people. But I believe they will allow you to leave. Are you not the lord of this manor?"

"I am. And I would have my bride retire," he said. "I will stay but a while longer."

Rhys stood until Caty and Rose were out of sight, then sat back down. His brother moved next to him. "Finally it's happened! I thought you would never settle down, brother! You must take care. Don't lose her. The people love her already. They are happy to see you at ease." Thoughtfully, he added, "Our friends from the Highlands left early, didn't they? Seems they got whatever they were looking for. You should move quickly, Rhys. You have little time. They may know about your bride. 'Twas an odd comment he left."

"True enough. In the morning, we will travel with Caty. She needs to see these lands and their boundaries. She is the mistress over many now. I will ask how she knows our 'friends,' as you call them." Rhys slipped out and slowly climbed the stairs, pleased with the day, anxious for the night, and planning for the time surely to come.

Caty opened the door to her lord's bedchamber. Candles were already lit, and the fireplace warmed the room. Crossing into her own chamber, she began to undress. Rose laid a beautiful white bed gown on her bed. "Whereever did you find this, Rose?"

"It is a gift from my lord. He wishes you to be comfortable on this night. He will be good to you, m'lady."

"This I believe. I think . . . ," Caty answered in a feeble voice. Shaking her head to bid the feeling pass, she continued, "You are kind to me, also, Rose. I am thankful for your companionship and care."

"'Tis I that thank you, m'lady. 'Tis my privilege for certain."

"Please think of others whom you would have share our time and work. I will need more help, I believe. In the morrow, or perhaps the next day, you and I will walk this castle and the grounds. From this, a plan to bring more help can be made." Caty touched Rose's hand. Rose curtsied; when she stood, her eyes were misty.

Once prepared for bed, Caty slowly entered Rhys's chamber. She sat near the fire and waited. This night would tell her what she might expect for her life. *Mother, my heart cries for your wisdom, now more than ever.* Her heart pounded, but she knew it was not only fear. Her heart beat with anticipation. His door opened. Turning to him, Caty sat quietly, not certain just what she should do now. Rhys stood still; her beauty and serene demeanor struck him. He stood speechless and motionless.

A small smile crept across her face. *Why, he is as nervous as I,* she thought. *Perhaps I could grow fond of him. Better to live in harmony if possible. He is Catholic. I think I can live here, happily.*

Crossing the room with building confidence, Rhys took her hand and gently pulled her out of her seat, to him. He took a small packet from his breast and slipped her mother's ring back onto her finger. Then on the left hand, he slipped a beautiful copy of his emerald ring onto her finger. She looked at her hands. "Rhys, you return my ring . . . and have given me yours." Her eyes were filled with emotion as she looked up at him.

He ran his hand through her hair; it smelled like flowers, soft and silky in his hand. Stepping back, he slowly turned her around. She seemed to float. Then he lifted her up, as if she were a child, and carried her to his bed. He laid her down, stood back, and began to remove his sword.

She watched him undress. He was strong and athletic. Several scars marked his chest. His arms were muscled and his chest broad. His breathing was deepening. He lay down beside her and slowly began to unbutton her gown. When he finished, he carefully lifted it away and pushed it aside, exposing her completely. His eyes leisurely moved over her naked body. Caty knew she blushed deeply; still she lay quietly, waiting. His warm, tender hands carefully and gently traveled over her body, exploring each crevice, curve, and swell. Caty felt herself drift away, into another world. He would not be rushed, and slowly continued exploring her body, his hand moving downward. A slight moan escaped her lips. When she felt she could stand no more, he moved atop her, gently, slowly. Involuntarily, she moved into him, with him. With a gasp and cry of pain, her body became rigid as he took her. With his gentle persuasion, this was followed by moans of pleasure as she relaxed. The hours of darkness stirred wave after wave of passion. Her passion rose to match his.

Morning light found them both spent. She lay curled against him; his arm encircled her. *She sleeps,* Rhys thought, looking down upon her. *My lady sleeps. She is mine. Last night was only a small taste of what will be, my love.* Gently, he moved his arm and covered her nakedness. Pausing, unable to resist, he removed the covers again, studying her body. He unhurriedly stroked her breasts, caressed her nipples, and then gradually moved his hand over her belly and down her body. Searching gently, he found what he was probing for. Moaning, she turned to him without opening her eyes. She let him in, easily, eagerly. When he was spent at last, he lay back. "Would that we could stay here all day," he whispered into her neck.

"No, my lord, better to have this to think upon all this day," Caty answered.

"You are no longer afraid of me? I please you?" he asked, his eyes closed.

"I was never afraid of you, my lord. Yes, you do please me." Turning to face him, she continued, "More than I could ever have imagined. How shall I stand to wait all day for you?"

Rhys smiled. "You will be with me this day, my love. We are to ride these lands. I want you to see your people; I want them to see you." He could see the warm light in her eyes. The light he had hoped for filled them. "I think, my lady, you do love me." His voice was soft.

Caty didn't answer, but instead kissed his mouth. "Yes, I do," she finally said. Then, slipping out of his embrace, she robed and left the chamber. "You must not tarry too long, my lord," she called from the next room. "We will break fast in the great room soon. And there will certainly be many of your people there." She could hear him moan. She smiled.

The great room filled with some guests from the evening before, as well as Rhys's men and their ladies, eager to catch another glimpse of the newly wed couple. Caty knew this was a good thing for these people. It would be a good thing to share food often. They would need a good cook, a baker, and someone to keep order in the kitchen and food stores. Her time in the kitchen had shown the lack of direction in that area. Though the meals were prepared in a timely fashion, the same woman had to bake, cook, and plan each one. With the varying numbers of guests, this was no small feat. So it began. Caty was the lady of the castle.

After eating, she stood to take her leave. "Will we be long this day, Rhys?"

"We'll be away from this house for at least a week. It would be best if you can pack lightly, but warmly. You will of course ride. If Rose is able, please take her with you, if you feel the need to do so. I will come for you shortly." He stood as she left the room.

"Well, brother?" said Bruce, grinning, once she had gone. "Is it going to be a good union?"

Rhys smiled. "Aye, and more." His face clouded. "We've escaped notice so far, but any day, the English may call us to their side. That would mean Caty is here alone. I have no doubt she will see to our people, but they do not know her yet. They need to. They must help her when this time comes. I fear that bad times may be upon us, brother. The Highlands have yet to accept the changes with the union. It will be clan against clan."

"I have a difficult time understanding why there is still such resistance when everyone can tell we are better off. We have new access to English markets, peoples are more prosperous, and it seems as if we may have some peace for a change," Bruce noted.

"Bruce," Rhys said patiently, "the clans of the Highlands are not much better off than they were before. They still speak of what once was and none can match their loyalty for the imagined king of Scotland. The best we can hope for is a quick end and no reprisals." He stood. "We will be ready to leave shortly, brother. I am always grateful for your presence. Yet, perhaps there would be some way for me to leave you to watch over our lands while I am away."

"I think not, Rhys. I'm going with you. We are so far from the edge of anything important, our holdings will be safe. I have no doubt many of the men will stay. Things will be fine; you will see."

Lord Dermoth was one of the few lords that allowed the men working the lands to actually own their plots. His actions created a stronger bond between him and those that lived on his lands.

"That all depends upon not being visited by any uprising clans until we return, brother." The brothers exchanged knowing glances.

TWENTY-TWO

WHEN HE OPENED THE DOOR to her bedchamber, Lord Rhys was pleased to see Caty already changed, with only a small package for the trip. "What have you packed?"

She opened the wrap, unfolding several woolen shawls that held caps, one change of shoes, several woolen leggings, some blankets, two heavy skirts, and two long shirts with long sleeves, high collars, and full vests. "Is this acceptable?"

"Yes. And Rose?"

"She has asked to be relieved of this duty," Caty said, laughing. "She is going to gather people for me to review to fill our house staff positions. I think I will teach someone to cook, but we need others."

Nodding his approval, he pulled her to him. "Pity we are expected below shortly. But tonight will come soon enough. Tell me," he chuckled, "I must know, who told you that to look me in the eye was punishable by death?" As her laughing eyes now looked into his, Rhys could hardly believe they were the same eyes he had worked so hard to see those many months ago.

Blushing, Caty shrugged slightly. "I was told that for a woman to look you squarely was deadly. I now believe they spoke of your reputation with your women, but I misunderstood. No matter, you have wonderful eyes." Smiling, she picked her small package up and left the room.

Rhys smiled to himself. *I really must do something about her habit of leaving before I am ready to have her gone. That needs work. Good that I will have many hours to teach her.*

Shortly thereafter, Rhys and Caty were riding through the settlement near his castle. People came to the streets to see them. Caty stopped often to speak to the women, to touch hands stretched out to her.

Near the outskirts of the hamlet just beyond the castle, an older lady limped forward slowly. Her thinning hair fell about her head, framing a wrinkled face. Those lines bore testament of her trials. The deep furrows between her brows and over her gentle gray eyes gave evidence of worries, both past and present. Her hands were thin, with knobs protruding around her arthritic fingers. A worn shawl was pulled about her stooped shoulders. She strained to see Caty. Caty felt the woman searching for her. She stopped her horse and dismounted. "Here, Mother, I am here," Caty said. When she reached the old woman, she took her hand and found herself looking into the kindest eyes she could ever remember having seen. "What can I do for you?"

"'Tis I that would do for you, m'lady. You are a healer?" The woman's eyes searched Caty's.

"Perhaps," Caty answered cautiously. The old woman's eyes were filled with questions.

"You helped my husband after the fight that brought you here. But for you, he would have died. You are a healer." Caty could scarcely remember all she had done on that night, but the woman's age, her gentle manner, and her story moved Caty. She nodded her head slightly. The old woman pulled Caty's very heart from her, as if she had taken it into her hands ever so gently. Caty was drawn to this woman.

"My mother's people were plagued with constant fighting, killing, and illnesses," Caty said softly. "If the families were to survive, the women had to learn how to help the men stay alive. My father was a leader, so my mother saw many men injured. She taught me well, and I helped from the time I was very small. I think all women are healers. Where is your husband now?"

"He works the fields. We have no children left. I can little stand to lose him too, m'lady. Because of you, he returned home." The woman now held both of Caty's hands in her own. "Would that I had a way to thank you."

"When your husband returns this evening, tell him I wish you both to go to the castle. Ask for Rose. Tell her I sent you. She will tell you what you are to do. You are to live with me, you and your husband. Now go pack what you would take with you. I will return soon, and would see you at our home."

132

The old lady smiled through tears. "Yes, m'lady. We would be proud to serve you."

Rhys and Bruce had been listening to the exchange with interest. Bruce grinned. "She could stand for position in the courts, you know."

Evening found them encamped near a river. Tents were erected and fires lit. The men had procured fresh game to add to the staples packed. Everyone ate well. The group was merry and Caty felt a certain companionship with these men. Later, lying in their tent, Rhys turned to her. "Tell me about Caterina, lady. Your people, parents—everything. I want to know everything about you."

Caty lay nestled within his arms. "My mother's mother was from Rome. She was wed to a merchant from England. The marriage was certainly one of convenience, but she carried a great deal of respect for my grandfather, and by the time they were elderly, she loved him deeply. He was a wealthy merchant who added to his fortunes by shipping tea from China. Unfortunately, he considered the opium trade a necessary evil, and nearly lost everything when England's monarchy changed."

She paused for a moment. "They had one daughter and six sons. I have no idea where or even who the sons are, as my mother—the daughter—was sent to court, to be educated. It seems someone in the court owed my grandfather a debt. For what, I am not certain. My father was already at court, as an apprentice to the court working with the ambassadors from Italy and France. He learned his lessons well, moved up quickly, and found himself embroiled in England's court intrigue. He eventually took my mother as his wife. When he was sent away for the first time, he took his wife, packed up his children, and sailed to the Indies, to secure England's rule.

"I remember little except fighting. Horrible fighting. My mother became an expert in caring for ill and wounded men. We moved about to many places. I spent nearly every waking hour next to my mother. Except when my brothers were about. During those times, my mother saw fit to allow me to roam with them. I learned a great deal from those boys. It was during that time that I came to love the horses."

Caty rolled over to face Rhys. "When my father felt the time was right, I was sent alone back to court. I never made it there. Our group was decimated in fighting, having been attacked by pirates, before we could land. Shortly after landing, I overheard the captain say my parents were killed . . . I know not the circumstances. My parents saw to it I was well educated, but passed before they could teach me how to survive. That I learned on my own. By God's protection I joined the band you attacked shortly after we landed. I have little doubt I would have been working in Glasgow or Edinburgh if we had been able to get that far. You could not have known we each were of different families and peoples. Not one knew the other—we were just together."

Rhys listened to each word. She believed she had no family, no money, and no obligation to anyone, except him and his people. She might never know that he knew well who she was and nearly everything about her family. That was for the best. She belonged to him now, and he loved her. He would do whatever was needed to protect her, this lady of such peace and calm.

Pulling her even closer, he gently guided her passion to the surface. The touch of his hand caused her to tremble. Removing her bed gown, he moved her arms above her head and left them there. When she once reached for him, he shook his head and placed her hands over her head again. Lying thus, open, he took possession of her. His hands moved over her body, and he teased her to the edge, then moved to other areas she knew not as alive before his touch. She could not contain herself any longer. Grasping him, she was again taken to his special world. For this, she had waited. As they lay together afterward, he requested she tell him more about herself. He wanted to hear her talk. Her voice was soft, easy, and melodic.

"I think you know all, Rhys. I was well educated, as were both my parents. My father believed I should have the same opportunities as my brothers, in education. My mother was a great healer, and given the circumstances we found ourselves in, this gift saved many a life. I was blessed to be at her side so long. She felt herself lucky to have been chosen by my father. They also loved deeply. Putting their life into words . . . their life was hard. Having lived it with them, it seemed not so."

Rhys pulled her closer. "Sleep, my lady. I cannot promise you a life free of labor or worry, but I can promise you a partner to share this life with. I will always love you, Caty. I have loved you from the moment I first saw you." He raised himself up on an elbow to look into her eyes. "I care not about having children. If we do, I will be happy; if you are barren, I will still be happy. I care deeply about my lands, my clan, and my country."

Rhys sank back down, lying with his hands under his head. "Scotland has had a troubled past, and is bound for more of the same, I fear. The clans, especially from the Northern Highlands, are not at ease with English influence, laws, or rulers. They have lived the same way for many generations, and see little value in any change. England's history regarding treatment of the Scots does little to dispel the distrust felt by so many. I still must guard my borders closely, and do all I can for the people that work the fields and mind the stock. There is always another clan leader willing to take what is mine."

He rolled back up on his elbow again as Caty lay listening. "I fear I will be called to side by the English, and must go," he continued. "Many will fight, but it will largely be Southern Highlanders against Northern Highlanders. Poor Scotland. This great land I love."

"I do not understand. If you love Scotland, which I believe you do, how can you fight with the English against her?" Caty asked.

"The Act of Union was signed, not so long ago, creating a parliament of Great Britain, abolishing both parliaments of England and Scotland. This union gives each one a common citizenship, and gives Scotsmen free access to the markets of England. While such an arrangement will certainly help us, it pushes the Northern Highlanders' long-held ways of life away. It is not long before their old way is lost forever. It matters not that I may agree or disagree with this life as they lived it. What will matter is that they will feel lost and betrayed, I believe. I am English, Caty. I feel more Scottish, but I am English. For this reason I must fight for the Crown. I fear our borders may become battle lines for roving clans looking to boost their holdings in a last big push to survive. Caty, I fear for my people while I am away, if I am called, as I feel I will be. You must do all you can to keep them safe." He turned to her. His face showed the enormity of his concern. "I am saddened to place such a burden upon you, but there is no other way, I fear."

Caty brushed his hair out of his face. "I will do all I can to be certain you only have your survival to think about. You must return to me. You took me; now your real burden is me, and you simply cannot leave me."

He smiled. "Such a burden one has never known, I am certain. I know you will do whatever is needed. My lady, my love."

The next week was spent moving about his lands, meeting peoples and surveying boundaries. Caty found that the land revealed great beauty. Grassy plains dotted with small hills gave way to steep northern mountains. Snow still capped these peaks, while rivers running throughout the land gave up sweet water following winter's fury. Evenings were cool, but the days were warm. Cattle and sheep grazed while men and women worked the fields. The children ran about, playing around the small huts that occasionally broke the landscape. It seemed unlikely that this could become a battleground, but Caty knew all too well how quickly the world could turn.

At last, after days of travel, she spotted the outline of bothies surrounding Dermoth Castle. When they arrived at the castle, Rhys helped her down. "You have made me proud, lady. You ride well, pack well, and certainly lay well," he noted softly. Caty blushed, and hurried inside.

TWENTY-THREE

WHEN CATY HAD CLEANED UP and changed, she hurried downstairs. Caty's small staff stood in the great room excitedly waiting. She was pleased to find the old woman had indeed come to the castle and had, by all indications, found a place with Rose. The smell of fresh-baked bread drifted from the kitchen, and candles were being lit throughout. Rhys had not yet returned from the stables, and staff hustled to be certain the meal would be ready for him. A large fire blazed, and Bruce was already warming his hands. He had spoken little during the trip, but Caty found him watching her frequently during their travels. "So, sister, how do you find our lands?" he said now.

Caty smiled. "Beautiful and peaceful."

"Not for long, I fear. Might I ask after your father? Was he Lord Tabor?" Bruce stared at the dancing flames in the fireplace. Like many of the young men of Scotland, Bruce had fought as a mercenary to bring badly needed monies to his family. By the time Rhys assumed control, the family fortune was stable and it was no longer necessary for either brother to fight for money. From the first time Bruce saw Caty, he felt he had seen her before. During their trek throughout Dermoth lands, he began to remember. It was not Caty he had seen, but one of her brothers, for sure. Their features, especially their eyes, were the same.

"Why would you think that?"

"You have the same features as your brother. I felt I had known you, when I first saw you, but I know now it was your brother. Your brother I knew well. Many Scots have fought in other lands, for foreign causes and peoples. I and your brother were together. He was one to be proud of. I still miss him. Indeed, Ricardo is probably missed by many a man—at least many women." At that he laughed out loud.

"For shame, Bruce," Caty admonished him gently. "He is gone and I too miss him. Though I must say, I knew him but little as a man. He was sent away when I was young. Yet, of all my brothers, he was the one who took me to heart the most. 'Tis true, I am the daughter of Lord Tabor. The only daughter. He had sons, many of them. I know not who is left alive, but I fear none are left. I do believe you and he could have been close. You make me think of him."

Bruce smiled. Looking into the fire, he spoke softly, sadly. "He was the bravest lad. We were taught how to fight, move forward, and give no quarter. He did all well. When our group was cornered, he alone was able to climb a ridge, pulling a few of us after him. We were able to stop the advancement, pushing huge rocks down onto the line below us. He then drew fire, himself killing several, allowing the rest of us to make our way back and pull what was left of our group out. Aye, I miss him still, lass."

The moment was broken when Rhys walked into the great chamber. His voice boomed off the walls as he strode in, followed by what seemed to Caty the whole of the small village that surrounded the castle. Everyone was in high spirits. As the dinner progressed, the fire warmed the air while ale and wine warmed the minds. Rhys smiled, watching his wife move about the hall, making certain each had been served, then taking her seat next to him. "You do well, wife, but you must let your ladies do such work when the hall is filled as this. Your place is next to me. I would entertain guests, soon, and would not care for them to see you as a servant."

"Of course, husband. Yet these women have but little experience in such matters, and must be shown what I would expect. Soon, this will not be necessary, as I believe Rose has chosen well the staff I need. You should have such a hall every evening. I would speak to you about your food stocks and preparations for winter, when you have a moment."

Rhys put his arm around her. "Of course, lady. Bruce tells me you are from good blood, and know the workings of such things well. Much more than you would have me believe." He smiled down at her. "What other small pieces of information did you see fit to leave out of your story, Caty?" While Rhys had shared Caty's story with Bruce, he was not willing to do so with Caty herself. There would come a time when he would be forced to tell his wife the reason for her abduction, but not yet. Not until he was sure she would stay with him, no matter the way she came to be in his care.

One of the young men attending the diners approached, interrupting them. "My lord, the man at the door would speak with you. He and the men with him come from Inverness."

Rhys nodded. "Bring him in to me."

The young man returned momentarily, and with a fleeting look, Caty gasped quietly at the man accompanying him. He was back—the one who had nearly taken her on the road after she freed the woman by the sea. Worse, Caty had not spoken to Rhys about him. What could he want? The impulse to look away was strong, but Caty ignored the feeling. She looked directly at the man. He strode to the table, nodded to Rhys, then looked frankly at her. "You prove well you are a lady. And you shine as happy. That is good."

Bruce exchanged glances with Rhys. Frowning, Rhys turned to his guest. "You are always welcome, and your men also. Make room for Clan Donroge." Servants scurried to follow his order. Turning to his visitor again, he asked, "What brings you here again, Donald?"

"I come to see with mine own eyes whether you be happily wedded. Every man is happy on the day of his wedding, many not so happy after. You are well suited to each other. Your fate seemed not to have plan for such. I ask that you speak with me, as man to man."

"Certainly." Rhys stood. Nodding to Bruce, Rhys led Donald and Bruce, followed by one of Donald's men, to a room away from the great room where they could talk in private.

Caty's stomach turned. Could he have found the woman she released? If so, what would he demand in payment? Deep in thought, Caty failed to notice Lord Rhys and Bruce's return until Rhys touched her elbow.

"Lady Caty, Clan Donroge would present you with a gift. Donald indicates that you and he may have met before." Rhys smiled down at her, but Caty could tell he was not pleased. "Again, I ask, what else have you neglected to share with me?" He spoke discreetly, but she knew Bruce heard. He too looked at her intently. Yet, in present company, she could not speak out. Her tale was too long. Pausing for the briefest moment, she responded softly.

"Sir, perhaps we should speak of such things again in your chambers, if it would please you."

"I hardly think 'perhaps' is the appropriate word. I think it would be better for you if you said 'we shall' speak, for indeed we shall." His voice had softened again, and he raised her hand to his lips. However, the look he gave her left no room for doubt: whatever Donald had told him now troubled his mind. Turning to the man now approaching them again, with a bundle, Rhys nodded and presented his wife. The leader of Clan Donroge presented Caty with a soft, beautifully woven cloak. Caty graciously accepted the gift, noting with relief the slight smile on Donald's face and the gleam in his eyes. His look told her that he knew more about her than she would have thought to share with him, but that he held no ill will toward her for her actions.

"I am well pleased with such a beautiful gift," she said. "Please tell your woman her handiwork is fit for a queen, as she must be."

Donald Donroge smiled slowly at her. "Aye, m'lady. I will tell her." He backed away and took his leave.

Caty and Rhys spent the rest of the evening listening to all that had taken place while they were touring his lands. Rhys's demeanor toward her did not change; though he frequently touched her hand or arm, she knew he was unhappy. She met his glances with open, honest trust. He may not approve of her tale, but Caty prayed he would not judge unjustly.

Listening to men talking with Rhys, Caty realized that her lord had men at court in England, others living in Salisbury, and still more in Edinburgh. After listening intently to each man, Rhys requested they be present at morning court. The men from Dermoth's fields and pastures received the same attention. Caty felt the undercurrent of worry in the conversations.

The talks also revealed to Caty that little had been done to prepare for any shortfall—winter, war, or anything else. This knowledge was unsettling. She knew very well what could happen to peoples that didn't prepare. She had a great deal of ground to make up before winter set in. *These poor people hardly know me, but I have to start tomorrow.* Making mental notes, she eventually requested her leave.

To her surprise, when she stood, Rhys also stood to leave. He took her hand, firmly placed it upon his arm, and led her through the long hall. They were heartily cheered as they walked together back into the kitchen, where he stood to inspect the workings. "'Tis good to see the old kitchen full and busy again. What do you think of our guests this evening?" he asked as he led her up the stairway.

"Winter and war make for hard talk. It seems that every man believes he will follow you if you are to fight. Is that so? For I still see one small group watching, always watching. They do not intend to fight with you, sir. In truth, it would seem most of the men you've asked to join your meetings in the afternoons are not fighters; they are surely the ones who tend the fields and stock. The men who meet us to break fast in the morns are different men. They would be your warriors. Is that correct?"

"Yes, Caty. You are very clever." For a short while, they walked in silence. Rhys was deep in thought. "I will take every man able to fight," he said. "That will leave you and the women. Some of the older men will stay. I had hoped some of the ones you see with us in the mornings would also stay, but I now think not. I do not look with favor on this, but I fear we cannot deny the request of England's command if we are to survive as a country." His gaze ran over the walls, with their paintings and tapestries, as if he wished to imprint them in his mind. "The changes wrought by the union have been for the betterment of the whole of Scotland, though the Highlanders find it difficult to believe. They are, for the most part, still unaffected by these changes and, as such, feel no need to fight for them. There are whispers of greater changes coming soon. Would that I could be here with you, not in some field fighting, but I must do what I must. You will be fine, of that I am certain." Rhys turned to his wife and smiled. "Your father did a great service to me, with you."

"I am not worried about being alone, Rhys. I am worried about what the winter might do to us. I know not what the winter brings with it in this land, except from my brief experience traveling. Even in temperate weather, the nights were cold. I must begin storing grains and other provisions to feed our people. Is that not what the women do here?"

"As much as they can, I suppose." He frowned, thinking. "In truth, love, I know not what they do."

"I hear from the people working your fields that you have a different way of farming. How is this way?" Caty hoped that his methods would hold his clan in good stead during the coming cold.

"Not so different from the English, I believe. I've had the good fortune to be advised on this matter by two gentlemen, Lord Hames and the Duke of Argyll. I have encouraged their methods on my lands here. We do such things as change the crop from season to season, and have added fertilizer to the soils. All this has yielded greater harvests. I charge no rent, so the people feel more at ease trying new approaches. If the processes fail, they are not faced with losing their lands. They help each other."

Caty looked up at him. "If you charge no rent, how do you earn enough to live, and to protect your lands?"

"Caty, these people do not belong to me; they work here. They hold the lands they work and pay a small fee. I suppose you could liken it to rent, except it is for protection they pay. However, if they should not be able to pay, I cannot make them leave. The land is theirs. If anything, I have a greater problem keeping the number of people down. We can only support so many. Word has spread of the Dermoth clan." Rhys added, "Of a greater nuisance, other clans are always eager to take over what is ours. Like yours, my father traveled to different places, bringing back ideas. The first was to sell the lands surrounding our castle to the people you now see. With the sale, the buyer had to agree that if he or his family no longer wished to live on the plot, he had to give it back to me. So far, not one has left. I place no restrictions on the game and use of the forest."

Caty noticed that Rhys had not answered her question. No matter—she liked the feel of her hand held by his, and his easy walk, as they wandered toward their quarters. She knew she loved him more with each passing day. And it would seem that his people loved him too.

Entering Caty's chamber, Rhys led her through, into his sleeping quarters. "I think we would do well to keep both chambers, but you are to sleep with me whenever I am here," he said. "If you feel the need to be in your chambers, you should feel free to do so. They are your rooms. The nights are to be spent here. Now, m'lady. I would hear about your family, and your travels while you ran from me, including the parts you failed to tell me. You are to have no secrets from me, Caty. This is my castle and land; I must know all there is to know. Talk."

He sat beside the fire and nodded toward the chair opposite him. With legs crossed, elbow on the arm of the chair, and fist at his mouth, he waited patiently for her to begin. Caty sat down. Looking squarely into his eyes, she began, "I will repeat some things, I fear. Memories of my mother's family are from her stories, told of an evening. My father was well known for his military acumen. Ours was not a traditional family. My family traveled with Father. At times, his fighting and work took him away from our home for short periods, but he always returned. In the later years, there was only Mother and I to follow him. She had a great gift for healing the men. Word of her gift spread. At each place we stayed, people came to her for help. So many were injured and ill. I had no other place to go, so I followed her. Soon, I began to work on my own. I knew not such work could ever be called evil. We ministered to so many people. It makes me sad, but I am always very frightened. 'Tis not always a good thing to be a healer, Rhys." Her voice had dropped; a sad note had crept in.

His brow was knit with concentration as he listened to each word. He nodded with sympathy. "You will be safe with me, and with my people. I dare to say you will be safe with most peoples of Scotland. Many of the women are familiar with herbs and treatments that our more learned friends south of the Tweed know little of. I know you to be very discreet, Caty. Do not deny someone comfort or healing because of fear. I have seen with my own eyes the effects of what you do." He indicated with a roll of his hand that she was to continue.

"While the English may field great armies, they frequently fail to heed the advice of the men at the front lines," she said. "Such was the case for my father's treatment by the throne. Still, he always managed to pull his men through. When I was sent away, I believe he knew the fighting would end badly for him. He and my mother talked deep into the night but she never faltered. She would not leave his side. I was sent away to court. The rest is as I told you. I doubt he had any money or houses in England, and in any case, by this time, I'm certain they have been taken. I knew my brothers went away to fight, as Bruce has confirmed to me. He tells me he fought alongside one of my brothers. At any rate, my lord, here I am, well educated and well traveled."

"No doubt, my lady. Please tell me just what you *did* while you traveled, without your lord, and without his permission." He spoke firmly. His words told of his concern and continued disapproval of her escape. He would hear every detail. "You think to fill me with tales of your life before us, but I would hear of life after you came to me, lady."

Caty started, eyes studying the fire as she spoke. She carefully recounted everything. He was amazed at her composure. He found himself pulled into her story and surprised at what he considered her occasionally hazardous judgment, especially with the men she met. Listening to her, Rhys felt the stirring of jealousy. That another man should have the privilege of keeping her safe angered him. Now he understood his friend's laughter and teasing in Stirling. Rhys closed his eyes briefly, trying to calm the rising anger. *I must be certain she knows she cannot do that again*, he thought. *Surely Carlos will come for her soon. I would have her kept safe within these walls, not running about unattended.*

As she neared the end, Caty paused. "Was Donald Donroge very angry I released the poor woman he left to die? For I am certain it was he. Why would anyone do that?"

"He says she was accused of stealing from him. He never indicated that he believed you let her go, but I feel he knows it sure. However, he was taken by your brazen answers and refusal to back down. I would say he accepts you now." His eyes remained closed. Slowly, the anger was abating.

"I pray you know all these things and can understand, Rhys. I had to try. I could not simply walk away from what I was and toward what I thought you to be. Nevertheless, believe me, husband—I know the value of perseverance and know, too, the value of a good man." Even as she spoke these words, she told herself that not even Lord Rhys would know her whole story.

Rhys stood, pulling her up to him. "Ah, and I, a good woman. Remember these things in the times to come." His lips caressed her cheek and mouth. He knew she still held what she believed was her secret, but was content to allow her this small concession. The time would come for him to correct her. It was not now. Instead, they came again to the moment he dreamed of all day, every day since the first time he saw her. After leading her to the great bed in his quarters, he began to undress her. He was gentle and unhurried. Caty was driven to distraction. He would not let her help, or even move. When she stood before him, naked, he ordered her to turn around. His eyes moved over the body he loved so well, and now knew so well. As she turned, he felt the warmth of his desire wash over him.

"Lie down, Caty," he ordered, his voice husky with longing. He undressed while watching her watch him. She smiled at him, her eyes nearly closed. Now also naked, he lay beside her. Caty was again taken to that place she found more intoxicating than the finest wine, the warmest sun, or the freshest rain. He took her again and again.

TWENTY-FOUR

THE BREAKING OF FAST EACH morning was quickly becoming a preamble for the lord's daily overseeing of petitions and conflicts. It was evident that the men attending the morning gathering were of a different turn than the gentle farmers and men who tended the stock. The morning group was educated, trained militarily, and astute regarding daily politics. Caty was learning fast.

This morning she planned to leave immediately after everyone had eaten and begin her assessment of the winter provisions. She would take Rose and at least two men. Caty had moved the young lad, Norman, who waited on her during her first days, up to the position of her personal attendant. He was a quick learner, and followed the steward whenever allowed to do so. Caty found he had some education, and she built on the same. He would come today also. Before the hearing sessions began, Caty spoke softly to Rhys. "I wish to begin reviewing what can be done to prepare for the winter and whatever else may come. I would take Norman, Rose, and two more men you would deem suitable. We will return this evening, and will probably leave like this several times each week, until I feel we have arrived at a plan. Are you agreeable to this?"

"Of course, Caty. Please take the men I will have waiting with your horses. When you return, we can decide how best to proceed. Take care, love. Remember that I need you here more than I do out there." He kissed her hand, brushed her unruly locks from her face, and smiled.

When Caty finally left the castle, she was in the company of ten men, as well as Rose and Norman. Making certain everyone knew everyone else, they moved out. The lord's colors were displayed on the blankets and reins of each horse and on the vests of each man. Caty, Norman, and Rose were dressed for riding and warmth. It felt good to be out and about. The fresh air lifted everyone's spirits.

Caty stopped first at the bothies closest to the castle. No sooner had she ridden in than people gathered to see her. Shortly, she had a group of men and women together, sharing ideas and planning what each group could contribute to the stores. They were pleased she was interested in caring for them. All had firsthand experience of bitter winters without adequate food. Many had lost young ones for just this reason. Caty wished to not ever have this happen again. With Norman taking notes while she asked questions and shared ideas, the morning flew by.

They rode to the next group of people after midday. Before she knew it, afternoon was nearly gone also. One of the men named Edward, the leader of her guard, suggested they start back soon. He did not want to have her out after dark with only these men to keep her. Caty smiled to herself. *'Tis not so bad to be out after dark, occasionally. I grew to enjoy those times.*

"I will finish in a short moment, sir, and we may be on our way," Caty said. She then continued to talk with the women and men surrounding her. Children came close, and as at the previous stop, she soon had a lap full of children. Then, suddenly, the sound of pounding hoofs broke through the talk and laughter. Everyone turned to see more of the lord's men thundering down upon them. People scattered.

Their leader pulled his horse close to her, boldly, sending dirt and rocks flying. "Lady Caty, you are to come with us at once." Turning to the men with her, he ordered, "Make ready to leave." He turned back to Caty. "Lady?"

At once angered and amused, she sat calmly with her arms around the children, most of whom had stayed with her. "Is the castle ablaze, sir?"

"No, my lady. But something else may be if you are not back soon." At that, he smiled, before turning to speak quietly with Edward.

Caty blushed at his implication. "Very well, to avoid any further delay in your mission, we will take our leave." Addressing the crowd, she said, "Thank you for taking the time to talk with me. With the work done between us, we will have a much better winter. I wish not to lose even one child to hunger or cold."

The crowd cheered, some calling out for her to come to them again. "I will, I promise. Soon," she responded.

Once away from the people, she addressed the man. "How is it you come for me with such urgency, sir?"

"Lord Dermoth sent me, lady. He was very clear with his instructions."

"I am certain he was. And so you may know, Edward asked me several times to leave, much earlier. I chose to stay. It was not easy to see some and not others. I chose to see all I could," Caty informed the gentleman Lord Rhys sent. She hoped to save the captain of her own guard, Edward, from anyone's displeasure.

The man watched Caty. "Lady, I spoke with Edward. He suggested you leave shortly before we arrived."

Surprised he would be so bold as to point out her inaccuracy, Caty studied him. She could see his eyes twinkle, and realized he toyed with her. There was nothing disrespectful about his actions. Caty knew he found the whole incident amusing. "And what am I to call you, sir?"

"My name is Thomas," he responded.

"Of course. Everyone is named Thomas. Very well, Thomas, I would ask that you accompany me every time I have need of an escort. I would assume my lord has not found my tarrying so long amusing."

"Your assumption would be most correct."

Caty's face broke into a broad smile as she urged her mount ahead. The group moved more quickly. She loved being out like this, but she would not worry Rhys. The very thought of him made her happy. This was indeed a good union.

When she stepped into her quarters to change, her door crashed open and Lord Rhys stormed into the room angrily. "Caterina! Where have you been? You should not be out so late without proper escort!" His voice thundered off the walls. "I would not have anyone think you are easy prey. You cannot just wander away! Had I known you planned to stay overnight, I would have forbidden you!"

"I took everyone you sent, Rhys," Caty answered softly. Her wide eyes and open face slowed him, but he was not fooled.

"Ten men is not very good security, should a neighboring clan have ideas." He shook his head in frustration. "You test my patience sorely, Caterina. I've a mind to—"

Before he could finish his sentence, Caty touched his hand and spoke. "Rhys, it was not my intent to cause you worry. The people are so eager to speak with us, and I lost track of time. Your men encouraged me to return, but I believed I could take just a few more moments."

"Enough—you know how I feel, and I trust you will act accordingly, Caty. Now, just what did you find out?" He pulled her onto his lap. *As usual, she gets by with me. Her independence, 'tis what I like,* he thought.

Caty shared with Rhys what she had learned and her plans. Then, over dinner, Rhys shared Caty's latest project with Bruce. Both men agreed—the winter was foretold by the old men to be very severe. Caty's work could save many.

"The most exciting for me," Caty was saying, "is how your—our—people have stepped forward to assist us. My lord, you would be so proud of all of them. They had wonderful ideas. I think, with your permission, I would like to ride out more often."

Rhys watched her. She was so animated. It was clear that she was happy taking care of his people. "Hmm," he said, "I would that you not do so if I am not here. Otherwise, it would be a good thing, for you and for them, I believe. I should like to go with you also."

"You realize that once winter comes to stay and people hear you have food, you will be crowded with the needy," Bruce noted. "Plan on that, if it is possible."

Caty made a mental note. *We will need to plan on extra people. Just in case. Can we get this all together before the snows come?*

Each morning found Caty adding to the food stores, both for man and animal. Word of the project spread quickly throughout the lord's holdings. Everyone wanted to do his or her share. Each bothy brought grains, wool, or whatever it could spare.

Near the eastern side of the castle wall, Caty located an area where water flowed rapidly. This stream, according to the castle's staff, had never run dry. Even in the warm weather it ran cold. Caty planned to store butter, milk, and cheeses there. Instructing the staff to dig deep into the ground close to the inside wall, Caty began to store potatoes and other vegetables there such as she could. Taking cue from her mother's people, she also began to salt-cure fish, venison, and beef. Slowly, the mound grew. Old Father, the husband of the old woman Caty had brought to the castle, was placed in charge of the stores, and he kept Caty abreast of the stockpile. Norman found several cats and set them loose in the storage area to keep away rodents. Even small children came to see what she was doing. At Old Father's suggestion, she created additional storage around the castle. If one store was destroyed by weather or man, others would still be safe. Caty and Old Mother, as the old woman was called, began drying bunches of herbs. Caty was pleased to find that Old Mother knew much about healing, and was eager to learn more from Caty. Caty's quarters began to resemble an herb shop in Edinburgh.

Rhys had an additional set of nearby rooms cleared out and furnished for her use, and slipped the key into her hand one evening. "Here, my lady. Do what you would with these rooms. I know you will make good use of them." Neither could have known that these rooms would save them all.

Rhys was gone for longer periods of time. Each return found him increasingly anxious. Nights found him and Caty clinging to each other as he shared with her his fears of an uprising. "Just who are these men that would rise against the British, and who keeps them united?" Caty asked him one evening.

"They are called Jacobites, believers in the deposed King James II. He was Catholic, and although many of his followers remain Catholic, most follow not because of a man or legion but because of an idea. That idea has its grounding in the belief that there is something about our old way of life to cling to. We have been starved, beaten down, and crumpled by the English. Yet, since the union, times have gotten better. I believe that in the beginning, Scots—myself included—believed the union would unite England and Scotland, for the good of both countries. This is not exactly what happened. Although some things have certainly gotten easier, the Scottish Privy Council has no power, the seat of government is in London, and England has direct control over everything, including taxes and the military. I think the worst is the taxes that keep popping out. Like the malt tax. Glasgow had a rather severe riot. Even lost some of the larger mansions—burned to the ground. An English general, General Wade, and his troops settled it down. Still, things boil underneath."

"Just what has gotten better?" Caty questioned.

"For one thing, Scottish merchants gained access to England's overseas markets, including America and India. And we can do much as we please. England is too busy to bother with us. Yet we do have the protection of her administration. We are already better with our trades. We nearly run the tobacco trade, bring in cotton, tea, and other goods. Our own goods, such as linen and finished cotton products, are filling ships daily."

"Has this greatly influenced your dealing with the people living on your lands?" Caty asked.

"No. I have watched as independence died for many Scots. When a man's independence dies, part of his soul dies too. My Scotland may not be a separate country, but we are a separate people. That has changed the way I deal with my people. I believe the way I govern is the best way. Each man can make of his life what he will. As with countries, families still need protection. Very simple, really."

"Perhaps not so simple, my lord. It seems the Scots to the north are not of your thinking. Will not these clans rise against the southern clans?"

"Aye, there lies the trouble. Times are hard for the Northern Highlanders. That gives reason for the attacks on lands south. Yet, to assist them would be madness. They still cling to the old ways. Improvements with trade and such have not helped the Northern Highlanders. The chieftains are as poor as the people they rule. But they can fight. Better than most men," Rhys admitted.

"That is not a comfort to me. Would that men found pleasure in other things—not fighting," Caty murmured.

"Oh, men have, Caty. Men have." With that, he began to kiss her face and neck, and then moved beyond. She gave way to the pleasures he offered. Worries were not to check the passion.

TWENTY-FIVE

SEVERAL DAYS LATER, RHYS ENTERED the great hall, followed by Bruce and several men Caty had never seen before. Caty and her staff were busy cleaning and setting fresh candles in the wall sconces. She watched Rhys come toward her. She could tell by the look in his eye that he would soon leave. Instructing the ladies to feed the men accompanying Rhys, Caty stood waiting for him. As always, she met his gaze.

"Come speak with me, lady," he said.

Once in her chamber, he faced her. Holding her shoulders, he began, "I must leave. I will be gone by sundown. Queen Anne vetoed a parliamentary bill intended to reorganize the Scottish militia. Scotland is on the verge of taking up arms. I take with me any able-bodied man. You will be safe, as the fighting Highlanders that wish to take up this cause are not after Scotsmen. Our holdings should be safe enough. You have readied our people for the winter we are in, and with fewer to feed, you will be easily into spring. Help me pack what I can carry. I shan't need much." He held her tightly.

Caty had helped her mother ready her father for battle many times. Now, Caty quickly prepared her own husband for his leave-taking. *I understand now, Mother, how action stays fear,* she thought. Caty would not let anyone see the anxiety and fear she kept at bay. Rhys must leave believing she would be fine. Soon, the two of them were in the courtyard, mounted men behind them.

Caty held him close once he had made ready to mount. "You must return, Rhys," she whispered into his ear. "I need you. Your child needs a father."

Lord Rhys's head jerked away. "You are with child? Why have you not told me before?"

"I wanted to be certain, first."

"And you are?"

"Yes, quite." Before she could say any more, he had picked her up and swung her around, his face beaming.

"My lady is with child!" he called to Bruce. Holding her again, he spoke to the crowd that had gathered to see them off. "Your lady will need you all to help. These lands are yours; do not forget that. She will see that you pass the winter well as you can. Take care of her, and of the child she bears for you. God stay with you."

"And with you!" The cry went out, and the people followed the lord's party to the great gate. He stood in the saddle to wave one last time, and Caty waved back, smiling through tears. With his standard flying, he and his men rode out.

There was still no news of Rhys or his men. Regardless, Caty was buried in work from sunup to sundown, struggling with one of the worst winters people could remember. Families began to move as close to the castle as they could, where food was given out each day. Pulling together, somehow the people made it, day after day. Christmas approached with little cause to celebrate. Yet the holiday's growing closeness filled Caty with hope that her husband would return. She knew the clans usually celebrated the new year more extravagantly than they did Christmas, but this year she would begin a different tradition for this place.

Born of a need to remind her people that God would indeed see them through, she instructed Rose to bake as many sweets as they could spare grain for. She gathered up most of the honey she had stored and a stack of new woolen blankets and capes. She found, to her delight, that the old men had been busy carving toys. She and the ladies set about laying fresh evergreen boughs throughout the great room. She tore an old gown into strips and fashioned bows from them, to lighten the mood of the room. Candles were placed everywhere. The priest had agreed to come to the castle following the evening mass. Any woman or child who could carry a tune was practicing. Many of the people played simple instruments, and those began to appear as well. It would be good. These poor people needed an uplifting time. They needed a celebration. The children needed to laugh again.

Christmas was a true celebration and renewal. Caty had managed to feed everyone, providing all with some sense of hope and belonging. The children were delighted with the simple gifts. There were wooden hoops to roll, wooden balls, and small poles for little hands to take fishing. The children played hopscotch and tag. The decorations were heartwarming, and stirring music filled the old hall. Blankets and other items she had been able to accumulate were gladly received by everyone present. The men missing were remembered by name. Caty cried herself to sleep that night. *Please bring our men back safe to us, Lord. Rhys, come back to me.*

The weeks after Christmas went by easier. The bond between Caty and the people was growing. She was welcomed everywhere she went. She found great peace in working each day to keep life as tranquil as possible for Rhys's people. *These people are kind and honest*, Caty noted to herself. *They care deeply about their children and for each other. God is central to them and honor is prized. What else is there?*

As January edged into February, the weather worsened and there was yet no word from Rhys. Caty had to fight herself to keep from becoming disheartened. Winds tore at the land and people. Snow fell as if a great hole had opened in the heavens. The temperature dropped lower. It became difficult to keep the castle warm. To save the wood, Caty had every unused room closed off. The inhabitants of the castle moved in together, allowing families without proper shelter to stay inside, especially those families without men. The gray skies were beginning to weigh on her. Sinking into the great chair near her fire one evening, Caty closed her eyes. The door to her quarters was closed and locked. Quiet at last. "Are you well, madam?" asked Rose.

"Yes," Caty replied, her eyes still closed. "I never expected this to happen. I believed I was too old to have a child. I am so glad feeling sick every morning has finally stopped." She paused, then quietly added, "Pray for our men, Rose."

"I do, every day and night, madam. Father has offered a mass every day they have been gone. They will be fine, you know."

"I know. Praying makes me feel like I am doing something for him, though. I miss him sorely, Rose."

Rose left to ensure that the doors had been locked for the night. Shortly after she left, Caty was roused by yelling and the sound of quick footsteps up the stairs. Her heart caught in her throat. Only a very serious matter would bring a visitor in this way, at this hour. The pounding at her door, though expected, still startled her. She could hear Rose arguing with whoever stood beyond. She arose to meet the visitor.

As Rose opened the door, an old man pushed his way inside. "M'lady," he said, "we have word they are attacking us. We have few men and are not able to hold off long. You have to send help."

Mud dripped onto the floor. The exhausted elderly man desperately appealed again. "Please m'lady. Please help us 'fore we fall."

Caty frowned in consternation. "Sir, who is attacking and where?"

"Clans from the south. They've come north. They look to take on greater lands. There is talk of building an army up for another fight in the spring. Many are sore for vengeance."

"Vengeance? What have we done to them?" Even as she asked, she knew. Her husband's clan had fought for the English. "I will get help. I need to think. Rose, get this man into clean clothes, feed him, and see that he rests. I will call on him soon."

Alone in her chamber, Caty tried to think. *I do not believe there are enough fighting men to be had, anywhere.* With resolve, she called to Rose. "Gather any blankets and foodstuffs we can spare. I leave at once to take what men we have. I would borrow breeches from Norman again. Move quickly, Rose! We must get to them before they are overrun."

"Lady, you are not thinking of going yourself?" Rose stood with an incredulous expression on her kindly face. Caty was a woman, and a pregnant woman at that.

"Certainly. I cannot leave the men to fight alone without help. Surely you would not have any less of me. Quickly, Rose. We must be ready to leave as soon as it is possible. Call Old Father; I would take him with me."

When Old Father knocked on her door, Caty herself answered. "Please come in. I know you have been in battle before. You must tell me what I need to take and what I can expect. We are fighting to save our lands."

"'Tis an old fight, m'lady. You can expect horrible wounds from swords. If they come from France, they may have guns also. I'll get what we can gather. You cannot think to go, m'lady. If we should not win, there will be no mercy given. You endanger both you and your child."

Gently, Caty replied, "This I know well. I spent many a day at my mother's side, near my father and his battles. But how could I live knowing I had let our people die? What would that leave my child and husband? No, we do what we must. I think I give reason to fight longer and harder."

It took little time for Caty to change and bundle up for the coming ride. She passed her ladies and the kitchen staff, all with worried faces, as she made her way to the castle yard. Speaking to the gathering crowd, Caty pointed out what she knew they were well aware of and requested that any able-bodied man among them step forward and come with her. She hoped for fifty men. To her surprise, she found herself surrounded by over one hundred. Many were from neighboring holds, having come to Dermoth Castle for food. Before dawn broke, the group was on the move. Grateful that she was barely showing and still able to ride, Caty resolutely headed the troop, with Norman at her side and Rhys's colors flying in the cold winter's wind. Wrapped though she was, the gale bit into her face, her eyes watered, and her hands ached. *How much worse the men must feel.* The band pushed onward.

TWENTY-SIX

IN ONE DAY'S TIME, THEY made the southern edge of the clan's holdings. Before her a rocky hill rose through the fog, its slopes broken by slick boulders, icy pockets of water, and little cover for either side. So far, there had been little fighting. The sides had been drawn, and fires blazed for both clans. Sadly she surveyed her side. Old men and boys. How could this turn out well? Caty had never actually been in a battle. She had only been on the receiving end: wounded and dying men brought to camp. Now, she stood looking at the men spread out before her. Most of them were men she had seen at one time or another. She could not see the intruders, but they were Scotsmen also, and probably looked like her men. A few men came to her, urging her to move farther behind the lines, as word of her arrival spread. The men Caty brought were already moving into positions with their clansmen. Caty moved farther behind the lines, her eyes riveted on the scene beyond her.

Nothing she had ever seen could have prepared her for what came next. Both sides rushed together. Men fought hand to hand. The men from the opposing clan, carrying swords and shields, led the onslaught; some even had guns. The defense, Caty's side, was armed with sickles, knives, and a few guns. It would be a bloodbath. Both sides screeched wildly as the men fought—one side for pride, the other for home and family, each determined to win. There seemed no order to the battle. When it ended at last, the field was strewn with bodies, and blood saturated the ground. Caty began immediately to move about the men, trying to help the wounded. *This cannot happen*, she thought. *We have not the men to do this again.*

She knew not which side the wounded men were on, as their weapons were scattered and blood and dirt covered any other signs. At least it seemed the ruthless marauders had retreated, and Caty noted so to the old man who had come to the castle with news of the fighting. "Nay, m'lady," he cautioned her. "'Tis but a time to regroup. They will be back. They want a settling of scores. 'Tis an honorable anger."

"Honorable? How can this be honor?" Caty snapped back. "They fight old men and boys, many who are without weapons. There is no honor in this fight, only cruelty!" She knew the reasons governments took up arms, she knew what was asked of men, and she knew well the type of thinking that men held when it came to fighting. *Mother was surely right. No man knows the real cost of war except those dying on the ground.*

"They are losing," the old man said. "They fight for Scotland. Lord Rhys is English, m'lady, and they know it well. These men need something to crush, to defeat. Because my lord is not with 'em, they know he is agin 'em. They still see themselves as true Scots. Perhaps they are." He walked sadly away, mumbling to himself.

After several hours with the men, Caty knew that if they were hit again, they would go down. The victor would move on northward, leaving nothing. Dermoth Castle would be easy prey. *Oh, Father, would that you could tell me what to do now. How do I stop this and save Dermoth lands? We are old and outmanned.* Unable to rest, she remained in the tent with the injured men. By this time, she could tell nearly half the wounded men were not hers. No matter, they all needed help. She moved from man to man, giving orders to the women who had followed. It took only a short while longer to realize that the men fighting hers were underfed, weak, and exhausted. From where the women came she knew not, only that they were there, and following her instructions. Suddenly, the tent became silent—only moaning, no talking.

A man spoke, but Caty could not understand his words; his voice was strong, not like someone injured. She knew he was speaking Gaelic, but could understand nothing more. However, she felt no threat. Slowly, she straightened. Turning to him, she listened as an old man spoke to this young, fierce-looking stranger. Before her stood a tall, muscular man with flying reddish hair. He was well armed and very intense. When he spoke again, he spoke in English.

"Would you be Rhys Dermoth's lady?"

"Yes," Caty answered. Her mind raced. Rhys would never concede. She must not either.

"I am Thain of Clan Macintosh. I have come to help. Lord Rhys defeated the man that held my lands. He could have kept the lands for himself; he did not. He returned them to me, along with my men. We're fighting men, lady. I swore allegiance to Lord Rhys." The young man's stance told Caty he would not be denied. He certainly looked the part of someone who could help.

Vaguely, Caty remembered Rhys's story about his fight with the clan to the north attempting to take his land. "I see," Caty replied. "You must give me a moment to think on this."

"I believe you would have thoughts about feeding and caring for more men. Please allow me to offer a suggestion to you as—"

"In truth," Caty interrupted, "I must give thought to how you might know this clan needs help. How did you know where to find me? Or to look for me?"

"Lady, word moves quickly in this country." He smiled briefly; then his tone changed. "You are to take the wounded back with you. This will soon be over. I will see you at Dermoth Castle. Some of your men will return as escort. You leave tonight." He left the tent. Caty stood watching after him.

Still, she hesitated. The old man, nodding approval, reassured her. "He speaks true. Make ready to leave soon, m'lady." The old man hobbled away. He was greatly relieved to see the younger man and his clan. Tired and unable to find a reason to doubt this man, Caty began the ordeal of getting the wounded men moved with her. They were ready before dawn.

Caty, now mounted, looked down at the young warrior. "Please, care for what I leave with you. It's the best I can do." She looked at him level, waiting for a response.

"I know what I do. I fight—and I win." He slapped the rump of her horse, sending him off.

The motion of her horse, the darkness, and her fatigue made staying mounted difficult. Stopping frequently to rest and tend to the wounded, the group moved slowly forward. Snow began to fall, wet and heavy. Dropping temperatures added to everyone's discomfort. Still, they moved on. After two days, they finally rode through the castle gates. Caty felt she could barely make it to her rooms. Rose nearly carried her up the stairs. Finally, once she was cleaned and warm, she slipped into the deep sleep of exhaustion.

The next several days, filled with families coming for their men—or what was left of them—and care being provided for the ones not of their clan, allowed Caty little time for herself. The great hall hummed with activity. Many of the men were taken away. Some died, but more left with family members or friends who would care for them. Caty knew that most of her clan probably knew the wounded men from other clans. She saw no harm in allowing someone to care for them. Caty supervised a careful distribution of stores and watched the southern road. More mouths to feed would be coming. She could not worry about Rhys. It would not help him anyway. Better to be certain he had something to come back to. Let God care for Rhys and Bruce.

The afternoon light slid gracefully below the hills. Temperatures again dropped, as if in angry protest to the fading sun. Fires were lit, as were candles, giving the great hall the untruthful appearance of peace and tranquility. The great hall was slowly regaining order again, except at mealtimes. It still held pallets of wounded, though every man with a family had been taken. Only those unfortunate souls without kin remained. Caty made certain she spoke with the wounded each day. Several women had come to her, timidly asking if they might care for the men. Always searching for companionship in the quest to survive, these people grasped at opportunities, no matter what the circumstances. Through the weeks, Caty had witnessed more than one match. Though little romance was felt, both parties would have a companion.

TWENTY-SEVEN

AS CATY MADE HER ROUNDS of the wounded one afternoon, several days following her return, the hall suddenly grew silent. Caty felt a stranger enter; immediately, she knew there was danger. The feeling was intense. She waited for the man who had caused this feeling to speak, continuing her rounds and assessing the wounded's conditions in the meantime.

"Might you be Lady Caterina?" the man asked in broken English when he eventually approached her.

Caty remained motionless. She could barely believe the question. The thick French accent cut the air. None but Rhys knew her given name. Everyone else knew her as Caty or Lady Dermoth. She doubted anyone present would recognize the accent or the menace it brought with it. Slowly, she raised herself up. "Who asks?" she said without turning, in flawless French.

"I do. I ask, might you be Lady Caterina?" the man insisted, slightly irritated and more than a little surprised to hear his native tongue from her. He too had switched to French.

Caty turned to face him. He was slim, dressed in what must have been the latest fashion. His dark hair was pulled tight, exposing a narrow face, black eyes with full lashes, and a large hooked nose. His mouth was thin and mean. His eyes, taking in all before him, were void of kindness. He looked like one who had known the easy life of the court, and seemed quite out of place with the fighting men lying about the floor. His manner indicated that he was accustomed to giving orders. Caty instinctively knew he would be cruel.

His gaze ran around the room at the wounded and dying men on makeshift beds. It seemed to Caty an appraisal; he was seeing what protection she might have on hand. She found this survey of her possessions both offensive and alarming. At last, he turned his critical gaze to Caty. "You are Lady Caterina for certain. The only daughter of Lord and Lady Tabor."

Calmly, she answered, "And by what, sir, do you make that judgment?" She in turn studied him, openly, without any hint of hospitality.

The man smiled, exposing even, white teeth and creating dimples that looked oddly out of place on such an ugly face. "Only the daughter of a woman such as Lady Isabella could do what you do for these people. Think you that your mother's 'gift' was a secret, my lady?" he asked sarcastically.

"Perhaps you would humor me and tell me who you are. I am at a disadvantage." Her voice was level and barely civil. Caty knew that her mother's gift was still persecuted in France—as witchcraft.

His face became serious again. He bowed stiffly. "Of course, my lady. I am Sir Frederic, brother to the king of France. I fought with your father."

Caty knew he was lying about this last part. Her father fought against the French, not with them. *What could he want, and how did he know I was here?* she thought. *Someone had to tell him, but who? And why? How does he know my parents?*

A second man entered and stood behind him. "I and my men will stay here in the castle," Sir Frederic was saying. "We can protect you from any scavenging clans. We have not eaten in a fortnight. I know you would be hospitable to those that would help you." With that, he ordered the second man to bring his men into the great hall. Fifty men stomped into the hall. They were rude, boorish, and loud, carelessly shoving aside the wounded scattered about.

Caty stood her ground. "I do not welcome you to this house, Sir Frederic. I can little feed my own people. I bid you leave, at once."

The man, surprised at her audacity, studied her with arched brows. Then, as his eyes narrowed, he replied, "You do not bid me to do anything, lady, and would do well to remember that. I am here, and here is where I intend to stay. If your husband was half a man, he would be here with you, not fighting alongside the English scum."

Caty bit her lip to keep from answering back. She had no intentions of giving him the pleasure of a verbal battle. She well knew that the real battle was yet to come.

As Caty entered the kitchen, Rose met her. The look on Rose's face spoke volumes. Caty gently touched her shoulder. "We must not let anyone see our concern. I will do whatever is necessary to protect these people. Keep everyone ready to leave if need be. We cannot fight, but we can make their stay very uncomfortable. For now, you need to send the young women away. These women are to take as many children as they can with them. Quietly get the word out; you will leave with them immediately. I do not think those of us that are older will be in any danger. But the young ones . . . Have Old Mother leave by the hidden stair in my quarters. She must take blankets and food. There is extra food and blankets in my storeroom, upstairs. Do this while these men are busy eating, before they begin to think of women and sleep. I fear I cannot keep them together after that. Now go, quickly. Move, Rose! We have little time."

"What about you, Lady Caty? I cannot leave you." Rose's eyes searched Caty's.

"Rose, you are the one I rely on the most. We must protect the children and younger women. Their need is greater. You are to do what I ask. This is not open for discussion." Caty spoke firmly, but kindly.

With the help of the older women of the castle staff, Caty began to prepare a feast she hoped would be eaten at leisure, with large quantities of wine. As the smell of bread drifted into the great room, calls for food rang out. Just when it seemed the men would come for the meal themselves, Caty and her women began to serve the men. She could feel Frederic's eyes following her every move. *Surely he can tell I carry a child. Please, God, protect this child and my people. Please give me the wisdom to make the best decisions and keep these men at bay.* Calmly, Caty continued to serve the men.

Her ladies followed her example and moved about the room quietly. When the Frenchmen had been served, Caty and the women fed the few wounded left in the hall. Back in the kitchen, Caty gave orders to the women helping her, instructing them to move the wounded out of harm's way. The tension was thick. The men with Frederic were not fighting men. They were scruffy, treated her servants with cruelty and disrespect, and appeared to have nothing in common with each other. *They are far beneath any of my people, servants or no,* Caty observed silently.

As he sat at the table picking over the remains of the feast, Sir Frederic frowned. This woman, the daughter of his nemesis, was clearly unaware of the peril threatening her. She would be aware soon enough. Taking this place would be easier than he planned. He knew the French would gladly aid Scotland, band together with them as allies against England. He himself, being banned from the court, could not represent France, but these people were not aware of this small detail. If he could take these lands, so close to the shore, who could tell? Perhaps he could redeem himself at court. At any rate, Lord Tabor's daughter would pay Lord Tabor's debt, many times over.

He would never forget—or forgive—what Lord Tabor had done. Tabor's advance into France had thwarted Frederic's plans to murder the older prince, thereby securing the throne for Frederic himself. Frederic was lucky he was only banished for not supporting the king. Had the king known the real plan, Frederic would most certainly be dead. He slit his narrow lips into a cruel smile. The pleasure it would give him to see Caty's fear and humiliation—this would be a time of reckoning.

Caty saw that every man had plenty of wine and ale but just enough food to keep them busy. As they began to drift away from the table and lie down around the room, she saw with satisfaction that most slid into the deep sleep of drunkenness. Her back ached and her feet were swollen. Her belly was now protruding noticeably. Still, she walked about cleaning up the mess left behind. Finally, as Frederic and several of his men were engaged in a heated argument, she slipped out. Closing the heavy door to her chambers behind her, she moved to lock and block the doors to Rhys's rooms. She was startled to see Rose pulling tight the shutters on the windows. "Rose, why are you still here?"

"Old Mother took the women and children long ago. You need someone near. That is my job, lady. Come, we must secure as much of this place as we can. Old Father has gone also, as have most of what older men are left. He felt they could protect the women and children."

Wordlessly, Caty touched Rose's hand. "Pray we are safe, Rose."

Morning crawled in, cold and damp, wrapping its fingers round Caty's soul. Rising slowly to face what she feared would come, Caty felt the child within her move downward. *You think to come early, I feel. I believe it would be better if you waited, little one. Time will not be gentle with you if you choose to visit now.* Once dressed, she went downstairs. Rose was already in the kitchen, with a morning meal well on the way. Caty slipped the keys to her chamber to Rose.

Sir Frederic awoke with a splitting headache. His mouth felt parched. Having slept in a chair all the night, his neck was so stiff he could hardly turn his head. "Woman, I would eat!" he yelled. Angrily he stood, clinging to the table to steady himself. He staggered toward the kitchen. Caty and the women were just emerging into the great room, carrying trays laden with food. Deftly avoiding his grasp in spite of her full belly, she moved into the room and began to awaken the men, offering coffee and a break from the night's fast.

"You should serve me first, do you hear?" he commanded loudly. "I decide when my men eat, not you. Come here, now, stupid wench!"

Fixing a steely gaze upon him, Caty replied evenly, "This is still my domicile, sir. We break fast this time in the morning. If your men do not wish to eat, we can certainly put these things away."

He paused. "You shall not have this place long, lady. Even in such a barbaric land as this, I keep what my wife brings to me. I will make you my wife, and I shall keep this. Your people and lands will soon be mine, to do with as I wish."

"If this is true, then you should know I bring little to you. Your men must know they will be taking lands that belong to the people, not me. I do not own these lands, sir. Each man owns his land. Your job will be to protect your men and their new lands from men such as you—for the lands you take will belong to your men. You did, of course, intend to give the land to your men, correct?"

Every eye in the room turned to Frederic. Own land? This could be better than the miserable wage he paid. Silently, the Frenchmen waited for his reply.

Frederic had no intention of giving anything away, certainly not to the ragtag company he brought with him. It would all belong to the French crown. How dare this woman! Mounting anger prevented him from further thought before he answered. "I give no such thing. When we are wed today, you and all that you have will be mine. I take these lands as mine. Do you hear, woman? These men will do as I tell them. They came with nothing, they will leave with nothing."

"I have little sir; however, I do have a husband. Unless you can bring to me proof of his death, you have no stake on me. The other thing I have is the responsibility of the safety of my people. I must assume that you will take over that burden, and that it will grow to include the safety of your people. Since your men will own their lands, you will have no cause to charge them for the use of their own lands. The protection you must provide will come from your own funds, which I must assume you have. You, sir, will be a very busy man. You certainly will not have time for any woman, especially one who refuses to wed you." Turning, Caty gracefully left the room.

Once out of his hearing, she leaned against the wall, breathing rapidly. She had wagered heavily; his men would see an opportunity now where none had existed before. She needed to create dissent within his rank and file—they would be easier to fend off if they fought each other, or at least distrusted one another. She was certain she had their attention. Now only time could tell if the seed planted would take root.

Back in the great room, Sir Frederic's fury erupted. His men were beginning to favor the bold woman. They knew he would never allow anyone to occupy the lands without heavy taxes. They also knew they would stand little chance of holding off any invader—they were, after all, only dockworkers and freed criminals, indentured to this madman. If this woman's husband were not dead, he would return, probably with warriors. What then?

Frederic jumped up and ran after Caty. He quickly caught up with her, wrenched her around, and struck her. The force of the blow bloodied her nose and split her lip. With Caty knocked against the opposite wall, Frederic advanced upon her. She turned to the wall, trying to protect her unborn child. Jerking her around and toward him, Frederic slapped her repeatedly, then shoved her up the stairs. Stumbling, she clung to the railing. He shoved her again as she struggled to keep her footing.

At the top of the staircase, he pushed her ahead of him and ordered her to open her door. With the door barely opened, he forced her into the room. "Now you will pay," he said. "Your father will see this, I'm certain. From wherever he stays. I will gladly beat you again. First, I intend to enjoy you. I will make your father proud. Of course, with me as the ruler over these lands, you will be little more than my plaything—something to amuse me. I must say, you are prettier than I had imagined. Pity you will not be so for long. Women do age with trials."

Caty backed away from him until she was forced against her bureau. He moved forward. Smoothly, he slid his hand around her neck while pressing his body against her, pinning her tight. With his free hand he tried to fondle her breast. Her body was rigid, and she could think only of the child within her. She tried but was unable to push him away. He laughed, his eyes still blazing. "Let us see what we have."

He grasped the top of her gown and with one powerful movement tore the garment to the waist, exposing Caty's swollen breasts and protruding belly. She attempted to cover herself, but he roughly pulled her arm away. "Look at you! I have been without a woman so long, even a milk-laden cow looks inviting." Caty pushed his hand aside and spat into his face. With a menacing growl, he slapped her again, hard. As she struggled to maintain her footing, her hand came in contact with the heavy metal candlestick on the bureau behind her.

He pushed her aside and walked unsteadily to the door. As he fumbled to slide the bar into place, he momentarily turned his back on her. Quickly, she moved to him. With all her strength, she smashed the candlestick into his face as he turned back toward her. He fell against the door and blood spewed. He cursed, staggering against the door. Blood splattered his face, and his teeth were smashed. Deftly lifting the heavy candlestick again, she brought it down onto his head as hard as she could. He crashed to the floor and lay still. Caty ran to her writing table, pulled out the dagger Rhys had recovered for her, leaned over the man, and slit his throat. Before she had time to catch her breath, Rose was banging on the door.

Caty opened the door and stumbled against the frame. Blood ran across the floor. As the knowledge of what she had just done sunk in, she shuddered. What would she do with the rest of his men? Surely, she and her women would pay in the worst way. Rose closed the door behind her and grabbed a blanket to cover Caty. Caty leaned against the wall, staring at the dead man. Rose was trying to move the man.

"Let him lie, Rose. Go get the rest of the women. Quickly. Bring them here." She grasped her gown to her, trying to cover her body. "We must move fast, before any of his men realize he is dead."

Several minutes later, Rose was back. As the women who remained in the castle flowed toward Caty's quarters, Rose shut and barred each door behind them. Carefully stepping over Frederic, the eight women left in the castle moved silently by. When they were all inside, Caty closed and locked the door, then turned and leaned against it. Rose scrambled to gather a change of clothes. "I have no idea what to do now. I need to think," Caty said. She could see the fear in the eyes of the women with her.

"The baby?" Rose asked, as she helped Caty change.

"The child is well, I would say. Only my face is pained." Suddenly, she held a finger to her lips. The sound of fighting reached the women; it seemed to come from the great room. More shouts and clashes could be heard from the window. Standing away from the windows, the women listened. What now? Were the Frenchmen doing battle with each other? Through the racket on the grounds below, the sounds of scratching came from the hidden door, the one usually concealed behind the tapestry. The room was otherwise silent inside. There it was again.

"Open," Caty whispered to a woman standing close to the concealed door.

"Are you certain, lady?" the woman asked.

"It must be someone who knows the door is there. Open," Caty ordered.

Old Father burst into the room as soon as the woman turned the latch. He spoke anxiously: "Lady Caty, are you hurt? What happened?" In reply, Caty pointed to the dead man. "Their lord? You did this?"

"I did." Caty shuddered when she looked at the fallen man.

"And you?" the old man peered up at her.

"I am fine, at least more than I could have been." She glanced back at the body.

"Hmm. I think he did not plan on such response." Old Father grinned. Calling softly, down the hidden stairway, he ordered the body removed. "Hide this body beneath the straw piled in back. Quick!"

"You must leave, lady," Old Father told Caty. He threw a heavy wrap around Caty and led her down the hidden stairs. Back when Rhys first revealed the hidden door to her, Caty never dreamed she would actually use it. The stairs were narrow, dark, and steep. With Old Father guiding her in front, Caty moved as quickly as possible. Rose and the women followed. The sounds of arguing men in the great room became fainter as the women and Old Father neared the outside door. This door was cleverly hidden from view by anyone at the front or side of the castle. Its proximity to the stables made a hasty escape possible. At the bottom, they were met by Old Mother and several older men. Three horses were saddled and waiting. Kissing his wife, Old Father helped her mount. Rose huffed and puffed to get mounted. "A few of us have returned to keep you safe if we can." Old Father waved at the men with him. "You will not be safe here, now. Go quickly." The sounds of men scuffling outside filled the castle yard.

As the realization of the danger they all now faced hit her, Caty said softly, "I fear I have placed you and all my people in grave danger. I cannot leave you now."

"You must go south and bring help, lady. We will be safe for this day and night. Some of his men have already left, not having the stomach to face Lord Rhys should he return. If I were able I would ride for help, but . . . Try one of the clans to the south. They fight with Lord Rhys and have no care for the French."

"I know." Caty touched the old man's face. "I will return soon."

Both the women with Caty were old and barely able to stay mounted. Caty knew Old Father had sent them with her because they stood a better chance getting out of harm's way on horseback than by trying to run. Caty would need to leave her companions somehow, if she were to reach help quickly. She remembered a place from an afternoon ride with Rhys. Turning down an overgrown path, Caty found an abandoned bothy, well hidden by brush, trees, and time.

Caty dismounted. "Here, ladies, you will be safe." She pushed the door open and quickly surveyed the inside. Sunlight poured in through the fallen roof. The horses and two women would easily fit into what was left of the old structure. "Quickly, come inside. Stay until I come for you."

"No," Rose protested. "You cannot leave us and go alone!"

"It is the only way," Caty countered. "I can ride much faster alone. Keep the horses out of sight. Do not let them loose, or they go home." Kissing both ladies, she mounted, despite their protests.

As her steed galloped away from the bothy, Caty guided him onto a well-worn path. She rode as hard as she dared, praying her child would not be harmed. As dawn broke, the sound of horses, gear, and men approaching on the road ahead reached Caty. Before she could see them, Caty quickly turned aside and rode into the trees and brush near the road. As the men rounded the curve and came into view, she felt relief wash over her. Clan Macintosh's plaid blew in the wind.

"Highlander!" she called. "Thain!"

The Highlander threw his hand up and brought the men to a halt.

"Thain, it is I, Lady Dermoth," Caty called as her horse stepped onto the road. She saw the Highlander start, then frown. He quickly rode closer, followed by several of his men. Caty realized how she looked. "I have met with trouble, and ask that you assist me once more, sir." She quietly watched him.

"And the trouble? How does he look?" he asked. Several of his men laughed.

"I fear he looks worse. He is dead. His men do not know it yet," Caty said. "We were overtaken by a Frenchman claiming to be a French prince, and his men. They are in the castle. I killed the prince. I sent the women and children away, but fear that when the Frenchman's men discover he is dead there will be trouble. None look to be fighting men, but we are not much better."

"I go ahead to Castle Dermoth with my men," Thain said in his rapid, singsong style. "These two will stay and come with you." He indicated two of the men who had ridden up with him. "Your child would do well with a rest." With that, he rode off to join the remainder of his band, leaving the two men at her side.

Caty and the two men rode back to the bothy and there joined Rose and Old Mother. The hour was late when the five of them reached Dermoth Castle. The grounds were awash with the living; it was not the killing field Caty had feared. Men were talking in groups among themselves. None of the French were in sight. Caty left her horse to the men who rode with her, while she and her ladies entered the castle from the back door. Slipping up to her rooms, she was grateful to find the bloody mess gone.

Once cleaned up, Caty and Rose entered the great room. Caty was astounded. A gasp escaped Rose's lips. Thain and his men had been busy. The French bodies were thrown into a pile on one side of the hall. Blood, broken dishes, and food littered the hall. "Be quick," said Caty to Rose. "We must clean this mess up. I will return shortly, and you will know how many we must feed this night." As she left, Rose began shouting orders, insisting that every trace of the unwanted guests be cleaned away.

Throwing a cloak about her shoulders, Caty stepped into the dark of the evening. In the center of the courtyard, a bonfire was raging. The Highlander and his men sat around it, warming themselves. Caty approached the Highlander and said, "First, sir, accept my gratitude to you and your men, for all you have done for my people and for me. Not just this day." She paused to survey his men.

"I see some of your men are wounded," she continued. "Please, we are preparing a meal for you all. Meanwhile, I will see what I can do for them. Afterward, the hall will be made ready for rest. You must all sleep inside. Come, follow me." Caty turned to the castle.

Inside the great room, the Highlander ordered his men to help the struggling women remove the bodies. Once this task had been completed, Caty had the food brought in. The men were hungry and ate heartily—but with gratitude and manners. She could not help but compare these men's behavior with that of her previous guests.

The Highlander and his clan talked long into the night but eventually began to move about, finding sleeping spots. Caty resisted the urge to open rooms upstairs to them. Keeping them together would keep everyone warmer. She was securing the castle when she felt a touch on her arm. The Highlander spoke softly. "I will see the place is locked. First, I would speak with you, m'lady."

"Yes?" Caty led him toward the kitchen, where he could speak freely and without causing undue notice.

"My wife is not educated. We wed for love, and not with the approval of our parents. I speak some English; she does not. She knows not the work of the wife of a clan leader. My request is that you might find it agreeable to teach my wife. Perhaps when the lord is returned, we may speak again, with him."

"Certainly. I would gladly help you and your family. When Rhys returns, we will speak. Thank you again for your service. You and your men have done well by Lord Dermoth and his clan. You and your clan will always be welcome at this place, sir." Caty gently touched his arm. "I am certain I could use the company of your woman. I believe we could each teach the other."

As the sleeping quarters were prepared, extra wood was brought in to keep the dropping temperatures out. Caty finally turned to leave the great room. "Lady, Lord Dermoth did well with you," the Highlander said as she moved away. Caty smiled back at him. The men around him nodded in agreement. She tipped her head forward in acknowledgement, then wearily waddled out. It seemed the child grew larger each hour.

TWENTY-EIGHT

WHEN CATY TRIED TO LIE down that evening, her weight hampered her breathing. Lying on her side just pulled at her aching back. She had not the strength to walk anymore. During the night, Rose heard her moving about and came to stand with her. "Let me fetch you hot tea, and I will fix the bed for you. We will bathe you. You cannot get into the water." Rose chuckled. "You do not fit. If you got in, we could not get you out! Water, cloths, and lavender are on hand. Old Mother is on her way. You must rest as much as you can. The babe comes tonight." Rose felt Caty's growing abdomen knowingly.

Caty had not been around anyone birthing but doubted the child would come this night. The baby no longer felt like it was moving down. Besides that, she reasoned, it was not yet time; she had two months yet. "Would that Rhys could be here to help his child come to us," Caty said to herself softly in the empty room. "I feel as though I am alone. Mother, let me know what I need to do, and help me—again."

With the bath and tea done, Caty finally drifted off to a blessed sleep. When she awoke, it was midmorning. Rose was right, at least about the bath—it had been badly needed. Caty felt energized and much better, in spite of her blackened eyes, swollen lip, and bruised cheek. *At least my hair is longer this time, and will hide the bruises on my neck*, she thought. Still the babe stayed safe in her belly. She would have to endure another long night.

During the next several days, which seemed to stretch endlessly, Caty tended to the wounded and hungry. Her own people had begun to straggle back to their homes, taking as much food as Caty could spare. She sent the

Highlander's men into the surrounding forests to hunt. They did well, bringing a good supply of meat back. The weather remained cold. "Perhaps the days will be warmer sometime before my hair turns gray," Caty grumbled to herself. "This cursed winter thinks to stay forever."

Eventually the child within her began to move downward. Trudging slowly up the stairs again, Caty felt tired to her very bones. *This night is going to be a long one,* Caty told herself. Her face still ached; the injured eye watered, and each time she remembered what she had done, she was filled with a feeling of dread. *I must speak with the priest,* she thought. *My heart cannot mend otherwise.* As Rose went around readying her for bed that evening, Caty touched her old friend's hand. "Rose, do you think it would be possible for me to see the Father this night? I know it is very late, but my heart is heavy and I feel I have done something evil. I wish to speak with him before this child arrives. Please, I need rest, and I feel this may be my only chance for it."

Rose nodded. "Of course, m'lady. I will send the page to get him at once."

When the priest tapped gently at her door, Rose let him enter, then excused herself and left the room. "Father, please forgive me for getting you out at such an hour. I am troubled, and my child thinks to come soon. I could not chance this time with my mind as it is."

"Child, the hour is not so late for one of my service. Please speak with me." He was a middle-aged man, with many years' experience. His eyes were kindly, his face serene. He pulled up a chair and sat down. He had witnessed all Caty had done for these people. This night, he could see that her mind was troubled.

While Caty had intended mainly to confess about the death of the Frenchman, she did much more. The worry and troubles of the past long months came out as water from a raging creek, including her activities healing people and ending with the intruder's demise. The priest listened quietly. When the storm had subsided, he spoke. His voice and manner were soft and gentle. He talked of her obligations to her people, to the unborn child, and to herself. He spoke of the defense of these same people and her child. After granting absolution, he rose to leave. Pausing at her door, he turned and walked back to the fire. "Lady, please listen carefully to me. There has been talk from the people who work this castle about your gift for healing. Fear not, for the peoples of this land often do whatever they can to heal. It is with God's help and blessing that such things can happen. You and your little one will be fine. What you have done for these people is more than I could have hoped from the lady of our land. Lord Dermoth chose well. If you have need of me, please call on me, my lady. When the child is born, I will be here to baptize him. Or her." He chuckled.

Caty felt her chest tighten. She knew too well the punishment for witchcraft. She hesitantly asked if that also could apply to her mother.

Growing more serious, he said, "You must know, lass, the Holy See does not condone nor recommend incantations to other gods or fairies. We try to stop it. Scottish peoples frequently mix their faith in God with superstition. You do nothing of this kind; I believe you learned what you know from your mother. You may rest in peace, my child." The priest thought on what Lord Rhys had shared with him when he wed Caty. He could relieve Caty of this burden, at least. "Lady Dermoth," he added gently, "you should know, your mother is with God." After blessing her, he left.

His words brought great relief to Caty's weary heart. She did not understand how he might know about her mother. It didn't matter; he was a priest. What he told her gave her peace. Grateful tears filled her eyes. *These long months my poor heart has ached. Now it is over. What happens to me is in God's hands.* God would see her through this time. God knew this child had need of a mother. Rose entered and began preparations for bed. Caty found that even after the meeting with the priest, she couldn't rest. She began to pace the floor.

"Lady, you must rest," Rose insisted, "your time will be soon. You should have been in confinement these long weeks ago. This is not good for your babe. Try to sleep, m'lady." Caty longed for the privilege of confinement while she awaited the birth of the child, but that was not possible given the events of this past month. No matter. The castle was more settled at least. Perhaps the babe would come soon, and bring relief. Yet sleeping proved impossible. She struggled out of bed. Her swollen belly hindered her breathing; she was barely able to sit or even walk. The hours dragged by.

TWENTY-NINE

RHYS FOUND HIMSELF EMBROILED IN an emotional battle. He was driven by a deep, long-held belief that Scotland was a sanctified country. She had been through horrible years under England's rule. There were many other insults to her, and yet Scotland held unyielding to her destiny. With every fiber of his being, Rhys believed her to be a great nation. His education and travels forced the truth on him. Scotland had to move away from her history. She needed a rebirth. She had to unite, or she would fall apart. He fought on the side that championed the changes the union had wrought on his Scotland. Yet he felt a great sadness as he watched the Highland clansmen lose their precarious hold. They never had a chance. *What man among us, living what they lived, would do differently?* In spite of everything, for Scotland to survive there could be no other way. Scotland would survive. She would fulfill that elusive destiny.

When Rhys arrived at the military camp, he found Bruce and most of his men. Bruce rushed to his brother's side and they clasped each other tightly. Neither man spoke of the atrocities. Rhys remembered Caty's work with all the wounded when he had taken her. He felt a stab of guilt over what the man who commanded their current division was doing. There would be bad blood over this, he feared, for many years. The Hanovarian commander sent soldiers, many of whom were Scots, to dispatch any of the Jacobite survivors. Guns, bayonets, and clubs were used. Not one man was knowingly left alive.

"I saw you go down, brother; I feared for your life. My horse later lost his footing and we both went down as well. Sadly, the horse never got up; gladly, I did," Bruce gripped his brother's shoulders. Rhys did not speak; he only searched the faces of his men. As the men gathered around, he shook his head. "In years to come, when they tell of this fight, I fear they will tell a story of Scots killing Scots. Sad, to my heart."

"No, Rhys, in years to come, because of what we do now, Scots will be able to tell their own story. There will still be a Scotland because of what we do now."

In his heart, Rhys prayed Bruce was right. He had to be right—else why did they leave the hills drenched with the blood from the sons of Scotland? Long into the hours of early morning, Rhys and his brother sat together, watching the flames of the fires around them. Groups of men huddled close. Somber. Many had killed for the first time. "I am ready to go home, Bruce." Rhys's voice was heavy with exhaustion and the toll fighting takes on a man. "This was a bad time. Scots against Scots. I long for the comfort of Caty and my home."

"I know your feeling well. It is time," Bruce said. The fighting was over for the time being. Groups of men who had volunteered to fight for the cause of a united Britain were breaking away to return home. There would be other battles in Scotland, but few of this magnitude. Before the first rays of sun found their camp, Rhys, Bruce, and their men rode toward peace and Dermoth Castle—at last.

Caty went about her work, struggling with exhaustion. Still the babe stayed within her. Carefully noting how foodstuffs had lasted, what needs were unmet, and what to do about the next harvest, she tried to fill the long afternoon hours. Days grew warmer, and she could feel winter making plans to leave. Nights still left ice covering the lakes and the edges of the rivers. Having closed off every unused room in the castle, Caty tried to save the wood. It was important to keep the great room warm, as most of the children and the very elderly now spent their time with her there. "Rose, pray tell me, what did these peoples do before we came? Without the support this castle provided this winter, half the people would have starved. These are not all from Lord Dermoth's land, surely. We have taken in carts of people who have traveled from afar to get here. From where do they all come?"

"They stayed close by their fires, in the bothies. Many people in this country died, mostly children, in the north—from no food and too much cold, I fear. The people you've seen come from the lord's lands, and beyond. Word has spread. They know you will care for the wee ones, you will. You have never asked where or why they come, you've just provided the best you can for them. Those that have food stay where they are." Rose looked kindly at Caty. "You chose one of the worst winters in my memory to come to our aid, lady. God bless you."

"We all worked together, Rose. Thank heaven it is finally getting warmer." Caty stifled a yawn. "I would go about the grounds in the morrow. Have Old Father come to me early."

"My lady, you should rest," Rose protested. "You are soon to be delivered. 'Tis not seemly."

"Rose, I can barely move. Any woman knows that it is best to stay busy about the work of living. I will know when my time is truly close. Until then, we go about our business, yes?" Gently, Caty nudged her friend.

The next morning, as the first light pushed the moon down beyond the hills, Caty pulled her wrap closer around her. The wind was dying down. She had listened to the howl all night and feared another storm. This day, though, looked to be a final eruption from the long months of cold and wet. Hoping she could keep up with Old Father, she opened her chamber door and waddled down the stairs. He met her at the bottom, smiling.

Caty's heart warmed at the sight of him. He and Old Mother had become like parents to her. "To what do I owe your gaiety, sir? For truth, you should feel great pity for me—a woman turned into a plump goose!"

At that, he laughed outright. "Nay, bairn, more a *fat* goose! You are well beyond plump. I smile because I know well the joy of children. Soon you will also."

"Hmm, if you believe so, I suppose." Caty smiled in return. Yet his eyes twinkled with a new light. "My child will have need of a grandfather. You should add that to your list." Old Father nodded happily. By early afternoon, she had made a tour of the families living outside the castle and listed every repair needed, knew who was ill, and had instructed Old Father where to send the most blankets, wood, and food supplies. She had not intended on going so far from the castle proper and with swollen aching feet began the trek back. Before she reached the outer wall, she heard it.

"Caterina!" His voice boomed through the halls, spilling out into the courtyard. Caty's heart stopped.

"Oh, Rhys!" Unable to run, she waddled as fast as she could.

Could this be the beautiful lady I left behind? he thought as he watched her come toward him. She glowed with the pregnancy, but he could see exhaustion written on her face, which still bore the signs of her beating. He had tried to imagine how she would look, but he was not prepared for this. And yet her beauty did shine through. He had forgotten how lovely her smile was and how it affected him. Her eyes—the glow in them was for him. He moved swiftly to meet her. She fell against him, laughing and crying. "You have grown since I last held you. I think this child comes any day now," he laughed. Caty nodded as he pulled her to him. Gently, he brushed the hair away from her face. "Come, love, we have much to share."

Together, they sat in his study and talked. Caty told him about all that had happened, and he ran his hand gently over her face. Anger and relief swept back and forth in his gaze. Later, though food had been set out in the great room for Bruce and the rest of his men, Caty and Rhys ate together near the fire in his room. Rhys held his wife closely. "You are doing well, Caty?" he asked with concern in his voice. She had been through a great deal since he last saw her.

"Better now," Caty said as she smiled. "I think this one waited for his father. I cannot tell you how happy I am to see you, my love. Now I can rest easy; I know you are safe."

Evening was on before Rose insisted Caty take to her quarters. "I will let you know when the babe comes, m'lord," Caty said as Rose ushered Rhys to the door. Rose closed the door firmly behind him and turned to her mistress. "You *must* go to bed, lady."

"I do not agree, Rose," Caty said softly. "My mother believed differently. There is always value in action. Also, be certain the doctor and Old Mother wash the instruments and their hands, many times. I insist on this matter, Rose. I know the value of cleanliness. The better care we take, the less chance something will happen to me or Rhys's child. You must promise me. The linens, tools, and hands that are near us must be clean. Promise."

"I do not understand why this is of such importance to you, but I vow to keep your wish. Now, please, at least try to rest. You will need all your strength." With that, Rose began boiling water to cleanse cloths, and gathering whatever else they might need. Many a mother had lain as Caty, without a physician to help her, but Rose feared the worst. Caty was a small woman; Rhys was a large man.

Caty did not sleep that night, but she was able to rest in her chair, by the warm fire. Rhys was home; she would be fine now. Before dawn of his second day back, she felt the first pains. Hesitant to awaken anyone else, she waited. The pains grew stronger.

Standing to relieve the pressure, she felt a sudden rush of fluid. Fearfully, she strained to see the pool spreading before her. It was not blood. The rush of liquid brought another pain, much stronger. Moaning, Caty grasped the foot of the bed. Rose awoke to find her mistress holding on to the bed, in active labor.

Rose sounded the alarm and went straight to work. She put Caty to bed and began heating water. As Old Mother came in, Rose made certain she was clean, much to the old woman's disgust. "Just who are the people that teach such nonsense?" she grumbled. However, knowing by this time their mistress and her determination, she and the other women who soon joined them each did as bid.

Caty closed her eyes, the better to concentrate on the job at hand. Her entire being was now focused on helping this child into the world. Biting on the wad of cloth given her, she kept silent in the beginning. The contractions came quicker and harder; Caty now moaned with each contraction. The sweat ran down her face, and she was unaware of anyone in the room. Wave after wave of pain racked her. Still, the baby did not move down. Old Mother said softly,

"Not yet time to push, but the babe is coming. This one wants to come out badly. You must rest between each pain, m'lady."

Caty had long since placed herself in the able hands of Old Mother. The two women at the head of her bed gave her something to grip. *Rest, she commands. Would that I could. It would seem this child is already as large as my lord,* Caty thought. She tried to relax, but the pains were nearly continuous.

Hours slowly crept on and on. Still the babe refused to come. Caty began to push, but the baby still held fast. Old Mother began to mumble. Now the pain was so severe that Caty cried out with each wave. Perspiration covered her body, dripping onto the bed. Her eyes were closed as she struggled. Her screams echoed down the halls.

THIRTY

SUDDENLY, THE DOOR TO CATY'S chambers swung open. Rhys charged into the room and toward the bed. "How does it go?"

The women were shocked to see him enter, but Old Mother spoke gently to him, her face etched with worry. "The babe doesn't move down, m'lord. It would seem it is not turned well. She tires. If the babe does not turn, we lose both."

"What do you do?" Rhys asked, his face blanched. He could see that Caty was barely able to stay the course. Old Mother simply shook her head. Rhys stood, frozen. "Nay, I will not let her go now. Not now."

He moved to the foot of the bed. Rose stopped him. "Stand aside," he said, pushing her roughly.

"My lord, I promised Lady Caty that each would clean their hands before touching her. You must; it was her most emphatic request."

After only a slight pause, he complied. Cleaning up gave him time to give quick orders. "Have swaddling clothes in the ready for this child. I will move this one myself."

"Sir, you could harm her, or the child!" Rose protested.

"I have been lord of this place for long years, alone. I would not go back to that solitude. No! I do not aim to injure either. I have delivered calves and foals; I can deliver my child. Step aside, woman, and do as I say," Rhys ordered curtly.

Caty became aware of his presence in the room. Weakly, she called, "Rhys? You come to me?" Her hair was plastered to her face and neck. Sweat and blood soaked the bed beneath her. She was weak and fading. Rhys leaned over her. Gently, he touched her face.

"Yes, my love, I come. It will be fine, now." He looked into her eyes. "Tell me when the next pain leaves you. Do this, and I will help you and the child." His voice was gentle, soft, and reassuring. Caty closed her eyes again.

Too tired to protest or even think, Caty nodded as the pain left.

"This will hurt greatly," his gentle voice said to her. "Take hope; it ends soon." With that, Rhys reached into Caty, felt the child, and turned it. The child was beginning to turn on its own, and the movement went quickly. Caty screamed, then began to pant as the next wave came. This time, the child's head began to show. The women stood in awe. Rhys slipped his hands under the small head and gently guided the child. "Now, Caty, push hard!"

Caty heard the cries of the infant before she closed her eyes and fell back. "You must continue to push, lady," Old Mother said quickly. "Everything must be delivered." She began to massage Caty's belly.

As Caty struggled to find the will to push more, she felt the final small rush, then relaxation. Rhys was at her side. "Look at your son, love." His voice was full of wonder. "I hold our son, Caty." Overcome with emotion, eyes filled with tears, he bent to kiss her brow. He then handed the child to her and watched them. "Caty, you must rest now. I will be here with you and the child." Rhys looked around the room. "Rose, open the windows; this place is hot as a kitchen. I think the deed is done. Clean the lady up, bring her some wine, and then leave us. Move." His voice was clear and even, with a tone that bade action. Leaning over Caty, he kissed her wet brow once more and pushed her hair from her face. "My love," he whispered gently.

One of the women took candles for the dessil. Fear the child might be abducted by evil spirits prompted some of the women to fall back on old beliefs. Circling Caty's bed, the woman spoke in low tones, hoping to ward off evil spirits, then left. Rose grumbled. She knew the old custom to ward off fairies would be difficult to stop, so she let it pass. "I will call the priest soon. He is the one we need now," Rose murmured.

As the women moved to clean the chamber and Caty, Rhys caught Rose by the sleeve. "Pray tell me why the physician was not in attendance? Who was to call him?" He was angry, his face flushed with the heat of the room and with outrage. His wife and son might have died. How could she have been left alone?

Rose shook her head. "He was killed in the fighting, early on. My lady has been both lady and physician to your people. She has done well. But it is good you are here. She finds the load heavy, Your Grace." Rhys frowned as he watched her walk away. He could not know what this winter had been for Caty. He had been gone far too long.

When Caty awoke, she thought she had dreamed her husband's voice. She could tell her belly was not filled with a child. "Rose?" she called.

Rhys was at her side immediately. "Lady Caterina, I am here. How can I serve you? What do you wish?"

"Rhys! You are not a dream; you are here. We do have a son?" Caty asked.

Rhys nodded. "Yes, you have given me a son, Caty."

"Oh, please let me feel your touch. Rhys, how I have missed you. You have returned." The memory of his return came back to her. Tears of relief ran down her face.

Rhys slipped his arms under her shoulders and knees, then lifted her as if she were weightless, carried her to the chair by the fire and sat with her in his lap. She rested her head on his chest, softly crying. "Hush, my love," he said. "We have every reason to be thankful."

"I knew you would return, but the days grew long and empty, one on another. To have you near again, and feel you, strong and protecting—I love you, Rhys. Perhaps I have always loved you, even when I knew you not." Caty lay contented within his arms.

Rhys held her closely. The door opened slowly and Rose entered with the babe in arm. "You must feed the wee one, lady. He cries for his mother. Perhaps for his father, too." Carefully laying the child in Caty's arms, Rose backed out of the room.

Rhys carried both mother and child to the bed. "Take care of our son. I believe we have need for a priest. Tell me, Caty, what have you for his name, this child of ours?"

"I think I shall leave that honor to you, Rhys. Look how like you he seems, already." Her eyes shone, and Rhys saw the mist of emotion. Tenderly brushing her cheek, he kissed the child, then his wife. He hated to leave them, but by now he was certain Bruce would have returned from making his rounds, to report on the men and arms found in his castle. The Highland clan leader Caty had told him about was not around when Rhys rode in, but he would be at hand now. They had much to discuss.

"I must leave you now, my lady." With love, he gazed at her. "I will return to spend this night with you. Rest now." He wanted to linger—and yet, the tale behind the men in his castle must be heard. In his mind, he was grateful Caty had been with child while he was away. *Caty I know and trust well*, he thought. *Other men, not so.*

THIRTY-ONE

RHYS SAT QUIETLY IN THE great room as he listened to stories told by Old Father and the few other men who had remained in the castle during his absence. Bruce sat nearby. The lord listened intently to every man, as well as several women who asked to be heard. The room fell silent when the Highlander and his men strode in. The clansman walked boldly up to the table and nodded to Rhys as one of his men announced, "'Tis Thain Macintosh, of Clan Macintosh."

"I would hear what you have to tell me, Thain Macintosh," Rhys said.

The Highlander waved to the full room. "You have already heard from your people. Let them speak for me."

"I ask you to speak. Nay, I command you speak. It would seem I owe you much, and would hear from where your duty to me comes." Rhys extended his hand to the man. Rhys remembered the man well, but wished the room to hear the man speak of the relationship between them.

The Highlander shook the lord's offered hand. Before he could speak, Rhys instructed that seats be provided for Thain and his men. Once seated, the Highlander said, "I came to you when the news came to me that your lands were under siege. At that time, I knew not the Lady Dermoth."

"But you knew I was not in attendance?" Rhys had no doubt that word of his absence had traveled quickly.

"For certain, Your Grace, or your lands would not have been under any threat." A slight smile rested on the Highlander's face.

Rhys studied Thain, frowning. "I remember you. Did you not fight me? In fact, you fought me well, as I recall."

At this, laughter broke out. Rhys raised his hand and silence ensued. The room waited for the Highlander to reply. "I did. I did fight you, and I did fight well." Again, men could be heard chuckling. "But," he continued, "not well enough. You won, Your Grace. You were just in your dealing with me. You gave my lands back to me. From that day, I and my men fight for you. My people have sworn loyalty to you. My lands are yours."

Rhys studied the man before him. "What would you ask in return?" He could use a man such as this. Honest and loyal, a fighter sure.

"A place by your side, after your brother. I will follow where you would lead, my lord. I am not meant to be a farmer, nor a lord, sir. I am a soldier, a warrior, as are my men. We fight. You may have need of such. I would also speak privately with you, when you deem it right for you. At that time, you will hear what I have yet to ask."

Rhys picked absentmindedly at the pork sitting in front of him. "Perhaps, Highlander, we should speak now. I would hear your request."

Standing, he motioned for Bruce to follow, and all three men stepped away. Rhys led the men to a small chamber. After lighting the fire, Bruce pulled seats up near a large round table in the center of the room. Motioning for everyone to sit, Rhys sat and waited for the Highlander to speak. After a moment, the man looked into Rhys's eyes. "I would ask that my young bride be allowed to serve your lady. My woman knows not the ways of a lady, or of a wife, for that matter. Well, some things she knows." He smiled. "There are no other women in my house. That is my request."

"You have children?"

"I do not yet. I would hope for babes someday."

"What would you do with them?" Rhys was pleased with the actions of this man, now and before his own return to the castle. He wanted to show what the Highlander's service had meant to him and to Caty. It would seem now he would have a way to do just that.

"If it pleased you, sir, I would bring them with me. They could stay in a bothy near. I will find a woman to look after them."

"Nay, Highlander. This is what will happen. I will accept your sworn loyalty, you and whoever of your men are willing to follow me. You will be at my table, after my brother Bruce. Your wife and any children that are born will live in this castle. My wife is not able to see to the arrangements, but her lady-in-waiting will. I would expect this to happen now. Is this agreeable?"

"Yes!" The Highlander was moved. He had never wanted to oversee farms, peoples, and lands. He wanted to command fighting men. He would protect these lands.

"It is done, then. Come, let us celebrate the birth of my son. My firstborn." Rhys clapped the Highlander on the shoulder, and the men returned to the great room.

The room went silent as Rhys reentered. "Let us eat and be of good cheer!" he said. "Tonight, we return from a hard time, but we return to find our homes and families intact, because of your Lady Dermoth and because of each of you that helped Lady Caty and each other. We also raise our cups in great joy for the birth of my son—Rhys Tabor Dermoth." The great hall erupted in delight. After so long at the fight, it was time to celebrate.

Bruce leaned in to his brother. "You cannot simply call this man 'Highlander.'"

"Why not? He is one, and a great piece of one, I would say!" Rhys countered.

Late in the evening, Rhys entered Caty's chambers. He found her sitting up in bed, nursing the babe in her arms. He stood silently by, watching. When Rose came to take the child, he sat on Caty's bed. "I have named our son, Caty. He shall be called Rhys Tabor Dermoth. The priest will baptize him tonight. Does that please you?"

Caty's tired face turned toward Rhys. "Yes, it does. You chose my father's name. This may be our last child, but I have no complaints."

"Nor do I." Rhys stretched out beside his wife. "When do I lie with you as a husband?"

"Soon, husband. I know it would trouble you to lie with me just so." Caty blushed, smiling. "Perhaps it would be better if you went to your own bed, sir. You will have need of sleep, and with a new babe I fear you will get little."

"I like that plan not. I intend to stay here. Soon enough the babe will be with his nurse, and we will both get rest. Now it is enough for me to be close to you. I have dreamed of you each night, these long months."

"As have I dreamed of you, Rhys." Caty lay back, nestled in his arms under the warmth of the blanket. Rhys held her until her even breathing told him she slept. Gently, he laid her aside, stood up, and slipped off his clothes. Sliding under the covers, he pulled her close to him. Holding her thus, he drifted off to sleep.

THIRTY-TWO

CATY WAS UP AND ABOUT soon. Her mother had often talked of the good that could be done if women would be up and about soon after any illness, birth, or tragedy. Her mother was right, although Old Mother worried and Rose muttered about Caty catching her death.

This day began as many before it. The great room was filled with people bringing disputes and other issues to Lord Dermoth. Old Mother limped to the back door of the kitchen on her way to the herb garden. At the door, she found a young girl. The girl begged to speak with the Lady Caty. After hearing her story, Old Mother led her to the kitchen, where Caty was giving instruction for the day's meals. "Lady, please hear this one. The bairn would speak with you."

The girl trembled. Her eyes were reddened and swollen. Her dirty, tear-streaked face was filled with fear. Caty was moved at the sight of her. "Speak, child. How can I help you?" She gently touched the girl's shoulder.

"My sister, she is before the Lord Dermoth now, accused of whoring. She will be run out of the lord's lands. She has two small children and me, that is all. There is no man to help her. If she has to leave, who will care for us? Please help her!"

Caty hesitated only a second, then marched to the great room. As she wove through the crowd, she heard a man speaking. "My son asks that you ban this woman from our lands. He bears shame unjustly."

Moving resolutely to the front, Caty stood off to the side, watching the scene as it unfolded. Rhys listened thoughtfully before finally asking the woman, "What have you to say for yourself?"

The woman was too afraid to even speak; she stood trembling, her eyes on the floor. Caty stepped into view and stood between the two opposing parties standing before Lord Rhys. Turning to her husband, she asked, "May I speak, Your Grace?"

Rhys was surprised to see her. He nodded his permission, frowning slightly. Bruce leaned toward him and noted, "Now 'twill be interesting, brother."

"Sir," Caty addressed the man, "it is your wish that this woman be banned for whoring with your son?"

"Yes!" he replied indignantly. "She is not fit for my son."

"Does your son have children of his own?" Caty continued.

Puzzled, the man replied, "Yes, of what concern is that?"

"I am just wondering, who will take care of those children when your son is banned?" Caty asked.

"My son? *Banned?* I think not. I ask *she* be banned!" The man growled with anger, gesturing wildly at the poor woman. There were murmurs from the crowded room.

"Please tell me, sir—when a table is set with food, two people sit down, serve themselves, and the food is taken in, what would you say happened to it?"

"Why it was eaten of course, but what does . . . ," he said, floundering.

"So you would say that both people were eating?" Caty asked. The room had gone silent.

"Certainly." The man clearly resented Caty's meddling.

"I agree with you, sir. Even though one is a man and one is a woman, both ate. So it would follow that if your son was with this woman, accused of whoring, he was also whoring, correct? If she must be banned, then your son must also be banned. I am certain you will happily take in and provide for the children and wife of your son. How many children does your son have, sir?" Caty was speaking rapidly but calmly, and with determination furrowing her brow.

"Five," he grumbled reluctantly. He was beginning to see where Caty was headed. To have his son banned as well as the woman was unthinkable. The thought of having his daughter-in-law in his house permanently was worse. As was the thought of the five children, two of whom were not even the children of his son. Men did not whore; they took mistresses. It was the norm. What place did this woman have to speak?

Rhys struggled to keep from smiling at the scene unfolding before him.

Unwilling as yet to give up, the man spoke up again. "It is customary to punish the wicked, is it not? This woman is wicked. I say she be punished."

Caty responded quickly, "While I do not under any circumstances approve of this activity, I am quite certain it did not take place without your son's actions, also. As both parties have other responsibilities, I maintain it would do no good to anyone to ban these young people, and would do great harm to the innocent children on both sides. I submit to you, sir, that *both* parties swear an oath to avoid such behavior and any contact with each other, under threat of fulfillment of said punishment to *both parties*. I trust your son would understand the gravity of his actions as I am certain this child, the woman of which you speak, understands well what she has done." Curtsying to her husband, she awaited Rhys's response.

Rhys had to admit that Caty's evaluation was rational, though highly unusual. Turning his attention to the man and both young people, he spoke sternly. "I agree with Lady Dermoth's recommendations. You both will be held to the oath you speak this day, and understand well what the consequences will be if you do not keep this oath. You, sir," he said, turning to the older man, "are, I am certain, thankful to Lady Caty for making a decision that would keep your days in advanced years peaceful."

The old man looked at Caty through narrowed eyes, then nodded. Shaking his head, he said gruffly to her, "The world needs more women who are truly ladies. My mother would approve of your decision, though I do not."

Caty tried to soften the man's defeat with grace. "Your mother raised a wise son, I see."

The man bowed and backed away as both young people swore to stay away from engaging in "unwed carnal activities." He then strode out with his hapless son scrambling to keep pace.

As Caty turned to take her leave of the great room, Rhys stepped down and held her elbow. "No, Caty. I bid you stay and hear with your brother and

I." He then led her to a chair on his left. As Caty sat down, Bruce took his seat on his brother's right. And so on this day, Caty heard about the conflicts of the lord's realm with the men. She kept all she was learning deep within her memory.

When the morning was finished, Caty rose to bring in their meal. Bruce laughed. "Sister," he noted, "you add fairness of a different color to this hearing." He was grinning widely, pleased to have something to break up what was often a boring morning.

Caty smiled, "Dear Bruce, you speak what you believe most times, but I feel you are speaking with kindness, not honesty, this time. It is not my desire to attend this function, if my husband would be so kind as to relieve me of the duty. I would much rather deal with the coming winter, illnesses, and entertainment we may have in this place." Nodding to Rhys, she left the room. She could hear Bruce laugh as she walked out. She met Rose in the hall and ordered that the girl from the morning incident be brought to her in the morn. "I would see that she not take this lightly. She cannot slip back. I suspect she does what she must to provide for her sister and children. I intend to remove worry about support from the poor woman."

THIRTY-THREE

CATY WATCHED THE CLOUDS DRIFT over the castle walls. The babe had been baptized and Rhys was once again gone, but she felt her husband was safe. Although some Highlanders continued to plunder hapless lands, so far none had crossed theirs. England and Scotland played a game of cat and mouse, as each raided the other across their common border. This was nothing new. *So why do I feel such a burden? The babe is healthy, my husband is well, our people are living in peace. What must be the worry I carry?* She felt a troubling ache in her heart. The warning was coming to her again. Once again, Caty felt the peril, but could not tell from where, or for whom. This time she saw nothing, only the heavy weight of troubles to come. Fall had begun to play with the leaves, weaving beautiful colors where before only green had stood. Winds blew colder, bringing with them a freshness that would like as not become bitter. The heavy feeling of dread clung to her as moss to a tree, growing ever stronger.

The feeling stayed with her all through the long dreary winter, yet nothing befell them. This winter proved not so cruel, and the people of Dermoth remembered well the lessons from past times. They were prepared. Rhys was with them most of the time. It had been a quiet, busy time, without turmoil. Nevertheless, Caty could not shake this feeling. Some days it was heavier than others, but it stubbornly clung to her.

The man and his companion, a friend of many years, rode in silence. They rode with bone-deep fatigue. The men were accustomed to fighting and had earned the reputations they carried. Tonight, however, the man's friend was afraid the fight would not so easily be won. The price for this victory would be much higher. Eventually, the friend spoke. "Carlos, we must stop. You do no favors to appear barely able to stand. I would rest, but if you cannot, I go also. Yet, think on what you run toward. If anything I know about you and the girl is accurate, you have not a need to worry." His words were spoken in love, for he loved the man as a brother. He felt no conviction, though. The girl was independent. What little time he watched her and the few times he spoke to her in Edinburgh had proved as much.

Lord Carlos rode in silence for a short while, lost in thought. Then he agreed: "You speak the truth, Henry. I can ride but little more this night. We stop here. Tomorrow we meet the rest of our men, God willing." The two rode deep into the underbrush and trees away from the usual travelers, finding a place to sleep out of the path of unwanted callers.

Morning sun brought a welcome respite from the cold wind of night. As the two men rode into a small hamlet, the horses tied outside the only inn proved that the men they expected were already in town. Carlos and Henry tied up their own animals, then stepped into the pub. There were men everywhere. The small room was so crowded that some were forced to stand along the walls. Several cheered when they recognized Carlos. Henry gave a bag of coins to the owner. When the man tried to return some of the money, Henry pushed it back into his hands. "I know you have earned this and more, my friend. We will be on our way and out of yours as soon as all have eaten," he promised. The owner shrugged as he tucked the bag into a pouch at his waist.

It took several hours to feed everyone, but eventually the deed was done. Some of the men wandered out onto the street, laughing and talking. "Strange there are no women here," one man noted.

"Oh, they are here for certain. Just had the good sense to hide when we hit town," his companion answered, laughing.

"Maybe we should find them, so they can taste what they are missing," another added.

An older soldier interrupted firmly, "No. No one leaves this company. Mount up and be ready to ride when Lord Carlos comes out. We are not here to cause trouble." At this, nearly half the men standing about followed the older soldier. They rode with this older man and were loyal to him, even when he had joined Carlos for unknown reasons. Now they sat atop their horses, unresponsive to the teasing coming from the remaining men, who jeered and snickered at the old man and would have no part of leaving without taking the women first.

"Stop there," Carlos called to the unruly bunch. "We leave immediately. There will be nothing said about our actions in this or any other place we stay. Is everyone clear?" Though there was some quiet grumbling, the men nodded, and soon the entire party was on its way.

The innkeeper stood on the steps, watching. He knew not where this bunch was bound, but he knew it could not be good. Only trouble would come with those men. *God care for the people where they travel,* he thought. Shaking his head, he returned to his inn.

After putting Tabor down for a nap, Caty walked to the great room. It was deserted, but clean and warm, with the aroma of the daily bread baking and winter stew cooking, floating throughout; one could hardly believe the violence it had witnessed. The sun had warmed the air, and the faint smell of spring was in the air. Pulling her wrap about her, Caty stepped into the bright daylight outside the castle. She began to wander slowly about the grounds. Women greeted her as they hurried into their homes, carrying milk and eggs. Children could be heard playing. Though Rhys was gone again, Caty felt as if perhaps the dread she felt during the last weeks and months were but a bad dream. She was behind the castle when the yells of men and the pounding of hoofs announced the arrival of visitors.

Hoping against hope, she turned toward the front gate. The standard that flew belonged neither to Rhys nor to the Highlander. These men were unknown to her and were not here for a social visit. The leader was instructing the men to secure the grounds and post to the entrance of the castle. Caty walked boldly up to him and his direct gaze. "Pray tell me to whom I might have the pleasure of speaking. I give the orders at this place."

He stared at her. The man's hair was jet black, hanging loosely to his collar. His skin was dark olive, his face hard and cold. But for the severe expression, the man would have been striking. His gaze was intense and penetrating. "Do you have anything you wish to say to me?" When the words left his mouth, Caty froze as if made of stone. She could barely breathe. As her eyes locked with the stranger's, she could neither move nor speak. Caty looked into an exact copy of her father's face, though she had never known her father to appear so harsh. She frantically searched her memory. As the youngest of seven children and having been separated for so many years, Caty found that the remembrance of her eldest siblings had begun to fade.

Caty started as her eyes took in the man next to the leader. He was the man who had come to her in Edinburgh, the one who, in the bookshop, had recognized her as a Tabor. "I do," she answered, struggling to regain her composure. "I know of fighting and leading. These things can be done by the same man but are not of themselves the same thing."

The leader dismounted, and his men followed suit. Stepping to her, he bowed deeply. "I have come for you. We leave within the hour, my lady."

Caty could not respond. She felt as if she were speaking to the spirits of the dead. Her legs felt weak. *Can this be?* Her mind refused to believe, but she knew what she saw. Could it be she did have family yet alive?

"Lady," he said again, this time in a gentle, soothing voice. "We leave now; you must make ready."

Caty faltered, "I cannot. I am responsible for these people. I have a husband and a child. I cannot leave them." Her voice was barely audible. Her face had lost its color, and she felt as if she would drop.

"What are you doing in Scotland, Caty?" the leader asked. "You belong where we go now."

In a flash, she understood that this was the impending trouble she had felt so persistently. Carlos was known to Caty, but only because of the stories—stories of his cruelty, his vicious temper, and his unscrupulous activities. Instinctively, Caty did not trust him. She feared both she and Tabor were in danger. "I cannot. Please do not make me leave. I have a child. I love the child's father. You must speak to him before you take me." Looking at the man, she felt the fingers of anger and fight; flight was not possible. Her mind failed to comprehend what she saw to be true. *Can this truly be Carlos? And why would he come for me?* Her thoughts raced. Surely, Rhys would return and save her. Still, with calm determination, she tried to stand against the man.

"Your husband broke a vow and an agreement. I owe him nothing," Carlos said, not unkindly.

"Broke a vow? How so?" Caty struggled to remain standing without letting the man know her fright.

"He was to take you, and he did. However, he was to bring you to me. I believe we can agree that he forgot the second part of his agreement."

Caty's mind now had more to unravel. This could not matter. She knew Rhys. Whatever he did, he did with honor. She loved him; they had a life together. "He knows you? He knows about all this? He knew who I was?"

"Yes. Come, lady, we leave now." He took Caty's arm and led her into the great room.

Resisting, Caty pleaded with him, "I would not leave my child. How does Lord Dermoth know you?"

"Of course, bring the child. My patience wears, lady. You must make ready to leave." He paused, then continued gently, "I know how you must doubt what you know to be true, much less what you see. There will be time later to talk. Now we must leave. If you love your man, as I believe you do, you know you should have no worry about him. Rather you should worry about your brother."

Desperately trying to gather her thoughts, Caty spoke rapidly, "I would take my ladies, my attendant, and my guard."

"Your ladies and attendant, yes. You have no need of a guard. Now hasten."

Firmly, Caty met his gaze. "I will take my ladies, my attendant, and my guard." She was regaining her composure. The more people she took, the more difficult travel would become.

The man regarded her thoughtfully for a moment. "How many men are in your guard, lady?"

"I . . . I am not certain." She hesitated, trying to remember just whom Rhys had left behind. He had only been gone one night, and she did not expect him for another five. Could she stall this man?

"Hmm. As I thought. You have no one here. If you do take anyone, you leave these people without protection. I think not."

Angry, Caty turned toward the stairs. *This is not over,* she thought. Speaking over her shoulder, she asked, "How much time do I have?"

"One hour."

Caty mounted the steps, two at a time. "Rose!" she called. "Come now."

As Caty told Rose what was going to happen, the other women made ready to leave. Caty tucked the knife Rhys had given her into her cape. Making certain she had her rings on, she folded the last bit of clothing into the chest. She, Rose, Old Mother, Old Father, Norman, and the child were down in the great room in less than one hour.

THIRTY-FOUR

THIS KIDNAPPING HAD BEEN WELL planned. Events took place so quickly that Caty's staff could do little but watch. As she left the castle, the people had begun to gather and many were crying. Addressing them, she reminded them they would need to care for each other and try to get word to Clan Macintosh for protection. Caty mounted her horse, then took the babe. Without looking back, she rode forward with her new captors.

After riding in silence for an hour, Caty spoke to the man. "You say my husband, Rhys, knows you?"

"Yes, he was to bring you to me, to keep you safe." The man rode stoically, without looking at Caty.

"He did that; he kept me safe," Caty answered softly.

"I would say he did that and more," the man responded gruffly. "You were to be brought to me. It seems my friend forgot that little detail." Carlos was intent on moving as fast as possible; an infant would slow them. His mind was already calculating how far they could travel this day. As an afterthought, nodding toward the sleeping babe in Caty's arms, he continued, "Your child? How old is the child?"

"My son is five months old."

The man turned to her sharply. "You have a son?" He had not planned on a babe, but a boy could bring more to his cause.

"I do, and a husband. I do not wish to go wherever it is you are going." Caty refused to let him see just how worried she was. She met his gaze without wavering.

He looked at her with compassion. "You are a queen now; you have no choice."

Caty gasped. "Queen of what . . . and whom?" *Perhaps this is not Carlos.*

Touching her hand, he said, "We will speak more of this when we are able. For now, know you are loved. I know better than anyone the price you are paying." He added bitterly, "But there is nothing to do about it."

"Mother and Father?" Caty asked. She needed to know for certain whether this was Carlos. Would he know about her family?

"Both dead. Because someone else desired what Mother did not want in the first place. The crown you go to claim."

Slowly, as Caty tried to put the pieces together, she turned to the man. "Rhys was with you from the beginning?" How could the man Caty knew Rhys to be get involved with Carlos? Her eyes were beginning to fill with tears. *Damn the tears!*

"Yes, but he never planned to fall in love with you. Once that happened, it changed everything." Carlos spoke quietly.

"He will come for me." She closed her eyes and looked away to keep the tears from falling.

"As well he should. His place is with you. You have provided an heir to the throne." Her brother spurred his horse ahead, leaving Caty alone with her heart and son.

Rose moved up to ride with Caty, perceiving her mistress's great sadness. For a while, both women rode in silence. Caty understood nothing; what strange kingdom was she to become queen of? Her mind reeled, but gradually she regained control. Turning, she surveyed the men behind her. None wore Carlos's colors. These men watched her, too. Tentatively, she nodded to them. The men who could see her nodded back. "Rose, I am afraid this bodes poorly for us."

"The lord will come for you, Lady Caty; have no fear," Rose insisted firmly.

"I hope so. I do hope so," Caty answered. She kissed the small head she held in her arms.

The babe began to fuss, and Caty pulled up. Immediately, the men behind her circled her and patiently waited. Caty called to the one closest to her horse. "Please, sir, be so kind as to assist me. I would dismount."

He hesitated for but a second before getting off his horse, then strode to her and extended his hands. She handed the now wailing child to him and dismounted unaided. She could hear the men around chuckle softly. Several long moments passed as Caty found what she needed to change the baby. The poor man holding little Tabor could not unhand him quick enough. He bowed and backed away, red faced. Before he could get away, Caty touched his arm. Looking into his worried eyes, she smiled.

"Thank you kindly, sir. Any man can fight; not every man has a gentle touch with his horse. I see you have a gentle touch and am certain the child was quite safe with you." She unwrapped the babe, changed him quickly, and dressed him again.

Addressing the man again, she noted, "I would feed my child; give me a moment."

Bowing slightly, the man quickly assisted her back onto the horse. The men stayed around her, patiently waiting until she was settled. Adjusting the wraps and herself, Caty nodded. One man took her reins, and they moved on.

Her brother watched this with interest. Shaking his head, he smiled. "Henry, I wonder if the realm is ready for this?" he said to his companion. His heart was lighter now, but there would still be hard times. Not the least of which would be dealing with Rhys. No matter, his sister was made from the best.

It took little time for Caty, Rose, and Old Mother to develop a routine around little Tabor, even while on the road. He was still sleeping most of the time, and Caty refused to ask for special treatment. She and her son, the son of Lord Rhys Dermoth, would be fine.

In the early afternoon, Carlos rode back to her side. "I would hold my nephew."

Caty looked at the sleeping bundle. "Certainly, brother. As gently as you once held me, I hope." She looked up at him. His eyes were misty.

"Even more so, Caterina. I have learned how short one's life can be," he answered softly. Holding the sleeping babe in his arms, he rode along in silence.

Gently, his hand brushed the blanket back so he could watch the baby's face. The realization came to Caty that Carlos had lost much.

"Have you children, brother?" she asked tenderly.

The spell was broken. Bitterly he replied, "Once, and a good woman, too. Not now. Now, I ride for you."

"I did not ask this of you," Caty countered.

He looked at her shrewdly and acknowledged this fact with a nod. "Still you will be queen, and I will ride for you. Is this not so?"

"I know nothing of what you speak, Carlos. I know only what you tell me. I must trust your better judgment in this matter." His behavior struck Caty as very unsettling. He appeared in control one moment; then, without warning, he would slide into an abyss nothing could enter. In this darkness, he was dangerous, even to her and the child.

He relaxed again, smiling at the baby. "'Tis a beautiful baby, Caterina. Worthy of the honor due him. A future king, son of the queen." Handing the baby back, he rode back to the lead.

Caty wanted to ask once more about where they were going, who and what she was to be queen of, but she thought better of it.

Carlos spent very little time with her over the next few days, but each exchange reinforced the fact that he had changed a great deal. Gone was the happy, carefree lad, eager to fight anything or anyone, that he must have been. He was now tall, dark, and scarred, and rode with a regal air. He and his men were armed and wore full battle dress. Though she was not certain whether this was for appearances or whether they truly expected to have trouble, Caty was impressed with the disciplined precision every man displayed. As evening shadows began to lengthen, she urged her mount ahead and rode through the men, up to the front. Carlos frowned when he saw her.

"I have come to request we make camp soon," she told him. "The baby and my attendants are weary. We need to rest." Caty spoke calmly, without any hint of confrontation in her voice.

Carlos looked around. "I am certain you can tell that this is not the place to stop, Caterina. We will stop soon, I promise. There is a small settlement near here, where we may find shelter for you and your child. Stay with me, sister," he replied, suddenly gay again. Glancing toward the men at his side, Caty took note that none shared his lighthearted disposition. Each wore the face of danger.

Caty nodded. "Thank you, Carlos." Pulling her mount up, she let the men pass until she was again with her household. Looking at Old Father, she gave a barely discernible shake of her head. He cast his eyes down. He knew what she thought. They were in trouble. Norman had ridden with the men behind, moving among them and talking to them. It was a strange troop.

As darkness enveloped the land, Carlos finally slowed the column down and gave orders to make camp. Caty was assisted off her horse by the elder man who rode at the head of the rear column. He was sympathetic and gentle with both her and the baby. Respectful with her attendants, he directed his men to set their area up quickly, to allow the women time to rest. He had water brought to her, and soon a fire was blazing before her tent. Too tired and worried to eat, Caty fed Tabor and made certain her staff had eaten. Handing the baby off to Rose, she pulled a cape over her head.

"You've a mind to walk among these men, lady?" Rose asked. "Take care. You know not what they have in their minds." Rose held baby Tabor close to her breast. Worry lined her face as she watched her mistress.

"Fear not, Rose. If I am indeed a queen, and I doubt this greatly, I would know my people. Rather, truthfully, I believe I may find out just what Carlos is about. Something is very wrong about this. I will find a way to the truth of all these things. Care for the baby, Rose." Slipping through the opening, she stepped into the shadows alongside her tent, moving away from the light cast by the fire's flames.

As she rounded her tent, she caught the movement of someone walking behind the circle of camps nearest her. Flattening against the tent wall, she watched. The man moved about quietly, fading in and out of view, as if guarding against any surprises. He was the same man who had come to her in Edinburgh. She watched him until he moved beyond her area. Taking a deep breath, she advanced confidently toward the men gathered around the larger fire. As she neared them, the first man to catch sight of her stood, then bowed. The rest of the men looked her way and followed suit. Caty walked among them, toward the elder man she felt was a friend.

"Please, sirs, allow me to stay in your company a short while. I would know you better," she began. As they stood awkwardly looking at one another, she spoke to the one nearest her. "From where do you come?"

He was a young lad, and he stumbled over his words, not certain just how to reply.

"Please, do not feel you might anger or alarm me," Caty said. "I spoke only to make conversation. I believe, from your confidence as you ride, that you are all fighting men. Am I correct?"

The men nodded, while one called out, "We are that sure, lady."

"Good. It is good to have men such as you with me. I would protect my small entourage. Have you been afield long?" Casually, Caty sat on a log and stretched her hands toward the fire.

"Not long, my lady," the elder man answered. He looked at her kindly, and from somewhere in the depths of her memory she felt a spark. She stood up and walked toward him, examining his face closely.

"Sir Nathan? Is it really you?" She felt her heart leap with hope and joy. She grasped his arm. "Tell me this is really you, sir!" Unable to contain herself, she threw her arms around his neck. Standing back, she could tell he was just as pleased to see her.

Caty wanted to ask more questions, but this was not the place. "Sirs, this man was by my father's side, as long as I can remember. I knew not life at our house without him. He was as my uncle, and my father felt to him as a brother. I thought I'd not see you again in this life, Sir Nathan."

He took her hand and made a grand introduction to his men. "This is Lady Caterina Tabor. Her mother was Lady Isabella Tabor. Her father, Lord Tabor, was the finest soldier I have ever had the pleasure of fighting alongside. I know that those of you who knew him would agree. Lady Caterina was not left in the house to sew and sing; she was put to horse, field, and arms. It is our pleasure to serve you, my lady." When he finished speaking, the men cheered. These men would keep her safe, of that she was certain.

"Come, let me not disturb your evening further," she said to the group. "I feel a renewed sense of security with you here." Smiling to the men, she stepped away from the fire.

Sir Nathan took her hand and, bowing, kissed it. "Nay, lady, 'tis we that feel blessed to be with you again. Come, I will escort you back to your tent." Glancing around to be certain they would not be heard, he spoke softly. "I felt it safer for you if I were not the one to bring attention to our history, Lady Caty. I would give Carlos no reason to discharge me, leaving you unprotected."

With a lighter step, she walked with him back to her tent. After looking carefully around also, she spoke quietly to him. "I am not pleased to be on this journey, sir. I fear my brother may have gotten into something he cannot finish." Sir Nathan nodded in agreement. "When it is safe, please come speak with me. I would not place you or your men in danger, so please take care." Standing on her tiptoes, she kissed his cheek. "I believe I am still allowed to do that, sir?"

"Of course, child. You will remain my niece as it were. I loved your parents deeply. Now, sleep peacefully, Lady Caterina." The older soldier briefly squeezed her hand.

Once Caty was safely inside the tent, Rose secured the entrance. She had moved all their belongings to the middle, and they huddled together for warmth. The baby slept peacefully. Caty kissed his small head. "What a sad place he may find himself in if I cannot get us out of this, Rose," she said in a low voice.

"What were you able to hear, m'lady?"

"These men are our guards. They will take care of us; of this I am certain, though I do not know why they ride with Carlos. Nor do I understand what my brother is doing, or for whom. I must speak with Carlos on the morrow. Tonight, we sleep in safety, Rose."

Caty clutched the ring around her finger, given to her by Rhys.

THIRTY-FIVE

MORNING CAME, COLD AND WET, as falling rain punished the camp. Caty refused to move out of the tent with the infant. Carlos came to the entrance, stomping and angry. "What is this I hear? You refuse to leave? I am not asking you, Caty—I am ordering you to leave. We must make good time; we have a boat to meet soon. I intend to have you on that boat when it arrives. I will not discuss it further."

As he turned to leave, Caty calmly answered, "I will not leave in this weather with an infant. Care you so little for the future king, as you called him? Would you bury him before he reaches his first birthday? What kind of protector or uncle would do such a thing? We wait. This should let up soon. In your haste to leave before Rhys's return, you thought not about the weather for this child. I do not mind getting drenched, but it will kill my son. We stay."

Carlos stood looking at her in astonishment. She did have a strong argument. What could he say to the child's death of cold? Begrudgingly he agreed. "We stay, but only for this day."

"No," Caty continued firmly. "We stay until the weather is safe for this child you have sworn to protect, sir." Her tone was cold. *This is not how my family could ever behave,* she told herself. He was under tremendous pressure. He must be, to even think of risking Tabor's life.

The rain lasted three days. During the third day, Carlos came to her tent. He entered quietly, stepping closer to watch the sleeping child. His mood was somber. "Caty, I must speak with you. Come sit with me. Let us not quarrel with one another. I have been too long away from you. I would have no arguments with you."

208

Caty nodded in agreement. "That would please me also, Carlos." She sat beside him, on the pallet she used as a bed. Rose moved to the far end of the tent. "Tell me, what have you done with your life? What can you tell me of our other brothers?"

Carlos told her of his travels, fighting for any country that needed an extra gun. He had learned from the best, and put it to good use. He knew little of his brothers. He had not been able to find any of them. He grew quiet, leaning forward, with his chin on his hands. He chose his words carefully when he continued.

"Our parents are both dead, Caty. Father was killed while trying to defend Mother." His eyes looked away into emptiness, but Caty could tell he saw images enough. She reached to touch his arm. "They took her, tried her, and condemned her to die at the stake." His voice was bitter and cold. "It was not the church; it was because of her family. Her mother and grandmother were of the family you go to protect, now."

The silence in the tent was powerful. "Burned her?" Caty could barely whisper. The rumors she had heard were true. Her mind filled with horror.

"No, they thought to, but I took that pleasure away from them. I shot her." Carlos's voice was flat, without emotion. His face had lost any sign of feeling.

Caty frowned, trying to understand. "You . . . shot her?"

"As soon as she was tied, I shot her. Even as they lit their damnable fire, I shot her. They knew not from where the shot came, nor who had pulled the trigger. No one knows I am still alive." His voice became louder. "Do you have any idea what it feels like in your soul to shoot your own mother? I am like a man dead, walking."

"Oh, Carlos." Caty hugged his neck. He began to cry, and great sobs filled the tent. Tabor awoke, wailing, but Caty sat still. Rose held the infant and quieted him. Still Carlos wept. When he finally stopped, he sat for a long time with his head on Caty's breast. Eventually, he sat up. His demeanor was calm again, but now he was cold to her. "You wish to not do your part for this family, sister? I think not. You will do as you are told. You are a queen, your son will be the king, and you will go wherever you need to go. Do I make it clear to you?"

"Where do you take us, Carlos? I would know what lies ahead for me and the child." Carlos only glowered at her. His eyes and face were like stone. Caty was stunned at the change in him. She moved away from him, to stand near her child. When he looked at her, he looked as if she were a stranger, not his own sister. Without another word, he left the tent. Caty stood watching the entrance, without speaking. *There is no family. We are in danger.* Caty's mind struggled to make sense of Carlos and his behavior.

At last, she turned to Rose. Rose crossed herself and the infant. "He is not right, m'lady. We are in a bad way," Rose warned. Caty had to agree with her.

Caty called Old Mother, Norman, and Old Father into her tent. "You must leave this night. Just after dark. Bring Rhys to us." Old Father protested, but Caty cut him off. "I do not ask; you must. You cannot keep up, and I will not endanger you. You can be of greater service to me if you bring help. Go with God." She hugged all three and watched them leave.

"If only I could keep him from traveling just a little longer. Perhaps it will rain again tomorrow." Caty began to pace. There had to be some way to stall Carlos.

The next morning, sunlight was filtering into her tent. For the first time in her life, she hated the sun. Carlos was already about, shouting at the men, and camp was breaking. Slowly, Caty and Rose readied themselves. The babe played, mindless of his grave danger. "So young you are, son. Please, God, let him see his father again. Let Rhys find us, somehow," Caty prayed, over and over.

"Caterina! We leave, now!" Carlos ordered as he entered the tent. His eyes surveyed the area. The women had already packed and now stood waiting. Caty was loath to anger him. He nodded, turned, and ordered the women to be mounted. Soon, everyone was moving again. Caty found comfort in the fact that Carlos again rode at the head, leaving her with Sir Nathan.

"You are shy three people, lady. Where are the old couple and young man you first brought with you?" Sir Nathan spoke without looking at Caty.

"I sent them back. The couple were too old to make a journey such as this. The young man is to be certain they arrived safely. Where are we bound, Sir Nathan?" Grateful Carlos had not noticed the three were missing, she prayed Norman would get to Rhys soon.

"He does not share information with me, but I believe he moves to keep you on one of the Hebrides. It would seem he knows of a castle there, where he can keep you hidden as long as necessary." Sir Nathan's voice was glum.

"I do not understand. What does he wish of me? There is no kingdom that would belong to my mother or her people. She was from Rome. 'Tis true enough, her father was of noble birth, but certainly did not have claims to any kingdom," Caty noted. Watching Carlos at the head, Caty tried to understand her brother. "Where did Carlos come up with this idea? How did you come to swear to him?"

Sir Nathan rode in silence for a while. Then, speaking carefully, he told her of his meeting with Carlos. Caty soon realized that he had met with Carlos as a tribute to their father. He could never have known what this would mean. Now, because of his deep respect for Lord Tabor, he and his men were caught.

"Your men, Sir Nathan, are they loyal to you, or to Carlos?" Caty's mind was working.

"To me, lady. They go where I go, without question. They are the best of the men I have fought with. Some fought with your father. The Crown saw fit to abandon them on foreign soils. When the offer was made, I believed Carlos had the best offer for our services. These services are specialized, as you can attest, Lady Caty."

"And the men with Carlos? What of them?"

"Most are men he has picked up along the way. Except for the man at his right. He goes by Henry. I know not his family name. He is a longtime friend of Carlos, and will never go against him, no matter what the consequences of staying with Carlos may be." Sir Nathan's voice was calm. His eyes regarded Caty with sympathy and kindness.

"Sir, we cannot get on a boat. Somehow, we must remain on this land, be it England or Scotland. How can we do this?" Caty could not keep the anxiety from her voice.

"Let me think on it, lady. We will speak again." With that, he turned his horse and rode back to his men.

THIRTY-SIX

RHYS AND BRUCE RODE IN silence. This foray, like many others, had been successful. Still, Rhys feared one day he would be called for a reckoning. His standard flew now, but was never seen in England. Glancing upward, Bruce said, "You were right, brother. Your standard now speaks to many. Perhaps too many. Think you to fight England, for the Scots? Surely, the men you have at your side will stay there, but each time we venture out, I believe we take a greater chance."

"I share your concern, Bruce. I believe England is destined to be a great power. I fear for Scotland, though. There is still much resentment over the union. I think I wish nothing more than to be with my wife and son. I have done much for both countries, and would now ask for a release to live my life as I see fit." He doubted that would be the case. No harm in wishing.

"Would be a pleasant dream, brother. I believe fate has other plans for us. What about Caty?" Bruce asked.

"She is mine, Bruce. She stays with me." Rhys smiled at the thought of her. "I earned her."

"Does she know about your agreement?" Bruce glanced at his brother.

"No. I know now that it would matter not anyway. She will stay with me."

As night plunged them into darkness, Rhys held his men up. He was unwilling to risk injury to either man or horse; they would stay the night. One more day would make little difference. His mind and heart were filled with images of Caty. Even now, he marveled that she loved him, more than he could ever have hoped. His mind recalled every detail of her face. Then, as he lay to sleep, he recalled his son's face and tiny body. How little and helpless. What a joy was his.

Early afternoon of the next day found them entering the castle grounds. Rhys surveyed the windows of their quarters, searching in vain for Caty's face. No matter, she would be in the great room. Nearing the door, he was instantly on guard at the sight of Old Father. The old man's face was drawn, anxious, and pale as he limped to them. He began talking before Rhys had a chance to enter the room. "She is gone, m'lord. Taken by someone she knew and gone now a week's time. She went not willingly. She and the child with Rose, too. Lady Caty sent me, my wife, and Norman back to tell you what took place here. You must go for her, m'lord. I would go with you. We must leave soon. I will alert Norman. He would go with you also."

He spoke so rapidly that Rhys had to calm him and get him to start over. Bruce was at his side by the time the story came out in an intelligible manner. "Carlos," Bruce said. "It has to be Carlos. Where would he take her?" Bruce studied his brother's face.

"I know not. What I do know is we leave soon. Carlos has a week on us. We cannot let him take her by boat. I will not let her go. I swear Carlos will rue the day he was born if he harms the child or Lady Caty. We eat, change horses, and leave. Eat, Bruce, then pull twenty men."

"That I will, brother. Tough men. For certain, we will fight." Bruce turned to Old Father. "And is there a man that sticks to Carlos like a burr? A fighting man. Does he still go with Carlos?"

Old Father nodded. "Aye, there is a man such as that. He is like a shadow, never leaving his side."

"Sad, I think. He is a good warrior, fights well. He is loyal," Bruce noted.

"Yes, Bruce, he is loyal, but to the wrong man," Rhys interjected. "In youth, I can see such, but as men, no. At some point one must stand for what one believes. Henry stands for Carlos, without looking beyond his childhood hero."

"True, but if one could change that view, think what you would have, in Henry."

"It will never happen." Rhys turned and took the stairs. He entered Caty's rooms and looked over the disarray left behind. She had packed in a hurry. He held her nightdress to his face. Breathing deeply, he closed his eyes and could see her smiling face before him. He pulled a ribbon from the gown and tucked it into his tunic. In his room, he found a note lying on his pillow.

Rhys, I pray you find this quickly. My brother, Carlos, comes for me. I do not remember him being the way he is, but it is he, surely. He talks nonsense, but is determined to take me; where, I know not. He believes I am to reclaim a crown, belonging to my mother. This cannot be; she was not royalty. I will travel as slowly as possible. Please come soon, my love. I fear for your son and your wife.

Rhys folded the note again, then slipped it beside the ribbon near his heart. With determination, he left the castle for the stables.

As he and his men rode out, the people around the castle called out to him. "Godspeed, lord. Bring our lady back." With him rode every warrior. Thomas was one of the first to mount up. He and Caty had remained friends, after he first cut short her visit with Rhys's people. There were others like Thomas. Though Rhys had originally planned to take only twenty, when word was out about the nature of the mission, men volunteered.

The legion rode steady, through the night. Early morning, Lord Rhys stopped them. "We rest the horses here. In four hours' time, we leave again."

When he led them off again, Bruce frowned. "Do we not ride to Stirling?"

"We ride to the Highlander. If anyone has passed through his lands, he will know. Carlos would not take her near a larger place, for fear she would be recognized or get away. The Highlander will have fresh horses, too."

"'Tis a gamble, brother." Bruce shook his head.

"Yes, one I must take." They rode without talking for several hours. Rhys turned to his brother. "Bruce, what do you remember of Carlos?"

"He had an evil mind when it came to fighting. No honor, just win. No cause, either. Whoever paid the most, he fought for. Not at all like Ricardo. Not like what I have heard about his father. And you, did you know him well?"

"Yes. Before he became as he is. He had a young wife and two small children. While he was away fighting, they were butchered and left out as a warning.

214

The French took no prisoners during that raid. They knew well whose wife she was, and made certain Carlos found her. She was staked naked. She had been raped and cut up, dying and watching while his children were slaughtered. Carlos never recovered. He went after the men with a vengeance I have never seen since. Every man paid in the worst way. When it was done, as it is with revenge, he felt no release, just a fire to destroy."

"What about Caty?"

"As for Caty, I only knew this—Caty's father sent more than his daughter to England. Carlos wanted a chest that was sent with Caty. I sent word to a Lord Richmond, in England, regarding Caty and the chest. He found the captain. The chest never made it. Knowing Carlos, I intended he not get his hands on Caty. I agreed to take her. My plan was to let Lord Richmond know when I found her. I never intended to keep her. I did, and I will."

"You will have to kill Carlos, Rhys." Bruce watched his brother closely.

"Yes."

"Caty would not know his history," Bruce added thoughtfully. "In truth, I doubt Caty really knows him at all."

"She does now." Rhys replied curtly.

THIRTY-SEVEN

CARLOS TURNED FREQUENTLY TO WATCH his sister. She looked so much like his mother; he had to look at her again and again. The child would be a blessing. A king in the family. His father would have been proud. Turning to Henry, he caught his friend's eye. "She is beautiful, is she not?"

"She is, Carlos, but with a mind of her own. I fear she may not take to your plans for her future. We cannot keep her hidden for too long. We must get back to Modena. There should be someone on the throne by Christmas. That was our promise."

"I know, Henry, I know. Do you not believe I do my best?" Carlos turned back to look at his sister again.

"I do. We make up for lost time. Winds should be strong this time of year. You planned perfectly." Henry understood little about this trip. He only knew his friend had changed and, it would seem, had gotten worse.

Carlos smiled. Henry had never failed him. The plan was brilliant. They would sail for the Outer Hebrides. The southernmost tip held a very defensible castle near craggy walls above the sea, wrought with rocks and shallows. He could keep her there for a year if need be. Better to be on their way sooner, but who could tell? His mind's eye saw the infant again. Strong boy, looked like his father. The child's mother, however, took Carlos back to a different time, a time he had worked to forget. His lips narrowed to a thin, bitter line. With eyes darkened by hate, he remembered his own wife and children. What did he care if his sister lived or not? Now that he knew about the boy, his plan would change. A king would have more power anyway. He would restore

216

Lady Isabella's family to its rightful place. A place of wealth, in a country near the hated French. From that point, he could make the French pay, dearly, for his family's destruction. He really only needed the child. He would act in the child's stead, until he came of age. *This is perfect. Even better than I thought.* Carlos felt new energy.

Henry rode in miserable silence. His love of Carlos was sore tested, of late. While Henry did play along with Carlos's so-called plan, Henry believed his friend was losing his mind. Carlos had horrific mood swings, became violently angry and completely unreasonable. While Henry had no doubts about the effects of the murder of Carlos's family, he also had to admit that these traits had been present long before that incident. He had ridden into battle with Carlos many times and shivered to see what his friend would do to anyone captured. Now, he dreaded every evening, fearing for the lady's life. If Carlos believed Caty held up his progress, he would take the child. Caty would not survive. Henry had never seen their mother, but from descriptions provided by Carlos, Caty was a replica. Henry had no misconceptions regarding Lord Dermoth's inevitable reaction to this kidnapping. If only they could board the ship without incident. If only . . .

As evening fell, Caty began to hang back. Eventually, Carlos noticed and rode to her side. "Of what do you think, woman? Are you not aware we must make the shore by the morrow? You either keep up, or I will take the child myself and you will be left. Do you understand me, lady?"

Leveling her defiant stare at him, Caty met his glare without once wavering. "Brother, I have no illusions regarding your value of me, but I believe you do value the child. He is ill, as I warned you he would be, traveling as we have. Look at him yourself. Feel his face and head. He lies with fever. Pray it is not the plague ravaging the boroughs you have taken us through. We must stop, so I may care for him, or you may be forced to bury your future king."

At the mention of the plague, Carlos drew his horse back with alarm. Peering into the blankets, he could tell Tabor was indeed hot with fever, attested to by his reddened face and hands. The babe cried weakly. The thought of losing his trump for French battles caused him to stop immediately. Giving orders to make camp, he put Caty and her lady off alone to prevent the spread of any disease to the rest of his men. Caty dismounted and entered her tent without speaking to her brother. She had gambled well on her brother's fear of the plague. Rose was silent until she was certain they were alone. "Lady, if the child is ill, 'tis certain you will be also. You must rest and take care. You cannot chance what will happen to you if you are ill."

"Fear not, Rose. The child is not ill, only drugged. Remember, my mother was a healer. My life is worth little, but he needs the child. If he thinks the child is in danger of dying, he stays, even for a short while. I must give Rhys time to reach us." Caty looked on her child with tender love. She felt bad about making him uncomfortable. Better uncomfortable than dead.

"Do you think he comes, lady?" Rose herself had begun to lose faith.

"Yes, I feel it, here." Caty touched her breast. "I know he comes, but he needs time. I intend to give him that time. If Carlos thinks the child ill with the plague, better for us. I know not if any of the places we have passed have the plague, but I hear talk of it. Rumors can only help us. Now, remember, this baby is ill. You may become so, or I, who can know? Who will be next?"

"Perhaps Carlos?" Rose suggested hopefully.

"Not likely, since I cannot get to him." With a quick kiss, Caty dismissed Rose to fetch water and make the tent ready for one who was ill. After Rose had gone, Caty fed Tabor and smiled at how heartily he ate. Her breasts were sore and swollen, and now glad to be rid of the milk the child needed. So intent was she with the child, she failed to hear the approach of Sir Nathan until he called out. Startled, she removed Tabor from her breast, to the child's great dissatisfaction. She bade Sir Nathan enter and then commenced walking around the tent with Tabor, attempting to soothe the agitated child.

Sir Nathan stood at the entrance, watching. Warily, he said, "Lady, Lord Carlos bids me see to the child. He fears the child may have the plague. Is this so, lady?"

Caty had to hide a smile. "Please come in, Sir Nathan. You come alone?"

"Yes, you have been set afar, for fear you infect the rest of the men." Sir Nathan had no intention of coming closer.

Caty hesitated briefly. She trusted this man, and had to place her life and the life of her son in his hands. "The child ails not, sir. I wish Carlos to believe he does. You cannot become ill with this child, Sir Nathan. He is not happy, he is tired, and he would rest, but he is not ill with the plague. Please take this message to Carlos: tell him the child is with fever, crying, and I am walking with the babe . . . that I await water to bathe him in, to try to keep the fever at bay. Can you tell me where we are?"

From outside came a shout from Carlos, who evidently stood a ways off from the tent. "Sir Nathan! Tell me of the child."

Sir Nathan nodded to Caty, backed out, and left. Caty put Tabor to breast again, knowing full well her brother would never come near the tent if he thought she or the child were with the plague. In fact, she would try to be certain his men thought so, also. Perhaps they would leave. Tabor finished eating and cried impatiently while Caty walked with him. When Rose returned with water, Caty bathed the child. As she laid the child down to sleep, she gave him several drops of something from a vial she removed from her bodice. Caty smiled at her sleeping son.

Morning found her walking with the child again, as he was up much of the night. The men near their tent could attest to the child's cries. Finally, she moved to the darker, quieter recesses of the tent, farthest from the entrance. Putting him to breast, she sang softly. When she had laid him down to rest, she stepped outside the tent. Any movement was watched by nearly everyone in camp. She could feel the fear. Perhaps this was not such a good idea. What would she do if someone decided to get rid of them, to save their own lives? *No matter*, she thought. *What is done, is done.*

THIRTY-EIGHT

RHYS AND HIS MEN RODE as long as they could. The horses were white with foam as they thundered into the Highlander's settlement, where the clansman was making ready to move his household to Dermoth Castle. As Lord Rhys's party approached, the Highlander emerged from the settlement to meet them. "Lord, what brings you here?" he asked. "You ride as if Lucifer himself were chasing you."

"My friend, I need fresh horses. Caty has been kidnapped. Her captor is believed to have one hundred and fifty armed men. They plan to take her to sea. I ride to stop them."

Instantly, the Highlander was in motion. "Change mounts with these men," he yelled to his clan. "Ready my horse; I take fifty with me. We eat, then leave. Move!" Men were already moving about quickly, taking gear off the horses, bringing other animals out. "Come, Lord Dermoth, inside. We have plenty of food ready. I and my men leave with you when you are ready." Lord Rhys and Bruce were led inside a small castle surrounded by bothies. There were no defensive walls or mounds around the area.

Rhys grasped the Highlander's shoulder. "You do not have to do this. The horses would be all that I ask."

"I do have to do this, lord. Your lady is our lady also, lord. My land and clan are yours. We ride together. Come, tell me about the one who has taken such a prize as Lady Caty."

As they ate, Rhys briefly filled the Highlander in. He did not reveal that Caty's kidnapper was her brother. He did not feel Carlos was much of a brother, anyway. When all had eaten, the men filed out, mounted, and rode.

"You stable fine horses, Highlander," Rhys said. "None look familiar." Forays into surrounding holdings were common, to take stock, women, and supplies.

The Highlander grinned. "They better not. If they do, you've been riding in fair England, I would say." Clearly, this stock came from south of the border.

"Where do we ride, brother?" Bruce asked.

"We ride to Fort William," said Rhys. "I would know if he has been there or about. He would not take her south—too many people."

The Highlander called to one of his men. "Ride to Clan Magnus. I would know if anyone has passed his lands. Such a band would be hard to hide. Do not wander like a maiden, boy; I would know tonight!" After a short while, he called another, repeating the instructions but giving a different destination. "Now we should have both sides covered. If they have been by, we will know."

With the Highlander's men and his, Rhys now had nearly two hundred men. It had to be enough. His only chance would be to keep Carlos's party from boarding any vessel. Surprise would have to be his trump. The men rode rapidly, taking little-known trails. After two days, they learned from one of the Highlander's returned riders that Carlos and his men had indeed passed through, and not long ago. They were moving slow. Slower than Rhys would have thought. Maybe, just maybe . . .

When several of Carlos's men became ill, as well as some of Sir Nathan's men, Carlos instructed that the camp be moved farther away from Caty and Sir Nathan. He made no attempt to leave without them, nor did he talk with Caty.

Walking into the brush, Caty relieved herself. After, leaning over a stream, she washed her hands and face. Her reflection looked haggard. Sadly, she sat back on her heels. Time was passing with no sign of help. She closed her eyes, praying. *I just cannot get onto a boat. Rhys will never find us. What happened to Carlos? He is evil, now. I fear for my life, and Tabor's.*

She got up and walked slowly upstream and past brush lining the bank. She detected movement behind her; it was so swift she was not certain she really saw something. Then the man's breath brushed her neck. Caty froze. "Lady, you will stop leaving without your husband's knowledge or permission. For shame."

She gasped at the voice. "Rhys?" she murmured weakly, hoping against hope.

"Speak not, nor move, lest you give us away. The child is ill?"

"No, it is a trick. We await your order, my lord," Caty whispered. She thrilled to feel his hand on her waist.

"Back to the tent," he said. "I will see you again soon." In a breath he was gone, but she stayed as he found her. Composing herself, she prayed no one had seen their meeting. She walked calmly back to the tent.

Inside, Rose was busy tidying up. She spoke to Caty without looking at her. "I slipped the potion to several of the men with Carlos as well as some with Sir Nathan. Felt bad about Sir Nathan's men, I did, m'lady. Still, your reason is sound, it is."

"Rose, I love you, you know. You are like a sister to me. Much more than just a lady-in-waiting. Someday, our lives will be quiet. You'll see."

Rose smiled at her friend doubtfully. "Whatever you say, lady."

Sir Nathan had years of experience. It served him well. When Rhys caught up with them the day before, Sir Nathan knew it. He felt certain Rhys would move this night. They were now close to the sea and Rhys would not chance losing his wife and son aboard a ship. Sir Nathan had expected Rhys to come, just as he expected there would be a fight. This time he felt no loyalty to the man he rode for, nor to the cause that that man represented. He did feel a great deal of regret at getting caught up in a snare such as this.

He had many long hours to think on it and make a decision. Carlos's fear of the plague proved strong. Taking advantage of the distance between his camp and Carlos's camp, Sir Nathan quietly spoke with his men. "You are my brothers in battle and peace. I have led you successfully for many raids and wars and would keep leading men such as you. This situation, I cannot abide. We change sides this night. We truly save Lady Caty and the babe. I will give the order. We move on Carlos this night."

He left them, pleased at the nods of approval from each man. They had not the stomach for Carlos either. When darkness was full upon them, Sir Nathan walked around the farther edge of his camp and paced behind the larger tent housing his men. Just as Sir Nathan had planned, Rhys found him.

"You keep bad company these days, Sir Nathan." Rhys's voice came from behind. Nathan could feel the tip of the sword at his back.

"That I have, but this day it is done. Your lady and child are safe, now. I would join you in your work this night, Rhys. I have not the heart for what I see in our friend. He is gone mad. He knows no reason, nor does he care for anyone, even himself or his friend, Henry. My men are ready for whatever you need from us."

By this time Nathan had turned to face Rhys. Years ago, they fought together more than once, for causes not well understood. Then it had mattered little. They had been young, and it was a long time ago. This was different. This time there was a clear cause and a dangerous enemy. Sir Nathan would fight for the life of the daughter of his old commander. Rhys fought for his family. Together, Rhys and Nathan devised a plan.

This time Sir Nathan entered Caty's tent without announcing himself. "Make ready to leave, lady. Stay inside, no matter what you hear. I will come for you. Take only what you can carry. Leave with no one but me, understand?"

"I do," Caty responded calmly.

"Be ready, we move quickly."

"Sir, some of your men are become ill. 'Tis not the plague, of that I am certain."

He nodded, then silently slipped into the dark shadows. Caty could feel her heart pound. Rhys was here; he had found her. Again, he would save her.

Hastily, she touched the tiny silver cross at her neck. *Please keep him safe, God. He is the hope of my son.*

Rose had already begun to pack what they would need for the child. Taking only what they could carry meant taking only those things necessary for Tabor. By now, he was sleeping soundly, and no longer feverish. She woke him gently and fed him again. He slept. "Just like a man," Rose observed. "Get food in his little belly, warm him, and he is with the angels. If he knew how, he would snore."

Packed and ready, they played the game of waiting. Caty could hear nothing for a long time; then the battle began. It sounded not like a field battle, but it was a fight just the same. Random shots rang out at first. Soon, the air was alive with gunfire from Carlos's camp. Then men yelled and Carlos could be heard above the mayhem, shouting orders. "Kill them all! Save the queen and her child! Kill them all! To the boats!"

Caty met Rose's eyes across the tent. They could not board! Yet, she had promised Sir Nathan she would wait. Rose leaned closer to Caty. "I am going to walk. These old legs get stiff, you know. Just a bit."

"Take care, Rose," Caty cautioned, as her eyes met Rose's. "Stay close." Rose waddled out of the tent. Caty might have need to stay put, but Rose did not. Rose intended to be certain Caty had help. If Carlos got to Caty first, Rose intended to let someone know.

THIRTY-NINE

BRUCE RODE THROUGH THE HEAVY mist that shrouded the shore. With the tide at its highest, a boat would have little trouble coming all the way up the finger. Bruce knew these waters well. "Blessing though this damned mist is for Rhys, I may lose the ship," he muttered. Moving slowly along the banks, he had to push the horse to continue.

The land was marshy and difficult to navigate. His horse struggled through the muck. Thick fog was moving into the bay and up the finger. Bruce doggedly moved forward. Scouring the finger carefully, he finally saw what he sought. The ship was well lit, casting an eerie glow through the fog as it danced with the water's movement. Bruce was certain the ship would be armed, made for speed, and well manned. After tying his horse inland, he removed his sword and rifle and held them aloft. He stepped off the bank and began sloshing slowly through the marsh and toward the ship. Deeper water soon demanded he swim. Moving quietly, he kept the distant glow in sight. Dressed in black and barely stirring the water as he swam, he was invisible even without the fog. It took little time to reach the vessel. Moving against the side, he rounded the bow and came up directly beneath it. He edged along the ship until he found the massive rope tied to the anchor. Pulling himself up, he hung precariously while he secured his weapons. Then slowly, hand over hand, he inched his way upward.

When he reached the anchor window, he pulled himself up and stood. Peering over the side of the ship, he smiled in satisfaction. His memory had served him well. He found the door to the captain's quarters secured, but quickly popped the lock and entered. The cabin was empty and dark. Feeling his way around, he slipped out of sight.

It was not long before the captain returned to his quarters, his first mate following closely behind. The captain slammed the door and angrily addressed the first mate. "Does he think to keep us here all night? We would do well to be on our way soon. I care not for the thought of finding ourselves with the English and Scots breathing down our bow. The tide is going down. It'll be up early morning. I wait until the tide is up, then no more. Alert the men. We sail at first morning light, Carlos or no. Is that clear?"

"Aye, I have a bad feeling about this," the man agreed.

When the captain was again alone, he sat down heavily at his desk. "Would have been better played to stay in Milan," he muttered to himself. "Some things are beyond money."

"True, captain, true. Things like one's life, perhaps?" Bruce's voice was light.

The captain jumped up but sat down again quickly, the point of Bruce's sword tipping his throat. "I think, sir," Bruce continued, "you would do well to shove off now. One word and the English and the Scots will be all over you and your crew like fleas. You and I both know your ship stands little chance. If you stay too long, the low tide will trap you. How easy is it to replace your crew? Or your ship, I might add? Perhaps you will do the best thing and leave now?"

The captain eyed his adversary warily. "Bruce Dermoth. Many a night I have cursed you. Leaving me in unfamiliar waters without so much as a good steersman. How goes it with you, lad?"

Bruce sheathed his sword and sat down, laughing. "It goes well, at least as well as it can go for one such as I. How come you to know this man, Carlos?"

"He came to me with the right weapons—money and the promise of a new ship. At my age, I get fooled seldom. This may be one time. The man is not on the same earth as you and I, Bruce. He talks normal one day, then is like one I have never met. I agree with you, and shall readily leave this cursed place. Let me take you to shore; then we leave. I have only two questions: Is the lady in question really his sister, and is she really as beautiful as I hear?"

"The answer to both is yes, my friend. Her heart is just as beautiful, but belongs to my brother. Lucky for him." Leaning against the captain's desk, Bruce asked, "Would you know why he takes her?"

"For certain, I overheard his talk with the man that stays with him. She is to claim her crown, but there is no crown—never has been. That man, Henry, pressed Carlos for an explanation. Carlos as much as admitted it. Don't think Henry understood. He doesn't seem too bright, that boy Henry. Carlos sails for the Outer Hebrides. He thinks to keep her hidden there. I say again, Bruce: he is mad and getting worse. Come, let me get you to shore."

"No need; I will go the way I came. Go with God, friend. When you decide to quit the seas, come look for me. I can use one such as you." The men stood and embraced, and Bruce took his leave. By the time he reached the shore, the ship's lights were moving beyond his sight and into the fading mist. Mounting his steed, he turned toward the fight he knew was now in progress. He dreaded it. Fog, mist, and the late hour would make this a tough confrontation. On the other hand he smiled to himself. Nothing like a good fight to warm a man's heart. He quickened the horse's pace.

Rhys had placed his men around the perimeter of the encampment. The Highlander had moved beyond, and waited for anyone trying to escape. Sir Nathan pulled his men between Carlos and the shore. Now, as the melee raged, Carlos ran to Caty's tent. "Come now, we leave, sister. Quick, take the babe and follow. The boat is waiting." His face was flushed, his eyes were wild, and he clearly intended to take the child.

Caty needed to stall him somehow. "I will not come with you, Carlos. If you must go, then you go alone. I stay here where I belong. I belong not to the country you represent, if indeed you represent one. Leave me in peace, brother."

He listened to her in silence, then bitterly responded, "Just as I thought. No matter, I care little what you do or not. But the child comes with me." He lunged toward her. Caty sidestepped him, but he caught her arm, nearly pulling Tabor loose. The baby began crying as Caty fought fiercely to pull herself and her child away. Swinging his arm around, he pushed his knife to her throat. "I care not if you live or die, woman. The choice is yours. Hand the babe to me."

"Will you care for him, Carlos?" Caty asked, crying, trying to buy time. She prayed Rose had been able to get help.

"I can offer him more than you or your man. I will give him a kingdom. Now loosen your hand and give him to me." Carlos was cold; an empty gleam filled his eyes.

Caty turned to give the wailing child to Carlos. Throwing his knife aside, he grabbed at the babe. Caty jerked Tabor back and turned to run. As she did, she was pulled back and pushed down, away from Carlos. Rhys stood between her and the madman. "How nice of you to visit, sir," Carlos sneered. He pulled out his sword and began the deadly dance he was so well known for.

"Rhys, they say he kills many with that weapon!" Caty cried.

"Not this time," Rhys said, low and quiet. The men sparred around the tent, and Caty was forced to move to stay out of harm's way. She watched the fight with her heart in her throat. Sir Nathan and several men came running. Entering the tent, they stopped in their tracks, unable to move in on either man. Carlos fought with the reckless abandon of one who thought little of his own life. Rhys fought as one who would save his family.

"You fight me now, Carlos? We fought together for the Crown. Now, you have no crown, no loyalty, no homeland. 'Tis not a good way to die, my friend," Rhys taunted.

"I have a place, and you are not my friend. You broke your promise to me. A friend does not do the things you have done," Carlos replied bitterly.

"No, Carlos, I kept my promise. I promised to take your sister for you. That I did. I promised to keep her safe. That I do, also. Even now. You are evil, Carlos. You have stepped into the sand, and now you sink." With that, he flicked the sword from Carlos's hand. Moving like lightning, Carlos drew his dagger and tried to throw it. Rhys dove forward and thrust his sword deep into Carlos. The man stood, a look of astonishment on his face. Slowly, he sank to his knees, blood pouring from his wound. Rhys pulled the sword out. With his foot, he pushed Carlos over. He turned to see his wife watching, her face contorted with horror. His heart went out to Caty. To have gone so long without any contact with her family, then have things turn this way. He looked back at the bloody scene.

"Come, Caty," Rhys said. He crossed the tent and folded her within his arms. "It is over. His men have already gone. Sir Nathan comes with us." The babe cried, Caty clung to Rhys, and Rose stood transfixed. Thomas stepped forward.

"Come, lady. We must leave quickly, lest we become entangled in the legal aspects of this incident. Lord, we await your command to leave. Travel tonight would be most advisable." Caty's eyes met Thomas. The tears were beginning to fill them.

"I agree. Come, Caty, we must leave now." Rhys gently pushed her toward the tent entrance.

"Please, Rhys," Caty whispered. "He is my brother. He once loved me, I am certain of it." As she spoke, she handed Tabor to his father, crossed to the lifeless body, knelt, and kissed the mouth, now relaxed and without the look of bitterness that had so long been a part of his life. "Forgive him, Father. Give him peace," she whispered. Tears fell as she walked back to Rhys. With his arm around his wife and son, he led the way to Caty's horse.

The men stood around silently. Mounting with Rhys's help, she looked down at her husband. "That man was not the man my parents would have raised."

Wordlessly, Rhys mounted and they moved out, headed for the Highlander's castle. The Northern Highlands would offer more protection than Dermoth, should anyone choose to pursue them. By this time, the battle might have drawn attention from authorities that may have been in the area. Little Tabor settled down and eventually slept in Caty's arms. She held him close to her breast. *Let me never forget how precious this life is, Lord. I came so close to losing him. Would that I remember that fear, always,* Caty prayed. The time wore on, and in spite of her resolve, Caty began to sway in the saddle. She longed for rest, but this night would see none.

The contingent had moved far beyond the township and onto a deserted road. Travel was slow but steady. Rhys was intent on putting distance between his party and the scene behind; none would be around to speak to the dead men left lying on the ground.

Caty struggled to stay awake through the night, and her mind ran ceaselessly over the ordeal she had just seen. Her thoughts were interrupted by the sounds of approaching men.

FORTY

"LORD RHYS?" THE MAN AT the head of the approaching party called. "Lord Rhys, I would speak with you." The man rode toward Rhys and his party. He was an older man, well spoken, at ease in the saddle, and confident. He and his men were armed but not threatening. He had a sense of urgency about him. Every man and every horse wore colors not seen in Scotland.

Rhys stopped his party. Silently, he waited. Caty had been moved into the middle of the troop, for safety. At once wide awake, she stared in disbelief at the standard flying above the other contingent. Barely visible in the early dawn, there was no mistaking its owner. Without taking her eyes from the approaching men, she said, "Thomas, you must tell Rhys we are met by Lord Lenitti from Tuscany." Her uncle had once fought under the same colors she saw now. Caty and her mother had stayed with Lord Lenitti and his family one Christmas, when her father was away.

The men talked at length. After a while, Rhys called to Bruce and Sir Nathan. Together, they talked. At last, Rhys came to Caty. "This man comes from King Marcus of Tuscany. They do battle with the French, soon. I have fought with one of the king's captains, the Duke of Lucca, more than once. Lucca has asked the king to send for me. He asks I come to his aid once more. I have agreed to do so." Caty felt a knot begin in her stomach. "I would ask that you go with me, lady. You can stay at the court of King Marcus. He is going to lead his men. Bruce will return to our home with the Highlander. Sir Nathan has asked to come with me." He stopped and gently touched her face. "I would not be without you, wife."

Caty nodded. "Wherever you would go, I go, Rhys." She held her small son closer. A crooked smile softened her voice as she said, "It seems I would take to the sea after all."

Lord Lenitti and the men with him joined Rhys and Sir Nathan. Bruce kissed his sister-in-law good-bye, held his nephew for a moment, and then, with another long look at Caty, rode with Rhys a distance from the horses and men milling around. The two spoke for a long period. Grasping his brother's hand, Rhys bid Bruce farewell. Rhys wheeled his horse, called to his men, and moved the troop out, bound for the docks and a waiting ship. Lord Lenitti rode closer to Caty. "You have grown, Lady Caty. You look just like your mother, you know." He smiled at her, his voice wistful.

Caty reached out and touched his arm. "What a wonderful surprise to see your kind face again, sir."

"It is good we will have time to visit aboard the ship. I shall see you then, lady." He took her hand and squeezed it gently, before moving away to his men.

The journey to Italy was much more pleasant than Caty remembered her last trip to be. Lord Lenitti visited frequently with Rhys and Caty, sharing time and wine. Caty and Rose were the only women on board, and every effort was made to make both comfortable. Rhys spent every night with his wife. Caty would have been quite happy if the trip never ended. But it did end. They finally docked at Piobino, a busy port on the Tuscany coast, just ahead of a horrific storm. After bustling to the nearest inn, every soul hunkered down to wait it out. The wind cried with anger, dashing everything in its path with freezing rain. At last, it broke.

The long trek to King Marcus Cassini and his court was undertaken with Caty the only one of the party in low spirits. The old feeling of dread had returned. As she had often noted before, her "gift" was more a burden.

Upon arrival at King Marcus's court, it was clear the king prepared for battle. Every person entering the walls was challenged. Men filled the court, readying weapons and supplies. Word had already reached the king that Lord Rhys traveled with his family. The women and Tabor were escorted away from the mayhem at court by an emissary of the king, who carried a personal note from King Marcus expressing his apologies for not seeing Caty himself. Also in the note were instructions to the emissary to be certain every need Caty might have was met. *Perhaps he would take this burden I feel from me,* Caty thought. Rhys and Sir Nathan were escorted to the king's council by Lord Lenitti.

Before three days had passed, the king's legion was leaving. King Marcus's colors now billowed in the wind. His men were bolstered by the reputation of Rhys and Sir Nathan's men. Caty's heart was heavy, but she smiled as she kissed Rhys good-bye, yet again.

In this place, Caty found the time passed quickly. Her son kept her busy. The ladies of the court played with him and entertained Caty. "He'll come back, m'lady," Rose assured her.

After four weeks of hard fighting, the French were defeated. Rhys had returned, as had King Marcus and most of his men. Sir Nathan pledged allegiance to King Marcus, and would stay there to secure the rest of his borders.

The first night following their return, the court was wild with celebration. Caty feared for Rhys, though. He had developed a nagging cough. He laughed at her, saying it was nothing. Caty tried to put it out of her mind, choosing to focus on his safe return instead.

As the celebration carried on, King Marcus watched his court, grateful to be at peace for a while again. His eyes roamed over the women, as usual. His own wife had died three years earlier, and although he tested the waters continually, he was still thirsty. He caught sight of Caty. She was dressed in a deep russet gown that was gathered at her tiny waist and flowed gently to the floor. The line was soft and smooth, not the usual rough brocade he saw frequently in court. Her hair was pulled atop her head, and shone in the candlelight. She was tiny, lively, and smiled frequently at Rhys. "Lord Rodolfo," King Marcus said to the man seated by his side, "tell me, who is Lord Dermoth's wife?"

"His wife, Your Grace? The daughter of Lord Tabor. You can't think on her, sire. Her husband just fought for you," Rodolfo laughed. Lord Rodolfo knew the king well; Marcus would not cross the line—yet.

"This is true. I would not insult him, nor myself, that way. But she is a beauty." He watched her most of that night.

The next few days, King Marcus found himself missing Lady Dermoth. She was never about court. Lord Dermoth was not around either. The second week, King Marcus asked for Lord Dermoth, assuming he had gone with Sir Nathan. His page reported the lord was ill, and that his wife was at his side.

"He looks to be dying, sire," the page reported.

Marcus frowned. "This is true? Send my doctor to him at once. How is it I have not been told this before?" Angrily, he rose to see Lord Dermoth himself.

The physician knocked on Lord Dermoth's door. "The king sends me to your service, sir." He entered to find the lord barely alive. "How is he ill?"

Caty looked into the old physician's kindly eyes. Her own eyes were reddened. She was exhausted. "He coughs, is feverish, and has not spoken in over a day."

"He looks to be dying," said the physician, moving to examine Rhys.

Caty's heart was breaking, though the physician's conclusion did not surprise her. *How could this happen?* She had no idea how he could have gotten so ill, so fast. No matter; he did and was. The words he had spoken last, the day previous, were of his love for her and his son. Now, she sat waiting for the end. She had seen death many times before, but never had it seemed so unfair.

The physician could do nothing more than what Caty had already done. He shook his head, sadly. He never would grow accustomed to meaningless dying. Fighting, yes—but this was not from some wound. He prayed whatever caused Lord Dermoth's suffering would not leave the room. The old physician patted Caty's hand. "Call for me, lady. I will do all I can for you."

King Marcus entered the chamber and stood behind Caty, watching the scene. This man, Rhys, had come to his aid. If his physician had been told earlier, perhaps the man would not be dying. His anger was sharpened by what he witnessed. Turning on his heel, he left to deal with whoever had let this go for so long. The physician followed and called after the king in the hallway outside. "He dies, Your Highness. Soon. It is not the plague." Even as he said it, the old physician prayed he was right. "He has a coughing illness. He cannot breathe. But he does not show signs of plague."

Back in the room, Caty could no longer watch Rhys suffer so. He moaned whenever he was touched; he grew more feeble by the hour, yet could not rest. Weakly, he gripped her hand. His eyes were filled with love as Caty bent to tenderly kiss his lips. She moved close to his ear and whispered, "I love you, Rhys. Please watch over me from heaven, my beloved." His eyes followed her, and he nodded. Caty fought the tears that threatened to wash over them both. Adding a potion to help him rest, she spooned warm wine down him. Rhys finally slept. Slowly, his breathing ceased. Caty collapsed upon his bed, weeping. When one of the ladies standing near touched her shoulder, Caty shook her head. "Leave us now. I would mourn my husband."

Hours later, she gathered herself together, calling for Rose.

"The king has offered a lord's burial, near the castle, lady," said Rose.

Numbly, Caty nodded. If only she could take him home. If only . . . It would be impossible. No ship would allow the body of a man who had died with a fever and cough on board. Caty hardly spoke during the next several days. She spent long hours with her son during the day and long hours weeping during the night. She wanted to take Tabor home, back to Dermoth Castle. Perhaps they could leave soon. It was not to be.

One week after Rhys's death, Tabor became ill. He awoke during the night with the fever and diarrhea that caused so many infant deaths. Caty did all she knew to do for her son. The old physician could add nothing. Tabor did not improve. *Is it not enough I give my husband up?* Caty pleaded to the heavens. *Please do not take my son also.* Even as she prayed, she realized it would not be as she wanted.

Caty held Tabor during the last dreary night. His fever would not go down, in spite of all her care and herbs. He too was dying. Holding him in her arms, she rocked the child. He nestled closely, sleeping fitfully. By afternoon, he had ceased to breathe. Rhys was not a week dead; now she would bury her son. She held the infant, weeping quietly. She had no desire to live, no desire to go on with this awful pain in her soul. Night was coming on, but Caty was not aware of the darkness outside. She was surrounded with darkness. A black, ugly darkness.

FORTY-ONE

ON THE AFTERNOON OF TABOR'S death, Rose left her mistress to find King Marcus. She timidly entered his court. As she approached his table, talking stopped. In the silence, Rose walked toward the king. One of the attendants had risen to remove her, but the king ordered her forward. "What brings you to court, Lady Rose?"

"Lady Dermoth's child is dead," she replied. "Would you have someone to help her, sire? Would you allow your priest to see to the lady, sire? She is saddened unto death herself." The king was stunned.

"The child or her husband?" the king frowned. Had he heard correctly?

"The child, Your Grace. You were at the burial of her husband," Rose replied patiently.

"His men have gone?" the king asked, looking around his court.

"All but Sir Nathan's, Your Highness. Lord Rhys ordered the others away when he became ill."

King Marcus remembered the men leaving. He had not been at court then, but his orders were to allow the men their leave whenever they so desired. He rewarded them well for their part in his service. He never questioned their leaving, even as he secretly hoped Rhys would stay, with Caty. Now, it seemed the poor lady had even more tragedy dealt to her. Rising, he left court and followed Rose to Caty's rooms. He watched Caty hold the child, singing softly. Numb, she never noticed his entrance. Rose touched her hand. "The king is here, my lady."

Caty looked at him with immeasurable sadness in her eyes. Marcus went to her; gently he touched the child, now cold. "Lady, the child is gone," he said with kindness, but his heart burned with anger. *How could this happen again to this lady, and I knew it not? Someone will surely pay!* he raged to himself.

"I know. I would hold him a while longer. He was my only child. There will be no more. He goes to his father." Her eyes filled with tears again. She resumed rocking with the babe in her arms, singing softly to him. After watching her for a moment, the king left and immediately sent for his priest.

The priest, Father Franco, brought an older woman from his household with him to Caty's rooms. Together, they were able to take the child from her. The next days were nearly more than Caty could bear. She didn't believe she could have hurt more than when Rhys died; now she knew that was incorrect. Her pain was beyond description. She felt a gaping hole in her heart.

Caty stayed in her rooms. She carried Tabor's small blanket around, slept in Rhys's shirt, and stood for hours at the window looking down on the gardens. Night after night she walked the floor, weeping. At his request, the king heard regularly from Rose regarding Lady Dermoth's welfare. The days slid into weeks, and those into months. Still, she mourned. At the king's order, she was provided every comfort, but was left in peace.

One morning, five months after Tabor's death, Caty dressed and quietly walked down the stairs, out into the gardens. Despondent, she walked the paths. *I find myself alone again, in a foreign land, without any direction. Rose is feeble. Soon she too will be gone. I will go back to Scotland,* Caty resolved. *I cannot stay here. 'Tis far too sad.* That afternoon, she requested an audience with the king.

As she entered his council, the room fell silent. Caty was now painfully thin. Dressed in black with her hair pulled back severely, she appeared even more so. A murmur rippled through the men gathered around the table. Although sorrow was etched on her face, she was still beautiful. Her golden eyes, surrounded with thick black lashes and underscored by dark circles, were deep pools against the pale tan of her skin. Sadness had given her a gentle grace born of deep faith. She stood quietly upon reaching the middle of the room now opened to her.

"Come, Lady Caterina," Marcus said kindly, rising to face her. "What can I do for you?" He could not remember seeing anyone like her before. Even in sorrow, she carried herself with dignity.

Caty spoke quietly, but without hesitation. "I would return to my home."

The king frowned. "Not yet, my lady. You have gone through a terrible battle in your own way. You must mend first. I will not consent to your leaving in such a state. Perhaps by summer's end. In two weeks' time, I ask you to attend court. You must be out and about with people. These people are saddened for you. They will help you walk the path you have been given."

Caty was speechless. She had not expected him to deny her travel, and certainly not to demand she attend court. She took a deep breath, her mind struggling to understand. *He cannot mean to keep me here against my will. He cannot deny me safe passage.* Admittedly, it would not be best discussing the matter further in front of everyone. Slowly, she raised her eyes to meet the king's. As she looked at him, she felt anger begin to fill her mind. Her eyes narrowed as she tried to think of some reply. At a loss, she simply curtsied and left court, head held high. Marcus watched her leave, noting her determined look, her simple elegance, and her silence.

They will never know how I feel, Caty thought as she marched back to her rooms. *How could he make me stay? How can he not let me leave? I've given both my husband and son to this place. I owe him nothing.* Her anger gave her resolve, yet back in her rooms, she felt defeated. Rose brushed her hair, now grown long, and readied a bath for her. Caty sank into the tub, wondering if she could ever get beyond what she now carried. "I will defy him, Rose. He cannot keep me here against my will." Her voice sounded more confident than she felt.

In the morning, she was greeted by a knock at her door. Rose answered the door, only to find a troupe of women outside. The king had sent them to wait on her. Caty sent them away. She barely had the presence of mind to care for herself and Rose, let alone a crowd of strangers. Early afternoon, a knock came again. Rose bowed to the man standing outside, and ushered him in. He was a well-dressed man, of medium height. His thinning hair was gray, as was his neatly trimmed beard. He carried himself with self-confidence and dignity.

When he spoke, his voice was calm and even. "My lady, I am the head of the king's council. My name is Sir Zonti. The king would know why you refuse his offer of help."

Caty replied simply, "Because they are not needed." She sat patiently, waiting for him to leave.

The king's man studied Caty. He felt as if an answer had been given only to humor him. "The king insists you have at least five more ladies to care for you. Your own lady-in-waiting is special, but she is aged. It is unfair to expect her to do all things for you. The women will return this afternoon. Choose five from the eight. Please let me know if I can be of further service to you, my lady." He positioned himself just inside her doors, a determined expression on his face.

Sighing, Caty rose, studying the man as he studied her. She realized she would have a fight on her hands. Without waiting for a reply, he at last nodded respectfully and left. As promised, eight young women came to her door several hours later. Caty sent them away. When they had gone, she had Rose start a fire for her and light the candles. She helped Rose clean up the quarters. Pulling a chair to the fire, Caty sipped a glass of wine and waited. Shortly, a knock at her door announced her visitor.

It was the head of the king's council again. From the look on his face, Caty could tell he was set on having his way this time. "Perhaps none of the women were to your liking, lady?" he began.

"Oh, I liked them all, but I'll have no extra help. Please thank His Majesty for me." She stood and walked him to the door. "I can care for myself quite well."

He left, reddened and angry, but more determined. Just as she was readying for bed, someone knocked at her door again. "This is becoming like the market, Rose," said Caty dryly. "Perhaps we should set booths up and sell something." Opening the door, Rose found the same man standing outside a third time.

"Please, Sir Zonti, I was just about to have a glass of wine with warmed apples," Caty said before he could speak. "Won't you join me? Since you must come so often, we should get to know one another." Caty stood and graciously indicated the chair opposite her. He was taken aback. The lady stood before him in her gown and robe, clearly ready for bed. He had not intended to enter her chambers.

"I cannot stay, Lady Caterina. I only—"

"Surely, you have no duties this late," Caty interrupted. "Rose, call the guards stationed down the hall and bid them come to my chambers at once. We wouldn't want any gossip. I'll stand outside in the hall until you return." Immediately, Rose waddled down the hall and Caty stepped through the doorway.

When the guards returned with Rose, Caty led them into her room. "Please stand inside," she said, "to witness there is nothing improper between myself and the councillor." With that, she sat down in her chair and gracefully waved to the remaining seat.

The poor man was unable to find a way out of the situation, and so sat. Rose brought him a drink. Caty waited to speak, aware of the man's increasing discomfort. He gave no indication that he intended to start the oncoming battle. "How many women wait on you, sir?" Caty asked him. One of the guards snickered.

"Only my wife and her staff," he replied gruffly.

"I see. Well, as you are aware, I have no husband, no child, and no duties. I have one lady-in-waiting. That is all I will allow in these quarters. Please thank the king for me, but I stand firm."

"So does he," the councillor replied under his breath, with resignation.

"Does he now? We shall see. Anyway, where would I put those girls? This space he has allowed me to occupy is just my size. When I have *mended*, as he called it, I will be leaving anyway. The question of help will be a dull point indeed." Now Caty stood.

The councillor rose to leave. Despite their differences, he found he liked her. She had wit, her actions were kind, and she was easy to be around. He smiled at her, shaking his head, "We've only had three rounds, my lady. His Majesty is quite able to go longer."

"As am I," Caty responded, nodding to him.

At the end of the third day, Caty answered her door, expecting to see the councillor, who was now becoming a friend. She found instead an angry king. He stood in the hallway, hands on his hips, a scowl on his face, and tenacity in his eyes. "Lady Caterina, you have worn my patience thin. I do not ask that you take more staff; I *order* you to do so. Furthermore, you will be moved to larger chambers in the morning. I would not have you crowded." His voice was level but resolved, its tone denying response.

"But, Your Grace——" Caty started.

"Enough! There will be no more discussion! I will see you at court tomorrow evening. If you are able to spar with me, you are able to attend court. Lady." He bowed, turned, and left.

Caty put her hand to her face. She could think of nothing to do at this point but give in. Closing the door, she and Rose stared at each other in disbelief. Caty began thinking. *He's angry. Yet, I think I might have won. He will send me on my way sooner than he thinks.*

Caty would soon find out how wrong she was.

FORTY-TWO

THE FOLLOWING DAY, SIX YOUNG women appeared at Caty's door just as she was being moved. At the sight of them, she threw up her hands and shrugged. "Come with me. Let's settle in and see how we fare, one with another." The women happily busied themselves with helping her move. Her new rooms were expansive and exquisite. Everything she could possibly need had been provided. *This is not a good sign*, she thought with alarm upon seeing the new quarters. *Why would he put me here? Pray I am wrong.*

Caty attended court that day, as King Marcus had commanded. She knew by their demeanor that the women of the court now deemed her their competition for the king's attention. She was determined to prove them wrong. She went out of her way to visit with the wives and stayed away from any men, thereby allowing the single women free access to the king, while pairing herself with women currently taken.

In the coming weeks, the priest who had been sent to help her months before now began to stop in and visit with her nearly every day. "Father," she said one day, "you cannot imagine how it feels to be able to practice one's faith without worry. It is truly a gift. My poor Scotland has struggled too long with this, as has England."

The old man nodded. "Sadly, lady, we too often take such simple things for granted." He added, as if an afterthought, "You must move on, lady. Life is a gift. You will find love again." He smiled at her kindly.

Caty sighed. "I do not think so, nor do I care to."

"Oh, trust me, child." He nodded sagely. "Trust me. You will." He knew the king well.

Each evening, Caty readied herself to do battle in King Marcus's court. She skillfully avoided the king, stayed with the women, and skirted the men. It was beginning to wear on her. As she dressed once more for the routine, she complained to Rose. "Does he not ever go anywhere? I am sick of court. Every night it is the same thing. I feel like I battle against him."

Rose was quiet. *You do, my lady*, she observed to herself. *You do. I think he might win.*

After nearly a month of cat and mouse, one of Caty's ladies dashed into her rooms. "Oh, lady, come look. You have new gowns being delivered. Beautiful new gowns."

Caty rose, frowning. "Whatever are you talking about, child?" She followed the girl into the foyer of her apartment and stopped suddenly. Before her were several men, each carrying four gowns. The colors and styles were the latest. "What . . . ," she started.

One of the pages smiled. "Where would you like them, lady? They are a gift from the king to you."

"Please tell the king that I thank him, but I have all the gowns I need. Perhaps he could give them to the women of his court." The page stood still, confused. He didn't dare take them back. Surely she jested. But she stood without speaking, holding the door open for them. The little line of crushed pages filed back out carrying the dresses.

The poor councillor was ushered into her quarters shortly thereafter. "Sir Zonti, how nice to see you again. I've missed you."

Zonti bowed, smiling. "I doubt that. How do you fare, lady?" His eyes roamed the room, nodding in approval of her decorating touches.

"I am well. Weary of the game we play, but well," Caty replied.

Zonti chuckled. "Lady, I beg you to take the gowns and keep me out of trouble."

"Fine," she replied. "Please bring them back. I will apologize to your staff." Caty had expected him, and had a plan. This time, when the gowns were delivered, she graciously took them, she begged the understanding of the pages, and everyone was happy. When the men had gone, Caty called her staff together. "Ladies, please each pick a gown. You may not have such things often, but your service has been more than I could have hoped for. Please." With a wave of her hand, she stood aside. Rose moaned and rolled her eyes. "Again, lady? The king will not be pleased," she warned.

Caty realized that one of her women liked the king and would become his mistress if given the chance. Caty already knew well how busy the king was with his personal life. Court gossip indicated he had taken women before. Many women. When Caty's ladies made their appearance at court on this evening, she made certain that this particular girl was close to the king, encouraged her to dance with the lords sitting around the king, and generally left the girl as close to him as she could. King Marcus was not interested. Moreover, he was confused by the gowns floating around the room, none of which contained Lady Caterina. Each evening, the ladies with Caty appeared dressed in new gowns. Meanwhile, Caty nudged the smitten girl to follow the king, hoping something would happen. Eventually, it did.

"Lady Caterina," Lord Rodolfo said to Caty, stepping in front of her as she and her ladies walked to court. Lord Rodolfo was King Marcus's most trusted friend, and his closest adviser. "The king would see you. This way." Deftly, he took her elbow and guided her away from her ladies and to the king. She was taken to a separate room, where the monarch sat with Sir Zonti and several other lords. When Caty entered the room, she realized she would have an audience with an angry king.

"Lady Caterina," King Marcus boomed, "what reason can you give me for the sudden unwanted attention of one of your ladies? Why are you encouraging this behavior? Surely you know this is not acceptable." This time, he really was angry. His flashing black eyes bored into hers. Momentarily intimidated by the men in the room, Caty was quiet.

She recovered quickly. "Sire, please forgive the misdirected plan. It was my intention to be certain you are not alone, as court gossip indicates."

"You listen to court gossip?" Marcus interrupted, his voice intense, eyes flashing.

"Not really," Caty admitted. "It was . . . I'm sorry, Your Highness. It was a bad idea, sire. Please understand it was not done with anything but the best wishes for your evenings," she said lamely. She saw more than one of the men standing about turn to hide smiles. "The girl is quite fond of you, Your Grace, and—"

"Stop! Say no more. This will cease at once!" he ordered, his face reddening. "Do you understand, lady?"

"Certainly, Majesty," Caty responded. "Is there anything else, sire?" She curtsied deeply with her head bowed, hoping fervently the meeting was ending.

"Yes, there is. I have sent at least fifteen new gowns to you, and I see them all over court, but not one on you. Explain, lady." He was now standing over her. While he had her here, he intended to clear the air.

"Of course, Your Grace," Caty began, her mind racing. What could she say without offending him or the men with him? They all had wives, and would undoubtedly share this incident with those women. "I had a problem with each gown, sire," Caty said slowly, planning as she spoke. "I am . . . er . . . smaller than the gowns. I am not accustomed to the food and court and am not as robust as . . ." When she stammered to a stop, several of the king's men had begun to laugh out loud. At first, Marcus scowled at them, but as what she tried to say so delicately sunk in, he too began to laugh.

"Your Majesty, please," Caty scolded him, looking up at him, "I did not intend to make fun of anyone. Please do not think so. The women here have been most gracious to me. I would never say or think anything to make them less than they are. They are very special, each one. I have been in a difficult place in my life recently and have not eaten as well . . ." The harder Caty tried to explain, the more the men laughed. Finally, exasperated, she asked if she might leave them. Waving his hand, as he continued to laugh, he let her go. Relieved, she sped out before he could think of something else.

"King Marcus, I believe you have found your queen," laughed Lord Rodolfo.

"That I have," Marcus agreed. "That I have."

Caty was discouraged. Nothing she had done so far had dissuaded him. He sent a seamstress to her the next morning, along with more new gowns. This time, Caty picked out several, stood for fittings, then allowed the gowns to be tailored for her. The rest she sent back. She could have sown them herself, but better to let him think otherwise.

I have to do something. I think it is time I leave. I think I cannot hold up much longer. Carefully, she devised a plan. She had run away from one man; she could do it again. She was older and more experienced now. This time it would be easier—or so she thought.

FORTY-THREE

ROSE WAS ASLEEP, CATY'S LADIES were in their rooms, and all was quiet. Caty slipped out of bed. Dressing in one of the kitchen maids' frocks, she locked the door to Rose's room and gently opened the door that led into the hallway. At this late hour, the guards were making rounds. She silently stepped down the stairs leading to the door near the kitchen. Once outside, she easily climbed over bushes, sneaked around fences, and finally made her way out the gates. She dared not take a horse. Using shadows for cover, Caty stole away from the castle. No one took notice of a servant girl leaving at this hour. The castle's inhabitants were used to the younger help occasionally leaving at odd hours, especially after dark. The castle activities lent themselves to young love.

Near the light of day, she stopped at an inn and requested to stay in exchange for her labor. The innkeeper's wife welcomed the help. In exchange for one meal a day, Caty worked the tables. Late in the afternoon of her second day, she watched as another woman who worked there talked to her man. Their child was ill; the father expected the baby to die. Caty was moved by the mother's anguish and her own memories. "Perhaps I can be of service. Wait here for me, then take me to the baby, lass," she requested of the woman. In the small room she shared with the female staff, she pulled her bag of herbs from under her cot. She followed the young woman and her husband to a small hut near the edge of town. By morning, the fever had broken, the child rested, and Caty rose to leave. The woman and her husband asked to pay. Caty refused what little they had to offer. *Would that I could have saved my poor son. While there is breath in me, I'll not let another mother suffer what I suffered*, she promised herself.

So it went. Caty moved through the towns, helping the sick people and always edging farther from the king. Word spread of her healing abilities. By the end of the week, she was at the outskirts of yet another town. Spurred by her success in previous jobs, she went to the largest inn. She easily got work, with food and lodging as her pay once again. This arrangement suited her well; she would have no cause to tempt a thief. Sometimes the men eating would tip her. This she was allowed to keep. Caty helped the sick during the nights, worked during the days, and planned where her next move should take her. The work was satisfying, but she had little money. Walking the streets at night, Caty felt the loneliest. *I will be old and wrinkled before I earn enough to make ship for Scotland. Perhaps I could hide away in some small village farther south.*

Caty kept her appearance as plain as she could. Her hair was dirty, her face smudged, legs muddied, and feet barely inside the worn shoes she had. There were so many people ill, she found she could not spend one day at a place without caring for someone. She was so intent on moving along that she failed to realize how word of her help was spreading. The innkeepers she worked for were more than happy to have her do all she could, as long as she did it on her own time. The people asking for help usually gathered at the back, but eventually more were coming into the inns and spending money. Caty was good for business.

A week earlier, a routine meeting of the king's council had once again been interrupted by Rose. She walked slowly toward Marcus, dreading the tale she must tell. The men surrounding the table fell silent. No one had ever interrupted his council before these ladies from Scotland had come to live in the king's castle. Frowning, King Marcus recognized Rose; he could see her concern. One of his attendants moved to intercept her. The king held his hand up. "Stop. Let her speak."

Rose hesitated.

"What have you to say to me?" he asked.

Taking a breath, she spoke at last. "Lady Caterina is gone." Rose had not been around the first time Lady Caty disappeared, from Lord Rhys, but the story was often told around Dermoth Castle. Now she had done it again, but this time in a different land. Rose feared for her mistress's safety.

King Marcus was dumfounded. "Gone? What do you mean?"

"When I awoke this morning, the door to my room was locked from the outside. I could not get out. I called from the window in my room, and one of your pages heard. He came to let me out. I have searched everywhere. The lady is gone." She stood quietly, waiting.

The king was immediately outraged. "Find her!" he bellowed. "There will be reward for the one that tells me of her presence, great suffering for the one who causes her any pain or discomfort. Damnation! What is it with that woman?" His voice rolled across the room. "So help me, I'll have her in chains!"

He stood, grabbed Rose, and headed for Caty's quarters. "How could she get out?" he demanded. "She cannot have gotten far. It is not common for one like her to wander about without escort." As he spoke, he examined her chambers.

"I suspect she will be disguised," Rose noted casually. "She was the first time."

King Marcus stopped walking and stared at Rose. "She's done this before?"

Rose nodded. "Yes. She ran from Lord Dermoth."

"Go on," Marcus prodded.

"He went after her," said Rose. "He found her and brought her back. It took a while, but eventually she came to love him. I suspect she will love you, too, Your Highness. If you can find her."

"I will find her," he responded firmly. His anger built with each resolute step. That afternoon, he and some of his men rode the streets and passageways in the village around his castle. The word was out. There would be good money for information and good money for her protection. For five days, they rode, searching. Nothing. "Surely someone must have seen one such as her roaming!" King Marcus fumed to Rodolfo after a day of seeking her. "A woman alone?"

Eventually, Marcus came to realize that the stories of a powerful healer going from hamlet to farm were about Caterina. They had to be. "She is the one healing and helping," he said to Lord Rodolfo. "It has to be her. I've heard of her healing powers. But where is she? Every place we come to, she has already gone from." Frustration was taking a toll. "We must find her soon, Rudy. I will be the laughing tale of every place the woman passes. When I catch her . . ."

Rudy watched his king and friend. King Marcus was angry, but Rudy could see that he was even more intrigued. "She's really very good at this, sire," Rudy noted. He couldn't help but admire the woman. Alone, no help, and she was making a go of it. "Not bad, lady, not bad," Rudy commented.

Marcus turned sharply to his friend. "'Not bad,' you say? Perhaps we could use her as a spy, after I rein her in." In the throes of this hunt, he was secretly enjoying himself. Provided he caught her before someone harmed her.

On the evening of the eighteenth day, they arrived at another inn. By now, the king and his men were also disguised as mercenaries, knowing full well that if she recognized the king before he caught her, he would lose her again. Besides, Marcus had no taste for his subjects being party to her escaping him, should the chance arise. She had helped so many, they would undoubtedly help her. Marcus was now worried he might not catch her before she crossed into another king's territory.

As Caty went about her work, passing trays of stew and bread to the tables, she deftly avoided the hands of men with too much ale in their bellies. Running an experienced eye over the crowd, she saw that the table at the back had not yet been served. She hoisted a tray, loaded it, and headed for the table. "Come sit with me," a man at the table asked.

Without looking at him, she answered, "I sit with no man, lest the rest of these men go hungry. You know where you can find comfort on a lonely night. Go there with a full belly. You'll be nicer to the woman." She expertly set the stew out.

The man replied quietly, "You misunderstand me. I did not ask, lady."

Shocked, Caty straightened, holding her breath. *I never saw him enter. It can't be*, she reasoned. Slowly, she looked at the man speaking. The moment she saw the face and fiery black eyes, she knew it was him. She was uncertain just what to do. She stared at him, speechless.

"Your hearing is poor? I bid you sit with me." At the command in his voice, several men turned to look at him. Aware he was now gathering unwanted attention, he moved this event along. Pulling the cloak away from his shoulders, he revealed his tunic and blade. He was recognized by several men and the cry went out through the inn: *the king!* Immediately, all men in sight rose and knelt. Caty stood looking around her in amazement.

"I would expect this, I'm certain," said King Marcus. "Only you remain standing, Lady Caterina."

Caty quickly attempted to kneel. He prevented her, instead rising to stand at her side. "Please rise and be seated," he said to the entire inn. When the room was silent again, he spoke. "I present to you your future queen, Lady Caterina. She has chosen to travel amongst you in disguise, to better see the people of this kingdom." Turning to Caty, he continued, "Tell me what you have found, lady."

Horrified, Caty looked from him to the people now staring at her. She was painfully aware of what she looked like. Every eye in the inn was on her. Carefully, desperately trying to think just what to say, she responded, "I have found people helping each other, although they have nothing in common. I have found people without anger, helping to raise children left orphaned. I have seen men and women working side by side, to make a life. I have heard of the love your people have for you, sire." Caty curtsied deeply to him, though her mind repeated, *I'll not let him win! I will not!*

The room erupted in cheers. "Long live King Marcus!"

One young woman stood timidly to speak. "Your Majesty?"

"Yes?" he responded. "Speak child; do not be afraid."

"This woman has healed many. She helps wherever she is found. She is like an angel to us. You have chosen well, sire." Again the inn rocked with cheers. Caty moaned. Marcus heard her, but ignored it. He graciously acknowledged the people who filled the inn, bowing slightly and holding his hands out to them. Instructing his men to pay the owners for each patron's bill, he ordered his coach be brought around and took firm hold of Caty.

Once she had been loaded into a well-guarded coach, he mounted. "Did you save your money, lady?" he called down to her.

"I made no money, Your Grace, else I would have bought a horse. Only the royal physician is rich. Normal healers are poor indeed," she noted wryly. "With a horse, I would have been long gone."

King Marcus laughed. "I see you have not lost your sense of humor. You will need it." With that, he closed the door firmly and rode away. The party moved out, following in his path.

Caty leaned back. The coach was richly appointed and its seats softly padded. *At least I will be warm*, she thought. *I seem to have lost my touch for running away. Perhaps I grow old.* She sighed, leaned back, and eventually dozed off. When the carriage stopped, she looked out to see they had arrived at a smaller castle. Caty rolled her eyes. *He cannot be serious. I am very poorly dressed, dirty, and probably smell. I would bet he knows the lord of this manor. Perhaps I will just stay in here all night.*

The king opened her door. "Lady Caterina," he said, taking her arm. As he marched in with her, Caty knew how awful she looked. She tried to imagine herself dressed in the finest of fashion. She passed the staring inhabitants as gracefully as she could, her face deep red beneath the dirt.

One of the older men in the service of the castle's earl, the head of his guard, eyed her keenly. "Might you be the daughter of Lord Tabor, lady?" he asked quietly as he led the group into the main room.

Caty stopped walking and turned to look at the man. "I am," she replied.

The man watched her carefully. "My name is Captain Tillea. I fought with your father, against the French."

King Marcus heard the exchange. "How did you see this lady was the same?" he asked.

The captain answered quickly, "Her eyes, Your Majesty, and her walk. She has her mother's eyes and looks. Her mother was beautiful, just like the daughter. She too seemed to float when she walked. Although"—he paused, frowning—"she had a different way of dressing." He pointed the way into the castle's great hall.

The king roared with laughter. Caty wanted to shrink. This was all so humil-
iating. She longed to escape to some hidden corner of the castle. Instead, they
were fed and entertained. Graciously, she praised both the actors and food.
She complimented the hostess and the earl. The king behaved as if she were at
his side willingly, paying no mind to her state. When the lady of the manor rose
to take Caty to her rooms, the king leaned close and spoke quietly in Caty's ear.
"If you are not still with me in the morn, these men will forfeit their lives." He
nodded to the men escorting her.

"That's horrible!" Caty gasped, appalled.

"Perhaps, but effective," he responded, without looking at her. Speechless,
Caty turned to follow the lady of the castle out of the great room. Once inside
her room, the lady asked if she could send some women to assist her. Caty
refused the help. When her door was closed, she waited a long moment, then
opened the door to peek out. There were several men standing outside her
door, plainly intent on keeping her inside.

"Please rest assured," she said to them through the cracked door. "I would
not endanger you by leaving. I will be here in the morning." The men nodded
nervously.

The next morning, Caty arose early and sat waiting for someone to come
for her. With the knock on her door, Caty rose to leave. A young woman stood
outside. "The king is ready to leave. Could you tell Lady Caterina he requests
her presence at the gate?" she asked pertly, her eyes moving over Caty's shabby
dress and dirty body, her disgust plainly evident.

Caty smiled back. "You tell her." With that, she stepped past the surprised
girl and made her way downstairs. Outside, refusing to allow the king's treatment of her to change her demeanor, she calmly walked toward her coach,
which was surrounded by King Marcus and his party. Remembering Captain
Tillea from the day before, she stopped before him with respect and smiled.
"I believe my poor mother is turning in her grave about now. Lord Tabor?
Well . . . he is probably laughing." She smiled at the man, noting the twinkle
in his eyes.

"Yes, my lady, on both counts," he responded.

The king watched Caty as she boarded the coach. She handled herself with such assurance and grace. He was now dressed in his usual finery, while Caty truly looked like a stable maid. A very beautiful stable maid. He rode near and leaned toward the coach's window. "You slept well?"

"Quite," she replied demurely, without looking at him.

He smiled to himself. As he sat atop his mount, it hit him. Captain Tillea knew Caty. He was just the person to keep an eye on her. The earl of the castle would surely release the captain to the king.

Marcus sent one of his men to speak with the earl. His messenger successfully enlisted the captain's services in the protection of Lady Caterina. The earl had relinquished the man without hesitation. As the king rode past the captain, he welcomed the elderly man.

"Thank you, Your Grace," Tillea replied. "You of course have realized that, dressed as she is, most men will assume she is a commoner, and as such, fair game." The captain could tell by the look that flew past the king's eye that he had not thought of that. Now he could think of nothing else. That any man would look on Caterina as a possible conquest angered him. He glanced back at the carriage. The day could not end fast enough for him. "Soon, we will be back in my own castle, and she will know what my temper can do," he muttered.

Upon arriving at the castle, he assisted Caty down from the coach. As he walked with her to the stairs that led to his quarters, Marcus spoke in a cool voice. "You have been moved. And you are expected to dine with me this evening, in the great hall." Curtly, he added, "And clean up. You smell." She was saved the humiliation of having to temper her reply, as he turned abruptly and strode angrily away.

Not certain just where she was supposed to go, Caty trudged up the stairs. Her adventure had only gotten her moved . . . again. Meeting several of the women previously assigned to care for her, she was greeted shyly at first. When they realized she was not angry with them, they crowded around her, leading her protectively to her new chambers. Once inside, she looked around, astounded. The rooms were beautiful, even more so than her last apartments.

The ladies-in-waiting gladly showed her the new abundance of gowns and jewels awaiting her. Any clothing she owned previously had been removed. Every new gown was already altered to fit her.

Wearily, Caty smiled. "May I have water, please? I wish to bathe. I think perhaps you wish I would also." The ladies all giggled and hustled about, helping her. "Where is Rose?" Caty asked. She missed her old friend.

"She is coming. She will be here this evening. She can tell you about her days. Tell us about your time, lady. Are you well? Was he angry? Is he still so?" They were excited to have her back and longed to hear the details of her adventure. That a lady such as Caty should venture out alone was quite unusual.

"For now, yes to everything. If you are still awake when I return, I will share my short time of freedom with you." Caty smiled at them, kindly. She knew they were fond of her, and she was growing fond of them. Caty's mind added, *Still, I pray I find a way from this tangle.*

FORTY-FOUR

BY THE TIME CATY ENTERED the great room, it was teeming with laughter. Music played, people danced, and the king's table was fully seated. Relieved, Caty could see there was no seating space with the king for her. She looked briefly around the room, then quietly slipped along the wall seeking a way out of the room.

She had never felt so alone and small. *What now, Mother?* she thought. She watched the people of King Marcus's court as they ate. More than one woman tried to catch the king's eye. *He still carries anger toward me, I'm certain,* Caty thought. *I know not how to resolve this.* She watched his lords and pages, his guards, and the couples dancing. So intent was she on the crowd before her that she failed to see Marcus send the king's newest court member, the new captain of Caty's guard, after her.

Marcus had seen Caterina sweep into the room. As always, his breathing quickened at the sight of her. This night, she wore a deep blue gown, form-fitting, flattering of her small waist, and falling softly to the floor. It was one of the gowns he had chosen for her. She stood straight and regal, watching his court.

Startled when her father's old captain approached her, Caty smiled with recognition. He too smiled. "You are your mother again, lady." He bowed, taking her hand and kissing it. "The king requests your presence."

"Am I not present now?" she asked innocently.

He simply took her elbow and gently guided her through the throng. Caty noted the daggers from more than one lady's eyes. *If you would only take him from me, I would be forever grateful,* she thought.

When she made it to King Marcus's table, he stood. Immediately, a chair was vacated on his right. He indicated she was to sit. The captain stood behind her chair. Caty could see the fire in the king's dark eyes. His desire was open and plain. Blushing under the scrutiny, Caty curtsied, then sat down. The king remained standing, watching her. "Lady Caterina, walk with me."

She looked up at him. Her eyes wide with foreboding of the upcoming battle between them, she slowly stood. As the revelers opened a path for them, she heard a woman' s whisper. "Look how skinny she is, and much too old to have children."

Hurt, she turned, but the captain shook his head slightly and blocked her. Quickly sidestepping him, she commented, with grace and not a trace of rancor, but in a voice that carried, "Please dance, people. Enjoy the food, wine, and music. Life passes swiftly. Too soon we bury our hearts along with our children. You have been more than kind to me, a stranger to your court. I thank you. As women, we must trudge forward. For who better to prepare men for battle than a woman."

The men and women both laughed. Several waved and called a good night to her. Caty waved and nodded back. Then, with the same grace, she turned to the waiting king. He was pleased.

Taking her arm, he led the entourage out to the gardens. "Lady, I have decided what your punishment will be. You are confined to the castle. You will attend every court function and take every evening meal with me. If I choose, you will break your fast with me, also. You have gotten much too thin. The door to your rooms will be locked after you enter, and remain so until I open them in the morning. Rose has been reassigned to teach the younger women court protocol. Captain Tillea will head your guard. You must have his permission to leave the castle proper, if I am unavailable. This will remain in place until it pleases me to change the order."

They walked on. Caty could not think of what to say, but she refused to let him see her anxiety. Instead, she concentrated on finding good in her sentence. *Maybe this is not so bad*, she decided. *I can read, sew, and wander the castle, perhaps even cook. This place is large enough to keep me busy for days.*

"Have you nothing to say?" Marcus asked.

"What would you have me say, Your Majesty?" She could tell he was well pleased with himself.

Self-assuredly, he replied, "I would have you say yes, cheerfully." Caty refused to answer or even look at him. The rest of their walk was in silence. He sent her to her chambers with one of his pages.

For the next two weeks, Caty shared the evening meal with him. They discussed everything: his political leanings, women's station, religion, and many other topics. She managed to keep him away from discussing their relationship. Frequently, they ended up arguing. Marcus allowed her to argue with him, often getting caught up in trying to prove her wrong. Pleased that she was well educated, he prodded her into heated exchanges.

No matter how he tried, she refused to admit that her rightful place was with him. He knew she had no choice; still, he would rather she agree happily. After one heated dinner argument, Caty stood in anger. "I am through for this night. I will spar with you no longer, sire." She gathered her gown about her and headed for the door.

"King Henry isn't the only king that could have a woman beheaded," Marcus remarked as she retreated. His voice was level and pointed. Caty paused.

Without turning, she replied tartly, "Then King Henry would not be the only king that would be known as cruel, arrogant, and a despot."

"You think I'm cruel, arrogant, and a despot?" he replied, leaning back lazily, a smile upon his face.

"No," she said, turning to face him. "You're not a despot and you're not cruel."

Marcus nodded. "Ah, you think me arrogant."

"Yes," she replied shortly.

He laughed. *How is it she can say what she pleases, and I care not? She must learn, though. I am her king.* "I am not through speaking to you, Lady Caterina." This time, his voice had a note of authority.

Caty acknowledged this fact with a slight nod of her head.

May as well just say it, he thought. "I want you."

"Then you would take a mistress, not a queen," Caty answered, raising her head to face him.

"You would be my mistress, lady?" he asked, amused. His eyes danced as he teased her.

"Not willingly," she answered, her chin level, her eyes meeting his without wavering.

He smiled and shrugged. "That would be fine with me." He eyed her over the rim of his goblet as he took a sip of wine.

"But not with your people," she countered. "People want to be proud of their monarchy, whether French, English, Spanish, or Italian. They want to be proud of their ruler. The ruler defines the country. Besides," Caty added, frowning slightly, "you need a younger woman. Someone that could give you an heir. You need a son."

"I have heirs. I have three beautiful daughters," Marcus replied smugly.

"Are they well educated?" Caty fired back quickly.

"I believe so," he said. "Each is prepared to reign if necessary."

"I am too old," Caty reminded him.

"Ah, you are older. But you are beautiful and graceful."

"I am not educated to be a queen. You should have someone well educated." Caty was pulling at straws now.

"You are not educated, lady?" he asked, feigning surprise. He knew otherwise.

"I am," she admitted, "but not about your country."

For a long moment, he was silent. "I could just take you, Caterina," he noted quietly. His eyes moved over her slowly.

"Then you would be proving me right," Caty stated flatly. "You want a mistress, not a queen."

He studied the lady before him as she fought to stay independent, refused to yield. "Ride with me on the morrow, lady. You *can* ride, can you not?" he teased.

"I can," Caty acknowledged. She felt her anger rising.

"You would ride with me?" Marcus asked.

"Yes, it would be most pleasant to be out of the confines of this castle." The moment the words were out of her mouth, Caty realized she had made a mistake. He now had a weapon against her. She glanced at him and knew she was correct. He smiled slowly at her, as if he had already won.

"I am an old woman," Caty reminded him. "I need my sleep. It is after midnight. Might I take my leave, Your Grace?"

He laughed out loud. "Yes, until tomorrow, then."

Caty curtsied. He quickly stood, moving to extend his hand to her. He helped her rise and kissed her hand. It was soft and smelled of flowers. He smiled again. Nodding, she left.

When she was out of sight, she stamped her foot. *How could I make such a stupid mistake?* she thought. *Now what might I do? He'll probably not show up in the morning. I'll be stuck in here another day. Again!* Shaking her head, she stormed to her apartments.

FORTY-FIVE

THE NEXT MORNING, CATY DRESSED as dowdily as possible. She turned before the mirror, then paused. *No, I'll not go down this way, if indeed I am to go down.* When she left her rooms, she was dressed in a deep-green riding gown with a full collar of ermine. The hood on her green cloak was edged with the same dark ermine. She still wore no jewelry. With her auburn hair, her olive skin, and her golden hazel eyes, Caty made more than one man turn and stare. Slowly, she moved down the stairs to the door. Her head held high, she nodded to the men as she floated by. *Perhaps I can muster support from these men. If nothing else, they will protect me should I find myself confined to this miserable structure.*

When she stepped out into the sunlight, her hair shone. Marcus caught his breath. He would have her, willingly or not; he would have her. He moved quickly to her side and helped her mount. She was light and agile. Pulling the hood over her head, she smiled at the men who stood around as Marcus mounted, then gently urged her horse ahead.

As they rode out, she rode slower and slipped behind the king, placing herself among his guards. King Marcus turned to her, frowning. "You ride *with* me, lady, not behind me." He stopped his horse, waiting until she was next to him. Satisfied, he moved them all out again.

Although she tried to disguise it, Caty was ecstatic with the ride. The air was fresh and clean, the sun warm, and her horse well trained. She frequently leaned forward to pet his neck. It was not long before Caty realized she had dressed too warmly. The hood was back, the cloak loosened, her gloves off, and still she was hot. Pulling up, she tried to remove the cloak without drawing attention. King Marcus stopped immediately and returned to her side. "You tire, lady?" he asked, concern in his voice.

"No." Caty blushed. "I have dressed too warm. I would remove this cloak." She proceeded to pull at it.

"Come," he instructed, bounding off his horse, "you need to dismount to remove the cloak." He stood at her horse's side, his arms upraised to assist her. As much as she hated to have him touch her, she knew he was right. With his help, she slipped off onto the ground and quickly removed the cloak. Thankful that her gown was lighter, she turned to mount again. Lord Marcus shook his head. "Come, lady," he said quietly. "It is unseemly to climb up like a man." He assisted her, a smile turning the corners of his mouth at her discomfort. Once both had mounted, they were off again.

Caty could feel her hair coming down, but there was little she could do about it. Before long, the horses were loping. Caty loved the wind in her face. Her hair flowed behind her like a mantle. He looked over at her, smiling. *She will make a wonderful queen.* He noted how his men reacted to her. She had found favor among them. Her ladies-in-waiting were loyal to her also. It would be a good match. Willing or not, she would take the crown.

The troop rode all morning, stopping occasionally to allow the horses to rest. King Marcus was pleased at how well she handled the horse. Nearing midday, they came to an area filled with trees. Caty could hear water bubbling in the background. Stopping, the king dismounted and helped her down. Holding her hand firmly on his arm, he walked her through the trees and into a little glade filled with soft grass and numerous flowers. Caty's eyes moved around the area, taking in its beauty and peace. "Thank you," she murmured.

She slipped away from him and walked slowly around the area. He watched her as she moved. Coming to a small stream, she bent down to touch the water. It felt cool and fresh. The horses had followed them, and were drinking nearby. After a moment, she stood and walked to her horse. For an instant, the king thought she might try to leave. Instead, she pulled the bridle off. The animal shook his head, nuzzled her, and turned back to the water. With the bridle over her arm, she turned back to the king, who stood watching her. Blushing, she dipped her head slightly, and self-consciously returned to him. He stood watching her intently. "You realize, Lady Caterina, you have just sealed your fate. You will make the perfect queen." He spoke softly, his black eyes on fire with passion.

"Perhaps we might come to some agreement," Caty replied weakly.

He laughed aloud. "Oh, there will be an end to our little war, lady. Whether you agree or not is up to you."

The page informed them their meal was ready. Caty had no appetite. If she were alone, she might have cried. With a heavy heart, she sat down. "Come, lady, you'll spoil your gown," said Marcus. He pulled her up, leading her instead to an area covered with a thick blanket upon which pillows awaited her. In short order, they were served lunch.

Caty couldn't bring herself to take a bite. The king watched her with interest. "Am I so undesirable that you lose your appetite, lady?" His tone strongly suggested he didn't care if she ate or not. He was helping himself to everything set out for them. He had already moved on. Caty had lost. Glancing at him, Caty shook her head.

Desperately, she looked around the glen. "I would ask that you reconsider, Your Grace. I am not who you need by your side. I have loved deeply before and still carry that love. A union would be unfair to you." She looked at him, her eyes pleading.

He was silent for a long while. "Give me the details of your love's face, lady. I would hear of him."

Horrified, Caty quickly turned to him. "How could you ask such a thing?"

"I do ask," he answered quietly. "If you choose not to answer, I demand. Whichever, I would know of him." He waited patiently for her response, continuing to pull his roasted chicken apart.

Caty looked down at her hands, which she found gripping each other. For a moment, she closed her eyes; then, shaking her head in defiance, she looked at Marcus. "I cannot. He stays within my heart. I cannot put him on display. He fought well for you. I know you remember him. Of what use is it to talk of him? When my heart is healed, perhaps. Not until then."

"Then I demand, lady," Marcus said firmly.

"So you said you would, Your Grace. The more you pull Lord Rhys out, the deeper the wound. Better to allow his memory to stay safe with me. I do not live in yesterday, sire. I know he is gone and life moves on." Caty met the king's eyes, unwavering. "He belonged to me."

"The sooner you talk of him, and finish with him, the sooner your life will move. Know this, lady. It will move. Now, tell me about Rhys."

"I cannot," Caty whispered. "I will not." She stood quickly and walked away from him. Standing at the edge of the forest, she leaned into a tree. She would not allow Marcus, or anyone else, into that corner of her world—that place belonging to Rhys. "Have I not suffered enough?" she murmured.

The king walked slowly to her side. With a masterfully smooth gesture, he pulled her to him. Caty did not resist. She allowed him to hold her closely. *She has not forgotten him*, he thought. *But it matters not. There will be nothing to stand between this lady and me. She is mine, now.*

Marcus stood silently with her in his arms. His hand gently brushed the hair from her face. "Come, lady, come walk with me." In a low, gentle voice, he continued, "Perhaps you are right, Caterina. We have each let go of things dear during our lives. It is in living that we pay the greatest respect to those we have lost. In our world, Caterina, yours and mine, women are a commodity. To me, you are a gift. A great gift. I will treasure my gift as long as there is breath in my body." With his arm around her, he continued to walk slowly around the edge of the glade.

Neither spoke for a long while. Then Marcus stopped and lifted Caty's face. "During your life, Caterina, you have known many men. Some with love, some as friends, and perhaps some as enemies. You have known only one son. A son to a mother is like nothing else in our time. You will never forget his face, nor the face of his father." His voice was still soothing and gentle. It was clear that she had lost her battle with him. Perhaps he would not push it. Perhaps he would let her have some time.

In the days that followed, the king spent all of his free time with Caty, walking through the beautiful gardens, beside fountains, and back. She was not allowed outside the castle unless in his company. Captain Tillea reported to her each morning, and each morning he had to let her know she was still under castle restraint. How she longed to ride free, to move about among the people, and to feel open again. She knew feelings were stirring for the king, feelings she fought to keep at bay. She knew the king had been patient, and in truth, she could find no fault with his treatment of her. Rhys no longer haunted her nights; rather he walked softly with her. Long visits with Father Franco gradually gave her peace, creating a new place for love to live. Still, the idea of being a queen made her resist. That, and the desire to not give in to the man.

One afternoon, with the sun shining down upon them gently, a breeze fresh against her face, Marcus turned to her. "Caterina, I grow tired of courting you." He spoke quietly, watching her face. He saw, with joy, the look of sadness that came to her. *I am right, she does care*, he thought. *She believes I think to court another. Now is the time.* He continued to walk in silence, curious how she would respond.

When Caty at last answered him, her voice was soft, with a hint of melancholy. "Perhaps you will find one at your court who pleases you more. One not burdened with a past such as mine, Your Grace."

He stopped and turned her about. "You misunderstand me, lady. I would make you my queen. We will be wed in one week's time. We will be wed in the afternoon, early. After which you and I will retire to my chambers. During that time, I will tell you when you will be crowned queen."

Caty was stunned. Words came to her, without thinking. "Are you certain? I could not live through another loss. Not now." She rushed on, "You know little about me, yet you seem to know all." She glanced downward, then lifted her face to find him smiling down at her.

For the second time, he took her in his arms, this time kissing her tenderly. "Come, we ride again this evening. Then we part until our marriage." They walked back to the castle in silence.

King Marcus took her immediately to the stables, and Caty saw Captain Tillea waiting, along with his guard and the king's men. "You are to choose a steed," said the king. "One that will be yours, to ride each day. Always with me, if I am here. With your guard, if I am not."

"Ah," Caty sighed, looking at the animals. "Better than jewels. Walking miles has proved it."

King Marcus laughed at that, then walked with her through the stables, giving a brief history of each horse. She stopped at the stall of a large, younger, nervous stallion. "This one is not for you, love," the king admonished. "He needs a stronger hand."

"Perhaps he needs a gentle hand, sire. Might I try him? You would please me to decide whether I can control him." She watched the animal; the horse watched her.

Captain Tillea smiled as he watched Caty with the horses. So like her mother.

Reluctantly, the king agreed. *I will see just what she can do*, he thought. Softly, Caty began to speak to the horse. All the while, she was walking toward him, opening the stall, and stepping inside. The king moved to stop her, but she was already with the animal. Marcus quickly stepped to the gate. To his surprise, the animal stretched his long neck toward Caty. She continued to speak with him.

Gently, she petted his nose, moved her hand to his neck, and caressed him with her voice. The horse turned to nuzzle her. She walked toward the gate, the animal following her, nuzzling her affectionately. "Sire, if it would please you, I take this animal. He is young, strong, and looks to have speed. All things I hope to never need, but would have if necessary."

The king studied his woman. "I can see we will have much to talk of, Caterina. Yes, the animal is yours. Captain?" Immediately, the horse was led out, saddled, and made ready for Caty.

"Place the reins over his neck, please," Caty asked. She called to the horse and stood near a fence, away from the men and near Marcus. The horse came to her, making soft noises, reaching to her. She petted him, kissed his nose softly, then went around to his side. The king helped her up.

FORTY-SIX

THE AFTERNOON RIDE WITH MARCUS was like no other Caty could remember. She had not felt this happy in so long. When she stopped her horse, the king, alarmed, came quickly to her side. "My lady, what ails you?"

She smiled at him. "I truly doubted I could ever feel this happy again, nor love again. How is it I deserve such a second chance, Your Grace?"

Riding closer to her, the king pulled her onto his horse. With his arms around her, he rode a short distance before answering. "You are my second chance, too, Caterina. I married for the good of my kingdom the first time. She was a good woman, a good mother, but cold to me and to my people. She never felt at home here. My daughters feel conflicted between loyalty to their country and loyalty to their beloved mother's memory. It was a union without passion, only courtesy." Looking down at Caty, he smiled as he held her close. "I have known only passion, love, and longing since you arrived here. Since first I saw you at my court. Out of respect for you and your husband, I kept my distance. When Lord Dermoth died, I ached for your sadness, but I knew our time would come. I could not have foreseen how determined you would be, lady. That is over." He paused. "There is not the need to have a great ceremony. How would you feel about a quiet arrangement, love?"

"I care not for the ceremony; I care only that you be there—and Father Franco." She leaned against him. "What of your daughters, Your Grace? I would hope not to be seen as an enemy."

He held her closer. "You knew it not, lady, but my daughters have been at court many times. They are ready to be with you whenever you are ready."

Caty shook her head. "You have planned well, I see."

He looked pleased with himself.

"Am I to be allowed Rose again, Majesty?" Caty asked. "She was a friend, not a lady-in-waiting."

"No, Caterina, that I cannot allow. What you did to her was wrong. This is as good a time as any to talk of this matter. Explain yourself."

"I see how you would think that," Caty acknowledged. "But you must remember, sire, I desired to leave and knew not how you might accept that action. I intended to protect Rose from your anger. If I shared my plans with her, she would be party to what you saw as my wrongdoing. If I left while she could move about freely, she would have not been able to disclaim knowledge. I did worry about her safety, should something happen while she was locked in her room. Knowing this, I removed the bars from her window and had the window replaced with one that would open. She knew the window was changed, and I am certain she knew why when she discovered the door locked."

"So you admit that running away was wrong?" he noted in triumph.

Caty corrected him. "No, sire, I admit placing her in any danger was wrong. Perhaps you could say I chose the least of two wrongs?"

"No, you chose a dangerous plan, lady. One which I trust will never be tried again." When Caty did not answer, he continued. "Tell me, lady. Admit you were wrong and will not do such a thing again." He spoke sternly, but Caty saw him smile.

"I will not do such a thing again, but I was not wrong," she answered demurely.

"Caterina, we really must work on your obedience, I see." He held her tighter and kissed her head. They were to be wed in one week's time. His heart was light. The world was a beautiful place.

The ceremony was intended to be quiet and simple, but word spread that the king would finally take a new wife. People flooded the castle and town.

Rumors surrounded Caty—of what was believed to be her poor station in life, her attempted escape, her parents, and her children. Exasperated, Caty asked one of her ladies, "Just where do people get these ideas?"

"People make up what they do not know," the girl replied. "I feel some of these people may have seen my lady when she was out and about, without His Majesty."

"Hmm, that's true," Caty admitted. She hoped the people would remember her kindly.

The evening before her wedding, Caty sat with her ladies for a meal. She quietly spoke to the women present about their behavior and what she would expect. They discussed dress, dance, and men. The mood was lighthearted and the room resounded with laughter. A page came to the door. "Sir? How may I help you?" one of the ladies asked.

He shifted nervously. "The king wishes to see Lady Caterina in his chambers—now."

Caty frowned. "Now? The hour is late."

"Yes, my lady, now," he confirmed, bowing.

"Is he ill?" she asked, rising quickly from her seat.

"No, my lady," the young man responded quietly.

"We are his servants, sir. Take me to him." She followed the page, praying the king was not ill. *But why else would he ask for me?*

When they arrived at his door, the page knocked gently and stepped aside.

"Enter," the king commanded from within.

"Would that you come to the door, sire," Caty responded, raising her voice to be heard through the door. "Tongues wag aplenty as it is. You asked to see me? Are you ill, sire?" She could hear him chuckle.

The door opened to reveal King Marcus in his riding clothes. "Come, Caterina, we are going for a ride." He smiled broadly, like a child with a secret.

"I'm not . . ." Caty stumbled for the words. "I'm . . . not dressed to ride, Your Highness." She was clad only in her nightclothes. Fear that he might be ill had made her forget to pull something more substantial about her slender form. "Might I change? I would be quick," she appealed to him hopefully.

"No," he answered simply. He took her hand and led her down the hall. She glanced back to see the king's attendants watching. None were smiling, but Caty could tell they wanted to.

This is just what I do not need. This man is impossible, she thought. The king strode with purpose down the stairs leading from his apartments out of the castle. Outside, he paused long enough to slip his cloak over her shoulders, then continued to the stables. There, Captain Tillea and his men waited. The king's and Caty's horses were saddled. Not questioning further, she simply followed his lead. The rest of the king's men rode after them.

After riding for several hours, they came to a small castle ablaze with light, flags, and life. "We come to your castle, Caterina," Marcus announced proudly, looking across the field.

Caty turned to the king, puzzled. "I don't understand, Your Grace. I am to stay here? Not with you?"

"There are times you will not be with me. I will be at my home; you will be here. Is it not to your liking?" He looked at the residence and then again at Caty.

Caty's heart sank. *He does not intend we stay in the same quarters? He even has me out of his sight, in another castle.* Trying to comprehend why he would do such a thing, a realization hit her. Anger followed. "Am I to do what you do when you are not with me?" she asked quietly.

Marcus drew his horse up to hers sharply. "Caterina! What did you say?"

She rode away from him, but he quickly caught up and seized the reins from her. Her horse tried to pull away, rearing slightly. Marcus held fast to the reins. Caty clung to the animal's mane. "I ask what it is you say to me. Answer!" His voice resonated in the night.

Caty turned to face him and spoke quietly. "I ask you, Majesty, if I am to do what you do when you are away from me."

His face flushed with anger. "You dare—"

"I would rather die now than be a queen you find on occasion," Caty interrupted. She quickly slid from the opposite side of her horse and walked rapidly away from him.

What is this she tells me? Marcus thought. Seeing her walk away from him only made his anger more acute. "Caterina!" His voice thundered after her. "You are not dismissed!" Caty paused, her back to him. He dropped her reins. The

271

great gray animal pranced anxiously to Caty. She spoke soothingly to him. Still not speaking to the king, she turned. Marcus remained seated in his saddle, glaring down at her, his anger evident with his every move.

"Speak!" His voice rolled over her. His hand moved to the sword at his side. He would hear it from her own lips before he moved with his anger.

"What would you do when I am not with you?" Caty said. "I fear you are toying with me."

"Toying with you? How so?" His anger still boiled, yet she had not admitted what he feared. He knew well what most men did when away from their women. That Caty would hint she might do the same while away from him fired his anger.

"You would have me as queen, but you would expect me to leave you and live elsewhere? I have only one marriage to draw experience from, Majesty. In that marriage, I did what my husband did, when he was gone from me."

"What!" the king said, incredulous. *She admits this openly?*

Captain Tillea frowned, shaking his head in disbelief.

Caty continued, with her eyes meeting his. "When he left to fight, I fought in his castle and at his borders. When he was called to see to the queen's people, I saw to his people, during one of the worst winters, when people were freezing and starving. So I ask you, what would you do when you send me away, so I might know what is expected of me where I stay." She stood silent, waiting.

Stunned, the king stared at her. Captain Tillea smiled to himself. *The king will do well to keep her close*, he thought.

Marcus dismounted. Standing before her, his anger was slowly quieting, replaced by a great relief. "Caterina, look at me," he commanded.

Caty stood still but took his outstretched hand. Her eyes were filled with determination. "Tell me whom you fought," Marcus ordered. His voice was still firm, but now quieter. His hold on her was firm also, but he sought to calm the shaking he felt in her hand.

"In my home, I fought the French," Caty told him quietly. "At our southern borders, I fought Highlanders, disillusioned with the war between England and Scotland."

"Tell me of these fights, Caterina." His voice was gentle now. He continued to hold her hand as they walked away from the hearing range of their men. Caty told him of her struggles with the Frenchman and his men. Trusting the feelings that came to her, Caty did not tell him about the Frenchman's death. She told him of the fighting over Lord Dermoth's lands and the Highlander's help. When she had finished, they both walked in silence.

King Marcus broke the quiet with another question. "You and Lord Dermoth—were you ever away from him when he was home?"

"No," she answered simply.

King Marcus looked deep in thought. "You slept with him, always?" He frowned, not quite believing. This was not the custom, and he knew it.

"Even the night our son was born. I was asleep and woke to find him asleep at my side. I believe you misunderstand me, Majesty. I would not take another man. I have room in my heart for only one man at a time. You are filling this heart. There is not room for another."

"And Lord Dermoth?" Marcus asked, studying the woodlands ahead of him.

"He is gone, Your Grace." Caty could feel peace settling over her. *'Tis true, Marcus*, Caty thought. *Until I spoke it, I realized it not. Rhys has freed my heart.*

The king gripped her shoulders and turned her to him. "My first queen came to my bed when I sent for her. She never spent even one night with me. You are correct. I did not understand." Thoughts ran quietly through his mind. Aloud, he added, "We have different tales to tell. It is time for us to live *our* story, yours and mine. This is your land, Caterina. I ask that you refrain from coming here, unless you have my permission. I rather favor Lord Rhys's arrangement. I would have you with me, in my bed and castle, whenever I am there. This will be a nice place for a retreat." They returned to their horses, and Marcus lifted Caty to her horse. Together with their men, they rode toward the small castle.

They crossed the moat, passed through the gate, and entered the castle yards. Fires were lit about the area, exposing men who lounged and ate. When the king entered, everyone scrambled to kneel. He acknowledged them but continued to the main castle door without slowing. He stepped from his horse, eased Caty down from hers, and took her with him. Inside the great hall, staff waited to serve them. The Tabor standard hung from one wall. Opposite it, behind the head table, hung the king's standard. Waiting for them stood Rose.

"Rose!" Caty called as she ran to her old friend. The women held onto each other. "You are well?" Caty asked.

"Certainly. I could have been with you sooner, but you are stubborn, my lady," Rose laughed. "I have been here making ready for your coming since you left his Majesty's shelter."

"The lady runs no longer, Rose," the king noted with authority. A great meal was spread before them. The hall had filled with people come to see Caty and to eat. Once the meal had been served but before anyone had begun, the king stood. The hall went silent. "Tomorrow, Lady Caterina and I will be wed. She is, from this moment forward, my queen. Protect her. This man," he continued, pointing to Captain Tillea, "is the captain of her guard. His orders carry the same authority as my own word. I tell all here present to witness my word. This castle and the lands with it, from this moment forward, belong to Caterina, my wife." He sat down. The hall was filled with merriment as the meal commenced.

After dinner, Marcus took Caty's hand and left the great hall. Outside, he kissed her. "My heart finds your heart a safe place. It will stay there, as long as I live. Come soon, my lady. I long for your touch." He mounted his horse and reached down for her hand. "Until tomorrow, Lady Caterina." He and his men rode into the darkness.

Caty talked with Rose long into the night. When Caty was ready for sleep, Rose began preparing her a bath. "What gown will you wear, my lady?"

"I have not thought on it, Rose. Since I knew not where we were bound, nor how long we would be gone, I am poorly prepared. When we rise, we will decide."

As she soaked in the water, she relaxed. A soft knock at her door brought her out of her musings. Caty quickly stepped from the tub and stood wrapped in a thick robe. Rose opened the door to find Captain Tillea outside. "At what hour would Lady Caterina leave?" he asked.

Caty smiled and called to the door, "Shortly after the sunlight warms this place, sir. I travel light. How is my horse?"

"He is spirited, like his mistress," he replied. He started to leave, then turned back. "Lady, you cannot understand how an old soldier's heart feels to know he will care for the only daughter of Lord Tabor." He bowed, then left her.

Morning came quickly. By sunrise, Caty was already dressed to ride, as were Rose and two other women. Walking through the great hall, Caty smiled to herself. *This is mine. I can hardly believe my mind. Today I wed another, Rhys. I know you still protect me and are with our son. Good-bye for now, Lord Rhys.* She blew a soft kiss toward heaven. As her steed galloped toward the king's castle, Caty felt the first blush of pleasure in anticipation.

FORTY-SEVEN

STANDING, WATCHING CATY COME TO him, the king could feel his pulse quicken. She was dressed in a gown of cream. The train of the dress was cream also, with thick embroidered vines of deep purple, the color of royalty. She walked proudly through the great hall toward him, her head high. Her eyes met his, and both smiled. In front of the gathered crowd, she promised to obey her husband and king. *I hope I can do that*, a small voice inside her head whispered.

Upon her finger he placed a smaller version of his signet ring. On the finger next to it, he placed a large ruby, surrounded by diamonds. He promised to protect and honor his wife. When they stood, turning to face his court, a cheer rose. His men began to chant, "Queen Caterina! Queen Caterina!" Caty was overwhelmed by the outpouring of love she felt from the great hall. Humbly, she curtsied to them and to her husband. He bowed to her, then, holding her hand, led her through the crowd and back to the head table.

Music filled the air, and Caty sat next to her king. "Are you happy?" he asked, leaning toward her.

"More than happy; I am at peace, too." Caty smiled back at him, her eyes bright with love.

"Would you dance with me, wife?" He took gentle possession of her hand again.

"Yes, gladly, husband," Caty responded. And so they danced. Caty was pleasantly surprised to find that Marcus loved to dance. Throughout the event, each of his men came to him, pledging allegiance to the new queen. When at last things were calmer, Caty asked, "Might I walk among the women, Majesty? I would be certain they feel no uneasiness toward me this night."

He frowned, but nodded. She left the table, her captain at her side, and wandered through his subjects, laughing and visiting with the women. The women were thrilled to have her attention. She picked up more than one small child, kissing the little hands and laughing with them. As she began to make her way back to Marcus, she felt a tug on her skirt.

"Oh, no, Santino, you mustn't." An anxious mother rushed to pull the lad away.

"Please," Caty said to the woman, "let me see what this little man wants." Kneeling down to look the child in the eye, she asked, "What can I do for you, sir?"

Suddenly shy, he paused, looked at his mother, then back at Caty. "Might I have a dance with you, lady?" His little voice was soft in Caty's ear.

"But of course, sir. I would be honored to have a dance with you. Your mother is worried I might step on you. I'll try not to be clumsy," Caty told the lad in a serious tone.

"Please do not worry, lady. I will not tell anyone. It will be our secret." With a determined frown on his little face, he took Caty's hand and led her to the floor. The dancers moved aside as Caty and the child stepped out to the music. A hush fell over the revelers. Rudy nudged Marcus. The king watched his wife dance with the lad. Neither missed a step. When the dance was finished, the boy, still unsmiling, led Caty back to the king. Bowing low, he thanked her for the dance. As he walked back toward his mother, he turned back and blew Caty a kiss. The room was hushed. Smoothly, Caty returned it.

Marcus watched her, his dark eyes filled with pride. "You have done well, madam. Would that more children would love their king and his wife as freely."

With tear-filled eyes, Caty turned back to the king. "I thank you for a moment of motherhood regained."

"Come, Caterina, come sit with me. I best reclaim you before any of the older boys follow suit." Amid laughter, she took her place beside Marcus. He leaned to her and said, "Caterina, you must take care to have an escort when you roam, no matter where that might be."

Caty's face grew grave. "I am sorry, sire. I did not think. It is important that the women know I am aware of the heavy burden they all bear. The child is special. I could not have refused that dance. You know, we now have a deeply loyal subject. He will bring others along with him. Someday, he will."

Later in the night, Marcus led his new wife to his royal suite. As they entered, the people crowded into the room to witness their first union. Marcus swiftly bade them leave. There was a slight hesitation. "Leave us," he ordered again. Taking both Caty's hands into his, he added, "We need no further witness to our union." With that, the room emptied while King Marcus kissed his bride.

When they were at last alone, he led her to a grand chair before the fireplace. The room was dark but for the gentle glow from the fire. He offered her a goblet of wine and sat opposite her. "Now, lady, tell me why you spoke the words that brought us to anger last night."

Caty blushed. "I fear I have misled you somewhat, Marcus." Her voice caressed his name.

"How so?" He frowned, his head cocked to one side, his brows raised in question.

"I knew you would find the very thought of me with someone else repugnant. I spoke hoping you would not feel the need to have another woman."

As he listened, a smile spread over his face. "This I already knew, Caterina. I intend to address that later. First, you must know, I will never feel the need to be with any other woman. Look about you, Caterina. This is our place. These are your chambers, also. Come, I'll show you." He took her hand and stood. Proudly, he led her around the quarters. They looked at every room, candles blazing a welcome.

As they returned to the bedroom, Caty spoke. "I find many of my possessions about these rooms."

"Yes. After we spoke last eve, I had all your possessions moved here. You will be with me. Caterina, you must never fear to tell me exactly what is in your heart. Come, I would walk with you in the gardens." He had waited this long;

a short while longer to make her more comfortable was not a great problem. Together, they stole into the soft darkness of night. Music drifted lazily along the winding walkways. Light from the great hall cast a short, soft glow near the windows.

"I think you will love me, soon," said King Marcus. "I wanted you at first glance. You give me peace." He strode along, his hand over her hand, which rested upon his arm.

After they had wandered through the grounds awhile, Marcus brought her back to the door of their chambers. Knowing what lay ahead, Caty was anxious. She turned her face to him, her brow furrowed. "It has been a hard road I have traveled, to you. I would ask your patience."

His voice was gentle as the cover of night. "Come, Caterina, come lie with your king." With that, he followed her inside, then closed and locked the door.

He walked to Caty, who stood watching the fire, and wrapped his arms around her. "Remember, Caterina. I am your absolute ruler," he whispered into her hair.

"My mother always said . . ." She stopped. What her mother said would not sit well with him. Her mother never foretold a marriage with a king.

"Well, what did your mother say?" he said into her neck.

She tried to brush it aside. "No matter."

"Caterina? It is too late. Now I command you to finish your thought." He was smiling, his eyes alight with mischief.

"My mother always said the only absolute ruler over a man is his woman."

A short silence was followed by laughter. "I would have loved your mother, Caterina." He then called for Rose. When she appeared with a pure white sleeping gown, he nodded toward his wife. Stepping into his dressing room, he called for his page and began to change. When Marcus returned, he found Caty in her bed gown, standing before the fire as before. He crossed to her and placed his hands on her shoulder. She was shaking slightly. Slowly, his hands caressed her as he shifted his hold to her small waist. In a powerful movement, he lifted her in his arms and carried her to the chair near the fire. With her securely in his lap, he began. He unbuttoned her gown, slowly, teasing her with his movements. Caty found herself shivering at his hands. Marcus's gentle expertise transported her beyond thinking. He watched her as he moved his hands over her body, slowly, carefully. He studied her face, her eyes, her mouth. As he carried her to their bed, he said, "You're even more than I imagined." His voice was hoarse with passion.

He stripped and lay next to her. He pulled her closer and softly scolded her. "Remember, Caterina, I am your king. I do what I want with you."

I think not, Caty silently countered. She began to rhythmically move with him, then suddenly he was moaning. Caty gave herself to him, to the night, and to their life together.

By morning, they were finally sleeping. A knock at the door awakened Marcus. He rolled to see his lady lying close, her hair spread around her, the covers thrown away. Quietly he watched her sleep. He wondered at her beauty. *More, she comes to me, willingly. She loves me and asks I love her, willingly. This is a good match.* Ignoring the knocking, he lay back and closed his eyes. Turning to her again, he began to tease her awake. His gentle touch set her afire again and again. *My wife stays with me, every night*, he thought. It was late afternoon before they emerged from their quarters. As they walked to the hall for the evening meal, they were greeted by his men and women. Caty found the women were very gracious and friendly, more so than she had expected. *This feels right*, she mused. Impulsively, she took his hand as they walked. He smiled, gripping her small hand within his. And so, Caty began another chapter in her life.

FORTY-EIGHT

THEIR TIME TOGETHER IN THE first year was spent well; he talked long during the nights. They shared laughter, love, and living. Marcus kept Caty close, not allowing her to go beyond the gardens below their chambers without him. The young boy, Santino, had become a regular attendant at the evening meals in the great hall. It was a soft, easy time.

Their second and third years together passed in much the same way, but Caty found herself called upon more often to help his people. The messages came to her quietly, through some of the pages and ladies-in-waiting, and occasionally through a lord or his wife. Word was spreading of her resourcefulness and generosity. Even the stable hands devised ways to ask for her help. Marcus had begun to allow her more freedom of movement. She took care to keep Captain Tillea and the rest of her guard near. Until recently, the people had come to her, waiting near a back gate of the castle. The crowds were getting larger.

There was no doubt: Caty was a healer. She feared the jealousy of Marcus's personal physician, but he proved to be a kindly old man, unimpressed with himself. He gladly shared his thoughts with her as she shared hers with him. A bond formed slowly. As she lay in the embrace of the king one night, while he was drifting off to a satisfied slumber, Caty whispered, "Would you allow me to visit the town, Marcus? I could take Captain Tillea with me. I would only take a short trip, sire. Better than having so many waiting for me."

He opened his eyes. Laughing, he moved her hair from her face. "And why would my queen go to the town? What would she seek there, love?"

Caty was not certain just what to tell him. She had never kept anything from him and would not start now. She was certain, though, that if he guessed the real reason she wanted to go, he would refuse her permission. She had to find a way to ask without upsetting him. Casually stifling a yawn, Caty suggested, "I would see if all goes well with the ones who were so kind to me when I traveled about in your service, just before our marriage." She giggled playfully.

"In my service, Caterina? Is that what you call misbehaving as you did?" He smiled at her.

"Not exactly, Marcus. I would have called it a mad dash to freedom, but you called it differently. In the inn, remember?"

He raised himself up on one elbow and traced her jaw with his finger, laughing. "So, you would ask my permission to be gone for weeks on end, without me? I have learned what your short trips are like. I think not. I am surprised you even ask." Shaking his head, he lay back down. "Mad dash to freedom, indeed," he mumbled.

"Silly man. I would only be gone a day. I would leave in the morning and return before you were ready for your evening meal. I cannot miss my time in your court, sire. It is much too entertaining. The games your lords and ladies play." Caty lay on her back, smiling to herself.

"You may go, Caterina. Take Captain Tillea and whomever he chooses to include. I would see you at court tomorrow evening. If you are late, you answer to me." He turned to her and pulled her closer.

"Thank you, Marcus. You indulge me." After kissing him good night, she snuggled against him and slept.

Early in the morning, she sent for Captain Tillea. "Sir, thank you for coming. I have been given permission to travel to the town. I will leave in thirty minutes. Please have my horse ready. Marcus said you would know who you need to take."

"How long are you to be away, Your Highness?" In his mind he was already choosing his men.

She laughed. "I must be back by evening meal."

He bowed. "I will see you downstairs, madam." Smiling, he added, "This is truly to be a short visit, Your Majesty?"

Caty impulsively kissed the old man's hand. With a light heart, she made ready to leave. Caty stopped by the physician's rooms on her way out. "Are you certain you would not go with me, sir?" she asked him. "I think you would add much needed advice."

The old man shook his head. "No, no. You go ahead, child. Tell me what you find, and if what we discussed works." He took her hand and kissed it. "Come see me; do not forget your old friend, Majesty." He walked her to the door of his quarters. There were several tables in this study of his, all strewn with herbs and various potent-smelling brews. His candles were always nearly burned down, such were the hours he kept. Papers lay scattered over his desk. Quills and ink pots sat everywhere. Caty loved the feeling of these rooms.

"Never could I forget you." She smiled at him fondly, making a mental note to order more candles for him.

Once they set out, Captain Tillea found that Caty knew just where she was bound. She explained where in the settlement they would find the man that needed her help. The farmer was surprised to see her, and stumbled over himself, not certain what to do. "Why would you doubt me?" she chided him amiably. "I said I would help!"

He nodded shyly, glancing at the men with her. "But when you helped before, you were alone, you were. And not dressed so . . . proper." His was the first family she had helped after trying to escape the king.

"I am the same woman that came that first time. Let us see to your problem." Caty smiled at him.

Captain Tillea looked around, shaking his head. A crowd of twenty or so people had gathered. *This is going to cause a stir, sure as I sit here with her*, he moaned inwardly. *She truly is her mother's daughter. The king will be none too happy about this. I think this day will try the king's patience.*

Caty got down from her horse and slung the reins over his neck. As always, the animal followed her. Once she entered the dark shed, she first ordered the loose boards covering a small window be removed. In the corner, she found the pig, separated from the rest of the animals.

Without hesitation, she knelt down onto the damp, mucky ground next to the farmer. The poor man was beside himself over the ailing animal. After she had carefully studied the symptoms and behavior of the man's sow, Caty handed him a packet of herbs. "You must see that this is all taken. If you mix it with water and mush, it is easier to get down. First, there will be a great activity of the bowels. That is as it should be. Keep water close. Next there will be drowsiness. When this passes, the illness will pass also. It is not something that will make the others ill. Now, let me see the cow, sir."

Captain Tillea moaned, rolling his eyes. Yet, he could not deny the reverence with which this lady was received. News of her arrival was still spreading. The little shed and corral were soon crowded with curious onlookers, both adults and children.

After looking at the cow, Caty shook her head. "This animal has eaten something bad. Keep her separate from the others, not because they might become ill, but because the cattle I've seen with this malady are very wild. She would seem to be getting better already." Rising, she tried to shake the debris from her skirts.

"She is getting better, 'tis true. Please take this as payment, Your Majesty," the man said. His extended hand held a small crucifix. "I know it is not much, but it is my most valuable possession."

Caty admonished him gently. "Sir, I believe your wife and daughters are your most valuable possessions. I would never think to take them. Someday I may have need of your services. I will know I can call on you." With that, she stepped, blinking, into the bright sunlight. Captain Tillea helped her mount.

"Caty, you know King Marcus will be wild with anger if he finds out what you just did," the old man said, a worried expression hovering over his face. "I pray he asks me not where I took you this day. We must ride like the storm coming. You are late, lady." The troop rode madly back to the castle, Caty in the middle, her horse's long strides easily keeping pace with the rest.

In her apartments, she rushed to bathe and change. The excursion had taken longer than she planned, though not unreasonably so. *Perhaps he will not notice*, she thought. Then she admitted to herself, *As if one could not notice a storm.* Entering court, she walked to her place as if nothing were amiss, stopping to visit with several men and their ladies.

Upon seeing her enter, Marcus took a deep breath and exhaled slowly. "Lord Rodolfo, can you find out just where she went?" The lord nodded and discreetly left.

FORTY-NINE

CATY SMILED AT MARCUS, A hopeful expression on her face. Leaning to her, he kissed her cheek before speaking into her ear. "You are late to dine, Caterina. That is not acceptable. I worried for your safety. You have a good reason? Did I not request you come back in time? I believe you agreed to our terms." He ended by setting his goblet of wine down, turning to her, and waiting. Their table had become silent.

"I beg your patience, sire. It took longer than expected to explain how to take the herbs. I planned poorly, apparently. Next time I will know better." The moment the words left her mouth, she would have given her best gown to have them back.

King Marcus scowled. His relief at her safe return was quickly being replaced by displeasure. "You think there will be a next time, Caterina? You are optimistic. Why did you not also take my physician?" He waited for her reply, his eyes narrowed and direct. Caty nodded to Lord Rodolfo, who had just sat down next to her.

"I did talk with him, before I left." Caty was doing her best to get Marcus off track.

"Caterina, you are ignoring my question. I will not ask again. Answer." He was becoming angrier.

"He could not go, sire," Caty answered softly. She bowed her head, closed her eyes, and tried to think. *This is not going so well. I think it will go even worse, soon.*

"Why is that, Caterina? Pray tell why he could not go." His voice was becoming quieter; if she had but known, she would have recognized the warning signs. Unaware of these, she fumbled blindly onward.

"Sire, he does not take care of pigs." The words tumbled out of her mouth.

Marcus could not believe what he heard from his wife. "Did I just hear you tell me he does not take care of *pigs*, Caterina?" He was frowning, leaning toward her. "Surely I heard wrong." His mind struggled to accept what his queen had said, his anger quickly rising.

"Yes, Your Majesty," Caty answered, her voice still barely audible.

"Speak up, Caterina!" He was now bellowing. "I would know what pigs have to do with this!"

Now the entire court had become quiet. Never before had Marcus taken Caty to task before their people, but it looked to be coming this time.

Lord Rodolfo attempted her rescue. Clearing his throat, he subtly nodded toward the crowded floor. "Sire, I spoke to Captain Tillea. While he was not pleased with the chore taken on this day, he reports that the populace served is loudly proclaiming your goodness and is even more bound to you." Lord Rodolfo calmly watched his friend.

Marcus was stunned. He turned, seeking the captain. When their eyes met, his questioning look was answered with a nod.

"Did I not just bid you to speak, Caterina?" Marcus pushed her. "I would understand what it is you have done this day." He had regained control of his voice, but Caty could clearly see the anger in his black eyes.

Caty cringed but spoke clearly. "I took care of a farmer's pig today."

Suppressed giggles could be heard from the king's table. Captain Tillea moaned inwardly. Marcus was momentarily speechless, but he soon found his tongue. "You *what*! My queen went to a pigsty today?"

"It was not just the pig, sire. The cow was ill too," Caty added hopefully. "Else I would not have been late."

Now open laughter rippled through the crowd. Marcus was embarrassed, and so angry that he could have throttled Caty. He could hardly speak.

The laughter of the hall bothered Caty more than the anger of her husband. When she spoke again, the hall fell silent. "You laugh, but this man has five children. The cow provides milk, butter, cream, and cheese to this family. The pig will be bred again, providing enough coins for this old man to keep his family sheltered. I have seen illness from animals kill entire villages, man and animal. Ask the physician whether this is not so. My choice was either to go see for myself and treat the animals, or to merely hope they get well. Not really a choice to my mind. Each one of you would do whatever it took to care for your children. The farmer would do the same for his. How could I not help him? Only by the grace of His Majesty did I go! You must know he loves all his subjects, and values them all, even the most insignificant of them."

Many of the crowd now bowed their heads in embarrassment. Captain Tillea smiled to himself. *How well I know this story*, he thought, *and the heroine*.

"Did you touch it?" someone called from the gathering. King Marcus dropped his head into his hands. Surely there could not be more to this tale.

With her chin tilted up in defiance, Caty spoke before she had time to think. "Yes, I touched both; I knelt in the stable on the hay with the farmer. I did." She realized how what she had just said must sound. With trepidation, she looked to Marcus. He was staring at her, dumbfounded. "When I returned, I bathed before coming to join my king." Her voice tapered off weakly. "I think I am in trouble," she murmured to herself.

King Marcus quickly found his tongue. "Go to your chambers. I will see you there at my pleasure." His eyes were flashing, his face dark, his jaw pulsating. Without speaking, Caty bowed and turned to leave.

"I will walk with you," a young voice called to her. "He cannot spank you, Majesty. You're all grown up." The words were plain to everyone in the hall. Santino stood at his usual place, and now ran to take her hand. His mother was horrified, but Caty took the hand. People sitting or standing near now roared with laughter.

Under his breath, Marcus muttered, "Don't count on it. I care not that she is an adult."

"I will send him back with Lord Rodolfo, lady," Caty said to the anxious mother.

The two, followed by Lord Rodolfo and Caty's ladies, left court.

"Did you really help a pig, Majesty?" the lad asked in wonder. He walked along with Caty, clinging happily to her hand.

"I did. Sometimes the things we look down on are the only things other people have. That pig being healthy means that his family will eat for a while. Besides, we wouldn't want other pigs to become ill. Still, you must remember, child, I was wrong to anger the king."

The boy nodded solemnly. "If I ever have pigs and they become ill, I would ask you to care for them." He looked at Caty with a serious furrow between his little brows.

She could see Lord Rodolfo's face break into a wide grin. He mouthed the words "me too" over the child's head, to Caty.

"And I would never be angry with you," the lad added in defense of his friend. At this declaration, Lord Rodolfo had to turn away to prevent the child from seeing his laughter.

When they reached Caty's rooms, the boy impulsively reached to hug her neck and kiss her, then turned to Lord Rodolfo. "Are you ready to go back? I'm hungry now." And off he ran, back the way they had come.

"Lord Rodolfo, thank you for escorting me," Caty said. "It was easier than having to walk out alone. That was kind of you." Caty noted his smile, which played about his face despite his best efforts to stay serious. *He wants to laugh*, she thought. As he bowed, she cautioned, "Don't laugh in front of Marcus." His smile broadened and he chuckled.

After sending her ladies away, Caty changed into her sleeping gown, built the fire up, and sat to wait for Marcus. When he did not return as the night wore on, Caty changed again, replacing her sleeping gown with a riding gown. *It looks like he will send me to my castle, certainly alone. I would be ready to go at once, to avoid anyone. No matter, the farmer and his family know the truth. As does my physician friend.* Sighing, she picked up her rosary and waited by the fire.

Back in the great hall, Marcus continued to talk with his men, trying to act as normal as he could, but his rage was visible to those closest to him. Finally he gave in to his wonder and anger. "Bring Captain Tillea to me," he told Lord Rodolfo. "I would hear how he let this happen."

Lord Rodolfo nodded, adding with carefully chosen words, "He would die before he allowed any harm to the queen. Still, he knows her nature. If he refused to take her, she would have found another way, I'm certain, sire. She is of a strong mind." As he turned to leave, he added quietly, "Fitting for one such as you, Marcus."

Marcus knew that Rodolfo was right. Better to have Tillea with her than have her running about unescorted. *Damnation!* he thought. *How do I handle this? I want to wring her neck like a duck, but*—he smiled to himself, despite his anger—*I would miss her sorely.*

Captain Tillea confirmed what Rodolfo had already told him. "Captain," Marcus said once the old man had finished his tale, "I would know—was the mother like the daughter? From where does this independence spring? How did Lord Tabor deal with the mother?" By now, the drama was over and the dancing had resumed. The wine was calming Marcus as well. The court was busy with itself, and Marcus could speak without worry.

"Her nature is of both parents, sire. Truly she is like her mother again. Both in beauty and temperament. Lord Tabor had times he felt as I believe you are feeling now; he could not be without her, though, sire. She loved him deeper than most men could ever dream of being loved. Because of this, she was totally honest and open with him. Spoke her mind clearly and"—he chuckled at the memory—"frequently. Lord Tabor's men loved her. To a man, we would have gladly died for Lady Tabor."

Marcus nodded as he listened. How well he knew the feeling. *Having allowed my temper to expose this problem to everyone here, I must handle it as publicly*, he thought. *She does speak the truth. The people she spent her day with love her more honestly than do most of the people in my court.*

Marcus turned to Rodolfo. "Tell me, Rudy, did she and the boy talk on the way back to her rooms?"

"She told him the farmer needed the pig and cow to keep his family. She added that she was wrong to anger you, and that he must never do that."

"Was the lad impressed with the advice?" Marcus asked dryly.

"It was hard to tell, sire, with one so young. He did hug and kiss her good-bye before running back to fill his hungry belly," Rodolfo said, laughing.

"Ah, and he promised to call on her if he ever had sick pigs." All within hearing laughed.

After a short while, Marcus spoke to Rodolfo, Captain Tillea, and all others within range of his voice. "I see she earns the love of the most helpless of my people. Perhaps we could all take a better look at how we care for these." Draining his goblet, he rose to go to his wife.

FIFTY

IN HER ROOMS, CATY WAS dozing off and on, by turns pacing and sitting before the fire. The longer she waited, the more she imagined how awful the consequences would be. *Please help me find the words to soothe his anger at me. Pray he is not angry with my poor captain.* Fear she may have placed Captain Tillea in an awkward position with the king bothered her more than her own fate.

When Marcus opened the door at last, he found an empty chair before the fire. Looking about the room, he found her at the window. Her silhouette was so still it seemed she had turned to stone. He also stood unmoving at the open door. He had half expected her to be in bed asleep. Pleased she was still up waiting for him, he locked the door behind him and walked slowly to her. Caty held her breath; she had no idea what might happen next.

"Caterina," he said, stopping before the blazing fire. "Come here." His voice was commanding and Caty knew he was still angry, but not as before.

With her heart pounding, she walked to him, her eyes never leaving his. When she reached him, she curtsied as she spoke. "Sire?"

He extended his hand to her. He helped her to stand, then released her hand and sat in his chair. He left Caty standing alone for a long moment. "Come stand before your king, Caterina. The king you saw well to leave in worry and anger until it pleased you to return."

Making her face calm, Caty studied the king as she stood before him, her hands clasped loosely in front of her. Marcus stared at this wisp before him. Her countenance was calm, serene, peaceful. For the first time tonight, he noticed that she had been crying. With satisfaction, he noted that she remained silent. He knew she was anxious but not frightened. That pleased him also. He would not have her afraid of him. He loved her too much for that. "I am going to give you a chance to explain yourself once more, Caterina, before I decide how best to punish you. Speak to me." His voice lacked the angry thrust of earlier.

Taking a breath, Caty looked down at this man she now loved more than she dreamed she ever could have. "Marcus," she began carefully, "all of my life I have had people coming to me and asking for help. In the beginning, my mother was the one they wanted. I learned from her, from my father's physician, and from the monastery near one of our encampments. It came easy to me."

She paused, collecting her thoughts. "Here, it has been not unlike other places. The people become ill, their animals become ill, life goes on. What I have come to see is this—when you lose a horse, you are saddened, as you reluctantly choose another." Caty looked kindly at Marcus. "When one of the lowest of your people loses a goat, a pig, a cow, or consequently, a child, his life becomes doubly more difficult. Hunger is a constant companion for many. It is difficult to appreciate the wonder of this world when one is holding a dying child. Of that I have firsthand knowledge."

Caty now moved closer to the king and knelt on the floor, looking into his face. "I have received many requests since I've come to your castle, Marcus. I cannot deny what I am, nor what I can do to help them. I would not anger you, husband. It is more difficult to go about the things I can do with all the trappings that come with my station in life now—but still, I must try. When this man today knew his animals would survive and his family would be safe for even the shortest time, his thankfulness was without expression." Her face, turned up to him, was filled with sincerity.

Marcus watched Caty. Her golden eyes caught the light from the fire, and it danced in their depths. "Caterina, you place me in a difficult position. You cannot simply crawl about the ground, take off and go where you are not protected, taking chances like this. I could not even begin to think on living without your love, your touch, and"—he smiled slightly—"your trick of touching just the spot that sets my anger aflame." He leaned back in his chair, his eyes closed. While she could think of a thousand things to say, she knew this was a time for silence.

His hand gently touched her face. "You are not dressed for bed, Caterina." Studying her, he thought, *She hesitates to speak. I know her better as time passes. Pray I have the patience to see our lives through.*

"I was dressed for sleep, sire," Caty responded hesitantly. "My fear you would send me away became strong. I would not stay here changing when I needed to be gone from you. I care not to cry in front of you." Caty looked down for a second. She missed the smile of victory that passed on his face.

"Caterina, on the morrow I will ask Lord Rodolfo, my physician, and Captain Tillea to meet with me. We will assign men to work with you. If you find it impossible to stay put, at least you will be cared for. My command is that each day, you will meet with Lord Rodolfo and Captain Tillea, go over what requests you have received, and decide how best to meet them. You are not to leave the castle or its grounds without my permission. Remember, Caterina, Captain Tillea is not your husband, nor your king. You must ask me first. My decision will direct your next steps. If you disobey me, Caterina, all arrangements are cancelled and you will no longer be allowed to help anyone. Am I quite clear, Caterina?" He had devised a way to keep her safe. He knew she would not jeopardize this chance he had given her to help the people. When she did not immediately answer, he frowned, reaching up and tipping her face toward him. "Caterina?"

Her face was beaming. "Yes, yes, Marcus. I would comply with what you have asked. Thank you, Marcus. Your people will know what you do for them."

"Hmm, I would rather know what *you* will do for *me*. What can I expect this night, lady?" He pulled her onto his lap. "Ah, before we go further, love, there is another matter to discuss. You have a very small knight. I would like to assign him to Lord Rodolfo directly, to learn to care for you. Perhaps he could be a companion for you." Marcus knew young Santino was attached to Caty. He waited faithfully for her each evening, before returning to his family. He was growing taller, and looked to have the potential to be a tough soldier.

"That pleases me more than I can express, sire. In the evening, he must go to his mother, though. Certainly she would miss him sorely." Caty could not fathom forcing the mother to lose a child.

"You need not worry about his mother, Caterina. She has five younger and four older than him, all boys. She will gladly take a break from one. It has come to my attention that she is well pleased with you and with his admiration for you. The match will be good, I am certain. Now, lady, take care of your husband." He set her back onto the floor and began undressing, leaving his clothes where they fell; such was his drive to lie with his prize, for a prize is how he felt about this small bundle of trouble he had the good fortune to claim. "Come, Caterina, remind me why I will have patience tomorrow when you ignite my anger again." He laughed softly, folding her within his embrace.

When Caty rose with morning's light, she flung wide the shutters. The sun was bright. Marcus had already gone. He was to hunt on this morning. That usually meant he would be gone all day. Happily, she went about making ready for her day. When Rose waddled through the door, Caty was already dressed and waiting. "Lady, I think as you get older, you rise like the cocks," the older woman said. "For the king's sake, pray you do not crow, too."

"I leave the crowing for His Majesty," Caty laughed. With the passing years, Rose had become more like a sister to Caty. Their easy banter was interrupted by the arrival of her ladies. The schedule for the day was agreed upon. Just as everyone began to scatter, one of the ladies ushered in Lord Rodolfo and Caty's small friend from the night before.

They both bowed, and Lord Rodolfo smiled at Caty. It was very hard to stay angry with her. *She grows prettier by the day*, he thought. *Livelier too, I would wager.* "I bring a new member of your staff, Your Majesty. Officially, I present Santino. Santino, you are supposed to bow now."

His young face turned to the lord, brows furrowed with the weight of such a new place. "I already did. Do I do it again?" It was clear he wanted to do everything right.

Suppressing a laugh, Caty answered, "Yes, unfortunately, we do lots of bow-ing around here." She stretched her hand to him and was surprised when he immediately flew into her arms. "Oh, I suppose we are old friends now. We shared a dance and you escorted me to my chamber. However, I must let you go. I know you have a busy day ahead of you. Please come see me before we dine, Santino. Thank you for agreeing to serve me. I know you will do very well. And Lord Rodolfo, thank you for bringing Santino by to see me. He has a place to stay?"

Lord Rodolfo smiled and nodded. Caty could see that the little man had already worked his magic on Lord Rodolfo, too. "You always please me with your thoughtfulness, sir," she said. "Marcus does well to love you as he does." Caty smiled graciously at Lord Rodolfo. "If you should find you need your rooms back for a while, please do not hesitate to allow your charge to come visit me. I expect I will see him frequently, in between lessons about being a proper companion for his queen."

Rodolfo bowed, nudging his small charge to do the same. They both left, Santino asking questions one after another.

Caty spent the morning visiting with the physician. "I hear you earned the king's displeasure, Majesty," the old man said, his face worried. "Is he still vexed with you?"

"No, he made his point well, however. He intends to assign specific men to a council with you, to review requests that might come to our attention; every-one will decide how best to proceed. My friend, when we are alone, let me ask that you please tell me what you think without hesitation. If you ever feel the need to see me alone, so be it. The king will, of course, see how we progress. I cannot leave the castle or property without his permission. I can live with that . . . I think."

The old man chuckled. "I expect you can, Caterina." He looked at her kindly. He was quite fond of her and did not care who might know. She was very intelligent and a quick learner. She was also willing to share all she knew. It was a new world he found himself working in, one that no longer required him to argue his way around. She was a strong supporter. They continued their business by discussing the ill pig and cow, and then Caty showed him the herbs she had collected for him and presented him with several bundles of candles.

The sun had moved well beyond its high point before she left his rooms. Hurrying through the halls, lest she be seen, Caty slipped out of the castle, hugging her cloak close. Already the seasons were changing. She would surprise Marcus when he returned. She had missed his banter this morning. Coming to the king's stable, she maneuvered into the stall with her horse, sharing an apple with him while she waited. She planned on stepping out to him when he returned. To her horror, she heard footsteps. Quickly, she crouched down. "It would do me no good to be seen alone without an escort," she whispered to the horse. "What was I thinking? I was not, as usual."

FIFTY-ONE

HARDLY DARING TO BREATHE, SHE hid. The horse was careful as he stepped about his stall. *Thank goodness he knows me. This would not be such a good idea with one of the other horses.* Hidden, she listened as a small group of men discussed the king. They had been allowed to attend court by order of one of the king's men, but she couldn't hear the name. Not unusual to have men from other courts attending. The men were French. As the men spoke, a sick feeling began to fill Caty, a feeling that grew with each moment. It did not take long for her to realize that these men plotted to take the king's life. Marcus hunted frequently during the week, and the traitor who had invited these two Frenchmen to court was to let them know the next time the hunt was called. The traitor had been spying on Marcus for some time. Upon the next hunt, the massacre would take place. Caty listened to every word. No name was spoken other than the king's. When at last the stables became quiet, Caty remained hidden. After only a few moments, Caty heard Marcus talking. She listened in vain for the Frenchmen. They had gone.

Slowly, she raised herself up. Captain Tillea saw her first. She shook her head and looked for Marcus, then slid back down when she realized several of his hunting party were riding into the stable corral. Taking the horse from Marcus, Captain Tillea leaned close and spoke quietly. "Sire, do not let it be known, but you have a small frightened visitor with her steed." Marcus looked with surprise at the captain, then glanced around his stables. He sauntered to the stall, speaking to Caty's horse, all the while searching the darkened areas for what he knew must be Caty. Not seeing her, he opened the stall door, stepped inside, and found his wife hidden against the darkest corner of the stall, behind her horse. Caty was unsure just who might still be in the stables. He watched his wife; through the dark, his eyes met hers.

"Captain, has Caterina taken this animal out to exercise it today?" he asked.

"Not that I know of, Your Majesty. That does not mean it has not been done, however."

"Hmm, you are right." He watched his wife. *She knows I am here. Why does she still cower in the corner?* "Boy, call Lord Rodolfo to me. I would visit with him. Close the gates after yourself. Be quick. I am hungry." The young stable hand who had met the king and his men as they returned acknowledged the order. Caty could hear him running away.

"In my heart, I know there is a good explanation for what I see. Please share it with me." The king reached down to take her hand. It was cold and clammy. She was trembling. "Caterina, what ails you?" He now spoke softly, with great concern.

"Take me to our rooms. I must not be seen coming from here," Caty answered, her voice calm, unlike her body.

Marcus looked to her captain. "How? Think quickly." Both men looked around the stable and toward the castle. Lord Rodolfo walked in at that moment.

"Marcus—in the loft there is a bundle," Caty said. "Lift me up, and I will change. Quickly."

The king knew his wife well enough to know she did not frighten easily. Not wasting time with questions, he did as she asked. Caty moved about the loft, located the bundle she had hidden there when she was running away from Marcus, and was changed in minutes. When she came to the edge to be assisted down, all three men were startled. They sent a queen up to the loft; they helped down a scruffy stable hand.

She handed her clothes to Marcus; he wrapped them in his cloak and tossed it over his arm. As other men began to arrive to work with the horses, Marcus played along with the charade. He cuffed her lightly on the shoulder and began scolding her. "You were asked to get my cloak, boy. Take this one; it's too heavy. Be quick about it." Then he resumed his discussion with the two men. All three wandered back to the castle slowly, deep in conversation, while Caty walked in plain sight through the kitchen entrance, took the back stairs, and slipped up into their rooms.

Hastily, she pulled the old clothes off, tossed them into the fire, donned her dress, and tried in vain to smooth out the wrinkles. Her ladies heard movement behind the closed door and entered. They were happily going about their afternoon duties. One noticed Caty's dress. "Majesty, your gown—you must change, quickly." Not waiting for an answer, she began to sift through Caty's gowns.

Caty nodded, and quickly responded. "I suppose I should change. Does this look too messy? We really must find better chairs and more room for the physician. Have any of you been in his apartments? Oh my goodness. No wonder he comes here so frequently," Caty noted casually, hoping to avoid any questions. "I would too, if I lived there!"

At that moment, King Marcus entered. He had long ago grown accustomed to the fact that when he came to see his wife, he would have to send everyone away. He did so now as he grabbed his wife and swung her around. The women left, Caty calling after them, "I will see you all downstairs. We must not be late." Her ladies hurried to change and make court on time.

Marcus walked to the door, locked it, and studied his wife as he returned to her. "I am listening, Caterina. This promises to be the best tale yet." He shook his head. Caty could tell he was not angry; he was reserving judgment until he heard from her. She quickly told him everything she had heard.

He stood but a moment in thought. "I must speak with Rodolfo and Tillea." He made the door in two long strides, unlocked it, and was nearly knocked over by a young bundle of energy dashing into their room.

The lad immediately stopped, bowed, and said, "Majesty?" With a worried face, he looked to Caty.

"Queen Caty," she interjected quickly. "Santino, can you keep a secret?"

"Mum says I am the best!" he proudly proclaimed.

"Do you know where Lord Rodolfo and Captain Tillea might be?" Caty quizzed him.

He leaned toward her, whispering. "I do, should I not tell you? I can keep it secret."

"No, child. I would ask you to run to both and tell them the king needs to see them, now, in his room. Can you remember that?" She knelt, with her hands on his small shoulders.

"Yes, Queen Caty." He stood straight and proud.

"You must take care no one else hears what it is you say, and you must go, fast as the wind. Run now." Caty turned him to the door and closed it behind his running little feet.

"I see we might use this little messenger. Tell me again what you heard, Caterina." Before she could finish the second telling, a soft knock at their door interrupted her. Caterina opened the door and stepped aside as Lord Rodolfo and Captain Tillea entered, followed by the lad.

"Santino," the king instructed, "you must stand quietly outside the door and see that no one else enters. You are protecting Queen Caty. If someone tries to come in, stand before the door and call out." Marcus led both men into his dressing room.

Nodding in satisfaction, Santino opened the door and stepped out. Caty followed the men into the king's dressing room and again told what she had overheard. "Did you recognize any of them, Majesty?" Lord Rodolfo asked her.

"No, I was much too low to see clearly. I could only hear." She could feel the heat of a blush. Lord Rodolfo did not ask for details. He simply nodded.

Marcus walked to the fire and stood staring into its flames, his hands clasped behind his back. His two most trusted men left by the king's private stairs. Caty went to her husband. Fear for his safety filled her heart. "Can you stop this, Marcus? What is this about?"

He pulled her close. "France would like to take Tuscany and other smaller countries. It has been a constant issue. Caterina, do you think you would recognize the voices, out of the five Frenchmen that attend my court, should you hear them again?"

"Certainly. Tell me what to do next." Her face was serious but calm. He bent to kiss the lips he so loved.

"You must walk through the court, as you always do, and"—he laughed softly—"as I always take you to task over. Start this night and do so every day. And, Caterina," his voice now becoming stern, "think carefully on why you were in my stables unescorted. We will discuss your latest adventure when we return this night. I trust it will be most entertaining." He kissed her again, long and with passion.

"Sire, you must not. If you continue, we will miss dining. I find I would rather lie with you." Caty was breathing heavily, her eyes closed.

He smiled down at her. "Soon, love." He gave her a quick kiss and started for the door. When he opened it, he found Santino still guarding his queen. Marcus smiled at the small boy, as the child bowed. "You did very well, Santino. I shall tell your uncle and grandfather how well you protect my wife."

"Santino," Caty asked, frowning, "who are your uncle and grandfather?"

"Why, Lord Rodolfo and Captain Tillea. That is what I am to call them, Lord Rodolfo told me. He said they are like an uncle and grandfather. I don't think I have an uncle, and my grandfather is dead. So it's all right. Is it time for us to eat? My stomach is calling for food." He looked at them both seriously.

Caty nodded. "You may go on and find your uncle or grandfather. Tell them your queen thanks them for allowing you to stay so long at your post. You make me very proud. I agree, it is time for you to eat."

His beaming face lit the halls as he ran happily to eat.

"We will certainly discuss the fact that I am your king and you as yet seem not to understand what obedience means, my lady," said Marcus. "Come, my stomach also calls for food." With Caty's arm on his, he headed for court. *This night promises to be most entertaining. Perhaps Caterina's wandering has a purpose*, Marcus thought.

As she was wont to do, Caty quietly moved to the floor after dinner had been eaten. Visiting with the women, she wandered about. Little Santino stayed at her heels, his face intent as he tried to keep up with his queen.

The night was nearly gone when a young man asked Caty to dance. His name was Gus, and he had been with Marcus for five years now as a member of the royal guard. Caty readily danced with him after getting her husband's nod of approval. She was tempted to share her fears for Marcus with him, but Marcus had asked that no one be told. As they moved about the floor, they talked instead about Santino. "He is a delight, Gus. So serious, though. I enjoy both his views on our doings and his questions. Life seen through the eyes of a child is quite simple, and much more meaningful."

"How so, my lady?" Gus said, puzzled. "How can a child know more than even a young adult? Do you not tire of his constant babbling?"

Caty laughed. "I see he has found you, also. Be patient with him, Gus. He will learn quickly who he can trust and who plays with his little mind. He is no fool, that boy."

Gus shook his head, and the conversation drifted to other things. Making a turn toward the back of the hall, Caty heard a man call to Gus. Gus paused, causing them to be nearly upended by another dancing couple. Grateful for the collision that hid her start, Caty turned to see who had called to Gus. She did not recognize the man, but knew that voice. She forced herself to be calm while Gus answered the man. Both spoke in perfect French. Gus agreed to a meeting, then swept Caty along. Her heart broke. She wanted to cry. She knew what must come next.

They had danced nearer to Marcus and his table by the time the dance ended. Santino was waiting jealously for her return. "Queen Caty, may I have this dance?" He looked up at her expectantly.

"In truth, Santino, I would rather sit and visit with you. Come sit near and let me catch my breath. I am a little older than you, and would have need of a short rest." She smiled at him, her stomach turning.

"I think you must be a lot older than I, Queen Caty. You look very different. You should sit." He led her to her chair.

Marcus could read her face; he knew her expressions intimately by now. This would be a good time for her to leave. He watched her search the crowd, her hand on Santino's shoulder. "Ah, I see who I search for, Santino. You must go and give your mother a kiss and a man's hug. Share some time with her. She loves you a great deal, to allow you to be with me." Caty nodded toward the woman watching her son with pride. Santino ran off.

Caty turned to Marcus. "I feel I must retire, Majesty. If it pleases you, perhaps you might come soon also."

Marcus nodded. "Lord Rodolfo, you and Captain Tillea please meet at my apartment shortly. Give Her Majesty time to be gone without drawing further notice." He could see the concern on Caty's face. "Caterina, this is nothing new," he said to her in a low voice. "Such things have gone on since there were rulers and ruled." Forcing a small smile, Caty bowed to him. As she turned to leave, he reached for her and whispered into her neck, "Worry not, love."

Santino saw that his lady would leave and, after kissing his mother, ran to Caty. Caty walked to the mother and thanked her again for allowing Santino to serve her. "You have done a beautiful job with this young man. He is well liked and trusted." Caty nodded to Santino. "Let us take our leave, Santino. I think these people would dance." The two, along with her ladies, left the great hall, followed by several of Tillea's men.

At her chamber door, Caty gave Santino a hug and kiss. It had become their routine. Though the lad was nearly walking in his sleep by this time, he would not think of leaving without his kiss from his queen. As he left her room, Caty prayed for his safety. *Marcus must take care that the child is protected. I could never forgive myself if something happened to him.*

Caty made certain the fire was blazing in Marcus's dressing room. Fresh candles were set about and lit. Wine and goblets were placed on a small service table nearby. Chairs were close to each other. Now she would wait.

FIFTY-TWO

THE FIRST TO ARRIVE WAS Rodolfo. He discreetly wandered to the hall's end, waiting for Tillea or Marcus. They arrived together, laughing and visiting. Both entered the king's dressing room, followed by Rodolfo. "Caterina," King Marcus said, "share what it is you heard that gives you such a heavy heart." His voice, gentle and comforting, came to her before she saw him.

She stood, hardly able to admit what she now knew as truth. All three men now stood around her. "Your groom, Gus, was not one of the voices in the stable. I know him well. Tonight, though, a man called to him while we danced. When he stopped to speak to the man, it was clear they knew each other well. The man carried a message to Gus from someone else. His voice I recognized. The man speaks in French and is dressed as a Frenchman. He asked Gus to confirm when you plan to start your progress, and then asked him to meet with him near the stables, at dawn. He expects that that will give Gus time to have your horse ready as usual." When she finished, her hand went to her throat. "I understand not. Gus? Why?"

"A good question, Caterina." He paused, watching his wife carefully. She was worried, he knew, but now the time was his. The problem and its solution were his. He would keep her safe and shield her from the unpleasantness at hand.

Before he could direct her, she noted, "I think perhaps you would like to visit with your men, Marcus? I would like to walk in the gardens below. 'Twill soon be too cold for such small pleasures. I would take the captain's men and my ladies." Bowing to him, she left. He smiled, watching her leave him to do his work.

After knocking lightly on the doors of her ladies' quarters, she soon had several ready and happy to take a turn about the grounds. The little group entered the gardens, happily visiting with the soldiers accompanying them. Caty was left to her own thoughts for most of the walk. At some point, one of the men, older than the others, stepped in time with her. "You seem troubled, Majesty. Is there something one of us can do for you? This is not usual for you, to wander about at night." His kind face looked upon her with concern.

"Thank you, sir. I am fine, really. I was just thinking on how life has swept me along, sometimes not so willingly, to this place. It is very different from the place whence I came, but not so different from where I spent much of my childhood. I have found the people here most kind and gentle, and with a foreign queen no less." Caty smiled at him.

"'Tis because of you they are kind, Majesty. You have made it easy for them to take you into their hearts. The people out there"—he waved beyond the castle walls—"love you."

One of the king's footmen caught up to them. "Majesty, the king requests your presence. He is in your chambers waiting." The young man bowed and left them.

"My father was a commander for England. He and his men had a hard job. At times, my heart goes out to the young men in every realm," Caty confided to the soldier who walked with her. "Many seem too young to understand the politics of a monarchy." She glanced at the older man. He was shaking his head in disagreement, ever so slightly.

"Have you something to add, sir?" Caty prompted him.

"Only that there is not an age of innocence. Kingdoms are passed on to infant kings. Children are ordered killed to protect the Crown. 'Tis the time we live in. Our king is just and kind. He *is* the king, though. He makes what decisions he must. I've only served King Marcus, but I believe they all rule much the same."

"You are right," Caty noted sadly. "I would add, it takes more than a crown to make a queen. I suppose I am still too ordinary," Caty admitted.

"Majesty, there is nothing ordinary about you. You are every inch a queen." Solemnly he added, "Perhaps a mite too independent, but a queen nonetheless."

Knocking gently on the doors leading to their quarters, Caty entered. The room was dark but for the light of a dying fire. She expected to see him seated at the fireplace, but he was not to be seen. She walked into his library. He was studying papers spread out before him on a large table. Sir Rodolfo and Captain Tillea were still with him, and several others had now joined the men. They looked up at her when she walked into the room. "I'm sorry, Your Grace, I believe I misunderstood." She bowed and backed away.

"Caterina, I sent for you. We will be here for a while. I have asked my page to stay up with me. Give me a moment; I would speak with you." He turned back to the map and the men resumed their talk. Caty had been in many such sessions with her father. She knew to keep lights strong and the fire going, and to have room for additional men as the need arose. Not certain how much she should do in Marcus's war room, she at first sat quietly. As candles burned down, she lit more. She added wood to the fires and kept the room secure.

Hours later, her king had still not called her. As she stood at one of the large windows in his library, she watched the sun rise. Its rays gave a gold shimmer to the lake below and bathed the land with a glimpse of newness. Caty sighed. So beautiful, yet so dangerous. Life is not forgiving, nor is it patient, when men are pushed to fight.

Marcus had passed the night planning their defense. Caty was hesitant to intrude, but she was bothered by something. At last, when all but Marcus, Tillea, and Rudy had gone, she spoke up. "Sire, are there so few of your court that speak French?"

Marcus looked up from his task to focus on her question. "Ask again, Caterina, I was not listening," he answered patiently. She repeated the question.

"Most of the court speaks French. It is likely there are more involved than we thought at first," Marcus replied. "Why do you ask?"

"I find it strange that Gus would speak so openly, with me as his dance partner. Possibly he assumed I did not speak French. Surely others heard the conversation. Has no one come forward?"

All three men looked at each other, then at her. "It is larger than we first thought," said Marcus. "We've spent some time talking with the court guests, and several have come forward, after overhearing Gus. Most have little to add, but were not comfortable with what was said. Most of those associated with the man Gus spoke to are now in custody. Not one of them could believe you speak French." He stood up, stretched, and yawned. "Gentlemen, I wish to spend some time with my wife. We will walk for a while. Page, send for food and drink. I think we have a long day before us." He took Caty's arm and led her out.

When they were away from prying ears, he gently spoke of Gus. "Gus was tried and sentenced last night. He is to hang today. Not in public, as we hope to catch three more men. Each of the men taken last night will be tried and sentenced accordingly."

Caty's heart was heavy, but she would not allow pity to excuse what Gus had attempted. "I want you safe," she replied. Marcus put his arm around her as they walked.

"You have set up a war room in my study without anyone knowing," he said. "From where did you learn that?"

"My father. I sat with him during most of his meetings. No one noticed a woman running around getting food and drink, bringing maps, or providing light and ink. I learned while I sat." They walked a bit farther. "After the men were all gone, I sat with Father and asked questions. He was well known for his military acumen." Her pride was strong in her voice.

"That he was," Marcus agreed. "Perhaps you would share with me how you came to be in the stables alone?" He continued to walk along the path, his hands behind his back.

Caty laughed at the irony of the situation. "I intended to surprise you when you returned from your ride. What a surprise, don't you think?"

"Caterina—" he started, his voice stern.

"I know, Marcus. I know. I would never even think of doing such a thing again, although it is truly a blessing I did just this once. You will be safe, at least this time, because of my errant ways, Your Grace."

Marcus had stopped walking and now stood staring at her, his brows raised in disbelief. "Your point is well taken," he admitted grudgingly. "However, the command—and this is, Caterina, a command—is that you are not to be without a guard. Now more than ever. Agreed?"

"Yes." Caty reached for his arm. "Agreed." Marcus pulled her close to him as they wandered back to the castle. Before he left their bedchamber, he kissed her. Shaking his head, he opened the door to his study.

Through that day, Marcus continued to meet in his study. Once she had slept a few hours, Caty kept the room quiet, kept food and supplies stocked, and waited for the day she knew would come. The intrigue deepened with time. This had been no rogue plot. France was already amassing forces at Marcus's northern border. Marcus would leave to fight.

Three months later, she kissed Marcus with fear in her heart. She had lost one husband; she could not lose another.

"Caterina, if something happens to me, you must leave immediately for your castle. Captain Tillea knows what to do. Take Santino and your ladies with you. I have assigned additional men to defend you; they will go also. You will be safe there. The castle belongs to you, and is in your maiden name only." He held her tightly. Then, standing away, his eyes moved over her slowly. He wanted to remember every detail of this woman. Caty walked him to his horse. His men were ready.

She waved to him, smiled through tear-filled eyes. "Go safely, husband. I care not to lose my love again."

Marcus returned in only two months' time. The fight went well for him. The battle had been short though furious. France would be held at bay for a while. Keen to get back to Caty, he bounded up the stairs to their quarters. She was not there. Asking for her, he found she had gone out to care for someone's horse, and was struggling to deliver its first colt.

Anger flared within Marcus. He had no desire to repeat the previous episode.

After asking for directions, he stormed outside and called for his horse again. Lord Rodolfo rode up, the king's tired horse in tow. "Sire, are you in need of assistance? I will go with you."

Marcus nodded as he mounted but spoke not about the mission he left for. Rudy motioned to several men who were just beginning to dismount; they climbed back on their steeds and rode after them. Once they were through the gates, Rudy noted casually to the king, "Where do we ride, Your Majesty? With so few men, I think we do not ride to do battle."

"We go to a certain village, for Caty. She may have need of protection," Marcus growled back. "I ride home expecting to find my wife, only to find she is delivering a colt. I go to bring her home."

Sir Rodolfo had to bite his tongue to prevent the laughter in his throat. Silently, they rode. After an hour's time, they came to the village. From the crowd gathered at the stables, and the presence of Caty's guard, Marcus was certain he would find his lady there. His men scattered about to ensure the safety of the king and queen. They need not have done so; this village loved Caty. She was in good hands here. A murmur went up from the crowd: "The king comes too."

Rudy noted softly to the king as they approached, "It would be to your advantage to save your anger for your chambers. These people believe you have come to assist also. Good for you, sire." He smiled innocently at Marcus.

Marcus was shaken from his thoughts by the crowd's reaction to him. "Humph," he muttered, but he knew Rodolfo was right, again.

As she knelt next to a pregnant mare in the stables, Caty was telling a farmer what he must do. It was clear the exhausted animal had been at this for a long time. Caty spoke gently, all the while moving slowly to the rear. Rolling her sleeves up, she began to reach up for the colt; the mare was unable to deliver it turned as it was. She kept talking to the mare. Strong men held the horse closely. The animal seemed to understand that help was at hand.

Once she found the colt, Caty encouraged the mare. "Push, mother! Push hard, one more time." She prayed the mare still had strength to do what was necessary. From deep within the horse a grunt rose, and the animal pushed again.

With the push, Caty turned and pulled. The mare moaned and tried again. Caty sensed the colt was moving and so did the mare. The next push brought the colt out. It had been difficult work, and so intense was Caty that she failed to notice the atmosphere in the now crowded stall had changed. She peeled the afterbirth away from the tiny colt and rubbed the animal with a large rag, checking to be certain its legs were not broken. Finally, she brought it to the mother's nose, letting the mother smell this small bundle that had just come near to killing her.

"Will she live, m'lady?" the farmer asked anxiously. He knelt at the mare's head, stroking her, talking to her. The mare was trying to stand.

"I hope so, sir," Caty answered, instructing the men around to help the mare. The tired mare now stood spread-legged, her head hanging. The colt suckled as if this afternoon had never been. It was at this point that Caty noticed the king standing nearby, watching her. She knew he was not certain whether to be angry or proud. Trying to sway him toward pride, Caty acknowledged him and stepped aside so he might examine the mare and colt. King Marcus stroked the mare's neck and ran his experienced hand down her chest and back.

"The mare will live," he said. "She will be weak for a few days, and someone should check on her often. The colt is like most children: only his appetite is important." Laughter answered him.

When Caty had finished with her parting instructions, she came to him, her face flushed with the day's work, her eyes lit with the excitement of the birth, and her clothes bearing evidence of her involvement. "Sire, you've come home! How I've missed you."

"I see you have found ways to occupy your time," he replied sarcastically. Silently, he helped his wife mount, then rode beside her as they left the village. As they rode past, people called to Caty, waving and blowing her kisses, and cheered the king. Near the edge of the little village, a group of children had gathered. As she rode by, they tossed flowers to her, cheering. Caty waved.

As the king and queen's party left the mayhem behind, Caty turned to her husband. "You are not pleased with my actions, Marcus. Would you be more pleased if I had let the mare die?"

"I came home hoping to find my wife. Imagine my disappointment when I wandered through an empty room. To find her, I must scour the countryside and search dark corners of a barn." His voice was low and stern.

"What did you find in the barn, Your Grace?" Caty pushed him.

He glanced at her. She rode beside him, serene, beautiful, filthy, still every inch a queen. How could he stay angry? He reached out and found her small hand. They rode this way for a long time.

After a while, Marcus stopped his horse, as did the rest of the party. Confused and waiting for his next move, Caty watched him dismount, throw his reins over the stallion's neck, and walk toward her. Her heart beat faster, but she forced herself to remain collected and calm.

Reaching for her, he helped her down from her horse. "You smell like a horse stable, Caterina. You're covered in blood and hay. I care not." With that observation he walked with her away from prying eyes and into the surrounding forest. Once they were sufficiently hidden, he wound his arms tightly around her. Brushing her hair back, he kissed her mouth, her neck, her eyes, her ears. Pushing her against a tree, he continued with increasing passion. Caty knew sounds would carry where sight was lost. She grasped his face, whispering and reminding him of the need for discretion. "We ride, lady," he said, his voice heavy with desire, "but I would have my time with you. It has been too long." He pulled her back out, toward the horses. "Do not think, lady, I have forgotten your little adventure." He lifted her easily up to her horse.

Caty's eyes were bright with love for this man. "Take me home, Majesty. I ache for your touch."

His face broke into a wide smile. "Home!" The ground shook with the thundering hoofs that took the royal couple toward their bedchamber.

Back at the castle, Caty entered her study and called for two baths to be prepared, one for her and one for the king. She quickly sank into the water; its lavender scent filled the room. Her hair was washed and combed out. Dried and dressed in a soft sleeping gown, she pulled a shawl over her long, damp ringlets. Opening the door to their sleeping chamber, Caty walked to the side of the king's tub. Marcus lay soaking, his eyes closed, a smile upon his face.

"Husband, tell me your smile is for me," she whispered as she dropped the shawl and began to wash him. He remained relaxed, his eyes still closed. Suddenly, his arm went around the tiny waist and with one swift movement he had pulled her into the tub. She slid directly on top of him. She shrieked as her head went under the water. Struggling to sit up, he pulled her up and turned her around to face him.

He was laughing out loud. For her part, Caty was still sputtering soapsuds and trying to free her hands from his grip. "Caterina, do you struggle against me? I have been gone too long, I see. Perhaps you are in need of a reminder. Your king owns you, Caterina. And what a prize you are!" He pulled her against his chest and began to kiss her mouth. Her gown was hindering his movements. It took him but seconds to remove it. There she lay, naked and warm in his arms. He found he could not control his desire. When they finally lay spent, the water was cold. "Come, Caterina, if we move quickly, we can make it to the bed before we freeze." Caty laughed with him as he jumped out of the tub, pulled her out too, and carried her to their bed. Snuggled warm and close, Marcus was again aroused. Caty responded with passion.

The night was nearly gone when the two at last lay within each other's arms, satisfied and sleepy. Caty's eyes were closed, a smile on her reddened and swollen lips, her fingers tracing lines on his chest. "I have missed you so, Marcus. Pray tell me you need not leave again for years hence."

Marcus raised himself up on one elbow. "I would remember you just like this—smiling, in love with me. Whatever comes, comes. You and I, love, have made our own story." Tenderly, he brushed her face with his hand.

Could Caty have foreseen the future, she may have wished life to stop here, as she peacefully lay in the arms of this man she had grown to love. Life, however, rolled onward.

FIFTY-THREE

TIME PASSED QUICKLY, AS TIME will when filled with work and living. Caty typically rose early each morning, made her rounds of the castle, and met with her staff. Today, however, for the first time in years, she slept in. Taking her time, she sauntered downstairs to meet with the staff much later than usual. Passing by Marcus's study, she overheard a heated argument. Two of her ladies were alone inside, and fighting over what to tell their queen. Curious, Caty stood motionless outside the door.

"I cannot be party to a tale that will surely break her heart," one woman insisted. "I will not!"

"She deserves to know," the second countered. "She should have been told before. It is not fair to her. I think we should tell her."

Just as Caty thought to step in and clear up the fight, the first one added, "He would not be the first king to keep a mistress. Besides, he knew that woman long before he knew our queen. Why he yet goes to her I cannot think. But it is only a day's ride, and he sees her whenever he pleases. The queen need not know. If you feel that way, you tell her. I will not."

Caty was stunned. Could she have heard correctly? She quickly took the stairs and reentered their chambers. Marcus was gone, but his fighting gear lay inside his trunk. He did not leave often, but he did leave. Always to secure his borders. Caty never thought to question him nor look through his trunks. All day, the thought of where he might be ran through her head. During a long night, she paced the floor. By morning, she had made a decision.

Captain Tillea was red-faced as he listened to her plan. The veins stood out on his neck and he had begun to raise his voice. Caty was unmoved. "If you do not wish to go with me, suit yourself, sir. I am going. With or without you and your escort, I am going."

"Why, Caty?" he pleaded. "'Twill do no good. Every king does the same. He was a widower for three or four years; what do you think he did? How will this make it any easier for you? Tell me!" He hated to see the hurt in Caty's eyes. "You have to know he truly loves you, Caty. He always has. But—"

"Tell me, Captain, did Lord Tabor do this to my mother?" Caty's great eyes, swollen from crying, sought his and held them.

"No, little one, no he did not—ever. How could he?" He sadly shook his head. How could Marcus do this to Caty? No matter, she would have to learn to live with it. Women did every day. Even beautiful, kind women like Caty. There was no denying that the king adored Caty, but . . . he was a powerful man and loved women. Always had. The woman Marcus spent time with was demanding, sharp-tongued, and haggard, and Captain Tillea never understood what Marcus saw in her. But who could know the workings of a man's need to take a woman to bed? Sadly, he watched the woman beside him as she dug for answers that would bring her more pain. She looked again like the young child he had watched grow.

Eventually he relented. He picked several men he knew would be discreet, and they rode. They stopped at the last rise before their destination. Caty dismounted and stood just under cover of the trees, looking down. Through the trees, she could see the castle below. The grounds were a mess. The structure was falling into pieces, just like Caty's heart. Caty moved as close as possible without detection. Clearly, Marcus was there. His large horse grazed in a fenced lot, along with others. His standard was raised over the castle gates. Caty's searching eyes found Marcus. There was an area near the wall of the castle itself, clearly used for men's sport—fighting. In the middle, with several of his men in attendance, stood Marcus. At first, she watched as he sparred with different men. Then a woman walked across the grounds and up to Marcus. Caty moaned, as if shot, when the woman and Marcus embraced. Marcus stood with his arms around the woman and kissed her again before they moved apart. The woman walked back into the castle.

Marcus and several of his men, including Lord Rodolfo, resumed jousting in the yard. Heartbroken, Caty could not take her eyes off the scene below. Captain Tillea touched her shoulder lightly. "Come away, Caterina. This is not for you to see." Caty had slid down to the ground. She started to stand as another moan escaped her lips. The woman appeared again and called. This time, Marcus came to her, lifted her, and carried her in his arms through a doorway. Without speaking, Caty finally mounted and rode back to Marcus's castle. Her world was no longer a nice place.

She thought of the castle Marcus had given her. They had spent many happy hours there. Caty decided she would never go there again. She could barely go back to the king's castle. The wind whipped her cloak around her, and her hair blew away from the hood. Tears came, flooding her face with icy fingers. It was so unlike the heat of the evenings she had spent with him. After exacting a promise from every man with her to keep her trip their secret, she left the stables. It would be days before Marcus returned. Caty spent hours on her knees, praying and crying, angry and hurt. Life would go on; it always did. But could she?

In the midst of this anguish, there was more. Rose, now grown quite old, had taken ill. In the evening after Caty's discovery, Caty sat with Rose as the life faded from her. The only mercy was that the woman's final days passed quietly. When she went, she went peacefully, while she slept. In a day's time, Caty found herself at another funeral, mourning once again. *This land has taken much from me. I have nothing left to give.*

For the next three years, Caty went about her days, refusing to allow Marcus or anyone else to see her heartache. Captain Tillea checked on her more frequently. "You know he loves you, Caty," he would say while he walked with her around the grounds, as was his habit every afternoon since that awful day. "He has loved you since the beginning. He is a king. He does what kings do. You must live beyond what the king does, Caty."

"I believe I have," she said one day. "At least as much as I can bear to. Nothing will ever be the same between Marcus and me. If a person were to believe all the rumors around, Marcus may have others, also. However"—Caty turned to her old friend—"I am what I am. There is naught to do for it. I am grateful the people keep me busy." She smiled at Captain Tillea. It was a small, sad smile. "And I am grateful to you, my dear friend." She kissed his cheek before leaving him.

For these three years, she had been able to keep from Marcus her knowledge of his wanderings. He asked, in the beginning, what bothered her. Again and again, he asked. "Caterina, you know I love you. I have loved you since I first saw you. Tell me what saddens you so."

Her answer was always the same. "I am fine, Marcus. I love you too. I am happy here, and we are lucky we have people that love us as they do." Over time, she came to believe her own lies. She also began to understand she did love Marcus, in spite of it all.

FIFTY-FOUR

THE WIND WHISTLED OFF THE castle turrets. Although the weather was not especially cold, Caty shivered, sitting near the fire. *These winds bring change*, she thought. *I fear 'tis not a good change.* Marcus had been gone for several weeks now. He and his men had left, as before, to defend his borders. This time she knew he meant it. He took a large army with him. He had laughed, telling her he would be back before the fourth night, and Caty had not worried. The days had passed by—but still no word from the king, nor from any of his men. After the tenth day, she had felt a growing sense of uneasiness. No matter what had happened between them, Caty knew she truly cared for Marcus. She also knew the waiting would soon be over.

The sound of men yelling and horses galloping brought Caty to her feet. Rushing to the window, she watched with fear gripping her throat, making it hard to breathe. Marcus was dead—she had felt it days ago. Today she had dressed in black. Hoping despite her intuition, she waited. The men riding into the courtyard carried not Marcus's flag, but another's. There were a few of Marcus's men in the mix, but this great body of soldiers rode for the new king, who rode with them. His dress and armament left no room for mistaken identity. Her lady rushed in. "You must escape, Majesty. Quickly! Run! You cannot let them catch you!"

Whirling around, Caty flung her cloak on and ran, stumbling, down the narrow stairway that led from the end of the hall to the far side of the castle. Her one thought was to flee. Too well she knew what happened to the queens of vanquished kings. There would be no need to dethrone his daughters. All three had long since given up any claim to the crown and moved back to Germany—the land of their mother. Seldom was a widowed queen allowed to stay or to live, lest she gather a rebellion.

In the harsh midday sun, Caty ran toward the stables. The old stable hand already stood waiting. He had watched out for this lady these past years. Now, he feared she would stand little chance. He intended to give her all the time he could. Her horse was saddled already. He kissed her hand, stepping back as the animal lunged away. Clinging to the mane and saddle, Caty felt the horse sail with little effort over the small fence surrounding the yards. People spread away from her, allowing rider and horse a clear path. A single gate leading to the land beyond the back castle wall was opened. It took only a few minutes for the great horse to fly through that gate.

As the rider and horse sped past, one of the new king's men spun to watch. Rounding the castle corner, he only caught sight of them dashing away. From the cloak flowing down over the horse, the man watching felt it must be one of the deposed king's grooms. This rider knew what he was doing. The witness nearly turned away, but then remembered the deference the people had given horse and rider as they left the grounds. He turned back around, thoughtful, watching, frowning. "Your Majesty!" he called, running toward the new king. "The queen! 'Tis she I saw!" The noise of the takeover was too loud; he had not been heard. Desperate, the man found his king and, gripping the monarch's reins with both hands, forced the snorting horse to stop.

"What is this!" The king angrily pulled up. "Unhand my horse or lose the hand."

"There is another gate yonder, Majesty. I believe the queen of Marcus just rode out. The rider is smaller. The crowd around gave way for her." He nodded toward the far wall. "She, if it is her, rides well on a horse meant for speed, sire."

The king's horse reared with the effort of turning sharply as the king pulled the reins aside. Several men with the king followed. He had not yet decided just what he would do with the wife of Marcus. To have finally taken over the lands was more than he had believed possible. But Marcus had grown careless, soft with age. Santino Giovanni was now king of a vast stretch of land, taking in the eastern shores of middle Italy, which curved along the coast southward. He was doing his part to fulfill his grandfather's dream.

Santino's first instinct was to let her go. After all, she was not from Italy. His goal of making the people proud of their Italian heritage was being realized. His vast military force was due in large part to just that—pride. Curiosity, more than anything else, prompted him to give chase. He could see a lone rider ahead. She was indeed small. Santino's horse was already tired. Unlike Caty, Santino was large and wore full armor, as did his horse. He knew his mount could not maintain against a fresh animal. Santino watched as the rider widened the distance between them. To his surprise, he felt no anger. Instead he felt an intense desire to overtake her. That she would try to leave was laughable.

Following the castle wall, he returned to the yard and called for a fresh horse. Without armor or heavy weapons, the new horse would do well. It was a great roan, anxious to run, hard to contain. Removing his own armor and all but his sword, the king was soon mounted and out the gate, closely followed by several of his guard.

They thundered away from the castle. *Where does she run to?* he wondered. *There is little shelter or support for her now. Still . . . it took great heart for a woman alone to try.*

Caty had seen her pursuer turn back, but it gave her little relief. *Where can I go?* she asked herself. *I cannot endanger the lives of these poor people who asked for none of this. There is not a neighboring king who would take into his protection a dowager queen. Especially one whose lands had been overtaken.* Caty realized as her mind uttered these words that she had no options. She was running in the wrong direction for the sea, with no strong neighbors and too many innocent peasants. Pulling her horse to a stop, she sat. The horse fought her, stomping and snorting. Before long, Caty heard the riders behind her. *Seems my choice is made for me. If he kills me, I gain my freedom, from everything.* And so, she sat, waiting.

Santino saw that the rider was no longer fleeing. In fact, she sat very still, her horse pulling to continue the race. The small figure atop the large horse did a superb job of controlling the animal. The king stopped several lengths behind her.

"Lady!" Santino called with authority.

"Majesty," Caty responded after a long moment, without turning.

"When I speak, you will look at me," he demanded with deadly calm.

For several heartbeats, Caty remained still. She was still a queen. Her point was not lost on the new king. Then, lightly touching her horse, she turned. "Majesty?"

Santino started, then held his breath. He could not take his eyes from her. He had heard the talk about this Caterina and her mother. She was all that and more. He moved slowly closer. Caty sat quietly. There was no anger or fear in her eyes, only sadness. A sadness he knew he had given her. Unexpectedly, he felt a stab of guilt. Not because he had killed Marcus, but because he had caused this creature before him sadness. In that instant, Santino made a decision.

"You think to escape?" he asked, his tone even and firm. "Do you know what happens to queens of vanquished kings?" She did not answer, nor did he expect her to. He nodded toward the road behind him, where his men were now gathered. Caty slowly approached him, and acknowledged his newly won status with a slight bow. "If you die, what do you have," he goaded, watching her keenly.

"My freedom," she answered quietly.

"You will not die," he replied, his voice low.

For a short while the party rode in silence. Caty sat straight, regally, concentrating on holding her composure, looking neither right nor left. The horse, carrying his mistress as he carried her often, responded to her gentle nudging and picked up speed. These men must never see her as weak. *This could well be my last ride. I must remain someone these people will remember after I have gone.* She refused to think on what might come. As the riders around her moved to keep pace, Caty nudged her horse yet again. She was beginning to move out ahead. Suddenly, the sounds of hoofs thundered around her.

"You think to lead us? You will not, lady." The anger in Santino's voice was clear. Caty slowed her mount, still looking straight ahead. She was maneuvered to the middle of the riders.

As the group passed through the castle walls, Caty's heart ached. When Santino spoke, she felt her world crack. "Take her to her chambers. See that she does not leave." He dismounted and walked to her. In one swift, powerful movement he lifted her from the saddle and set her down firmly. She swayed, nearly falling. Santino was quick to steady her. His mouth near her ear, he commanded curtly, "You are a queen, lady. Act like one."

Caty took a deep breath and forced herself to walk. As she moved forward, she heard a voice cry out, "Queen Caty!" Turning, she saw a small crowd of the castle staff and groundskeepers looking on. She smiled briefly and nodded to them. Her concentration was fixed on not losing control.

How can I go into this house again? With a stranger, she heard the voice in her heart calling, *a stranger who murdered my husband*. She was to be taken to her own quarters, the rooms where she and Marcus had lived and loved. The rooms where she tried in vain to mend a shattered heart and an unkept promise. *How can I do this? Better to have died*. Caty's hands were clutched tightly together. When her escort opened the door, she gasped. The room was entirely changed. Gone were any remnants of their lives. Now, the room was empty, save for a thin straw mat. She stopped and turned. "I cannot." She glanced back at the rooms.

"Lady," the man behind her urged. His stance told her she would have no choice. Shaking, she stepped beyond the door and froze. She felt the door close and heard a board slide into place.

"What am I to do now?" she said aloud, though she was alone. She turned and surveyed the room. One other item remained, a heavy golden cross the priest had given her the day she wed Marcus. It still stood in the corner. Crossing the room, she knelt beneath the cross and ran her fingers along its edges. "What am I to do?" she repeated to an empty room.

FIFTY-FIVE

SANTINO STRODE TOWARD THE STABLES. A quick inspection told him the animals had been well cared for. His men had already secured the grounds. Some had begun to clear the houses that had been home to an army now decimated. Santino gave strict orders that not one person was to be harmed. He knew that if the people lived as well or better than before, they would quickly forget King Marcus. Loyalty was seldom to a king; it was to the one who made life easiest. After an inspection of the castle grounds, he wound up at the entrance of the building itself. It was a strange mixture of styles. The arches and tile work spoke of Italy. The turrets and domes revealed Moorish influence. The castle would be easily defensible with its walls, numerous catwalks, and towers on every side that allowed one to see well beyond the fields outside the walls.

Inside, a great hall was lit with candles and burning fireplaces. Santino watched as the kitchen staff moved about serving his men. He knew that, later, there would be knights coming to swear allegiance to a new king. Santino was tall, standing well over six feet. Powerfully built, he had a reputation for his prowess with weapons. He was known as a superb tactician, too, and for his fierce temper. His black eyes surveyed the world through thick lashes. His hair was dark, curly, and long. Most of his men were intensely loyal. This had been a hard-fought victory, and he knew his warriors were exhausted. They could relax now. For Santino, this night would be an important time. There were men here with him, *his* men, who were bound by more than money. Most of those closest to him had a long history with him. At home, however, many of the men at his council table were not so loyal. With this latest conquest settled, he could take care of those whose loyalty wavered like the wind itself.

"Majesty, have you seen the queen since your return?" his cousin, Gabriel, asked. Gabriel was much shorter than Santino, but with the same dark eyes and hair. A deadly man with a sword, he had been raised along with his cousin by Santino's mother. Both had been treated cruelly without favoritism, but Gabriel understood well that his cousin was the king, while he, Gabriel, was one of the king's most trusted friends and followers. His status was shared only by the king's brother. It was a role he took great pride in keeping. He would gladly die for Santino.

"No, there will be time enough for that," said Santino. "Now we see who comes." Santino sat down at the table he knew had been used by King Marcus before him. The hall was already filling up with men. A subdued air hung about the room. Santino's war council sat at a long table below him, to the side. They too were interested in the solemn line of men who now entered. Slowly, one by one, the men knelt before the king, pledging allegiance to a new ruler. Methodically, Santino made note of the men he felt he might trust, and of those he knew he must keep under watch.

This was one of the aspects of conquest Santino and Gabriel most enjoyed. Both could read men well. When the dust settled, they would compare notes, placing bets on whose judgment was most accurate. Which of these men could be the first to strike? The night was nearly gone before the room emptied. Yawning, Santino thought briefly about the woman sitting upstairs. *Not this night*, he decided. *There will be other nights. It's evident she is the people's queen. She could be very valuable indeed.* The past weeks had been good. He never expected that Marcus would be so easily overcome. *I can see why*, he mused, thinking about Caty. *Time spent with the queen, instead of reigning over his realm.*

Walking through the rooms and down halls, he noted the paintings, tapestries, and statues adorning the area. Studying them, he felt certain none of the furnishings had been chosen by Marcus's queen, not that it mattered. Stifling a yawn, he searched for a place to sleep uninterrupted. After weeks on the battlefield, he slumbered soundly in a quiet chamber.

FIFTY-SIX

FOR THE FIRST TIME IN many years, Caty cried herself to sleep, leaning against the wall near the fireplace. The room was dark and cold now. There were no rugs, nor were there tapestries to hold the cold from the stone walls at bay. It made a strong statement. There was a new king now. Caty and Marcus were gone. Without fire, candles, and Marcus, the room felt more like a prison than her chambers. By the fall of the third night, she had yet seen nothing of her captor. She had not eaten since her attempted escape. A jug of wine was slipped through the door shortly after she was first locked away. She shivered from the cold and could no longer stand the silence. *I must do something. I will not sit around waiting for him to finish what he's started. Tonight I leave.* Marcus had been proud of this castle and its secrets. He had shown her one passage, in his study, and now she prayed that this room too held a secret. Caty started at the wall opposite the door. As high as she could reach, then down to the floor, she began pushing the wall, stone by stone. Slowly, keeping her ears open to avoid possible discovery, she worked her way around the room. Finally, the old castle shared its secret with her when she felt a stone begin to slide inward. Holding her breath, she pushed against the stone. A small section of the wall swung slowly back into the darkness. Caty stepped through, then pushed to close the section. It groaned as it moved back into place.

Wearing her mourning dress, black as this night promised to be, she hurried down the stairs and away from the castle. On familiar ground, she hustled along the wall toward the back gate she had used before. This time she had no horse beneath her to make her escape. She ran well beyond the castle. Forced to rest after some minutes of running, she stopped, gasping. Her eyes ran over the outline of the castle one last time before she turned away.

Caty realized her only chance lay in her ability to somehow reach the docks, where she might trade jewels or what coins she had for safe passage. Having ridden and walked these lands many times, she knew where she was. She began to walk the road. When a merchant and his wife came around the curve, she stepped toward them. Immediately, the man stopped his cart. Without waiting for her to speak, he helped her into the back and covered her with the blankets and straw headed for market. The man urged his donkeys on. For several hours Caty lay beneath her cover. When the man stopped again, he helped her down. "Majesty, you must walk now. Where we are bound is crowded and you will be seen."

He refused the ring she offered in payment. "But for you, Majesty, my child would have died, years ago," he said. "I had not seen you since, but I will never forget. Pray you get away safely." Tears ran down his wife's face as she kissed Caty's hand.

Caty touched the woman's face gently. "God keep you both." After watching them move away, Caty climbed a roadside embankment and walked along the edge of a small grove of trees. *I will be at the docks well before morning*, she told herself.

The lights from home fires glowed in the darkness. Dogs barked, and sounds of life floated through the night. It took little time for Caty to reach the small port. She stopped to braid her hair, trying to give it some order. She brushed the straw and dirt from her gown and tried to clean her mud-caked shoes. Still, Caty did not look like a queen.

Closer to the wharf, the activity took on a more roguish nature. Moving in the shadows, she walked unnoticed. One pair of eyes caught sight of her when she stepped into an alley leading to the dock, but the person passed without stopping or speaking. With only a short distance to several large ships gently pulling at their ropes as they rolled with the tide, she felt a wave of relief. Nearly safe, she was completely taken off guard when she felt a hand grip her arm from behind and jerk her close. Forced to walk with the man, she was pulled toward a doorway.

"Well, well, if it is not our lovely widowed queen," the man sneered. Caty recognized the colors he wore when he stepped into the lit entryway of the barn where they now stood. She tried in vain to pull away, but the man's grip was far too tight. He mashed her against the side of the building with his body while he grasped the neck of her gown and tore it away.

I may die this night, she thought, *but he'll not get what he thinks to steal from me.* With all her might, she swung her free arm around and smashed her ringed hand into his eye. He yelled, cursing, losing his grip of her. She could hear other men laughing behind her. Suddenly she was surrounded by four men. With a sinking feeling, she realized all wore Santino's colors. Now, with any hope of escape taken away, Caty knew she would not survive this attack. She would have to be killed and the crime covered up, or surely the people who loved her would rise against Santino. The uprising would no doubt be fruitless, but lives would be lost on her account.

Angry and frightened, Caty fought with a fury born of loss and desperation. The men were not expecting that she would try to fight them—at least not like this. She was slapped around so severely that she felt herself losing control of her balance. From the depths of her being, she screamed aloud, "Let me be! Four men against one woman? What manner of men are you?" Caty's mouth was bleeding from lacerations caused when her teeth cut into her jaw and lip. Blood from her nose ran down her face and splattered when she was struck. The skirt of her gown was ripped, her back scraped from being repeatedly shoved against the rough walls, and her arms were bruised where the first man's hand had held her fast. She bit, kicked, and scratched in a futile effort to free herself. Thrown to the ground, she was held firmly while one man tore at her skirts.

Drawn by the woman's screams, three men suddenly appeared in the barn doorway. "If any of you move, I'll run you through," the deep voice of one of the new arrivals calmly announced. Surprised, the men holding Caty froze. Walking through the doorway, a tall, thick man, with sword drawn, advanced. Behind him, two other armed men entered. "Stand away from the lady. Allow her to leave," he ordered. Caty's aggressors all stood and stepped back. Caty immediately rolled toward the armed men. When she did, one of the king's guards quickly pulled his sword.

"Do you know who it is you deal with?" the guard asked, an evil smile on his face. "Before morning, you will all hang; then your heads will adorn spikes." Caty shuddered. Crawling out of the way, she staggered, then stood, trying to cover herself.

"Perhaps I should introduce myself to you," the stranger responded, stepping into the light. By this time, every man was armed. Caty started for the now vacant doorway. "Stay, lady," the stranger called without looking away from his quarry. "You should not be seen like that. You are a queen, Caterina."

Stunned, Caty tried, in the dim light, to recognize any of the men who came to her rescue. She could not. She moved against the wall and stood, holding her gown together. The ensuing fight drew several spectators. Painfully aware of how she must appear to the onlookers, Caty sought cover deep within the shadows.

Santino's guardsmen were expert swordsmen, but surprise, then fear, when they recognized Caty's champion and his companions made them falter. The three men confronting them were at ease and comfortable. One of the guardsmen broke away and ran. One was soon lying in a growing pool of blood. The remaining two were wounded, but alive. An order was given to bind them, then bring them along. The stranger also ordered that the runaway be caught and brought back. Caty waited, unsure what to do.

The apparent leader of the three approached her. "Lady, you need not be afraid. It is over." He removed his cloak and wrapped it around her. "Come, I'll take you to shelter." She moved with him, not speaking. Hidden beneath the cloak, with only her muddy shoes and torn skirt visible, she appeared to the crowd as someone's mistress. With the fight over, the crowd dispersed. Caty was escorted onto a ship. Too numb from what had just transpired, she allowed herself to be led to a small but very well-appointed cabin.

Her escort bowed and turned to leave. "Please, tell me who you are," Caty asked, handing the cloak back to its owner while holding her gown in place. "I cannot repay you now, but would know who it is that holds my debt."

The man rummaged through a drawer and found a long shirt. After giving it to her, he looked at her, his face serious, though there was no mistaking the mischief in his deep brown eyes. "There will be plenty of time for that. You will be treated well aboard." He turned to leave again.

"Where am I bound?" she asked, but the man was already gone. Grateful for the shirt, she buttoned it up.

FIFTY-SEVEN

AT THE DOOR OF MARCUS'S old study, a young woman stood, refusing to move. Santino was holding council there now. She knew women were not allowed into the room, but the new king should hear. It was plain that no one else would tell him. Maybe no one knew. She knew. She had grown very fond of her queen. Fear for Caty's life overshadowed fear for her own. The woman waiting nervously was the youngest of Caty's ladies and the newest to court. As such, she was not aware of the fate that likely awaited Caty if she were captured and forced to stay.

Inside the study, Gabriel frowned. "Santino, a woman has stood at the door all this day. She waits to speak to you. Looks to be one of Caterina's staff. Perhaps you'd have time to speak with her?"

"I would much rather speak with Caterina, but since the lady has kept her post for so long, let us see what she has to say." Santino stood and stretched. He grew bored with the constant line of problems coming to him, and was now relieved that most had been settled. "Perhaps the queen would grace us with her presence next," he suggested sarcastically.

Once ushered into the king's study, the woman stood, uncertain how to say what must be said.

Santino studied her. "You wished to speak with me?" he said. She was pretty, in a childish way, and visibly shaking. The king stood, patiently waiting for her to begin, taking note of how well dressed she was.

"The queen has gone," the young woman stated, almost below hearing.

"Speak up, child!" Santino ordered. "You'll not be harmed. What did you say?"

Again the young woman spoke, but now she raised her head and spoke clearly, looking directly at Santino. "The queen has gone. She is no longer in her chambers."

Santino and Gabriel exchanged glances. "Have the guards left her door?" Gabriel asked quickly.

"No, Your Grace, they have not," the woman promptly answered, surprised he would think they might have abandoned their post. The guards were clearly afraid of both the king and his companion. "I went in alone, and have told no one. I do not believe the guards are aware."

"Are there other doors she might use?" Santino asked. "When did she leave?" His mind raced. How long had she been gone? Why did he not check on her before? Who would think she might try escaping now? Was it not clear her previous life was over? If he were still in this frame of mind when he found her, her present life might also be over.

"I am not certain when she left. I only found this out today, when I tried to see her. There are many doors and halls, Majesty. She stays in the chambers she and the king . . ." She paused. "That she and her husband shared. She knows this castle well."

Santino called for his horse and his guard. His page returned shortly. "All are ready but four, Majesty," the page announced. "The missing four rode into town late last night but have not returned. Your horses await." The page turned and led the way for Gabriel and Santino. Still in disbelief, Santino realized his only choice was to go after the minx. In little time, the men were riding out.

Without hesitation, Santino rode toward the small hamlet built up around the closest harbor. "How do you know which way she takes?" Gabriel asked.

"You made certain there are no horses missing. She would not be able to run far afoot, without staying with someone," Santino explained. "I do not believe she would risk someone's life for her own. That means she had to go to the harbor, hoping to catch a boat out." Neither man voiced the possibility that she might already be aboard a vessel and at sea. Exactly when she left was uncertain.

When the troop rode in, the town was bustling with activity. Several merchant ships were being loaded. Santino's boats were still moored, waiting. He searched for his captains. The first two he found knew nothing. They did know that four ships had already departed. Determined to find Caterina, Gabriel split the men up. *While out, I'll find the rest of the guard*, he promised himself. *They'll spend a long time behind walls thinking up reasons why they should never have left.*

Darkness crept over the western walls of the town. A fading sun glinted off the water. Santino's anxiety increased with each passing hour. None of the men they spoke with recalled seeing Caterina. Perhaps he had been wrong. Perhaps she did not come this way.

Santino entered the last establishment secured by his men. By this time, he was clearly known to the men crowded into the room, although he had entered the town only hours ago. His dress and very manner spoke volumes. He longed to be back at home, where he could move about with relative safety, and not be impeded by so many men. Sinking onto a bench across from Gabriel, he shook his head. Neither spoke.

Behind them, a man approached. "Majesty, you've been looking for me?" The man was dressed well, armed well, and grinning. "I think I may have something that belongs to you, sire."

"Pray tell what that might be." Santino smiled at his younger brother, Prince Carlo. He hoped against hope it would be Caterina. The two men accompanying the prince pulled up stools. Santino stood to hug Carlo while Gabriel ordered more ale and food. Carlo clamped Gabriel's shoulder affectionately and reached for a mug.

"We arrived sooner than planned," said Carlo. "Lucky for you, and for the little lady now sheltered on your boat." Carlo proceeded to tell Santino of the attack on Caterina. He saw the darkening of Santino's eyes. "I killed one of the men, one fled, and the other two are on the boat. Awaiting your pleasure, Majesty." Again Carlo's face broke into a grin. "Of interest to you, brother— they wear your colors."

"Not for long," Santino announced, through clenched teeth. With the knowledge that Caty was safe and secure, the men ate their fill. After giving directions to Gabriel regarding the captive guards, Santino turned to his brother. "Now, take me to the lady. I will deal with her before we leave. After I have spoken to her, let her sit for a couple of hours. Then bring her to me. I will see her in council."

"Late for council, is it not?" Carlo noted, raising a tankard of ale to his mouth.

"Not under these circumstances, brother." Santino stood and clasped his brother's shoulder. "Take me to Marcus's queen." His face was still dark.

Carlo nodded. He stood up to take a very angry Santino to a lady waiting.

Caty wandered around the cabin as the sun marked the waning hours. Hoping to feel the vessel move out soon, she was unable to rest, let alone sleep. She had not traveled by boat very often, and only once had it been pleasant. The fine wood of the desk and chairs felt smooth as she ran her hand along the patterns. The bed was narrow, but soft. Under different circumstances, this would have been very comfortable. Today it was not. Caty paced—something she had grown quite good at.

Eventually, she heard voices and approaching footsteps. "At last," she sighed, "maybe now we set sail."

Caterina jumped at the sound of the door bursting open. As she stood in the far corner, she found herself looking at the dark form of Santino. Paralyzed, she held her breath.

"Did you think I would allow you to walk away, lady?" He moved toward Caty. His steps were slow, his movements menacing. Caty was taken aback. She had not expected to see him here, in this place. Worse, she could think of nothing to say. She stepped back slightly, blocked by the wall. He now towered over her. His eyes took in the disarray of her hair and clothing. She looked him in the eye, without flinching. "Have you nothing to say?" he prodded.

Caty shook her head. What could she say? It was over. There would be no escape.

333

"Believe what I say: we will talk again, this night." His voice was low and cold. "You *will* speak to me then, and this will be settled." The stillness of the room was overwhelming. His eyes bored into hers.

"You do not love me!" Caty's words sliced the silence. "Let me go."

Santino had not expected to meet such resistance from Caty. "Do you not know this is what a king can do when he defeats the sitting monarch? He takes the deposed king's wife."

"Begging your pardon, Your Majesty. If this is true, your castle must be over-run with wives. You most certainly have no need of me," Caty calmly pointed out. She heard muffled chuckles behind the king. Santino's scowl deepened. "I have no interest in challenging your rule," she continued. "I wish to be released to go home." Caty's voice was quiet, almost pleading. "I cannot do this again. I have been twice widowed. I cannot play the game any longer. I want to go home. Let me go, please."

"You said you would gain your freedom by dying, did you not? I was quite clear. You will not be free, by dying or any other means." Santino paused, studying the lady before him. "What does love have to do with any of this?" He turned and left her standing alone.

"What, indeed," Caty whispered, watching him walk away. She heard the sound of a metal rod as it was slid into place, securing the door. Her thoughts turned to Marcus. Still sore from Marcus, Caty certainly did not trust Santino. *Kings do not feel bound by promises once the deed is done. You, Santino, will do what all kings do. I cannot do this. I never wanted to be a queen.* She sank into the bed, defeated. Another round? Her spirit was beaten. On edge, she stood and walked around the cabin, again and again. There had to be a way . . . some way to go home. Home to Scotland. Touching the wood, feeling the ornate carvings, and brushing the tapestries, she tried not to think on what was sure to come.

FIFTY-EIGHT

AS SHE STARTED AROUND THE cabin once more, she hesitated before a panel. Studying it carefully, she frowned. *This looks like a door. Could it be?* With a light touch, she grasped the carved wooden knob. The door swung open easily. *Of course,* she thought. *Many vessels have a door in the captain's quarters. It's very common.* Well hidden from the bow of the vessel, Caty stepped out onto a small deck at the stern of the ship. Listening and watching for any sign of the king's guards, she stood still. Silence greeted her. Hoping against hope, Caty hastened to the side rail. Leaning over the side, she gasped. The water, lapping against the ship, appeared far below her.

Caty took a deep breath. *If I would be free, I must take this chance, now.* She climbed onto the side, took another deep breath, and dove into the water. She plummeted deep into the sea. Her skirts swirled around her as she came up fighting for air. Caty scanned the water. The pier was close. One ship, the farthest from her, seemed to have no activity around or lights on it. She swam toward it. Pulling herself onto the dock's edge, she carefully slipped between barrels and some stacked boxes of goods awaiting shipment. It was already dark, so most men were gone.

Men working late to load and outfit other ships took little notice of Caty. Walking to the darkened boat, she tentatively climbed the ladder, thinking to hide before the ship was manned. Caty was at the top when she was met by a man who was leaving. "Lady? You are on the wrong boat, perhaps?" Startled at the sound of a voice, Caty nearly fell off the ladder.

She quickly gathered her wits. "I'm not certain. Might I ask where you are bound, sir?"

The man stepped closer, and scrutinized Caty before answering. "Where did you want to go, m'lady?"

"I would like to return to my home, in Scotland, sir," Caty replied. "Would it be possible to travel with you and your ship? I can cook, and I have some money with me." She waited for him to respond. She was dripping wet, her hair was plastered to her neck, and her shoes were long gone. "Please," she begged him softly.

The captain looked around at the docks beyond and back at Caty. "I am bound for English shores. I will take you that far. Follow me; I will show you where you'll work." He walked rapidly across the ship to the kitchen, handed her a lit lamp, then left. "Do not burn my ship down, lady," he called over his shoulder.

Caty surveyed the area. It was filthy. In the middle sat a long table with side benches. Both benches and the table were covered with supplies. Caty looked through the cabinets and shelves. The area clearly had not been used recently. Starting at one end, Caty cleaned every shelf and drawer. In the midst of storing the supplies, she failed to notice the men standing at the doorway, watching.

Caty jumped when one of them asked, "Are you the cook?" The men moved into the area and looked over what she had already stocked. Several began tightening drawers, latches, and handles. A quick glance out the door proved that the once dark ship was now a hive of activity.

"Yes, I am," Caty replied with a great deal more self-confidence than she felt.

"'Tis plain you have not sailed before. Everything has to be tied down or secured, someway," said a short, portly man who stood in the middle of the room. "Don't just stand around, men; get busy. Get the supplies up. And move it!" At his order, a flurry of activity began.

When the men had finished and moved on to another area, Caty tried to take stock of all the supplies. The door to the galley was open, and Caty could hear the captain arguing with someone. As the conversation grew more heated, the voice of the man shouting at the captain carried easily to Caty. When the man had gone, the captain came in. His face was red with rage. "You had best be off. We are going to have a fight, soon. Not a place for ladies." His tone was curt.

Before Caty could get across the room, mayhem broke out on deck. The owner of the voice from the argument strutted into the galley. He was a very heavy man; his graying, wavy hair was greasy and hung around his collar. His full beard was dirty, with pieces of his last meal clinging to the hairs. His clothes were crumpled and stained. The man was so intent on his battle with the captain that he failed to notice Caty.

"You will load every keg, box, and bundle onto this ship, at once!" he yelled. Caty could tell he tried to appear threatening, but he looked more like a giant gnome.

Calmly, the captain repeated what Caty had heard him state before. "I tell you, I will not take stolen goods aboard this ship. This is my property. Now, get off!"

The gnome-like man grew even more enraged. "Arrest them all—everyone! They are charged with piracy! I will see them in court in two hours!" With that command, armed men swarmed the ship, taking everyone on board prisoner. Caty gasped. *Piracy. That means hanging.* She tried to slip off but was nabbed before she even walked three feet.

After an appearance before the same gnome, who proved to be the city's magistrate, Caty found herself imprisoned as a pirate. No amount of argument swayed the man. He sentenced everyone to hang, come morning. Caty was dumbstruck. This could not be happening. She didn't dare tell him who she was. How could she explain her appearance, or why she was unescorted? Moreover, why would he believe her?

The magistrate waddled up to Caty, his breath turning her aside. He grabbed her arm and jerked her closer. Peering into her face, he snickered. "Maybe I'll help myself to you, before you hang." Caty shuddered. He swaggered away, laughing, and the door swung closed behind him. Caty could scarce believe what had happened in so few hours. She stumbled, numb, along the cold, dark corridor with the rest of the prisoners, being shoved by silent guards.

The captain, now held with his crew in a cell close to Caty, called to her. "Lady, you do not belong here with us. I will find a way to get you out."

"Thank you, sir. I would add that neither you nor your crew belong in here, either," Caty called back. "I fear I can be of little service. I do not know anyone to help us." She did not dare try to send word to Santino. Anyway, even if she wanted to do so, how could she?

"I do," the captain responded. "Stay quiet, and pray."

FIFTY-NINE

AFTER ROAMING AROUND THE DOCKS, flirting with the inn maids, visiting with the king's captains, and securing another horse for Caty, Carlo opened the cabin door, ready to return the dowager queen to his brother. A quick survey of the cabin dumbfounded him—she was no longer aboard the king's ship. Immediately, he and his men began a search of the docks and adjacent ships. A quick visit with the port authorities proved that no ships had left the dock since Carlo last saw Caty.

Sitting on a barrel, waiting to load his ship, an older man watched the activity with interest. Finally, he stepped up to Carlo. "You look for a lady, do you?" His wrinkled face bore evidence of a hard life. He was clearly a seafaring man, armed and unimpressed with Carlo. His speech was rough, and he walked with the rolling gait of one who is far more comfortable at sea than on land.

"I do," Carlo confirmed. "Have you information for me?" As he asked, he reached into a pouch at his waist and fingered several coins.

"The magistrate in this place is in need of judgment. Just this afternoon, he arrested the whole crew of that ship there." He pointed toward the ship at the far end of the dock. "He tried them just an hour ago, and they are all to hang, as pirates." The seafarer shook his head in disgust. "They not be pirates. I know the captain. He is no more pirate than you, Your Grace. Anyway, there was a lady on that ship. Little thing, she is. She is to hang in the morning with the rest." He looked at Carlo. "Keep your money, Your Grace. Take care of the outlaw magistrate."

Carlo was stunned. Frowning, he asked the man to describe the lady. The man could not, other than that she was small. "Do you know where the lady is now?" Carlo questioned.

"She is in a cell, in that building over there. Wish someone would take the trouble to the new king. Maybe he could stop it . . ."

"Why has no one spoken up about this man before?" Carlo asked, eyeing the old man critically.

The old man shrugged. "Who is going to believe one of us? King Marcus did not. There's no fighting the likes of him on our own." He turned away, adding, "You'd best be getting to the prison. Think the lady may have trouble if she is alone. Not a good place, that prison, especially at night."

The walls of the prison were thick; the door into the structure was massive. Entering the prison with a phalanx of men behind him, Carlo was hit with the foul odor of human excrement and the stale water that sat around in puddles. The very walls were damp. Green mold covered the steps that led down into the area where the cells were. The sound of dripping water echoed in the hall. Two guards stepped up to prevent the visitors from advancing farther. When Carlo spoke, his cold voice gave clear evidence that he was not going to accept anything less than what he asked. "You best step aside, or you will find yourself at the wrong end of my sword. Take me to the man in charge of this prison. Now!" One guard started to resist, but as he stepped up, he noticed the men with Carlo.

"Who are you?" the second guard asked. "The magistrate will want to know." He tried to speak with authority but failed miserably, as his voice did not match his actions.

"I said *now!*" Carlo advanced toward the guard, ignoring the request for identity. The guard retreated so rapidly that he stumbled and nearly fell.

In only moments, Carlo was standing before the head jailer. "I will speak to the prisoners sentenced this day to hang," Carlo demanded. "Starting with the lady. You, sir, should pray that all is well with everyone."

The man had no idea who Carlo was, nor did he recognize the king's colors. He did read the danger in Carlo's voice. Hastily, he stood, grabbed keys, and led Carlos into the bowels of the prison. They first passed the cell that held prisoners the jailer identified as the ship's captain and his men. "Free these men," Carlo ordered. To the ship's captain, he added, "Join my men behind me. I would speak with you about your day, sir." To the head jailer he demanded, "The lady?" Carlo stepped closer to tower over the man, who was now shaking. His pay was too little to fight so many men so well armed.

"Best you get to the lady," the ship's captain urged. "She is not part of my crew. I only traded her work in the kitchen for safe passage this afternoon. She looks to have never been aboard a boat before—at least not as crew. And she is no pirate."

"The magistrate knew this?" Carlo asked through narrowed eyes.

"He did, not that he cared," the captain assured Carlo.

Carlo turned to the head jailer. "Move!" His order was crisp and cold.

Only a sliver of light sneaked inside the narrow slit of a window in Caty's cell. The floor, walls, and air were damp. Roaches and other insects scampered ahead of her as she paced. Rats could be heard squeaking and scurrying around. An overpowering odor permeated the cell. Time crept through the prison, causing decay. Caty had only one thought: she would have been better served had she chosen one of the more active vessels. Too late for that now. There would be no escape from her sentence. Caty shuddered with a dreadful realization. This would be her last night. Closing her eyes, she began praying. Tears slowly trickled down her face, dripping onto the floor.

When a noise in the hall came ever closer, Caty froze, her heart pounding. The magistrate would make good with his threat. Caty backed away from the door, determined to give him a fight. When the cell door creaked open, Carlo entered. Her relief at seeing him again was so great that she felt weak. "Lady, it is time we traveled," Carlo said. "Would you like something to eat before we leave?" His voice was kind. He smiled at her, as if nothing were amiss.

"Whom do I have the pleasure of thanking for saving both my honor and life—again?" Caty asked, her voice breaking. The man's smile broadened.

"Carlo, brother of the king, at your service, Lady Caterina." He bowed deeply. Caty was staggered by this news. Of all the possibilities she could think of, having Santino's brother come to her rescue—not once, but twice—was not on the list.

"Might I be correct in assuming that that was your ship I was held on?" Caty inquired. Carlo took her arm and guided her from the cell.

"Such an assumption would be incorrect. That vessel and the two next to it belong to the king." He grinned at Caty, obviously enjoying the moment.

Her shoulders sagged. This could not be happening. Shaking her head, she stepped into the hall. As she passed Carlo, he again draped his cloak around her. When everyone had gathered in the office of the prison head, Carlo turned to the ship's captain. "Tell me, captain, what happened to you today?" The captain related his account of the incident and following imprisonment.

"I would add," Caty's soft voice broke in, "that the captain refused to load the ship because he believed the goods were stolen. The magistrate said he would see that the captain never sailed again if he did not load up. Not one time did the magistrate deny the merchandise was stolen." Caty added, "That court was meant for a jester. It was but a platform for the magistrate to bully from." Caty's voice had become indignant. Carlo's mind had already been made up, but Caty's version of the story sealed his decision.

"Mr. Leighton," he said to one of his men, "lock the men who run this prison in the cells below. And send several men to arrest the magistrate. He is to be locked in the last cell. No one, and I do mean no one, is to speak with them, or go to them. They will remain locked up until such time as the king makes his decision regarding the disposition of them all." Looking around the room, he asked, "Is everyone clear on this?" Leighton had already sent men for the magistrate.

"Lady Caterina." Carlo led Caty out into the evening.

SIXTY

RIDING HARD, THE PARTY MADE quick time reaching the castle.
As Carlo helped Caty from her horse, he firmly took her elbow. Clearly
he had no intention of letting her go anywhere. Obeying his brother's
command, Carlo immediately took Caty to where Santino had set up a
receiving room. Although the hour was late, the room was still full. When
Caty and Carlo entered, all talk ceased. Carlo nodded toward where Santino sat, a fierce scowl on his face. As she walked by, Caty handed Carlo's
cloak to him, revealing her pitiful state. If Santino was to explode, he
should see that the day had not been easy for Caty, either.

For a brief moment, Caty's eyes ran over familiar walls, paintings, and tapestries. So quickly had things changed—objects were the same, the atmosphere
was not. Caty took a small breath, then moved toward Santino. Her shame at
her appearance was being replaced with anger—and it began to boil. Santino
stood to look at her. He walked around her as she knelt to him. "You are sickly
thin, dirty, wear an ugly black gown, and smell bad. You would not have been
attacked had you stayed where I put you. You do not look like a queen, Caterina. I am told the people actually *miss* their queen. One must wonder. What
have you to say?"

Caty rose, her back straight. To his surprise, and to the amusement of his
brother and his cousin, she spoke clearly. Her anger was evident, although
her voice was even and controlled. If he hoped to humiliate her into sub-
mission, he had underestimated her. "I am thin by nature, but sickly thin by
your design, Your Grace. I have not been allowed to eat these days, since you
brought me back. I put on this black gown the day you entered the castle.

Surely you remember that day, sire. My husband was killed." She paused for a breath. "Ah yes, you would know that."

Carlo and Gabriel exchanged glances, impressed with her brazen attitude.

Caty looked defiantly at Santino. "I cannot change gowns, Your Grace. Every gown has been removed from the chambers where you keep me. I have no water to bathe with—well, there is that small jug of wine. I suppose I could use that." The sarcasm in her voice was edged out by anger. "I will gain my freedom either way, by starvation or through your anger." She was speaking so rapidly that those listening had to concentrate closely to pick up her meaning. "The people do not miss a queen, Your Majesty; they miss a healer. I have traveled this land without harm or threat. I do not know the men who attacked me, but they wore your colors, Your Grace. Although"—Caty paused for a moment—"they did not get that which they sought." Caty shrugged. "And the imprisonment was false."

When she finished, the room was silent. Carlo worked hard to keep from laughing. Gabriel was standing just inside the room, staring at Caty. Santino was stunned. Who did she think she was that she would be allowed to talk to him in this manner? He spoke through clenched teeth, such was the effort it took not to shake the maddening woman. "Tell me, Caterina. Do you see before you any of the men that injured you?" His voice dripped with sarcasm. He was squaring off to do battle with her. "I hardly believe you can call my cabin, aboard my ship, a prison." At this, Carlo groaned. Santino had no idea what else Caterina had been up to.

Caty refused to look around. With her eyes on Santino, she quietly replied. "I was in a prison. Locked in a cell, Your Majesty. The kind with no windows and bars." The room was silent as a tomb. "You are the king, sire. I trust that you have or will find and judge those involved in both instances."

Santino could not believe his ears. Did she really imagine she could best him? In the presence of Marcus's men, no less? She had been detained in her personal quarters; it was her own actions that resulted in the attack against her. How could she think to compare his cabin to a cell in a prison? "To be imprisoned, one must be guilty of a crime. Of what crime were you guilty, Lady Caterina?" Santino's tone was smug. He stood looking out a window, waiting for her reply. When she did not answer, he half turned toward her. Though surprised, he was pleased to see she was struggling to find an answer. "I am waiting, Lady Caterina," he urged her, sternly.

Caty glanced at Carlo. Carlo half shrugged to her, his expression telling her that she was on her own. In a quiet voice, Caty admitted, "I was accused of piracy."

"What!" Santino said incredulously as he whirled around. "I cannot hear you—speak up!"

In a slightly louder voice, Caty repeated, "Piracy, Your Grace. I was accused of piracy."

"Piracy! Carlo, is this true?" When Santino saw his brother take a deep breath before answering, he knew it would be true. Caty had been in prison, a real prison, and was accused of piracy. "Never mind, Carlo. Best I speak with you in private. I only ask, is Lady Caterina guilty of piracy?"

Carlo shook his head. "Definitely not, Majesty. No, she is not."

Santino knew that to continue this discussion would not do. Every eye in the room was on Queen Caterina. He had not had time to speak with Carlo, had no idea what had transpired to keep them so late, and by Caty's tone, knew it would not go well. In view of this, he chose to change tactics. Perhaps her latest troubles would make life as his queen more appealing. She would understand that nothing is secure. He looked at the pitiful figure standing before him. "When we return to my castle, I am entertaining the crown prince of France and his sister," Santino said as he walked around the room. "She is offered to me as a wife." He looked at Caty with disdain as he walked back toward his chair. "I look forward to meeting her. It will be a pleasant change indeed, to be around a *normal* woman."

The French prince had tried unsuccessfully to marry off his poor sister for years. Caty remembered clearly what the princess looked like. "Perfect. Exactly what you need," Caty muttered under her breath, looking at the floor. She could hear Santino's footsteps stop, then come back toward her. Aghast, she quickly turned to look sweetly at Santino. "She is young and very healthy—good for a king."

Santino cursed in his mind to think she had recovered so well, but he could not think how to catch her again. Instead, grasping her arm, he ordered, "Come with me." Caty had to run to keep up with him as she was dragged from the room. On his way out, Santino barked, "Not one man is to leave this room! Everyone is to give up their arms. Everyone! Carlo, see to it!" Until he knew more details about the piracy charge, he would not take a chance on some ambitious soldier of Marcus trying to rebel.

Santino took Caty back toward her chambers. He was so angry now, he seriously considered stopping to wallop her. *No,* he told himself, *first things first.* He would not be gentle or soon forgiving of this lie. She thought to greatly exaggerate his supposed mistreatment of her? In the company of his men and those of Marcus? He must be able to trust her, and better she learn now what would happen if she ever tried to flee him or lie to him again.

At the door of her chambers, he questioned the guards. "Has anyone come in or out of this door, but the queen's lady-in-waiting?" Both guards denied that anyone had been in the rooms, other than Caty's lady. Santino then swept the door open. "Light, I need light!" His voice echoed ominously into the empty space. When a lamp was brought, he stepped into the room.

The silence was palpable. It was just as she had said. There was not one piece of furniture, the walls and floor were bare, and even the candles were gone. A thin straw mat was thrown in one corner. He walked around the area in disbelief. Who would do such a thing? Now *he* could not think of what to say. When he looked at Caty, he saw not the sign of triumph he expected. She simply watched him. He walked around the rooms again, trying to think what he could say. As he walked, the anger he had felt when told what his guards had done came back twofold.

Taking her arm again, Santino left the room. Though still firm, his grasp was not as harsh. "I would have the person who prepared this chamber sent to me," he growled to one of the guards at the door. "Tonight!" He continued with Caty along the corridor, pausing to study each door. They came to an ornate entrance. Opening the door, he held the lamp to light the area. He walked throughout, examining each of the four rooms carefully. "Light these rooms up. Get a fire going." Turning to Caty, he added, "I will send for you shortly, lady. We will eat then. You and I will speak." He paused, then continued, his eyes never leaving hers. "I apologize for this. I did not know—"

Impulsively, Caty touched his arm and interrupted. "I know. Many things happen when a new king moves in. I'm none the worse for it all, Your Grace." As the candles were lit, he noticed again the bruising about her mouth and eye. Pulling her nearer the light, he brushed her hair away. His eyes flashed with renewed anger. Nodding to her, he left her alone in the room. As he passed the guards, he grumbled, "The lady needs a bath. Bring water—a lot of it!"

With the water came three women Caty had never seen before. *I see he has replaced my ladies-in-waiting,* she thought. *It's to be expected, I suppose. I have given him cause to worry.* While she bathed, several of her gowns were laid out. Once cleaned and wrapped in a towel, she paced back and forth, trying to decide between them. When she was dressed and her hair done, the ladies around her were silent. "Did I make the right choice? Is this too bold?"

"No, m'lady. This is perfect," one answered. Caty had chosen a deep purple gown. The royal color made the exact statement Caty hoped it would. Form-fitting to an empire waist, the gown flowed softly to the floor. The sleeves were long and straight. The high neckline was edged in a soft gray lace. Attached to the shoulders of her gown, a train of gray silk cascaded to the floor behind her. Her hair was piled upon her head, the curls dropping loosely down the nape of her neck. She did not wear any jewelry, save her mother's signet ring and the ring Marcus had given her when they wed.

When the king's man knocked at her doors, Caty was ready. "Shall we?" she asked.

As Caty entered, a heated argument was ending. Santino's voice rolled around the room and off the walls. "I am the king! Did you not hear me? Any man not loyal is gone!" Santino pointed at one of the men seated nearby. "That would include your brothers." The man paled, nodding, anxious. "Gabriel," Santino continued, "take care of the man that would call himself magistrate yet behave like a tyrant. Carlo, hang the guards you captured. Let it be known why." As he surveyed the men around him, he caught sight of Caty. He stood motionless, staring. Caty serenely walked toward him.

"Sire?" She curtsied deeply. Santino quickly moved to assist her up. He could not hide the glint of victory in his eyes. He had taken Marcus's lands and now he would take his wife. Both beyond description. The moment the thought entered his mind, he knew he would bed this lady, pirate or no. He took Caty's elbow and led her out. Glancing back, he spoke to the men around the room. "I am going to dine. Then we take up this conversation. Before this night is ended, we *will* agree." Ignoring the glances that flew between the men, he left.

With Caty's hand on his, Santino led the way to a nearby room made ready for a meal. His cousin, brother, and several other men followed. The hour was late, but with the wine and Santino's much-improved mood, the meal was a loud and riotous event. After several hours of listening to the men banter, Caty leaned toward Santino. "If it please you, Majesty, I beg to take leave of this evening." Her day had been long, to say the least.

He looked at her, at the men laughing and talking around him, then back at Caty. "It pleases me not. You stay." He turned back to his brother and continued their conversation. Caty's brows shot up.

She sat looking at her plate, then leaned back. *I suppose, under the present circumstances, I stay.* Studying the men around the new king, Caty wondered about each man's place. The time ahead of her held no promise of happiness. Could she play the game yet again? A new court, new gossip, new intrigue—new problems. *I cannot. I will not.* She was beyond exhausted; she could not think on today, let alone tomorrow. *Somehow I shall get out of this.*

At length, Santino stood and yawned. "I think this day has gone on long enough. I would spend some time with Lady Caterina. We will resume our discussion later on today. Excuse the council. None are to leave the grounds." To Caty he spoke softly, "I believe some time to think on my request of them would be in order."

Santino knew Gabriel would handle the wayward magistrate, who would stay in prison until it could be determined whether he was shipping stolen goods. The man's future depended upon that investigation. While several of the men with Santino spoke with the king, Caty's eyes roamed around the halls. It no longer felt like the place she called home these last years.

The king led Caty back to a receiving room. A small number of his men followed. Caty groaned inwardly. She was so tired. Every fiber of her being cried for rest. She knew she would struggle to stay awake and alert. Determined this man would not win their battle of wills, she tried to think of what he might speak about. Seated at a small table in a quiet corner, Santino began talking with her.

Caty answered every question graciously, although she never volunteered anything extra. No details. Santino could see she was holding back and that she remained cautious. *So would I*, he noted to himself as he watched her. *So would I*. When offered more wine, she waved the page away, shaking her head.

Santino decided to change his approach. "You have been married twice before, I am told. Tell me about your first husband—Lord Rhys Dermoth, I believe." He waited for her to respond, watching her keenly.

Caty was surprised by the question and took a moment to decide just what to say. She smiled, speaking softly. "He was very kind to me. His temper was legendary. In the beginning, I believe he spent most of his time angry with me. I was captured when he and his men overtook the ones with whom I traveled." Remembering her first year with Rhys, she laughed softly to herself. "He was very angry when he finally caught me. He soon left the anger behind."

"Caught you? You tried to leave him also?" Santino asked, his interest deepened. "Tell me. I would like to know if you have gotten any better at sneaking away." His voice was dry but his eyes were twinkling. Admittedly, he was having a good time with this lady, despite his apprehension.

Caty answered with a shrug, "I would rather not bore you, Majesty. I am certain much more important things need your attention." She glanced at him, hoping she could shift Santino's attention elsewhere.

Smiling lazily, Santino replied, "I have nothing else to do at this moment. You have my full attention, lady. Please." He urged her to continue with a wave of his hand, then sat back in his chair with his long legs stretched out before him.

I cannot believe how this goes on, Caty thought to herself. "I did leave," she began, "but was not very successful. It was a great adventure, I must admit." She smiled openly at Santino. "Looking back on the time, it was rather enjoyable."

"Share. What did you do while you were running around?" He leaned forward in his chair, his eyes laughing. He wanted that smile back. Besides, what could this genteel lady call an adventure?

"You are determined!" Caty observed. "Very well." For the next hour, Caty spoke of what she had done until Rhys ended her little escapade. She did not provide any details of that moment, only that he had found her. For his part, Santino immensely enjoyed the tale, laughing frequently. It was clear there was more to Caterina than a title. Santino was taken with her.

SIXTY-ONE

TO HIS SURPRISE, SANTINO REALIZED he could have listened to Caterina for hours. He could tell, however, that she was struggling to stay alert. This had indeed been a long day; the sun was already beginning its climb for a new one. He stood, took her hand in his, and lifting it to his lips, kissed it. "I see the talk is true. Marcus lost all because he was absorbed by a woman. Until now I never understood." As he spoke, he lifted her chin to look into her eyes. When he finished speaking, he saw emotion flit into her eyes. It only lasted a breath, but he saw.

It was not the sadness of loss, but rather the pain of betrayal. He stood for a second longer, but the look had gone. Her eyes were controlled and calm. *I know that look*, Santino thought. *I find it hard to believe, but Marcus may have lost everything over a woman—just not* this *woman. So* all *the rumors are true.* He held his hand out to her. "Come, Caterina. You need to rest today. We leave at first light tomorrow. I am taking you home with me. I had planned to send you by boat, but have changed my mind. I think you have seen enough of my cabin. We ride together, you and I." He helped her stand.

When they reached her door, Santino opened it and ordered the fires lit. "Caterina, have you a favorite steed you would take with you?" His voice was low. He was drawn to her; his black eyes sought hers. He could see she was no longer irritated with him; nor was he with her. It was a start.

"I believe you would know which would be the best—perhaps not the swiftest?" A soft smile crossed her face. "I leave that to you, sire." She bowed. Santino smiled back at her. As he closed the door behind her and turned down the hall, he called for Carlo.

"I have a job, Carlo. I know you too are weary, brother, but this cannot wait. Find out about a possible problem. The rumors of another woman are true. If that woman has sons, it could lead to trouble. I do not want to deal with rogue heirs to Marcus's throne. Take care of it for me, and"—he nodded toward Caty's room—"your future queen."

"At once, brother." Carlo sighed with relief. He felt in his bones this would be a good union. Someone like Caty could pull Santino from his self-imposed emotional prison. Not averse to the task at hand, he left. Curiosity rode with him.

Getting the information Carlo needed proved simple enough. Since the people loved their queen, they were more than happy to talk of the other woman—the Evil One, they called her. Now Carlo would clean up this last hurdle.

Several of Marcus's old guard rode with Carlo and his men. Taking the shortest route, the riders were soon on a rolling hill overlooking a castle below. The area surrounding the small castle was poorly kept. The castle itself was sadly in need of repair. Riding through the streets of the small town, Carlo felt the fear hanging over the people. They moved away from the riders, closed doors as the horses and men passed, and pulled children off the streets. Inside the castle proper, the new king's brother and several of his men rode into a courtyard in disarray. Carlo's practiced eye took in every detail. This was not a place in which to waste one's time, though his own behavior betrayed no indication he found anything amiss.

He confronted a man he caught scurrying around a corner. "You! Is there a man or lady of this place I might speak with?" The man's eyes darted back and forth, and eventually he realized that Carlo was not going away without an answer.

"Yes, m'lord. She be the one in the rooms yonder. 'Tis not a good day to speak with her," he stammered.

"And why would that be?" Carlo asked, moving his horse to block the man's escape.

"There were a fight, Your Grace. Her three sons agin' the one. That man won. All the sons are dead. She intends to hang the man. Set on quartering him first." The man shook his head. It was clear he disagreed with the plan for the hapless winner.

"Take me to the lady," Carlo demanded. "Now." He stepped off his horse and followed his wary guide. The door leading into the castle keep was large, with great metal hinges that creaked notice of any arrival. Once inside, Carlo was struck by the state of the room. Filth was everywhere, the fire was dying, the candles were burned out, and wailing filled the hall, giving eerie evidence of life. Food was rotting on the tables; chairs were overturned. Carlo surveyed the area as he was led through, looking for exits. He nodded to one of his men, in the direction of another exit beyond the hall. Several of his men took that exit.

The frightened man working at the castle led Carlo up a dark, narrow stairway. Stopping at the first door, he knocked softly. There was no answer. Carlo stepped past the man, who gratefully beat a retreat. Carlo pounded on the door, demanding it be opened. Years at the king's side came in handy, as Carlo maintained his composure when the door opened. The woman was, he decided, the ugliest woman he had ever seen. Surely this was not the woman Marcus kept. Her matted hair stuck out around her head like some windblown weed, long since dead and dried. The black gown she wore had seen a better day. Its front was stained with both old and new splatters. Her long nails were dirty. Her eyes were reddened and swollen from weeping, but the bitter lines around her lips and the scowl on her brow were not from recent events. They were the remnants left after years of a hateful nature. When she opened her mouth, vile words spewed forth, followed by dribble.

"Who are you?" she hissed. "Can you not tell I have neither the time nor the inclination to entertain? Be gone before I have you thrown into the dungeon below!" She would have slammed the door but for Carlo's foot.

"Take me to the man you plan to put to death. Do not waste my time; the new king is not patient." He stood to the side, waiting for her. She protested, and cursing, tried to close the door on him again.

Turning to one of his men, he ordered, "Bring her." He pointed to a man from the small crowd now gathered at the stair's bottom. "You. Take us to the dungeon. I would see the prisoner." The man hesitated, looking from the now screeching woman to Carlo. The man quickly decided that Carlo was the more dangerous of the two, even though he was deathly afraid of the woman. After all, this stranger had more men—and he represented the new king. The peasant led the group down into a dank, dark area. There a fire blazed, and instruments of pain filled the room. At the far end, a bloodied man was chained to the wall. He hung, unable to stand. He was young, had been burned and beaten, and was barely alive.

"Free him and take him upstairs—to her room," Carlo ordered. "If there is a physician here, bring him." Shoving the woman into a cell, Carlo chained the door closed. "I'll personally run through the one who frees this witch," he said, tossing the keys to a man standing at the fire. Turning, he followed the men carrying the injured man up the stairs. Profanities from the screaming woman followed him. Laid onto the bed, the man closed his eyes. He could scarcely speak, and was dying.

"Did you indeed kill the sons of that mad woman?" Carlo asked. He sat on the bed, his heart saddened at the condition of the young man—the result, Carlo knew, of the actions of the odious woman below.

"I did," the man replied with his eyes still closed.

"Why did you fight?" Carlo asked quietly.

"I was a guard for Queen Caterina. When it became clear that Marcus was defeated, I came here. This woman is evil. I cared not to have her endanger the queen's life. She would have Queen Caterina killed before your king ever got there. That would leave three other heirs to the throne."

"The king would not have allowed them to take the throne," Carlo noted. "Why go after the queen, when it would be King Santino that was a greater threat?"

"The witch was crazy. She swore to me she could take your king, and he would not have another . . . the same way she took King Marcus." The man continued, his voice weak. "King Marcus . . . he kept this woman for years, long before he took the queen. He was not worthy of Queen Caterina," the young man added bitterly. He paused, his face contorted in pain. "I hoped the queen would never know Marcus betrayed her, but she found out. It broke her heart." He looked away, as if the memory were too painful. Sighing, he continued, "No matter, the bastard sons of Marcus are gone. I did not intend to kill them. I came for her, but they goaded the fight." He paused. Opening his swollen and bloodied eyes, he spoke with the calm of an older man. "I am dying, but the price is small for my queen." He struggled to lift his hand. With measured movement, he dug beneath his knotted belt. The young man then held his hand out to Carlo. "For the queen." Into Carlo's hand, he dropped a ring given him by Caty.

"What is your name, lad?" Carlo asked gently.

"I am called Santino—as is your king, I believe. Pray he will care for the lady I love. She was more dear to me than my own mother. I loved Caterina well . . ." His voice trailed off. He closed his eyes. In a moment, he no longer breathed. Carlo left the room and headed back to the dungeon.

When he entered, he saw that someone had been there ahead of him. Several men stood around the fire, avoiding Carlo's eyes. The woman's body was crumpled on the floor; her severed head lay against a wall. Even in death, there was an evil expression on the grotesque face. "This place will see a new lord, and a better life," Carlo told all present. "King Santino promises." The men around the fire looked to each other, then hesitantly knelt to Carlo. Nodding, Carlo left the rooms of pain and evil. "Bring the lad," he called. "We bury him away from this place."

SIXTY-TWO

CATY STOOD IN THE SOFT light of dawn, stretched her aching back, and began walking slowly down the stairwell. She was surprised she had slept through the day and night. Now here she was, dressed to leave this place, probably forever. She used to love how the light played in all the rooms in Marcus's castle, and along the halls. Not anymore; the last three years had been long and dreary. Nights had usually found her pacing the downstairs halls, trying to understand the man lying asleep above her. By dawn, she would make certain she was back in their room, determined he would never know the pain in her heart.

By the time Marcus left the last time, the pain had numbed to a dull ache. She was not the first woman forced to share her husband, nor would she be the last. At least with the current events, she would not be subjected to a public fight over Marcus's throne. Let this new man fight Marcus's woman; Caty was out. She stepped through the door and felt the rush of cold from the storm that had crept in while she slept. One of the men standing around informed her that the king had left for his own castle the evening before after all. He had urgent business awaiting him, but she would still leave today.

Caty was relieved. She loved to ride, and now she would not have to entertain, nor listen—only ride. She mounted, settled in the middle of the guard, and waited for the captain. A woman rushing around the corner of the castle caught Caty's attention. She called out, "Please, lady! My child is ill. I fear she dies. Please, she is all I have . . ." Her pleading eyes looked into eyes that understood the mother's pain.

"Of course, Mother. Show me where." Without acknowledging the men surrounding her, Caty urged her horse quickly through the gathered men and followed the woman. Both left the courtyard before the guard could gather themselves enough to start after them.

Unaccustomed to chaperoning a woman and not certain what Caty's exact station was, the captain of the guard was still trying to gather his younger members from the great room, incorrectly assuming Caty was not up and about yet. Upon hearing the commotion coming from the yard, he stepped out to find men rushing through the side gate. By the time he had gathered those men and realized his charge was no longer with them, Caty and the mother had disappeared into the homes surrounding the castle. He found her riderless horse grazing with other animals outside the castle wall.

"Find them!" he yelled, dashing through the narrow streets, while visions of his own demise flashed before him. Chickens, children, and dogs scattered with the onslaught of men.

An hour went by, then another, before he spotted a crowd gathered outside one small hut. He rode in that direction. He dismounted and pushed his way through the throng of people who strained to catch a glimpse of the healer. Caty was inside, rocking a sleeping young girl whose curls lay wet around her face and on her neck, the only remaining evidence of the high fever that had gripped her just hours before. Exhaustion had won over irritability, and the child now slept, unaware of the activity surrounding her.

Caty could hear the captain of the guard ordering people aside. Handing off the child, she stepped to the door. "Please, sir, the child has need of a quiet rest. I will be outside in a moment. I have but a few directions for the mother; then I will be with you. My horse is yonder." To the people gathered around she announced, "King Santino sent this man to care for me. So that his subjects will be cared for, this man sees to my safety. He is not a rough man, but a man who takes seriously his duties." At her words, the people stepped aside and nodded or bowed respectfully to the captain and his men. The captain was unwillingly forced to wait.

It was three hours more before Caty and her escorts left. The streets were lined with people waving good-bye and crying. Caty's eyes were filled with tears as she bid these simple people she had grown to love farewell.

For a long while, they rode in silence. Caty knew the captain was angry with her, with himself for losing control of his charge, and with the people who had refused to give up their friend. He looked to be the sort of man who displayed his talents best on a battlefield, not chasing down a captive woman.

"Sir, I know you are angry with me. I beg you to forgive me. These have been my people for many years. The kings change; the lives of these villagers will only be worse unless your king is able to protect them. How much easier it will be for him to do what a king must do when the ones he protects love him. You are an extension of the king. You are much better at your job than I was at mine. Forgive me. When the king rages over our late arrival to his home, if he does—"

At this the captain interrupted her. "He will. You have no idea how his temper runs." He shook his head. "Make no mistake, lady, that it will be me that bears the brunt of that anger."

"No, it is me he will rage at. I will see to that. I promise." She looked at the man riding beside her, sullenly staring ahead. They rode a long distance in silence before he spoke again.

"What you did for that mother was a good thing, lady. How is it you come to know such things?" He turned to look at her. Gone was the anger, and with it, the scowl. Dressed in a soft green gown with a long darker-green cloak, Caty cut a striking figure. Her auburn hair caught the sunlight. Golden eyes looked at him with kindness.

"My mother taught me many things," she responded, "but the best thing she did for me was send me to a monastery outside Rome, her hometown. I studied with the monks, and learned Latin, French, and healing." Caty smiled at him.

He smiled back. The rest of the ride was pleasant.

When King Santino's castle came into view, Caty pulled her horse up. Breathless, she stared. With the whisper of dusk, lights within gave the huge edifice a soft ambience. Protected by massive stone walls, great towers inside rose at each corner. While care had been taken to preserve the security of the king's home, the castle itself was built to blend with the surrounding countryside. "It's beautiful," she whispered. "So large!" She hesitated to ride further. The castle was spread out across the hill, covering the area with buildings, all beautiful from what was visible.

The captain smiled at her childlike wonder. "Come, Lady Caterina. I believe this is your new home. It is still cold during the nights, but on this night, I have no doubt it will be hot . . . for both of us." He chuckled.

"Hmm, I believe you are right, sir," Caty agreed seriously. The ride had given her time to plan her response to Santino. If she judged him correctly, she would indeed need to help the captain.

As they rode onto the grounds surrounding the castle, Caty took in the beautiful arches, turrets, stained-glass windows, gardens, pools, and trees. It was like a piece of Eden set in Italy, peaceful and quiet. Her wonder was dashed by the reserved reception her party received from those taking the horses. "I think I am in trouble, sir," she acknowledged softly to the guard captain. He nodded solemnly.

A page gave the captain a message from the king. "It seems we are expected immediately in his presence. There will be others in attendance, lady. You have been a queen, and have proved to be one yet again today. Remember that. He has a terrible temper, but he is fair. Your Majesty." The man spoke with respect as he assisted her to dismount.

"Thank you, sir. I am so sorry I may have caused you undue trouble. Please believe me, I will not forget what you have done for me this day." Caty's hand rested a moment on the captain's arm. The captain nodded, studying this small woman who had such an aura about her. This was one he would find easy to protect.

Following the messenger, Caty and the captain were led through winding halls and into a large receiving room. Much more opulent than the great room of Marcus, this room had polished floors, thick tapestries hanging on the walls, and large candles placed strategically along its exterior. Great arches broke up the walls, as did large windows placed near the ceilings. Through each arch, a soft glow beckoned one to wander the hall. Men milled around, talking together in small groups. Attendants filled goblets with wine, passed out cheeses and breads, and kept the tables cleaned. The room fell silent when the newly arrived party entered. Santino sat on a raised platform. The captain dropped to one knee before him. Caty knelt as well.

Santino stepped down from his chair and approached. Addressing the captain, he sternly asked, "Did you not agree to bring Lady Caterina here at early light? Perhaps the lady slept until midday. Perhaps you were overtaken by robbers, or maybe you became confused and were lost. Pray tell me"—his voice dropped—"and it had best be a good tale you tell. Share with me your reason for keeping me waiting." There was an ominous tone to his voice.

Before the captain could answer, Caty spoke, still kneeling with a bowed head. "I must confess the fault is mine, Majesty. I was not with the captain and his guard, having slipped away. He was forced to search for me."

"Lady, I do not believe I have spoken to you. You will wait until I address you. Captain?" Santino stood with his arms folded across his chest. His eyes flashed and his face flushed with the anger that consumed him. He had paced the floor for hours, worried some mishap had taken his men and Caty. He would not be soon forgiving this day.

Caty began to pray in a loud, clear voice: "Dear God, please help your king Santino listen with an open mind to the humble testimony of his servant. He must know I was caring for his people, who now know he cares for them. Knowing how he cares for them, they will gladly give what they can for his taxes, tell him whenever there is unrest, and pray for his continued health." She spoke so fast, Santino could barely follow her. The men present had quieted, and listened, unbelieving. "Father, I ask you to help him understand it was I, not the captain, who caused the long delay. The captain took me to task when he found me. Let the king know I meant no harm, but only did what a healer does—I helped an ill child." Caty paused. "If it might be possible, move him to forgive us, his servants—"

"Enough!" Santino barked. "Think you that I do not see what you do?

Captain, I should reward you for putting up with this. You are excused. You, lady, will remain."

The captain shot Caty a quick look of relief as he beat a hasty retreat.

Santino paced the floor, struggling to decide what he should do. That everyone returned safe was a blessing, given all that could have gone wrong. But this woman must not be allowed such freedoms. She was not one to know her place; she proved it again today. "Lady Caterina, rise; I would hear what business kept you from doing what you were ordered to do and why you would keep my men looking after you." His voice was still low and held the weight of danger.

Rising, Caty stood to look up at him. He was so tall; she would have loved to move up the steps the better to look him in the eye. Knowing there was little chance of that, she raised her chin and met his gaze without wavering. Speaking as if he were a child, she carefully explained. "I was ready to ride at first light, when I was approached by a woman crying. While I am quite aware such a sight would not move Your Highness, it did move me. I asked the reason for the sadness and she spoke with me—"

"When you speak to me, woman, do so with caution," the king interrupted. "I care not for the tone nor the message your voice sends me. You will learn to be a proper lady in this court." So saying, he waited for her to continue.

Knowing the room was full of people who just heard their king chastise her, Caty continued without change in either her tone or her stance. Better he understand what he dealt with. That way there was a chance he would send her away rather than fight with her. "I followed the mother to her home, where her child lay burning with fever. I knew the child's affliction." She paused a moment, and her head tipped to the side. "It is life's cruelest turn to take a child from its mother. I searched the land beyond her home until I found what I needed. The child was treated and sleeping without fever when I took my leave. From then, we rode with great haste to this place."

When her story was finished, Santino felt his anger beginning to ebb. Loath to let her see it, he stepped around her to leave. "You will be at court this night," he ordered curtly. "The crown prince of France is presenting his sister, the princess Dominique. She is of marriageable age. I will seriously consider the advantages of such a union." Santino turned to storm out.

"Ah, a match from heaven, for sure. You are perfect for each other," Caty noted sarcastically, under her breath. To her horror, she heard Santino's footsteps suddenly stop, then come back toward her. Once more, she had slipped. Glancing up at Santino who again towered over her, she added, "She looks able to have healthy children. A king needs heirs. To have someone at your side for a lifetime—what a blessing, do you not agree?" Her face bore no sign of sarcasm or humor.

Santino studied her, trying to decide if she were being pert with him or serious. "Tread lightly, lady. I am king. You would do well to remember what that means. Get rid of that hideous riding gown. Burn the gown when you take it off. You will be at court. Do not enter late, Caterina. You are the entertainment tonight." He heard her gasp. He had not intended to say that; it just slipped out. No matter, it was effective. Smiling to himself, he took his leave. *I'll break her yet*, he thought. *She has run free far too long.*

SIXTY-THREE

CATY STARED AFTER HIM. SURELY he was jesting. *What fault could he find in this gown? What do the women of this court wear?* She could not change clothing; her trunks and boxes had not yet arrived. Entertain? She had no talent for song, dance, or even poetry. She seriously doubted he wanted her to apply a poultice to everyone.

Her first reaction was despair. It moved to fear but then settled on determination. *If it is entertainment he wants, that he shall have.*

Several women came to escort Caty to her chambers. Stepping inside, she surveyed the rooms in amazement. Slowly, she walked through them all. The windows and huge doors were placed to flood the rooms with sunlight. A beautiful balcony overlooked a pool and garden. For all their opulence, the rooms still felt comfortable and inviting. Thick tapestries covered walls, floors, and furniture. The bed was large, soft to her touch, and curtained for privacy. Hesitantly, she crossed to the armoire. Empty.

Standing out on the balcony, Caty tried to think. Watching the sun complete its slide below the sea's horizon, she decided upon a plan. Gathering the women around her, Caty gave instructions. The women scurried about gathering odd bits of material. The pieces of cloth were fit to her and altered rapidly, with Caty helping. The time for court would come soon. Excitement from Caty rubbed off on the women with her. At last, Caty was dressed and ready.

"Well, what do you think of our work?" Caty turned around. First one giggled, then another, until all the women were dissolved in laughter. "I take it you think it a success. Entertaining? For certain. Dangerous? Possibly. Different? Definitely. Come, our hour is here." She led the way through a long hallway, nearly skipping. *I think I've beaten him,* she thought. *I do not know any of these people. They will remember me.*

Nearing a massive door that opened to the enormous hall beyond, Caty could hear the music. It was beautiful—music made for dancers. "Tell me when the king begins to dance with Princess Dominique," she told her women. "I will enter then—not a moment before." After sending them off to keep watch, Caty leaned against a wall and closed her eyes. After all that had happened, she could hardly believe she dared do this—but what choice was left her? For the first time in a long time, her thoughts roamed to Rhys. "I miss you, Rhys," she whispered.

One of the girls came running back. "He dances, m'lady. He looks none too pleased, but he dances. The French princess is not very . . . well, she is . . . poor thing," the girl finished lamely.

Caty took a deep breath and entered the room. Candles and fireplaces filled the room with light. The furnishings were rich and colorful. Decorations set about gave the hall a festive air. Caty walked toward a table near the rear of the room. Several couples sat visiting. Indicating an empty chair, she asked, "May I?" The group looked at her, hesitating. One of the men stood up.

He smiled, trying to decide just what she was—male or female. "Certainly. Join us. We're here to witness the king's meeting with the princess of France. It is thought she is a possible match for him." All eyes were on Caty. She graciously sat, thankful the table was near a door.

"I am new to this area and court," Caty said. "It is quite beautiful. I've traveled a great deal and have not seen a place like this before." She smiled warmly at the guests with her. For a moment, the people she sat with were silent, staring.

"I doubt you have," another man finally laughed. "Indeed, I must say, you look rather like a pirate. A very pretty pirate, but a pirate nonetheless. From where do you come?" Caty wore a long white shirt, with full gathers at the cuffs and shoulders. The shirt hung over black pants. A wide red band encircled her tiny waist. The pant legs were gathered and stuffed into high-top red boots.

Her long hair was tucked under a black hat with a large brim. An oversized white feather was tucked into the headband.

Those sitting at the table all laughed with the man—Caty too. "I am not a pirate, sir, but agree with your supposition. I am from Scotland. My trunks and things have not yet made it here, so I was forced to be creative." At this, everyone relaxed.

Santino's time was taken with the French princess and her brother. He was irritated and anxious for Caty to come. As the evening progressed, Caty began to share tales of her travels. Her comments and descriptions had the table roaring. Men and women alike joined in the conversation. Santino had not come or called for her. Just when she had begun to think she could carry this evening off without any problems, she felt a tap at her shoulder.

"Lady, would you allow me the privilege of a dance with you?" The prince of France stood politely waiting, his hand extended. A hush fell over the table. Every eye was on her. Caty took his hand, her heart in her throat. Before her stood the exact duplicate of the Frenchman she had killed so long ago.

Gathering her wits about her, she curtsied. "Of course, Your Grace." The man took her hand and led her to the floor, and they danced. Caty concentrated on not allowing her distress to show. *This must be his son, or perhaps a younger brother . . .*

The dancers circled the floor, with the men and women alternating in lines, changing partners. To her horror, her next partner in line was King Santino. At first he did not recognize her, and thought a boy had slipped into the wrong circle. He caught his mistake as he surveyed the slight figure before him. "So you come to my court as a pirate, lady? Quite appropriate I would say," he noted dryly. Before he could comment further, Princess Dominique was at his side. Caty could not resist smiling sweetly at Santino. His expression made clear he saw no reason for smiling. He remembered all too well Caty's supposition regarding the match between Santino and the princess.

At that point, she was whirled around and was suddenly with another partner. Each man dancing with her delighted in the surprise. Regardless of how she tried to slip from the circles moving about, she was taken by another partner. *Well, I suppose I am the entertainment,* Caty admitted to herself.

When the dance finally ended, Caty tried to quickly leave the floor, but was met by the prince again. He talked with her, not allowing her to return to her seat. "I feel I know you from somewhere," he commented, standing in her path. Caty's heart was in her throat. "You are much too young, though. Could not be the same woman," he concluded, studying Caty.

With a start, Caty realized he mistook her for her mother. He knew her mother. He had to; someone from his country had sentenced her to burn. Could it be he knew about Lady Tabor? As the facts jumped before her, she knew she had to get away from this man. Desperate, she glanced toward the king's table, catching Carlo's eye. "Look, Your Grace, the king would like to speak with you." Caty nodded toward the front.

Immediately, the man released her hand and headed for the table. Without looking at anyone, Caty began to weave her way out of the room. Once in the corridor, she walked faster and faster until she was running, all the while trying to open doors that might lead outside. Eventually, she came to an arch with a large door, pushed the door, and was met with cold air. Outside, finally. The choking sensation was leaving. After looking around, she ran onto one of the paths that wound through the grounds. Running until she was forced to stop and catch her breath, she crumpled to the ground, against a tree, and began to sob. The floodgates that had held back so many tears from so many heartaches opened. She wept uncontrollably.

Santino had waited impatiently for the French prince and his sister to enter. Maybe she would be as beautiful as many Frenchwomen were, he had hoped. He had groaned inwardly when he saw Princess Dominique and her brother approach. The woman was nearly six feet in height—and in width. Her thinning hair was pulled severely back into a tiny bun at the top of her head, over which rested her crown. Her face was heavily scarred from the pox, and as she got closer he had to fight the impulse to stand back. When she smiled, he saw that several of her front teeth were missing, and others were already blackened. As he rose to walk around the table to greet the woman and her brother, he could see both Carlo and Gabriel were struggling mightily to keep from laughing.

"You'd best not," he snarled under his breath to Carlo. "Find Caterina," he ordered. "'A match from the heavens!' she says. When I get my hands on her . . . ," he muttered to himself. Carlo and Gabriel exchanged glances, grateful for the diversion. They both stepped aside. Safely away from the crowd, the two men dissolved into laughter.

"My money rests with Queen Caterina," Gabriel noted when he could finally catch his breath. "She handles our brother with ease. This will be an interesting evening."

Carlo and Gabriel began searching for Caty. They wandered by women dancing, seated at the tables, and talking in groups, but no Caty. When Carlo finally recognized Caterina, the Frenchman was leading her to the floor. "This gets better and better," Carlo whispered into Gabriel's ear, pointing Caterina out. The small pirate was being turned through the circle of dancers.

Gabriel agreed. "This lady has great courage. A pirate!" Both men watched as Santino and the princess danced, then watched Caterina and the prince. As the end of the dance neared, Carlo and Gabriel split up, each taking a side and moving toward Caterina. Carlo caught her eye, nodding to her. In the crowded room, however, both he and Gabriel soon lost her.

Unable to find her, Carlo and Gabriel returned to Santino's table, where they stood on the raised platform, searching the crowd. Carlo was positive she had seen him; then, suddenly, she was nowhere to be found. The prince was talking with Santino, as they walked toward the head table. Gabriel and Carlo quickly took up the search again, broadening the hunt.

First one, then two hours went by. The men stood at the entrance of the hall. "We have looked everywhere," Gabriel lamented. "She is not in her chambers. Every room she could have entered is empty. The stables have not been disturbed. Where?" Neither wanted to be the one to inform Santino she had gone—again.

"I know the first thing I intend to do when we find her," said Carlo. "I intend to reassign her ladies-in-waiting and her guard. This cannot happen again." He was now angry. Angry at Caterina, at her ladies, and at himself for failing to take enough precautions.

"We have not looked in the gardens beyond those near," said Gabriel. "We should have searched those closer to Santino's chambers. If she came from where he housed her, down that way"—he pointed to a side entrance—"she would have left that way, as she does not know this castle." He was already moving in the indicated direction.

Outside, both men moved silently along the pathways. They walked a fair distance before they heard the sound of someone weeping. Not the wailing done by professional mourners, but the weeping of a soul damaged. Seeing Caterina on the ground, they stood but a moment watching. Gabriel spoke first. "Stay here, Carlo. I will bring Santino. This is partially his doing." Carlo nodded before moving deeper into the shadows. He could not bring himself to disturb Caty.

In the hall, Gabriel sat down next to Santino, who was trying to avoid dancing. When he leaned in and spoke to the king, Santino immediately rose. Both men left, moving through the dark halls. "Tell me again," Santino said on the way.

"Something is terribly wrong, cousin. She weeps as one whose heart is torn. She vomits with the emotions tearing at her. I have never seen one so distraught. She is there, alone."

When Gabriel and Santino approached, Carlo stepped from the shadows onto the path. "She still weeps," he reported softly. "She is not aware of my presence. She just rocks side to side, weeping."

The king stood and watched Caty for a moment. He knew she was strong, independent, and self-assured. Everything she had said and done proved it. Seeing her in such misery moved Santino. His anger at her forgotten, he stepped to her and knelt on one knee. He gently brushed her hair from her face. "Come, Caterina. You cannot stay out here."

Caterina looked up, hardly recognizing him. Numbly nodding, she tried to stand. Santino helped her, then swept her up into his arms. She was even lighter than he expected; his arms tightened around her as he walked with her. She seemed unaware of anything around her. She only knew the sorrow of her heart, and wept. Inside her chambers, Santino sat on the bed with her on his lap, still holding her closely, his deep voice gently soothing her. Slowly, the sobs began to subside. At last she lay still within his arms. Her ladies-in-waiting stood inside the room, not certain what to do. "Get her ready for bed," the king commanded. "I will return shortly." Solemnly he left the room. Outside, he spoke to his brother and cousin.

"I want a guard for her. Find ladies-in-waiting, not children-in-waiting. She is not to be left alone until I agree. Starting now. Both of you are to meet me back at the hall. I will dispense with our two visitors tonight. Seeing the princess, one can almost forgive the tactics her brother used to get her married."

The three women who sat with Caterina that night were middle-aged. All widowed, they were well known at court. None were interested in husbands, nor in court intrigue. Talking softly, they watched over their charge and discussed how best to go about this new assignment. It was made clear to them that this woman was pursued by King Santino.

When Caty awoke, it was nearly dawn. She lay very still, trying to remember where she was. As it came to her, she sat up suddenly. She was on a bed, in the softest bed gown she had ever worn. The room was still. At her stirring, a large figure rose from a chair near the dimming fireplace and walked to her. Santino sat on the bed and took her hand. He kissed it.

"Our plans, yours and mine, whatever they were, have now changed." His voice was deep and gentle. "To begin, Caterina, you will never be called Caty again. Caterina speaks to your Italian heritage. Next, I must know why you wept so. What is it that broke such a strong heart, Caterina?"

Caty looked at Santino, trying to think. His eyes looked even darker than usual in the dim light. "Women cry . . . ," she began hesitantly.

"Yes, some do. Some do not, as they have no heart to feel." A savage expression passed over his face. "But you, Lady Caterina, you do not cry. You mourn. Your heart has an ache deep within. I would know what gives you such a pain." When he finished speaking, he sat very still, watching her, praying it was not him that caused so much pain.

At first she looked away. Shortly, she turned back to him. He remained silent, patiently waiting.

"The Frenchman," she began, "looked very much like a Frenchman I killed." Santino frowned, his surprise at this news evident. Caty added, "While in Scotland."

"I am listening," he encouraged her softly. *Killed?* He thought she had told him all about herself. He had guessed she had a history, but he had never thought of this.

Caty told him about the time she defended Dermoth Castle. "I have a difficult time with the French, sire," she added softly. "They ordered my mother burned at the stake as a witch. She was a healer, not a witch. The priest with Marcus gave me a letter from the Holy See regarding my mother. They condemned the action of the French government. Her own son shot and killed her before the flames could touch her, to save her the pain."

She winced and leaned back onto the pillows stacked behind her. "There are women who have lost much more, I know. I tried to keep the pain inside. For so long, I have held back my heart's tears. I apologize for losing control." She ducked her head. "I would release you, my lord. I would not be queen. Please, Santino," she begged him softly. The sound of his name on her lips stirred him. "I know love is not important for a union such as ours. But life is hard enough. I do not care to take on any more pain. I would not play the games courts play. Not yet. I wish to go home, back to Scotland—please." Slowly, her eyes met his.

He listened to her intently. "I believe Lady Isabella was from Rome. Is that correct?"

Caterina nodded. "Yes. Why do you ask?"

"You are home, Caterina." His voice was gentle. He watched her eyes fill with tears. "Do you find me repulsive, Caterina?" he asked, sitting back. He studied her, watching her thoughts move across her face. Unguarded as she was now, he could tell she did not find him unpleasant. In truth, he now believed she had feelings for him, too. He sat coolly waiting, not wanting to give her any reason to hide what he now was certain she felt.

"No, I do not find you repulsive, Majesty. You have been most kind, considering the circumstances of our meeting. I . . ." She struggled to find the right words. "I find myself in an unfamiliar arena. I long for the comfort of things already known."

"I have never taken a wife," said Santino. "My mother made certain I never cared to share my days and nights with a woman. You changed that." He paused, his head tipped so he could see directly into her eyes. "Our life may not be easy, but it will be shared. And you *will* be queen," he finished firmly. Caty looked at him for a long moment. His eyes were kind, but they also had passion within. She could see the emotion. "Do you love me, Caterina?" His voice was so low she could barely hear. "Even a little? I believe you could."

"I have loved before, and I know the fire. It burns small, but it burns." Her eyes sought his. "It is a love I cannot allow to grow. You embody the promise of much, but too easily a man's heart cools. I never sought a kingdom, a crown, or a king. Now is the time for you to step aside and let me go. Before we have both moved beyond our control." Her eyes pleaded with him.

"That small fire you speak of rages within me, Caterina. I see your eyes in the stars, feel your smile in the sun, see your face in every moment that makes this life better. That fire consumes me. I will never share my love, nor another's bed. I swear." When he finished, he lifted her chin and kissed her soft lips. He kissed her cheek, her swollen eyes, and her lips again. "I will never allow you to leave. Do not ask again. It is futile to ask for something that will never be granted. You were made for this, Caterina—can you not see? Your life is formed by everything you have touched. Just as you changed lives, your life has changed. No, Caterina, you will not leave. You will be my queen; more importantly, you will be my wife." When he finished speaking, he watched for her reaction. He already knew something of this lady. She could love him, of that he was sure. It mattered little to the men in his world whether the woman they chose loved them. To Santino, however, it did matter. Instinctively he realized that if Caterina did not love him, this thing that bound them would unwind. He would do all in his power to bind her heart, not just her life, to him.

Caterina rose, pulled a blanket around her shoulders, and walked away from Santino.

"Have you children, Caterina?" Santino asked, watching her move away.

"Yes," she answered, without looking back, "a son."

Having previously believed she had no children, Santino's face lost the soft expression that hovered about his eyes. "Where is this son?" He held his breath, awaiting her answer.

"In a grave, next to his father. He was ten months old. I will not let any other mother suffer what I felt, if I can help it," Caterina replied quietly. "You make me feel important to you," she continued, speaking quietly. "I watch you and . . ." She stopped walking. She had not intended to say that—it just came out. She slowly began to walk again.

He wanted to see her face. By this time, the sun tossed rays into the room, filling it with light. *Like she fills the room with light,* he thought. "Caterina! Since when is it proper to walk unexcused from your king?" Santino stood with his arms crossed.

"When one has spoken without thought and is humiliated. My hope is the king might fail to see or hear," she admitted.

He laughed. "Look at me." He waited for her to turn around. "You blush! How refreshing. My hearing is excellent, as is my sight." He began to walk toward her. "I could never not hear or see you, Caterina. You *are* important to me." Caterina stopped walking and waited for him to reach her.

She looked up at him. "Am I forgiven for last evening?"

"I am thinking." He smiled, then reached for her hand and pulled her closer. "You are much more entertaining than I could have imagined." For several seconds, he merely stood, holding her. "You think it so objectionable to be my queen?"

When she did not answer, he changed the question. "Are there other things I should know?" he asked. He brushed her hair away from her face again.

"All of it?" she asked, nervously.

"Everything," he answered firmly, wondering what there could be that caused her nervousness. He led her back to the bed and held the covers while she slipped beneath them. Sitting on the edge, he waited for her words.

She had been asked that question by every man she was tied to. Each telling was longer, though every tale ended the same—in sadness. Caterina Tabor Dermoth Cassini told King Santino Giovanni her life's story. Everything. When she was finished, he sat studying her, thinking. Finally, he smiled. "My life has been rather dull, Caterina. I must assume you will change that." Yet, he would see she did not run as freely as she apparently had with Marcus. He would be a husband and her king. She would have protection, whether she wanted it or not. "You should know, lady, I would have been much harder on you—even though you healed the pig."

"Perhaps." Caterina shrugged.

"No, not perhaps." His voice was firm. "You would only have wandered once."

After lighting a fire, he called for food. Once it had been delivered, he took her hand, led her to a small table, and sat opposite. "You and I will be wed. Until now, I've thought my life too busy to take a wife. Now I know I want to have you waiting for me, living with me, and sharing my work, both successes and failures. However, we must have an understanding." With that, Santino began to carefully lay his rules down, making certain there could be no misunderstanding.

When Santino finished, Caty eyed him keenly. "It would seem you own me," she noted.

"It would seem," he agreed firmly. For several heartbeats, the room was silent. "The job will be with its own rewards and pleasures, I promise. I could never be very tough with you, Caterina. I will not waver on the point of knowing where you are, always. Your safety is too precious, as are you. I will be your husband, Caterina. Your king in every sense of the word. Agreed?"

"Yes," she replied simply. *What choice do I have?* Then, frowning, she added, "If my guard agrees to come with me, am I free to roam about as long as my whereabouts are known?"

"No, you are not. Unless I say so. Pray, little lady, I never have to go looking for you again." His tone was dead serious. His eyes never left hers.

Caty looked around the room. "Might I ask where we are?" If she was to live her life here, she would make the most of it.

"You are in your chambers, my lady," Santino answered quietly.

Silence enveloped them again. Caty saw the passion rise in his expression. At that moment, a woman entered the room. "Majesty, the ladies are waiting for your approval, as is the guard." Caty turned to see an elderly woman standing to one side. Caty glanced at Santino in time to see him smile with satisfaction.

Caty stood at the doorway while Santino looked over the people standing beyond, in the foyer of Caty's chambers. Carlo was standing with the men, and introduced everyone. Caty would have protection and chaperones. Santino was taking no chances. When all had gone, he sat down with her and they ate. He talked of the castle, how it grew with each successive generation, and how his grandmother started the gardens. Caty began to relax. She watched his eyes light up when speaking of his brother and cousin. "I must leave," he said at last. "There is work to be done. I have sent for material and a seamstress. In case you wonder, the pirate clothes were destroyed last night." He smiled at her. "You provided great entertainment, I must say." He stood, kissed the top of her head, and left.

For the next eight weeks, Santino came every day to see Caterina. He came in the morning, then joined her for every evening meal. When he came, he would talk with her about his people. Sometimes he walked with her around the grounds. Always attentive and respectful, he took every opportunity to fan the fire she admitted having for him. He had never taken a wife, but he had taken women—many of them. Now he used everything he knew to win her favor. To his surprise and pleasure, she was not so impressed with the gowns, jewels, or finery he gave her. She was more impressed with the stained-glass windows in his castle, the gardens, the flowers, and the people who worked the grounds. She loved the king's chapel with its towering statues, paintings, and tapestries. She began each day in that chapel.

Before long, every man and woman working around her made certain they were close enough to greet Caty while she walked. Fresh flowers were brought every morning with her meal. The word spread; the king pursued a woman to wed.

Caty was not allowed at court. Santino took no chance that some conniving mother or former lover would have an issue with her. She only left her chambers if Santino was with her. Her ladies-in-waiting were well trained and her guard kept a close eye on her. Caty wondered that she was not bothered by the restrictions. She had nothing to do but heal. Slowly, that's what she did. Each day Caty grew more comfortable with Santino. He had been successful—the fire was growing within her.

Santino's fire grew also. He was pleasantly surprised to find that Caty had a good head for management. He discussed more and more of his official business with her. He frequently included Carlo and Gabriel in the evening meals, as well as in the wanderings around the gardens. To the king's delight, Carlo and Gabriel were genuinely fond of Lady Caterina, as if she had always been one of them. The days passed easily for Caty.

SIXTY-FOUR

IN THE WEEKS LEADING UP to the wedding, word of Caty's healing knowledge had spread. Santino waited for her to tell him of the requests coming to her. Each day, a messenger found his or her way into the castle, asking for the ladies-in-waiting. When the first had come, Santino himself had questioned the lad. Since that time, each afternoon, one of Caty's ladies met with Santino to tell him of the requests coming in. He expected that Caty would at some time ask to go see someone ill. No matter how he argued with himself, he had to admit he did not know what he would say when that time came.

The day came when King Santino would make Lady Caterina his wife. The bells in the cathedral tower beckoned. Men and women, clothed in their finest, crammed into every pew, stool, and vestibule, both upstairs and down. Grand stained-glass windows spread the afternoon sun across the wide center aisle. Vivid reds, blues, and greens bathed the marble floor. A profusion of candles were lit, making the walls come alive with the reflected dancing flames. Fresh flowers adorned the entrance, with ropes of garland draped along the pews. The church was charged with anticipation and curiosity. The increased presence of guardsmen only added to the anticipation of the event.

Santino chose his uncle to escort his bride to him. It had taken great effort for Santino to move past what his mother had been. He knew that to hold her brother guilty was not fair, but Santino's heart had been cold. For years now, the old man had tried to win forgiveness. Today would be the day. Santino had spent his adult life refusing to even think he would one day marry. He had little love for his natural father and hated his mother. She had proved to be one of the cruelest people he ever knew. After all these years the thought of her still roused the hatred inside him. When he had her executed, he slept through the night for the first time in his memory. Only the devotion and love of his brother, Carlo, and cousin, Gabriel, kept him sane. The man he thought of and loved as a father was an old priest. That man had died several years ago, but Santino still heard the man's voice chiding him whenever he thought to do something the old man would not have liked. Santino's mind wandered to the woman who had been Caty's mother. He could not imagine how her husband must have felt when she was taken away, then sentenced to die—in the most terrible of ways.

Now, here Santino stood, waiting for a small genteel woman to promise she would love him above all others. He would promise the same. Perhaps peace was finally coming into his life to stay.

Santino watched Caty enter the cathedral. Her dress was soft and billowed around her small frame. On her head, she wore a diadem of silver. It nestled in her hair, encircling her head. From this, a train of white silk flowed. He hardly noticed the dress or anything else. He was stunned. Caty looked for all the world as if she had planned on this day all her life. She walked regally, her head high, her movements comfortable and confident. *Gabriel is right*, Santino thought. *She does float.*

To maintain her composure, Caty kept her eyes focused on the man waiting at the altar for her. Her gown was crafted from a material Santino had chosen, draped in layer upon layer of gentle gathers from the raised waist and sweeping the floor. When she and her escort entered, the very walls seemed to move in. The silence that followed was unbroken but for the rustle of her gown and her soft steps. As she walked slowly forward, the occupants stood, row after row.

When she reached the kneeling bench before the altar, Santino knelt with her. The ceremony began. The heat of the candles and bodies made Caty long for an open window or door, anything that would allow a breeze to cool the hall. She found her mind wandering while the bishop's voice droned on and on. She remembered the other times she had made the walk to an altar, and the other men. This felt familiar, yet very different. She heard the bishop begin anew. He spoke of loyalty, honesty, and obedience. She stopped herself before she laughed when the sound of someone snoring drifted to the front. She could imagine the embarrassment of the wife who was probably pinching the poor man.

Then she was aware that the tone of the bishop had changed. She quickly brought her wandering mind back to business. Just as the bishop indicated they should stand, someone behind them fainted. There was a collective gasp. Caty laughed under her breath as she stole a quick glance at Santino. He was watching her, his eyes twinkling as he fought to not laugh. Several more poor souls crashed to the floor. Santino leaned toward the bishop, speaking softly. The bishop stuttered; then, nodding, he finished quickly. He blessed them both after they had taken communion.

Santino turned to Caty. Holding her hands in his, he looked into her eyes. "I give you my name, Caterina. You already possess my heart. A wise man loves not lightly, if he finds one who touches his very soul. You have touched mine," he said softly. He turned to the congregation behind them. "My wife, Caterina." The silence was broken again, but this time with a cheering that filled the large church, crowded the rafters, and spilled out the great doors that were now opened.

With Caty's hand on his arm, Santino walked down the aisle. The crowd that had stood when Caty entered now bowed low before their newly wed king and his wife.

The crowd moved out, following the king and Caterina. People rode horseback, walked, and filled carts on their way to the celebration that would surely fill the castle's great hall. Santino, Caterina, his brother and cousin, and a small party of followers led the way. As the wedding party moved slowly away from the cathedral, Santino leaned back toward his brother. "Is it all ready?"

Carlo grinned. "Of course." Santino smiled with satisfaction. Caterina may have been married before, but this wedding would be the one she always remembered—the one she would remember when they were both old.

Santino's eyes shone with mischief. "We are going on a trip, you and I," he said to his bride. "Without all the pomp and circumstance that usually follows a king's wedding. I want you to myself for a while. Impossible if we stay in the castle." His face bore a wide grin. "Will you come?"

Caty smiled. "'Tis late for me to say no. I think I go wherever you go."

"Trust me, Caterina." He heeled his horse. Arriving at the castle, Santino and Caty walked through the crowded great hall, now decorated and filled with music and laughter. When they reached the middle of the room, Santino stood still, holding Caty's hand. The music softened, the floor cleared, and the new couple danced. There was food, wine, and all manner of sweet dishes. Tumblers, poets, and dancers provided entertainment. Into the night, the merriment continued.

Gabriel requested a dance with the bride, then courteously escorted Caty to the floor. When the dance ended, he introduced her to several lords and ladies who stood nearby. After returning her to Santino, he and Carlo left the hall.

As night closed around them, Santino took Caty's hand and led her outside. "I know, Caterina, that you have had other husbands," he began, his face grave in the moonlight. "I know none of them could love you as I do. Nor will there ever be any man who loves you as I do." He walked with her down paths, past pools and fountains. When they passed a bench, he sat her down. Gently, he lifted her chin with his hand, running his thumb over her lips. "Caterina, I must have your promise that you will do as I ask. I have great responsibilities. I will not spend time worrying you might be away from the protection of me or my men, wandering about in the manner to which you have grown accustomed. You will never leave my presence without my knowledge of your destination. Do you understand me?" He could see Caty's face, her great eyes watching him. When he finished speaking, she turned away. Although she seemed to be looking over the grounds, he knew she thought on what he had just asked of her.

"I promise you, Santino. Not because you are my king, or my husband. I promise because I love you." Her reply was simple and honest. He pulled her up, then held her face with both hands. Gently, he kissed her. Ever so slowly, her hands moved until her arms encircled his neck. Still, the kiss stayed on. At length, he withdrew, his hands still on her face.

"Come, wife, I have a surprise for you, when this celebration is over." With his arm around her shoulders, he led her back toward the castle.

Carlo watched his brother and sister-in-law. They may as well have been the only ones in the hall. With satisfaction, he could see how happy his brother was. When the couple walked back to the table, Carlo asked permission to dance with Caterina. As Caty and Carlo moved around the room, away from the greater crowd, Carlo pulled her off the floor. "I have something for you, Caterina. I was asked to see you received this." He lifted her hand and placed a ring in her palm.

Closing her fingers around the ring, he explained, "When I found the boy, he was dying. Not by our hands, nor the hands of any of the king's men. By the hands of the sons of the woman Marcus kept." Carlo saw sadness flash across Caty's face. "She planned to do away with you and claim the crown for one of her sons. When this young knight realized the battle was lost for Marcus, he left for that castle. They were three, he but one. The three died during the fight. He was mortally wounded. He lived long enough to tell me the story, give me the ring, and exact a promise that I would protect you with my life." When his story was told, he raised her hand to his lips. "A promise I intend to keep, sister."

Caty's eyes misted. She squeezed Carlo's hand. "Thank you, Carlo, for so much," she whispered.

Carlo walked Caty back to the king. Nodding slightly to Santino, he returned to the dance floor. For a long moment, Caty sat with the ring clutched tightly in her hand. When she looked around, suddenly aware someone had spoken to her, she could see Santino watching her closely. "You're troubled?" he asked.

"Saddened." Caty opened her hand, exposing the ring. "This belonged to my father. I gave it to a very young member of the court of Marcus."

"He was rather like a son to you, was he not?" Santino asked, slipping his arm around Caty.

Startled, Caty looked at Santino. "You knew of him?"

"Yes, there are not many things about my kingdom I do not know." He studied her eyes. "I pray you do not stay sad for long, Caterina."

"What is done, is done, Your Grace." She gently touched his hand.

Watching his new wife, Santino knew, for the first time in his life, the only real treasure he possessed he had taken from Marcus: Caterina. He stood with Caty's hand in his. Together, they quietly left the hall. He escorted her down a hall, out a door, and across the grounds. "Hmm, we are bound for the hay, are we?" Caty murmured. Santino laughed heartily.

"No, but I shall keep that thought in mind for future reference, Caterina." Santino led her along the paths at a leisurely pace, visiting with his new wife. Caty had learned long ago that everything reveals itself with time, and so did not question the king. They entered a courtyard where horses, guards, and Carlo and Gabriel milled around. Still, Caty kept her own counsel. Helping her onto a horse, Santino noted, "You ask not where we are bound?"

"I belong to you, Your Grace. I choose to believe I am in good care." She smiled down at him. Caty's skill at interpreting the intuitions she felt was by now keen. She no longer tried to push the feelings aside. Now, she listened. She knew this union would be a good one. She was loved by a man of honor. She would never take for granted his love.

SIXTY-FIVE

THE RIDE WAS PLEASANT, IF slow. Accompanied by his brother, his cousin, and his guard, the party rode toward the port at Orbetello. Though the road was well known to all but Caty, darkness demanded caution. When the lights from their destination gave way to the black sea beyond, Caty stiffened. She glanced at Santino, frowning slightly. He was visiting with his brother, but Gabriel saw the apprehension on her face. "Your Majesty, I believe your surprise is revealed," he called to his cousin.

"Ah, yes. We have arrived. Caterina, since you have struggled so valiantly to get aboard a ship and travel, I decided we would go together." Caty opened her mouth to speak, but Santino leaned toward her and placed his finger over her lips. "Not yet, Caterina. You are not allowed to ask questions. Trust is a wonderful thing." Smiling at her discomfort, he led them onto the dock. Assisting her off the horse, he waved toward the opulent ship gently bobbing in the water. "This is my favorite vessel, if we are not going to fight, of course. Please." After leading her up the plank to board, he called to the crew on ship. "I present to you my wife and your queen, Caterina." The crew and staff broke into cheers and clapped. Caty curtsied, then took Santino's arm. He took her on a quick tour, greeting the crew, staff, and several women, including the wives of Gabriel and Carlo. The royal party ended up in a sitting room, where staff waited to pour wine.

After a short while, Santino stood and led Caty down a long hall to his private sleeping quarters. It was plush, with every convenience possible on a ship, yet mindful of the need to limit weight. The bed sat against a wall, but took up most of the room. Floor coverings, blankets, and a small changing closet and chest completed the decor. The king and his new wife were followed by his brother, his cousin, their women, and several pages and ladies-in-waiting. While the quiet colors and few lit candles created a sensual feeling in the room, the audience did not. Caty looked to Santino, then at the crowd. Santino pulled her closer. "I have not been married before, Caterina," he reminded her. "The king's marriage must be consummated—as testified by witnesses." He saw the look of horror that shot across her face. Taking her face in his hands, he spoke with care. "Do not think of these people, Caterina. Think on me, and you, and what we now are committed to. They will soon be gone; you will not even know when they leave." Caty looked at him doubtfully, trying to work up the courage to stay and not run out of the room. She glanced at the door. He smiled, reading her mind. "Do not do what you think on, Caterina. We would wind up on the deck of this vessel, before more than these few eyes."

Caty's mouth fell open briefly at the thought. Numbly, she nodded. Taking a deep breath, she turned to the young women waiting to assist her. *I was a queen before Santino, and I will behave like one*, she reminded herself over and over. Desperate to think of how to deal with what could easily become a disaster, an idea burst into her mind. *The power! I need to use the power Mother spoke of.* The idea grew rapidly, exploding in her head. *He wants them to witness us; well, they will not soon forget what they see.* Santino had walked through his sleeping quarters and now stood at the door of a small changing room, watching Caty. The witnesses stood in a half circle near the foot of the king's bed. Caty's marriage gown and other clothing were removed. One of her attendants held a soft white bed gown and began to dress her.

"Caterina," Santino called, softly. "Come here." The attendant stepped back, still holding the bed gown, not certain what to do. The new wife stood before the witnesses, naked.

I am a queen. If this is to be, I will see he stays in my bed. Caty slowly turned toward Santino. She began, bit by bit, to remove the pins from her hair, letting it roll softly around her shoulders and down her back. "Your Grace?" Her voice was low, sultry, and smooth. For a moment, Santino stared at her. Her steps were careful, as if she walked on a ledge. Her eyes held his. She seemed not to notice that there was anyone in the room but him. Her body moved seductively toward him. Santino shook his head, trying to take control again. He quickly stepped to Caty, urgently waving the people in his room out. No one moved. "You called, husband?" Caty murmured. She looked into his eyes as her hands softly touched his chest. Santino could feel his manhood pulsating. He reached out to touch her, as if trying to assure himself she was real. She stood still, her full lips turned up in a slight smile. "I am here," she whispered. Waving the crowd away, Santino's eyes locked on to Caty's. There would be no doubt about this union now.

Santino lifted Caty and carried her to the bed. Silently, Gabriel and Carlo ushered the witnesses out, closing the door behind them. Quickly, Santino undressed, his eyes still on Caty. He lay beside her. He wanted her so badly that he had to concentrate on taking her slowly. His breathing quickened. Caty was not expecting his touch to thrill her as it did. She could hardly breathe. As his hand moved over her breasts and slowly down her belly, she closed her eyes and moved with him, moaning. At last, Caty let him take her. Santino soon realized that although Marcus had slept with Caty every night he was home, he had not made love to this lady in a long time. Santino took his time, promising himself she would remember this husband above all others. As the night moved, so did the lovers. Santino rolled over onto his back, bringing Caty with him. She moved in rhythm with him, her head back, moaning slightly. When dawn pushed aside the night, its light found Santino and Caterina finally asleep. She lay nestled in his arms.

When Santino awoke, he lay still, listening to Caterina's even breathing. She had responded in ways he hadn't expected during the night. *How could Marcus ever leave this bed?* he wondered. *More, how could he sleep with her next to him and not take her every night?* Pleased with his prize, he looked down at her. She lay awake, staring at the window. "Of what do you think, Caterina?" he whispered into her ear.

She glanced at him self-consciously. "I thought how grateful I am that you did not let me get away."

Santino held her closely. In his mind, he reviewed the antics of his wife. *Had*

I known then what I now know, your return to me would have been dark for you. The very chance that you might have been taken by another . . . he thought, looking at his wife.

"Remember what I expect, Caterina. I will take no exception. When you and I are old, you will thank me again." Caty did not answer; she only smiled at Santino. He watched Caty's eyes follow the rays of light as they moved across the ceiling. "We sail for several days before I must return. Come, stand on the deck and watch the sun rise over our land. It is my favorite place for peace. Although," he added softly, "I think that may change." He kissed her tenderly.

Caty dreaded seeing the witnesses to her wedding night in the glare of daylight. She sat up, hugging her knees. "Does it not trouble you that so many of your court have seen me naked?" she asked Santino.

"Your wedding night with Marcus was not witnessed?" Santino pulled her back down.

"No." Caty moaned in embarrassment.

Santino laughed. "Let me remember—the people last night have seen you as a pirate, with your gown torn in revealing places, or in a prison cell—"

"I know, Santino, but I was dressed," Caty interrupted. "At least most of me was."

"However, you were in a more honorable position last night, my lady," he reminded her, laughing. "You are beautiful, even naked. Caterina, I think you will find much with me is different. I find I love you more each time we talk—and make love." He laughed again. "You did not look at them; you looked at me. You knew not when they left. They are my family and friends." His voice was gentle. "You belong to me, and so, to them. Soon you will be crowned my queen. I am certain you and I will have a good life, love." He held her closely. She kissed him with a gentleness that, before Caterina, was unknown to him.

When the royal couple returned to their home, Caty quickly fell into a routine with his household. She always believed that kings may come and go, but the needs of the people were a constant. One afternoon, one of her ladies brought a request for the queen's attention, Caty agreed to hear the man out. After meeting with the man and hearing about his problem, Caty promised that she would speak with him again before the day's end.

Santino sat in his study, working with Gabriel, Carlo, and several others. Caty never entered the room unless she knew he was alone. For a moment, she stood at the closed door, then spoke to the page standing near. "Is it ever permissible to speak to the king while he is working? I have something I must discuss with him, and fear I cannot wait until later." She watched the young man trying to decide whether the queen's request trumped the discussion going on in the room. He looked at the quiet lady before him and decided a favored queen would be a good one to help. It was a simple request, after all.

When he emerged from the study, he was smiling. "His Majesty will see you now. I think he needs a break."

Caty thanked the young man and followed him into the room. As always, Santino's eyes lit up when he saw Caty. "Caterina, please, how can I be of service?" His voice was kind and inviting.

Glancing around the room, Caty replied, "Please pardon my interruption, sirs. I will be gone quickly." Turning to Santino, she spoke quietly. "I made a promise to you, Your Grace. I come now, keeping that promise." Santino frowned slightly. He remembered everything he had ever asked of his wife. This could only be a request for her skill with healing. Taking her elbow, he led her away from the table.

"Someone has an ill pig?" He smiled, waiting for her to explain.

Caty laughed softly. Telling Santino of the man's request, she added, "I would need to see the animals myself, to know what the problem might be." She waited while her husband thought on her request. He walked to the window, thinking. The time had come. After a long moment, he turned to Caty.

"You do need to go. I will go with you." He walked to her and brushed her face with his hand. "I would see what you do." Santino knew he had resolved his one problem with Queen Caty. Like all problems he dealt with, Caterina Giovanni's gift would be handled one request at a time.

Santino kept his promise to Caterina. Their life was different, but it was good. He never hurt her. He teased her, saying she gave him little time for other women. In truth, he found he had no interest in any but his wife. Santino never lost the firm edge, but he was always gentle with Caterina. The years passed quickly. Yet, even after twenty-two years, Caterina's love for Santino grew. His feelings for her were stronger at each turn of their lives.

On this morning, Caterina sat on the bed for a moment longer. Her joints ached during the winter months, and winter had shrouded the land with snow and ice. Last night had been especially long for Caty again. She had sat by the fire for several hours and then walked the floor most of the night, before eventually lying down to sleep.

Santino had been up with her during the night, and now lay watching her. "Are you better?" Santino asked with concern in his voice. His wife was very active every day, yet she was slowing down. They both were, he knew, but it was hard to see her trying to deal with the pain.

"I am." Caterina turned to him, smiling. His hair was now white. Her own hair was still soft, though silver. She lay back down and he pulled her closer. "I believe I am getting older," she admitted. "I never think on it, but my joints remind me."

"We both are. When I look at you, I only see the same beautiful woman I fell in love with, Caterina. You are still the keeper of my heart." His smile was warm and tender.

Caterina laid her head on his chest as his arms held her close. Until now, she had never understood what her father meant when he said that each trial prepares one for the winter of life. Their fall was nearly over. Winter no longer frightened Caterina.

ABOUT THE
AUTHOR

BORN AND RAISED IN COLORADO, I was the second of four children. I spent my youth on a ranch twenty-three miles from town. My high school class had twenty-nine graduates. Living so far from town, my family seldom made the trip unless groceries or other supplies were needed. During the winter, we traveled over frozen roads. Most days the school bus made it through, but occasionally we were snowbound.

It was a working cattle ranch: the steers arrived in early spring, were fattened up all summer, and shipped out early fall. Men arrived early in the spring, before the steers, to mend fences and make ready for the cattle. There were several large hay fields; the harvested hay was baled and kept for the horses through the harsh winters. The ranch was beautiful, with meadows, pine- and spruce-covered mountains, rapid flowing creeks, and great rock walls rising from the earth, remnants of past geological activities.

Mine was an ideal childhood. I rode horseback to help move cattle, drove a tractor pulling a flatbed of hay, and worked the garden. Although everyone did their fair share of the work, there was plenty of time to roam the country, both hiking and riding horses. Nearly every Sunday, after Mass and lunch, my older brother would ride with me beside every creek and past every beaver pond on the property. When he could not ride with me, I walked alone. As I walked the many, many miles on that ranch, stories traveled through my mind. Characters came and left, knocking on the door of my memory whenever a certain sound like the ripple of the creek or a familiar sight such as the quivering

389

aspen awoke them. For much of this time, I felt as if I were an observer of life. Watching how people interacted, how animals interacted, and how what we do affects both.

My father worked every day, including Sundays. My mother kept a welcoming home for every cowboy, ranch hand, and child who found their way into our kitchen. There was always a pot of coffee and a kettle of beans on the stove while a pan of bread sat rising nearby. My mother never locked her doors. Not even when she and Dad moved into a small town in New Mexico. She believed if someone broke in, they needed what they might take more than she did.

When I left home to start nursing school, the youngest in my class, it was an entirely different world. Most notable for me was the fact that there were so many people in every class. And boys! Thousands of them! Unlike current living arrangements at colleges and universities, our school had male and female dorms. Since the school was a Catholic university with a history of being a convent, the boys were three miles off campus. Life was definitely interesting.

My first job as an RN was on the evening shift. I found myself observing people, as usual. Only now, the people were ill—usually very ill and frequently alone. We once let a dog come into the room of his owner, a tiny blind woman dying of cancer who was without family or friends. I'll never forget the look on her face in response to that simple act. The dog stayed all shift. He was taken back down the fire stairs before the night crew came. The lady died shortly thereafter, but at least she had had "family" with her for a while.

I moved to Carlsbad, New Mexico, in 1970. It is a small town, with a population of around twenty-eight thousand, with one high school and one hospital. It was there that I raised my only child. Lucky for me, my son shares my passion for baseball.

I continued to work as a nurse. My career choice provided a marvelous opportunity to observe human greatness as well as the depths of depravity we are capable of displaying. Nursing was, for me, a gift. I actually got paid to help people.

When my son went away to college, I was totally alone for the first time in my life. I stayed at work as long as possible to avoid the empty house. One can only wallow in self-pity so long. I began to write every evening. I hardly knew where the story should go or how to get it there, but go it did. The characters developed a personality of their own. They moved my story along, demanding additional twists or requiring that I leave some individuals by the wayside. They gave new life to me.

I remarried, and my husband made the decision to move back to his roots, so to speak. We moved to Edinburg, Texas, in 1998. Only forty-five minutes from Mexico, the change was dramatic. The language barrier, disease prevalence (more than 60 percent of the population is diabetic, bringing with it increased incidences of heart disease, kidney disease, among others), and horrendous poverty must share the stage with the violence along the Texas-Mexico border. Small but steady lights shining through these problems are the very strong family ties and the persistence to move forward and upward the area clings to. I have found the people to be kind, good-humored, and always willing to offer assistance to those in need.

I stopped writing for a period of about eight years while we set up my husband's medical practice and I settled into a new hospital. Eventually I took up my computer once again. How great it felt to be back at my desk. It was like seeing an old friend. However, my perspective on life had changed and so, too, did my book. It took on a new feel, a much more comfortable feel. My writing is no longer a way to pass time. My writing is my time.

READER'S GUIDE

1. Which of Caty's husbands do you think she was most suited to? Had Rhys lived, do you think she would have been as happy with him as she ended up with Santino?

2. How would the story have changed had Carlos come to fetch Caty from Rhys sooner? Would Rhys have given her up to him, given that he seemed to fall for her very quickly?

3. Many characters in the book do reprehensible things, but often we see another side of them that softens our opinion of them. For example, Marcus lied to Caty and abused her trust, yet this does not entirely ruin him in Caty's eyes. Carlos succumbs to evil, but only because of the pain of his past. Given the book's unwillingness to paint most characters as fully "bad," who or what is the villain of the story, if there is one at all?

4. What about Caty makes her so attractive to other people? Yes, she is physically appealing, but she's also headstrong and disobedient to men who expect obedience from women. Is her rebelliousness part of the appeal?

5. What did you make of young Santino's sacrifice for Caty? Do you think he was right to not tell Caty about Marcus's mistress out of fear of breaking her heart?

6. How did you react to the prologue? When it's revealed much later who these characters were, did you immediately remember the burning-at-the-stake scene?

7. Caty goes through three distinct cycles, each anchored by a different man. Do you think she learned and evolved through these cycles, or do you feel her character was relatively consistent throughout?

8. Under Queen Anne's reign, Scotland and England united to become the Kingdom of Great Britain. How did that political development play into the story? Given the strife—and the fact that many still advocate for Scottish independence—does the merge seem like a positive development?

9. What in Caty's background do you think gave her the strength and resourcefulness we see on display in the novel? When we first meet her, she's a captive laborer, yet everyone around her is awed by her calm and relative happiness. Are there any hints as to how her upbringing might have shaped who she became?

10. How much of a role do you think religion plays in Caty's motivations? When she leaves Castle Dermoth, she tells Rhys in a note that she's doing so because the household worships differently than she does, and the same objection arises just before the marriage ceremony. Do you think the strength of her Catholic convictions is what propels her choices, or is it a more fundamental desire for freedom?

AUTHOR Q&A

1. Your previous book, *Dancing with the Boss*, was set in modern times, but with *Come Winter*, you step deep into the past. How heavy was your research before and during the writing process?

   Very heavy. I wanted to make the story come alive for the reader; they should be able to see and feel Caty's world. I needed to know what foods they ate, what their houses were like. How did they live, dress, give birth, treat illnesses, relate to different members of a very structured society. And how would a woman weave her way through this, even a woman who admittedly came with a certain amount of station by birth. What was the weather like then (during that time frame the earth actually suffered a mini ice age), and how did countries relate to each other. I did a great deal of research . . . all the time. It was part of the fun. Thank goodness for the Internet!

2. As someone who grew up in rural Colorado, what drew your interest to Scotland? Do you have ties to that part of the world?

   No, but I had the idea for the story, and for it to work, I needed a time frame in which such a life could be lived. It was also important to find a country where the story could happen as a matter of course. Certainly things such as wifenapping would cause a stir now! Back then, not so much.

3. Caty is an uncommonly independent and free-spirited woman for the time and society she lives in. We see her repeatedly chafe against the expectations of women in eighteenth-century Britain. Were Caty alive today, what boundaries do you think she would be pushing in our society?

Much of Caty's attitude was influenced by both her parents and her faith. I believe she would have been a strong advocate for anyone of less fortune. Heaven knows there are plenty in that bucket today. She would have been active in raising awareness of illnesses. I doubt she would be married yet.

4. Did you have a model in mind when you created the character of Caty? You write in your author's note about wanting to shed light on the lives of women who were tossed about by misfortune but who found love none-theless. Did any historical characters in particular provoke your interest in this angle?

My comments make notice of the fact that women today struggle with tremendous difficulties, including diseases, divorces, loss of jobs, families, etc., etc. The times are different but the scars left are still just as painful. Not all nurturing should imply finding love. Women care for children, strangers, co-workers, and countless others. Women triumph in so many ways, though as a society, I doubt most of us think twice about it . . . including the women themselves.

5. How would you characterize Caty's gift? To many, her abilities raise the specter of witchcraft, but when we see her at work in the novel, she seems to simply have more medical knowledge than most, and a kind, nurturing manner. Was that enough, back then, to be labeled a practitioner of the dark arts?

Yes. Some peoples (such as the Scots) implemented such activity as part of their survival. Others, including so-called physicians, rejected these "dark arts" not in a small way because of jealousy. At times, religious representatives also feared such activity. So much of what they could not explain away became the subject of superstitions.

6. Caty repeatedly finds true love with men who she initially feels she could never marry, let alone be romantically happy with. What does this say about the general attitude toward love and marriage in our culture? Is there more to long-term relationships than the intense rush of romance at the outset that slowly wears off as the couple moves into married life?

   I believe so. Relationships were often planned by someone other than the couple. Love, if it came, happened quickly. Remember, women married much younger. It was not uncommon for a man or woman to have three mates during their lifetime, due to deaths during childbirth, illnesses, combat, etc. Although Henry VIII is a well-known exception, divorce was not common. Couples simply made the best of it. Women who were born of some station were used as a commodity. Love appears to have been a by-product of circumstance, although history reveals many arranged marriages found the couple in love. Today's notion of love and marriage has certainly changed. We wed older, take longer to have children, and have a stronger voice in the choice of mates. Divorce is common. I'm not certain we are comfortable with just what love is, yet.

7. One memorable scene in the book finds Caty and Santino having the consummation of their marriage "witnessed." Was this common practice at the time?

   This was not uncommon for royal marriages. This was seen as a way to prevent dissention over the legitimacy of an heir, and would prevent annulments on the grounds of an unconsummated marriage.

8. What is your writing process like? Do you stick to a schedule, or do you just write when inspiration strikes?

I suppose I'm a little weird. I write. Sometimes during the day, sometimes most of the night, and often, both. Once I'm "into" the story, I stay with it, if at all possible.

9. Did you learn anything from the process of writing your first novel that helped you write this one?

A great deal, actually. I spent more time re-reading—taking out unnecessary words, over-used phrases, etc. I am much more comfortable standing by what I want the story to say, what I want the characters to say, etc. I have been lucky. Both editors have been great to work with. Editors are not all created equal, either. But that's OK. It gives me a larger arena to play within.

10. What are some of your favorite entries in the historical fiction genre?

Some of my favorite authors are Bernard Cornwell and Philippa Gregory. I also enjoy Dan Silva, Mario Puzo, and some of Dan Brown's work. I think one can garner ideas from many avenues. For me, researching the times my characters live in gives my story body. Sometimes that research moves your story in a totally new direction.

11. Were *Come Winter* to be adapted for the screen, who would be your top choice to play Caty?

Wow, that's a hard one. I'm not certain. Someone who is strong but not hard.

12. Do you have any advice for first-time novelists?

Don't quit. Keep plugging and never think it is not worth the sweat. By the same token, relax. Let the story come out, meet your characters, and enjoy the trip.

13. What are your plans for your next book? Are you staying in the past or coming back to the present?

I'm actually working on one in the present. However, since my way of dealing with pauses in productivity is to work on something else, I have several projects resting in my computer . . . both past and present.

14. And, finally, let's say you're banished from your kingdom and can only take three books with you. What are they?

   My Bible, a thesaurus, and a HUGE notebook (does that qualify as a book??), or maybe the third would be my MacBook Pro. Is that a book?

DATE DUE

PRINTED IN U.S.A.